AND SO IT BEGINS...

A gust of wind caressed Natalia's hair as she stood on the deck of the *Vigilant*, the sky nearly cloudless on this glorious spring day. As the waters of the Great Northern Sea rose and fell around her, she couldn't help but imagine their embrace, then a pair of arms encircled her waist from behind.

"I was wondering when you would join me," she said.

Athgar chuckled. "I woke up, and you were gone. I guess I should have expected it, what with the sea around us. You really can feel it, can't you?"

"Of course. Considering my gift for Water Magic, it's only natural, but it doesn't compare to your arms around me."

He went quiet, and she laughed. "You're blushing."

"How in the name of the Ancestors could you tell that?"

She twisted to face him, then smiled. "I know my husband."

He shivered, and she wrapped her arms around him, burying her head into his chest.

"How much farther?" he asked.

"We should see the coast of Carlingen later this afternoon. Captain Grazynia assures me we'll make landfall well before dark."

"It's been too long," said Athgar. "We shouldn't have waited."

"Nonsense. Things don't fix themselves simply because a battle is won. It takes patience and understanding to ensure a lasting peace, and the Duke of Reinwick needed our help."

"And the King of Andover, don't forget him."

"Yes," said Natalia, "and because of our efforts, both realms have now banished the family." She paused, luxuriating in his embrace. "I am looking forward to getting home, though."

"Me too. Oswyn must be enormous by now. It's been a year since we saw her."

"Is that all? It seems longer.

"We left Ebenstadt last spring."

"We did, yet so much has happened since then. I was beginning to feel like we'd never see her again."

"I'm sure she's in fine spirits," said Athgar. "After all, Kargen and Shaluhk are looking after her."

"Don't forget Agar," she added.

ALSO BY PAUL J BENNETT

Heir to the Crown Series

Servant of the Crown

Sword of the Crown

Mercerian Tales: Stories of the Past

Heart of the Crown

Shadow of the Crown

Mercerian Tales: The Call of Magic

Fate of the Crown

Burden of the Crown

Mercerian Tales: The Making of a Man

Defender of the Crown

Fury of the Crown

Mercerian Tales: Honour Thy Ancestors

War of the Crown

Triumph of the Crown

Mercerian Tales: Into the Forge

Guardian of the Crown

Enemy of the Crown

Peril of the Crown

The Frozen Flame Series

Awakening - Prequels

Ashes | Embers | Flames | Inferno | Maelstrom | Vortex | Torrent | Cataclysm

Power Ascending Series

Tempered Steel: Prequel

Temple Knight | Warrior Knight

Temple Captain | Warrior Lord

Temple Commander | Warrior Prince

The Chronicles of Cyric

TORRENT

THE FROZEN FLAME: BOOK SEVEN

PAUL J BENNETT

Copyright © 2023 Paul J Bennett
Cover Illustration Copyright © 2023 Carol Bennett
Portrait Copyright © 2023 Amaleigh Photography

All rights reserved. No part of this book may be reproduced, stored in a retrieval system, or transmitted in any form, or by any means, electronic, mechanical, photocopying, recording or otherwise, without prior permission of the author.

First Edition: May 2023

ePub ISBN: 978-1-990073-52-6
Mobi ISBN: 978-1-990073-53-3
Print ISBN: 978-1-990073-55-7

This book is a work of fiction. Any similarity to any person, living or dead is entirely coincidental.

THE LAND OF
N
GREAT NORT
THE
NETHERWOOD
HALVARIAN
EMPIRE
SEA OF STORMS
WILDERNESS

DDENWERTHE
SEA
WILDERNESS
THE
PETTY
KINGDOMS
THE
WILDLANDS
CORASSUS
HIMMERING SEA
THE GREAT SEA

Petty Kingdoms

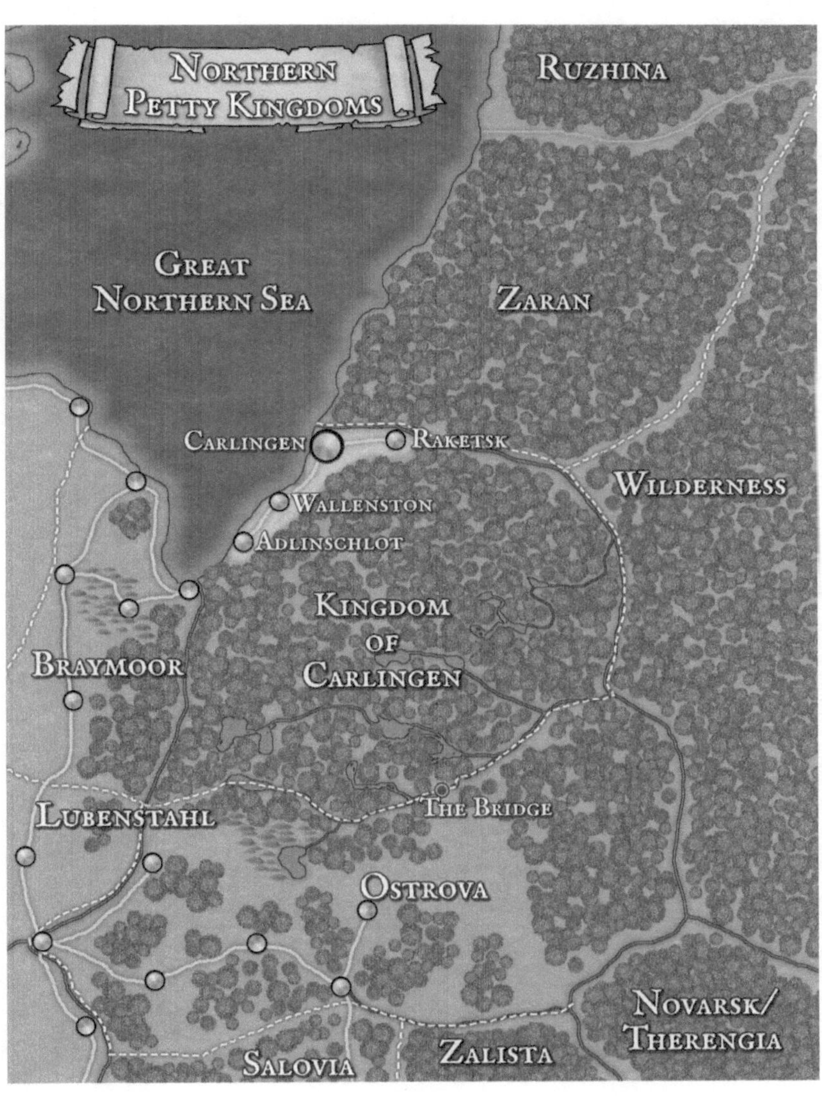

Northern Petty Kingdoms

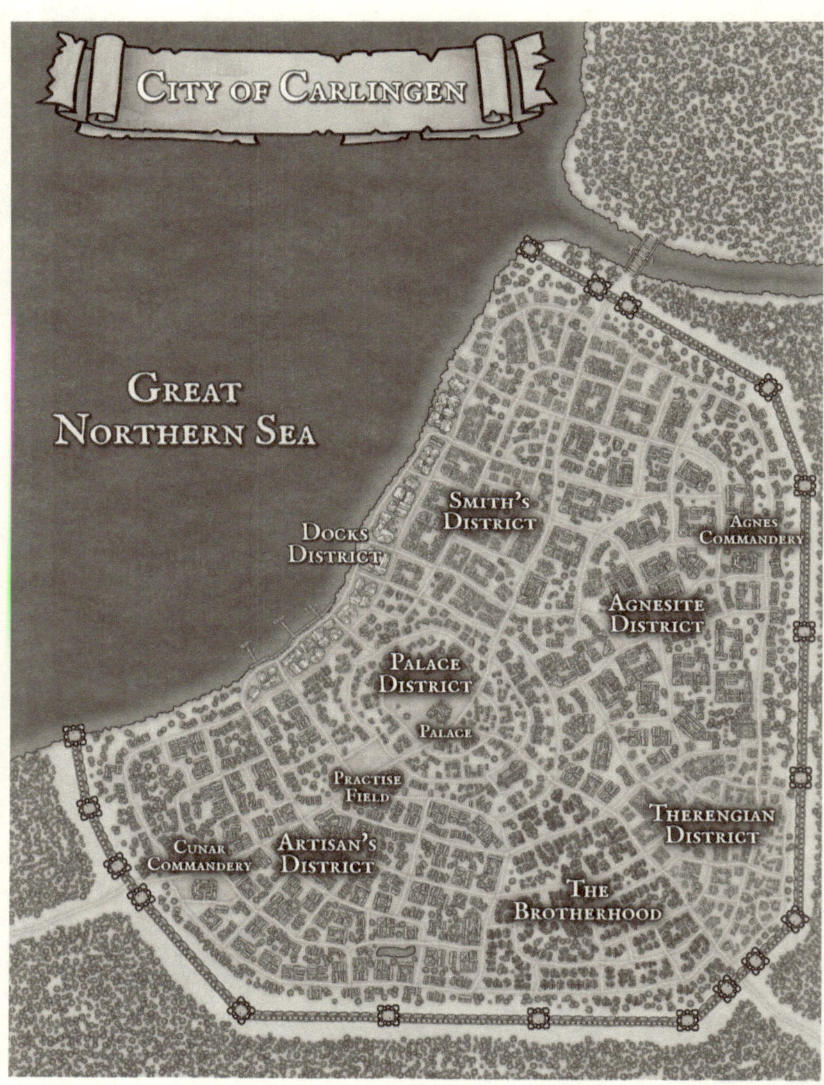

City of Harlingen

PLOTTING

WINTER 1109 SR* (*SAINTS RECKONING)

Graxion Stormwind looked around the room at the largest gathering of Stormwinds in decades, for Marakhova had insisted anyone of import must attend. It was strange to be back in the Volstrum after all these years, but since the burning of Stormwind Manor last fall, few other places could house an event of this magnitude.

He risked a glance at Gregori, who'd failed so spectacularly in Andover. Graxion's own ineptitude paled in comparison to the disgrace the family suffered due to that fellow's incompetence, and that thought, above all others, led him to relax.

The room was abuzz with chatter, but it died down the moment the head of the family, Marakhova Stormwind, entered. She cut an imposing figure, especially considering her advanced years, her eyes boring into several of her guests, causing them to look away in shame. She strode to the front of the room, sitting stiffly at the head table.

"No doubt by now, you are all wondering why I've called this assembly." She didn't wait long before continuing. "Our family, indeed, this very institution we call the Volstrum, has suffered much these last few years, and all of it can be attributed to one cause—the renegade Natalia Stormwind."

Graxion noticed looks of confusion on many faces, for much of what had transpired of late had been kept from the family at large. He turned back to the matriarch as she continued. "Natalia and her companions mock our institution, spreading lies throughout the Petty Kingdoms. Last year, they even dared burn Stormwind Manor, an act we cannot let go unpunished."

Marakhova scanned the crowd, her eyes finally locking on Gregori. "In

Andover, we suffered a defeat of such magnitude it calls into question our ability to influence courts across the Petty Kingdoms. Reinwick and Hadenfeld banned our people some time ago, but now, Andover has seen fit to do the same. I ask you, how long before the rest of the Petty Kingdoms also refuse our presence?"

Marakhova paused, letting her words sink in before continuing. "And it's not just Natalia. The influence of the Temple Knights grows with the Agnesites roaming the Great Northern Sea at will, putting all our efforts in jeopardy. I am but one woman, so I gathered you here this day to hear what counsel you urge. Speak freely, and know none will be punished for their opinions." She sat back in her chair, staring at those assembled before her. Would they answer the call? She knew some would remain quiet rather than risk upsetting their matron but hoped a few might prove bold enough to offer their ideas. An older fellow at the back of the room raised his hand.

Marakhova strained to recognize him. "Aramon? Is that you?"

"It is," he replied, standing.

"It has been some time since you graced the Volstrum with your presence. How are things in Ilea?"

"Quiet, Matriarch, and far too dull without someone like you there."

"I see you still have a silver tongue, despite your advancing years. Speak freely, my old friend, and fear no repercussions."

"I've heard disturbing reports of late," said Aramon. "Rumours the Old Kingdom is reborn. Is there any truth in them?"

"Regrettably, yes. A new kingdom has arisen on the eastern fringes of the Petty Kingdoms, one styling itself on the Therengia of old, even going so far as to adopt its name as their own. We sent someone to find a place at their court, but they rebuffed his efforts." She sought out someone in the crowd. "Ah, there you are. Perhaps you'd care to provide more details, Lord Graxion?"

He stood, feeling a heavy weight on his shoulders. "It's true," he began. "Last autumn, I travelled to their capital, Runewald, where I met with their thane's representative."

"And?" asked Aramon.

"He turned out to be an Orc."

The room burst into a cacophony of shouts.

"Let him continue," called out Marakhova, her voice rising above all others.

Graxion took a deep breath. "Unfortunately, I never met their leader face to face. They call him High Thane, doubtless a Therengian custom, although I'm led to understand kings ruled the Old Kingdom. I never learned his name, but it soon became evident he refused to see me. Not only that, but this self-proclaimed chieftain knew a lot about our affairs, leading me to conclude the renegade has spent time in their company."

"How much do they know?" asked Aramon.

"Where we're from and that we use a form of selective breeding. There was also evidence they employ mages of their own."

"Come now. Orcs are savages. Everyone knows it takes an educated mind to master the arcane arts."

"It would be foolish of us to assume that," replied Graxion. "We know from our own records we are not the only souls to use magic. They, too, have mastered spells, though not to our level."

"How is this of concern to the Stormwinds?"

"This new kingdom represents a challenge to our supremacy."

"It is more than that," shouted a voice.

All eyes turned to a woman standing off to one side. "I believe the renegade has taken control of this new kingdom."

"And you are?" said Aramon.

"Larissa Stormwind."

"Ah, yes. The one who caused us some embarrassment in Reinwick. I find it difficult to believe someone of your ineptitude has anything meaningful to add to this conversation."

"Quite the contrary. In the years since my unfortunate failure, I've been digging deep into the politics of the Petty Kingdoms."

"That is the stock-in-trade of all of us," said Aramon.

"Agreed, but whereas the rest of you concentrate on events local to your assignments, I've put together a grander picture, which I think you'll agree is a much greater danger to us."

"Ridiculous!"

"Quiet!" barked out Marakhova. "Let her speak."

"Thank you, Matriarch. As I said, I've been studying reports from all across the Continent, and a disturbing trend has emerged."

"Which is?"

"Our influence is waning, and unless we do something drastic, I fear we shall soon find ourselves banished from all the courts of the Petty Kingdoms."

"Tell us more," pressed the matriarch.

"In the last few years, there's been a great disturbance in the balance of power." This statement brought cajoles from the assemblage, but Larissa held up her hand, quieting them. "We've spent decades keeping the Petty Kingdoms weak and at each other's throats, but a new trifecta is rising, one that I fear we will be unable to stop."

She paused, considering her next words carefully. "The Church has been of grave concern to us for many years, and while recent developments reward our efforts, we've also suffered losses. The Temple Knights of Saint Agnes have built a fleet, and even though the Church itself is waning, their ship numbers are on the increase."

"And the second point?"

"Our efforts to gain influence in Hadenfeld were rebuffed some years ago. Now, with the kingdom reunited despite our attempts to incite a civil war, it holds one of the largest standing armies on the Continent." She gave her audience a chance to digest this information. "The third and final threat is the emergence of the new Kingdom of Therengia."

"Come now," said Gregori. "They are little more than barbarians. How could they possibly pose a threat to us?"

"Those barbarians defeated a Holy Army, and that's no small accomplishment. There's also their subjugation of Novarsk, one of the more powerful Petty Kingdoms. I tell you, if we don't stop them soon, they will grow stronger still."

"It's true," called out Graxion. He stood, drawing the attention of all in the room. "I saw the great beasts they somehow tamed. These are no ordinary barbarians, for they have a well-trained and disciplined army."

"Also true," added Larissa, "but the most disturbing development of all are the reports that they have dozens of mages in their employ."

"Dozens?" said Gregori. "Surely you exaggerate?"

"Survivors claim there were at least six present at the Battle of the Wilderness, and reports from Novarsk identify over ten during their failed campaign to conquer Therengia."

"Dire news indeed," said Marakhova, "but I'm more interested in how we counter these new threats politically."

"The first step is to rid the Great Northern Sea of the accursed Temple ships. Once we accomplish that, we can use our command of seaborne trade to worm our way back into courts across the northern kingdoms."

"We have no ships," said Graxion, "save for a few flying Ruzhina's flag."

"Carlingen has some," replied Larissa, "and our agent there has a strong influence over the king. With a little pressure, I'm certain we can convince him to begin a shipbuilding program. A stronger presence there will also give us a jumping-off point for a potential military campaign against Therengia."

"A military campaign? Don't be absurd! We have no army."

"We do not need one. All across the Continent, people fear the Old Kingdom reborn. We must capitalize on that fear, and men will come flocking east, weapons in hand."

"An interesting strategy," said Marakhova. "Prepare yourself, Larissa. I expect a full explanation of your plan by the end of the week."

Maksim the Fourth, King of Carlingen, looked down at the table, where he'd laid out a map of his kingdom. It was a curious work of art, inaccurate and oftentimes confusing, but served to at least illustrate their current conundrum.

"Tell me again what they want?" he said.

Svetlana Stormwind pointed to the border regions to the south. "They are yet to make specific demands, but there can be little doubt they seek to annex this area."

"What is it about the area that attracts their interest?"

"No one knows. I suppose there might be traces of shadowbark there?"

"Enough to warrant a war?" said the king. "I find that very difficult to believe." His gaze turned to the man on his left. "What are your thoughts, Lord Thalmund?"

The baron peered down at the map. "Difficult to say with any certainty, sire. One thing's for certain, though; it's not out of any desire for settlement. Their lands directly across the river are sparsely populated."

"And you, Lord Flarik?"

"I must agree with my fellow baron, Majesty. There is little of worth in those parts."

"How do we know?"

"I beg your pardon?"

The king winced. "It is a simple enough question, my lords. There must be something they want, or else they wouldn't be considering its acquisition."

"It's not about the land," offered the newest baron, Lord Tanger. "It's about forcing our hand."

"By asking us to give up some useless land?"

"Handing over that land reveals we will buckle under pressure, sire. Our only option is to defend it with our army."

"Army?" said Maksim. "We have few enough men as it is, and they're needed here, in Carlingen. They are the only thing preventing us from falling into complete chaos."

"I sympathize, sire, but what other choice have we? If we do not answer this threat, others will treat us with contempt."

"Perhaps your future bride might provide some help?" said Flarik. "She is well-connected, is she not?" All eyes turned to Svetlana.

"I've sent off letters to Karslev," she replied, "but have yet to receive any response. I'm afraid Carlingen holds little of interest to the Volstrum."

"Yet they sent you. Surely that accounts for something?"

"You honour me, Lord Flarik, but I'm afraid I am of little importance to the Stormwinds in the grand scheme of things."

"You bear their name."

"I do, but it's a large, extended family, with members spread across the entire Continent. I am but one of hundreds in a kingdom that, while important in its own right, holds little sway compared to the greater realms of the Petty Kingdoms."

"So, that's it, then? We are to be left to our own devices?"

"Come," said the king. "We are not yet under the sword of the enemy. Perhaps our southern neighbour will prove reasonable and allow us to keep the land to ourselves?"

"And if they don't?"

"Then we shall cross that bridge when we come to it. For now, at least, winter keeps them at bay. Who knows? By spring, there may be other alternatives."

"There is another option," replied Svetlana. "I could travel to Karslev and plead our case in person?"

Lord Flarik looked pleased. "Now we're talking."

"No," said Maksim. "You might find yourself reassigned to another court, which would be unacceptable. I would rather keep you here by my side."

"Even at the risk of the kingdom?" said Tanger. "You place too much value on this woman, sire."

"This 'woman' is to be my wife, my lord, making her your future queen. You would do well to remember that."

The new Baron of Raketsk fell silent.

Lord Flarik tried another approach. "Could we send envoys of our own to Karslev?"

"To do what?" demanded Maksim. "There are no spare coins to pay for help or enough warriors to march to an ally's assistance should it prove necessary. In short, we have nothing to offer, save for land, which is precisely the problem."

"Then let us increase the size of our army."

"And how, pray tell, would we pay for it?"

"That can all be sorted out later, surely? After all, the kingdom's safety is at stake."

"It's all well and good to speak in those terms, but the reality is an army still requires the forging of weapons and armour, which does not come without a cost."

"Then raise the taxes, Majesty."

"On whom? The collection of taxes assumes those burdened have the funds to actually pay. We gain nothing by taking what little remains to the destitute and poor of the kingdom."

"But there are merchants, surely?"

"There are," replied the king. "Are we then to assume they will shoulder the weight of supporting the army?"

"It is only just," said Lord Flarik. "After all, they're the ones who benefit from the safety and stability the army provides."

"I could say the same of you, my lord. Perhaps I should institute a further tax on my barons?"

They all held their breath.

"Then again, there are only three of you, so I doubt that would contribute much to the treasury."

Lord Thalmund snapped his finger. "That's it—trade!"

"Would you care to explain," said Svetlana, "or are we expected to guess what you're proposing?"

"My pardon. I was merely thinking out loud, but it occurs to me there may be merit in the idea."

"What idea?"

"That the king imposes a further tax on shipping. Saints know, ship's captains can certainly afford it."

"That wouldn't work," said Svetlana. "They would simply take their goods to another port where they can make a higher profit."

"There must be something we can do, surely?"

"What of that friend of yours?" replied Maksim. "The one who visited us last fall. What was her name?"

"You mean Natalia?" replied Svetlana.

"Yes, that's her. She returned to Karslev, didn't she?"

"She did, though I'm not sure she's still there."

"Perhaps you should write and ask her to intercede on our behalf?"

"To what end, sire?"

"To convince those around her to support our cause. A word from the family in the right places could do wonders. Who knows, they might even persuade Ostrova to leave us alone."

Svetlana blushed. "I'm afraid my pleas would fall on deaf ears, Lord King. My treatment of her during our time at the Volstrum was abysmal, as was that of my classmates."

"She seemed friendly enough when I met them."

"She is a Stormwind through and through, trained in diplomacy and etiquette. I'm afraid the appearance of friendliness was simply the result of her upbringing. To act in any other way would go against her strict code of conduct."

"Perhaps," said the king, "but I did them a favour by arranging their transport to Porovka. Surely that accounts for something?"

"You raise an interesting point, sire. I'll enquire about Natalia's current position, although I must warn you if she's been reassigned, it may take some time for my letter to reach her."

"And what will this letter say?" asked Lord Thalmund. "You can't just simply beg for assistance."

"I shall remind her of the great favour His Majesty bestowed upon them and ask her to use her influence to convince the family to take up our cause."

"Our cause being?"

"That we desire peace with Ostrova," replied Svetlana.

Thalmund frowned. "I doubt that will work."

"And yet we must try something," said the king, then his face softened. "Thank you, my dear. I appreciate your efforts, even if others don't." He sent a scathing look towards Lord Thalmund, but the fellow was too engrossed in his drink to notice. "We shall meet again in the spring. We can but hope Ostrova finds something else to occupy its time by then."

The three barons departed, leaving Svetlana and the king alone in the room. She moved closer to Maksim, taking his hand in hers. "Is it truly as bad as you say?"

"At the risk of sounding like a defeatist, there's a real possibility that the Kingdom of Carlingen will no longer exist by this time next year."

ARRIVAL

SPRING 1109 SR

Agust of wind caressed Natalia's hair as she stood on the deck of the *Vigilant*, the sky nearly cloudless on this glorious spring day. As the waters of the Great Northern Sea rose and fell around her, she couldn't help but imagine their embrace, then a pair of arms encircled her waist from behind.

"I was wondering when you would join me," she said.

Athgar chuckled. "I woke up, and you were gone. I guess I should have expected it, what with the sea around us. You really can feel it, can't you?"

"Of course. Considering my gift for Water Magic, it's only natural, but it doesn't compare to your arms around me."

He went quiet, and she laughed. "You're blushing."

"How in the name of the Ancestors could you tell that?"

She twisted to face him, then smiled. "I know my husband."

He shivered, and she wrapped her arms around him, burying her head into his chest.

"How much farther?" he asked.

"We should see the coast of Carlingen later this afternoon. Captain Grazynia assures me we'll make landfall well before dark."

"It's been too long," said Athgar. "We shouldn't have waited."

"Nonsense. Things don't fix themselves simply because a battle is won. It takes patience and understanding to ensure a lasting peace, and the Duke of Reinwick needed our help."

"And the King of Andover, don't forget him."

"Yes," said Natalia, "and because of our efforts, both realms have now banished the family." She paused, luxuriating in his embrace. "I am looking forward to getting home, though."

"Me too. Oswyn must be enormous by now. It's been a year since we saw her."

"Is that all? It seems longer.

"We left Ebenstadt last spring."

"We did, yet so much has happened since then. I was beginning to feel like we'd never see her again."

"I'm sure she's in fine spirits," said Athgar. "After all, Kargen and Shaluhk are looking after her."

"Don't forget Agar," she added. "And admittedly, we heard from them before we left, thanks to the shamans of the Ashwalkers. Are you sure they don't mind meeting us in Carlingen?"

"I'm told Shaluhk was quite pleased by the prospect of travel, although I imagine they won't be there for some time yet. It's a relatively long trip cross-country."

"I hope they don't run across trouble as we did going downriver."

"I'm sure they'll be fine. If I know Kargen, he'll bring extra hunters, likely with their warbows. Those things can penetrate the armour of Temple Knights, so I don't imagine they'd have any troubles with the wildlife."

"You forget the wyvern that menaced us when we made that same trip."

"We killed that, if you recall."

"So we did." She let out a pent-up breath. "Sorry, Athgar. I'm just worried about them."

"Let's change the subject, then, shall we? What do you remember about Carlingen?"

"King Maksim was a decent enough fellow."

"He was," said Athgar. "He had a thing for Svetlana, didn't he? I wonder if anything came of that."

"Perhaps we'll visit them. We must be careful, though."

"Why? They were friendly enough the last time we visited."

"Yes, but that was before we torched Stormwind Manor. If the family saw fit to inform Svetlana of our actions, we could find ourselves thrown into a dungeon."

"You never told Svetlana of our true intentions, did you?"

"No. As far as she knew, I was returning to the Volstrum for my next assignment."

"Then let us hope she still thinks that's true." He paused for a moment. "You know, we should have some reason for coming back."

"I'll tell them my new assignment is taking me deeper into the Petty

Kingdoms, and we decided to visit on the way."

"I suppose I should get used to acting as a servant again."

"Nonsense," said Natalia. "I'll simply tell her I received permission to breed with you. You are a Fire Mage, even if you're not a Sartellian."

Athgar laughed. "Breed. What a strange thing to say."

"Agreed, but that's the way the family does things."

"But we've already bred, or is that breeded?"

She laughed. "I'm sure she'll figure that out once Oswyn arrives. Don't worry. Things like this happen on occasion. It might raise some suspicions, but nothing I can't handle."

"Providing she doesn't know of our actions in Karslev."

"Precisely. We'll spend a week or two in Carlingen until Kargen and Shaluhk arrive, then head back to Runewald. Think of it as a nice vacation."

"Vacation? What in the name of the Gods is a vacation?"

"The wealthy of the Continent often go on a trip to get away from the politics at court."

"Like a pilgrimage?"

"More or less," said Natalia, "but not necessarily for religious reasons."

"Why would someone want to leave their home and family?"

"Not everyone is as pleased with their lives as we are. Don't you sometimes feel being High Thane is a burden?"

"Yes, but I'm not the sort of person who runs away and hides. The only reason we left Runewald was to get the family off our backs."

Captain Grazynia appeared on deck, the sun glinting off her armour.

"Expecting trouble?" asked Athgar.

"We are off the coast of Carlingen," she replied, "and our ships have not sailed this area for some months. We must be ever vigilant."

"Your ship is clearly well-named."

The captain merely stared back.

"I don't think she quite understood the jest," whispered Athgar.

"Oh, I understood it," replied the Temple Knight, "but this is not the time for such things." Her gaze swept over the water, paying particular attention to the distant shoreline. Then she grunted, her entire demeanour changing from alertness to relaxation. "Fishing boats," she said. "A good sign. Were there pirates in the region, they wouldn't be out."

"I assumed fishing boats would be a poor target."

"You'd be surprised what a thief will take. The fishing here is plentiful, and some harbours along the coast don't ask too many questions."

"Yes, but fish?"

"They like anything they can sell, especially if it offers little in the way of opposition. How much of a fight would a fisherman put up?"

"Likely none," replied Athgar.

"Now you understand."

Natalia glanced at the coast, then followed it eastward, finding no sign of Carlingen, but had no doubt it would soon come into view. "Will you remain in Carlingen for long, Captain?"

"We'll take on fresh water and purchase some food stores, but I know of no pressing matters requiring our presence beyond that."

"My lord, you shouldn't be here without an escort." Athgar turned as Herulf came up on deck. The Therengian had taken it upon himself to become the High Thane's right-hand man and took his responsibilities seriously.

"I'm sure Natalia is more than capable of keeping me safe."

Herulf's gaze roamed over the *Vigilant's* crew. Despite their efforts in the last war, the fellow still mistrusted them, particularly the scarlet-clad Temple Knights.

Athgar ignored the man's implication. "Where's Katrin?" he asked, hoping to change the conversation.

"Down below," replied Natalia. "I'm afraid she's suffering."

"From?"

"Sea sickness, if you can believe it."

"She was fine when we sailed from Karslev last year."

"She was, but the water has been choppier the last few days."

Athgar laughed. "She's a Water Mage. Isn't that a little like a Fire Mage not liking fire?"

"You like food. Have you never eaten something that upset your stomach?"

"Yes, I suppose I have. I apologize for the remark. I assume Greta is looking after her?"

"She is."

"And how is she coping?"

"Quite well, which is more than I can say for Belgast. He's refusing to come up on deck."

"Why?"

"Why do you think? In his opinion, Dwarves are not made for going to sea."

"So, he's sick?"

"No. He doesn't like the idea of the wide-open sea. Says he much prefers a crowded city, or at least some hills or trees to look at."

"He's just sitting below decks doing nothing?"

"Hardly that," said Natalia. "He's been playing cards with Stanislav, but that won't last much longer."

"It won't? Why not?"

"Our dear mage hunter is losing badly. Unless I miss my guess, he'll be out of coins before we make landfall."

"I don't recall Belgast being much of a gambler."

"That's because he usually keeps himself busy with other things, but there is little for him to do aboard ship."

"There's Carlingen," announced Grazynia. "We made better time than I expected. The sea has been kind to us this trip."

Unlike the other ports of the Petty Kingdoms that sat astride the Great Norther Sea, Carlingen had no breakwater nor spit of land to protect it, leaving the salt-stained, weather-beaten buildings along the coast open to the ravages of the elements.

The docks here, nowhere near the size of Kovoran's, still held an impressive number of ships. Unlike its western cousin, however, most were small, the vast majority fishing boats. The few large boats present were open-topped and, much like those of old, were incapable of spending extended periods out at sea.

The *Vigilant* slowed and then dropped anchor just offshore. Katrin and Greta came up on deck, followed shortly afterwards by Stanislav and Belgast.

"This is a fine ship, Captain," said the Dwarf. "My compliments to the crew."

"Thank you, Master Ridgehand. I shall be sure to pass on your remarks to all."

Natalia watched as they lowered the ship's boat into the water. "It was nice of you to provide us with transport," she said. "I hope we didn't put you to too much trouble?"

"Not at all," replied Grazynia. "And it was the least we could do after the service you did us in Reinwick."

Athgar cleared his throat. "Allow me to extend an invitation to your order," he said. "The Temple Knights of Saint Agnes will always be welcome in Therengia."

"I thank you. Rest assured, I'll inform my superiors upon our return to Temple Bay. Now, at the risk of sounding brusque, you'd best get aboard that boat."

The seven of them climbed over the side and into the ship's boat, then the crewmen pushed them away from the *Vigilant* and took up the oars.

Natalia scanned the docks, checking for any signs of trouble. A pair of soldiers in the king's livery wandered through the crowd but appeared to have little interest in the new arrivals. When the boat finally bumped up against the dock, Natalia was the first ashore, followed closely by Athgar.

"Well, we're here," he said. "Shall we seek rooms or go straight to the Palace?"

She waited until the others disembarked. "The Palace first. If there's going to be any trouble, best we know about it before Oswyn arrives."

Herulf pushed past them. "I assume that is where we intend to go?" He pointed at the Palace's distant roof.

"Yes," said Athgar. "Lead on."

They all fell in behind the Therengian warrior, making quite an imposing sight as they traversed the city streets. They garnered some interesting looks from people they passed, but no one interfered with their progress.

Two guards stopped them when they reached the Palace's front door. Natalia took a step forward. "I am Natalia Stormwind. My companions and I are here seeking an audience with His Majesty, King Maksim the Fourth."

One of the guards nodded. "I remember you, my lady. You're a friend of Lady Svetlana, aren't you?"

"I am. I trust she is well?"

"She is indeed, ma'am. If you would be so kind as to follow me, I'll see you're served refreshments while we wait for word from His Majesty." He called another guard to take his place, then led them into the Palace and down a hallway. "There's a waiting room down here, my lady." He paused as a servant opened the door. "I'll come and get you when the king grants you an audience."

They stepped inside a sizable room with a large fireplace at one end, although it wasn't lit. A long carpet ran the room's length, with numerous chairs scattered around the perimeter, none looking particularly comfortable.

"Oh, dear," said Katrin. "I hope this doesn't bode ill."

"Nonsense," replied Natalia. "The king was quite polite to us last time."

"True," said Athgar, "but we don't know what's happened since then."

Belgast went down on one knee to examine a chair. "Terrible work this. You would think the king could afford something better."

"If I recall, you didn't like the building last time we were here."

"Well, it wasn't up to the quality of a Dwarven stronghold."

Stanislav shook his head. "You're too particular, my friend. Not all of us are obsessed with the principles of architecture."

"It's not only the architecture. Work like this displays a general lack of interest in producing quality."

"Sometimes, it's more about the price than the quality."

The Dwarf looked as though someone had slapped him. He opened his mouth to speak, but Greta jumped into a chair.

"They're quite comfortable to me," she announced.

"Says the girl who used to sleep on the floor."

"Come, come," said Katrin. "That's hardly her fault."

"Sorry," grumbled Belgast. "I shall refrain from further comment."

The rest sat, except for Stanislav, who wandered around the room, his head bent, indicating he was deep in thought. "The last time we were here, one of their barons was abusing his position, wasn't he?"

"Yes," said Natalia. "Georgi Kulikov, the previous Baron of Raketsk. We informed the king of his misdeeds, but I wonder what happened to him?"

"Probably executed," said Herulf. "That seems to be the favoured punishment in the Petty Kingdoms. Hopefully, it's not what they intend for us."

"Well, no guards are storming in, so that's surely a good sign."

"What was King Maksim like?" asked Katrin.

"He seemed quite reasonable to me," replied Natalia. "And he lent us a ship with very little effort, although I suppose Svetlana is likely the one who arranged all that."

"Svetlana? The same Svetlana we knew at the Volstrum?"

"Yes. Didn't I mention her?"

"Not to me."

"Why does it matter?" asked Athgar. "Have you a history?"

"You might say that. I'm one of the Disgraced."

"Yes, but we rescued you."

"And I am truly thankful for that, but I doubt Svetlana will see it that way. To her, I am an outcast whose name has been stricken from all records."

"Let's not judge her too harshly," said Natalia. "The very fact you're here and in my company suggests otherwise. We'll tell her you left because they selected you for special training. She won't question that."

"I hope you're right."

"I think we have bigger issues," offered Herulf. "There were Therengians on the streets."

"Are you sure?" said Athgar. "I didn't see any."

"That's because they avoided you, Lord. Instead of making themselves known, they skulked about in the alleyways."

"Are they a threat?" asked Katrin.

"I don't see why they would be," replied Athgar. "But we shall be on the alert, regardless. If there's one thing I've learned after leaving Athelwald, it's that things are not always as they seem."

"Are you suggesting we're in danger?"

Natalia chuckled. "Athgar and I have been courting danger ever since we first met. You might say, it's become a way of life for us."

"She's exaggerating," said Belgast, "although I can't deny they've faced more troubles than most."

"So, what do we do?" asked Katrin.

"What we always do," said Athgar. "Watch each other's backs for any signs of trouble."

"I'll second that," added Stanislav. His hand went to the hilt of his sword. "At least they didn't take away our weapons."

"They know Natalia's a Stormwind; it's not as if they could take away her magic."

"On the contrary," offered the mage hunter. "They could use magebane."

"That's been tried before," said Natalia, "and it didn't go over well. In any case, I haven't eaten any food or drunk any liquid since leaving the *Vigilant*, so no one's had a chance to administer any."

"All right," said Stanislav. "I concede the point."

"Look at it on the bright side," said Belgast. "They clearly mean us no harm."

"Perhaps they mean to bore us to death," offered Greta, swinging her legs back and forth. "I don't know about you, but I'd be more excited watching water dry."

A knock at the door announced the arrival of servants bearing trays of drinks. "With His Majesty's compliments," one said as they handed them around. Natalia refused the offer, instead watching them closely.

Having completed their assigned duties, the servants removed themselves from the room, but just as the door closed behind them, a woman's hand appeared, keeping it open. Moments later, Svetlana Stormwind entered.

"Natalia!" she called out, a smile breaking across her features. "I thought I heard your name mentioned. Good to see you."

"And I, you."

Svetlana locked eyes with those of the Disgraced mage. There was only a brief moment of confusion before the hint of a smile. "Katrin? It's good to see you again, although I'm at a loss to understand why you're here?"

"She's on her way to the court at Hadenfeld," offered Natalia before Katrin had an opportunity to answer. "She and I are travelling together while our paths converge." She lowered her voice ever so slightly. "She will be doing some special work for the Volstrum, but we're not allowed to speak of it."

A look of relief flooded over Svetlana. "I'm pleased to hear it. Now, come with me, and I'll take you to meet the king."

AUDIENCE

SPRING 1109 SR

King Maksim stared out the window to where clouds had blown in from the west, bringing a light rain, giving the rooftops of Carlingen an ethereal beauty. It all looked peaceful, yet a seething chaos lay beneath the surface. At any time, the streets could erupt into violence, and he felt the weight of it pressing down on him.

"You have visitors, Majesty."

"Thank you," he said. He was about to send them away, but the servant's next words changed his mind.

"It's Lady Svetlana, sire, and she's brought guests with her."

"Show them in." He couldn't help but smile as she entered with a few familiar faces mingled in amongst those who followed her.

"Your Majesty," said Svetlana. "You remember Natalia Stormwind?"

"Ah, yes. A fellow student from the Volstrum, if I recall. We provided her with a ship, didn't we?"

"We did, sire. The *Bergannon*. It returned some months ago after dropping them in Porovka."

Maksim turned to Natalia. "I assume the trip was a success?"

"It was indeed, Majesty. We now find ourselves passing through your lands once more and seek to offer our gratitude for your assistance."

"You are most welcome, my lady." He glanced at the others. "I seem to recall you had fewer companions the last time. Could I prevail upon you to introduce them?"

"Of course. This is Athgar, my husband—"

"Athgar?" interrupted Svetlana. "Didn't you say his name was Rothgar last time?"

"My pardon," said Natalia, recovering quickly. "He is known as Athgar, son of Rothgar, names I often confuse. If you recall, the last time I was here, I revealed I'd given birth to a daughter?"

"Yes. I remember."

"This is the girl's father."

Svetlana clapped her hands together, breaking into a wide grin. "How marvellous!"

"As for the rest of my companions, this is the esteemed mage hunter Stanislav Voronsky, who discovered my gift for magic many years ago."

"A mage hunter," said the king. "We are blessed to have you in our lands."

"And this is Belgast Ridgehand, one of my advisors. He was with us last time we visited."

"And these other two?"

"Katrin Stormwind, another graduate of the Volstrum, and Greta, a girl under her care."

"It seems the family has seen fit to bless us with three Stormwinds," said the king. "Or is it four?" He looked at Greta.

"Greta served in the Royal Court of Andover, Majesty," replied Natalia, avoiding the matter of the family.

"This will not do. We can't have visitors of such import without a celebration. At the very least, you must allow us to show you our hospitality."

"We have plenty of room in the Palace," offered Svetlana.

"Yes, we do, and I insist that while you're in Carlingen, you stay here as our guests."

"We'd greatly appreciate that," said Natalia. "Thank you, Your Majesty."

"It's the least I can do for friends of Svetlana. You mentioned you were passing through our lands. Might I ask where you're going?"

"Katrin has received an appointment to the Kingdom of Hadenfeld while the rest of us are heading towards Corassus."

"Corassus? That's quite the trip. I do hope you're not in a hurry?"

"Not at all, sire. We shall be meeting some others here in your fine city before we continue on our way."

"Others?"

"Yes. Someone to guide us to our destination."

"Ah yes, of course. It only makes sense, considering the wild lands hereabouts. Any idea when these guides will arrive?"

"I don't have an exact date, but based upon the distance they must travel to get here, I think at least a ten-day, maybe more."

"A ten-day?" said the king. "What a curious turn of phrase. Where in the name of the Saints did you come up with that one?"

"Ah, that's my fault," offered Belgast. "It's a Dwarven term I use quite frequently. She's just become accustomed to it."

"Yes," agreed Natalia. "My apologies for the confusion, Majesty."

"No need to apologize," said Maksim. "I was simply curious. In any event, welcome to Carlingen. Svetlana can show you around the city while you're here. Your last visit was far too short to see anything of interest." He fell silent before a smile broke out. "Your appearance here doesn't have anything to do with our impending nuptials, does it?"

"There is to be a marriage?"

"Yes. Lady Svetlana agreed to become my queen, and we are to be married in two weeks. Could we, by chance, convince you to remain for the wedding? I know Svetlana would dearly love for someone to support her during the ceremony."

Natalia looked at Athgar, who nodded. "We shall be delighted to help in any way we can," she said.

"Good. Then it's settled. Unfortunately, affairs of state preclude an extended visit at this precise time, but I hope to see you at dinner this evening. Svetlana, would you do me the honour of showing these fine people to their rooms?"

"Of course, sire."

They left, following their hostess through the Palace's labyrinthine corridors.

"My goodness," said Katrin. "How in the name of the Saints do you keep your bearings? This place is like a giant maze."

"Not to me," said Greta. "It's no worse than the Palace in Andover."

"The girl has a fine sense of direction," said Svetlana. "I myself took months to become accustomed to the layout of this place. What think you, Master Dwarf? I understand the mountain folk are used to complex tunnels and halls."

Belgast grunted. "I'll agree it might be a bit confusing to you Human folk, but to my mind, the layout is quite basic." He paused a moment. "No offence, my lady. I assume that's the title we use when addressing you?"

"Please. You're friends of Natalia; feel free to call me Svetlana."

"That would hardly be proper."

"Nonsense." She halted at a set of double doors. "This is the ambassador's suite. The king's predecessor built it to house any important delegates visiting Carlingen. Unfortunately, your arrival here surprised us, so it may need a light dusting. I'll have some servants bring you fresh linens and clean the place up. Have you any belongings?"

"Yes, aboard the *Vigilant*. We thought we'd settle our lodgings before retrieving them."

"The *Vigilant*? That's a Temple Ship, isn't it?"

"It is," said Natalia. "Why? Is that a problem?"

"I was under the impression they only carried out Church business."

"Ordinarily, that would be true, but we learned it was the only ship sailing for Carlingen without necessitating a long delay. Thankfully, we convinced its captain to take us aboard."

"But I thought you weren't in a hurry?"

"We aren't, but if we are to wait, I'd much prefer to do it here, where we can visit. After all, it's not every day I get to see a fellow graduate, aside from Katrin, of course."

"Give me a few minutes," said Svetlana, "and I'll arrange some servants to fetch your belongings unless you'd prefer to get them yourselves?"

"That would be nice. Thank you."

"In the meantime, you can look around your suite. I'll be back shortly."

She left them, heading down the corridor with a light step.

"She seems happy to see you," noted Belgast. "I get the impression she doesn't have many friends."

"That's not surprising," said Katrin. "I remember learning about Carlingen back at the Volstrum. Mistress Nina referred to it as the armpit of the Continent, not exactly the most ringing endorsement."

"What else do you recall?"

"Carlingen was founded by treasure hunters, or so claim older texts. After the fall of the Old Kingdom, there were persistent rumours the wealth of Therengia was taken east to avoid it falling into the hands of its enemies."

"That's right," said Stanislav. "I should have remembered that. People came from far and wide trying to make their fortunes."

"And you were there for that?" asked Katrin.

"Come now, even I'm not that old. No, this would have been about a century after the fall of Therengia. King Maksim is the descendant of one of those very adventurers. Unfortunately, those who came here failed to find any treasure worthy of the name, but it didn't stop others from trying."

"That might explain all the grey eyes I saw," said Herulf. "Perhaps they built the city on the ruins of a Therengian outpost?"

"That's unlikely. From what I know, Carlingen was built from the ground up. If there was ever a city from the Old Kingdom around here, there's no record of it."

"That's because it's farther south," said Belgast. "If you recall, Ebenstadt used to be called Dunmere."

"Even so, there's no proof it was ever part of the Old Kingdom."

"All this is interesting," said Natalia, "but of little consequence to us unless you're thinking of sending out an exploring party?" She looked at Athgar.

He shrugged. "If the entire population of Carlingen couldn't find it, what chance have we?"

"I find that surprising," said Stanislav. "I thought you, of all people, would be interested in learning more about your ancestors."

"And under other circumstances, I would, but I'm much more concerned with seeing my daughter right now."

"Yes, of course. My apologies. I should have realized."

A knock on the door announced the return of Svetlana, along with a veritable army of servants. They quietly entered the room and began cleaning while Svetlana spoke with her guests. "The king informed me he freed up some time. Would you care to join us for a longer visit while your rooms are prepared?"

"By all means," said Natalia.

They headed down the hall, with Natalia and their host leading, Athgar right behind, while the rest followed at a respectful distance.

"Tell me," said Athgar. "Why are there so many Therengians in Carlingen?"

"That is a fairly recent development," Svetlana replied. "It seems word of the rebirth of that once mighty kingdom has driven many to come east hoping to find a new home."

"And do they not continue on?"

"Some do, but the vast majority lack the funds to purchase the provisions for such a trip."

"Why is that?"

"I'm afraid some within the city are willing to cheat people out of their hard-won earnings."

"And the king does nothing?"

"King Maksim has attempted to take control of the streets, but I'm afraid he's fighting an uphill battle. For many years, his predecessors ignored the plight of those outside the Palace. Thus, the effort has been a difficult one."

"Yes," said Natalia. "The last time we visited, each section of the city was run by a different group."

"Surely the king's men could restore order?" said Stanislav.

"I'm afraid it's not for want of trying. The fact of the matter is the depleted Royal Treasury restricts us. The number of soldiers it would take to subdue the streets would soon see us emptying our coffers." She paused at the door, knocking three times.

"Enter," came the king's voice.

Svetlana stepped through the doorway, standing to one side to allow the others entry. King Maksim sat by a fire, drink in hand, but rose as he spotted his guests.

"Welcome," he said. "Please, come and sit." He nodded at a servant who moved around the room, offering a tray of drinks.

"My congratulations," said Natalia. "It's not every day we have a chance to witness a Royal Wedding."

Maksim smiled. "Your arrival is well-timed. I feared my dear betrothed would have no family to participate in the ceremony."

"And what of yourself, Majesty? Have you any family here in Carlingen?"

"No, though I am gifted with friends, if for no other reason than I am their king." He chuckled. "Still, I suppose that's the burden of ruling."

"They say a king's life is a lonely one," said Stanislav, "and to a certain extent, I would agree, but it doesn't need to be that way."

"Oh? Have you met many kings?"

"More than my fair share. As a mage hunter, I travelled the length and breadth of the Continent over the years, and it was customary to pay my respects at court when I arrived in an area. There's no doubting the burden of rule tends to isolate individuals, but some believe in keeping their friends close at hand. Of course, such a person would have to be willing to accept advice occasionally."

"Wise words. Are you sure you weren't trained at the Volstrum?"

"I assure you, sire, I have no magical potential whatsoever."

"Then how did you find new mages?"

"That," said Stanislav, "is a fair question. The answer, however, requires some explanation. Typically, I would travel the Continent investigating rumours and idle gossip."

"What type of gossip? Can you be more specific?"

"Well, in my case, they paid me to find potential Water Mages, so anything to do with water caught my interest. In the case of Natalia here, there were rumours of someone who could command fish and calm streams. Mind you, she was particularly gifted for one so young."

"And is it always so easy?"

"Not at all. In fact, ninety percent of the time, the rumours led nowhere. I once travelled all the way to Rizela only to find out a jealous husband was spreading the rumours."

"But isn't that hundreds of miles from Karslev? How in the name of the Saints would you even hear of such things?"

"As you know, Stormwind mages are at most courts of the Petty Kingdoms. They act as the Volstrum's eyes and ears, reporting such things back to their superiors."

King Maksim looked at his future bride. "Is that correct, Svetlana? Have you made such reports?"

"There is nothing to report, Majesty. I am aware of no such rumours in Carlingen."

"That's unfortunate. It would at least have given us some leverage with Karslev." He paused, mulling things over. "Did you ever hear anything back about that other matter?"

"I'm afraid not, sire."

"A pity."

"If I may," said Natalia. "If you don't think it impudent, could you tell us of what you speak? We are an experienced group and might be of some assistance."

The king looked at Svetlana.

"Natalia is a powerful mage," she urged, "and one of the Volstrum's brightest students. If anyone knows the goings-on in Karslev, it's likely to be her."

Maksim nodded. "Very well. I shall tell you of my troubles. What do you know of our neighbours?"

"Let me see," said Natalia, placing her finger against her chin as she thought. "Braymoor lies to the west, although they've been weak for years. That must mean Ostrova is giving you trouble."

"Remarkable. How did you know?"

"It is a simple deduction, Majesty. The only other neighbouring realm is Zaran, and that's little more than an unexplored wilderness. Might I ask the nature of the problem?"

"Their king wishes me to cede him a significant portion of our land. At least, that's what we believe."

"And by significant, you mean?"

"A large stretch of land this side of our southern border."

"I had no idea you had any cities that far south."

"That's just it," said the king, "I don't. The area's nothing but wilderness, which only adds to the confusion."

"There must be something else of value there," offered Belgast.

"Such as?"

The Dwarf shrugged. "Godstone, perhaps?"

"Godstone?"

"Aye, also called skymetal. A rare mineral that falls from the sky from time to time. We found some back in Ord-Kurgad."

"Ord-Kurgad?" asked Maksim.

"Aye, you wouldn't have heard of it, sire. It lies to the south, beyond the Grey Spire Mountains. In any event, it's possibly the most valuable metal on the Continent."

"What is it used for?"

"We Dwarves make weapons out of it. The properties of godstone are such that they can hold powerful magic."

"The stone is magical?"

"No, but a mage can empower it with their own magic. Surely you've heard stories of magical swords?"

"Of course, but I always assumed they were crafted from steel."

"Most are, but those of a legendary nature are forged from a metal that falls from the sky. Such a find would be worth a king's ransom, although I daresay they'd have difficulty finding someone who could smelt the stuff."

"Why is that?"

"It takes a special forge to generate enough heat even to melt it, let alone fashion it into something usable. I've heard of a hammer far to the west, but I've yet to see it with my own eyes." He paused, staring up at the sky, deep in thought. "Such a thing would be glorious."

"And you believe this godstone might be found along our southern border?"

"I merely offer it as one possibility, Your Majesty. Godstone is extremely rare; someone would have had to witness it falling from the sky."

"In that case," said the king, "we can say with some certainty its presence would be unlikely. That area of the country is nothing but thick forest. The only way to navigate it with any real success is by boat, and I don't see that happening. My understanding is the other side of the border is just as bad."

"Still, they want something," said Natalia. "Have they made any actual demands? These may be merely rumours meant to spread distrust and disharmony."

"I hadn't considered that, although our two kingdoms never really got along. Did you hear anything at the Volstrum?"

"The Volstrum?"

"Yes. You went there after your last visit, didn't you?"

"We did, but I'm afraid we learned nothing new regarding Ostrova." She noted Athgar taking an interest. "Have you something you'd care to share?"

"I recently heard some rumours," replied her bondmate. "It seems there has been some friction of late between Ostrova and Novarsk, one of the kingdoms lying farther south."

"What kind of friction?" asked Maksim. "Are you suggesting they're threatened with war? Surely if that were true, they'd be asking for our help instead of making threats."

"Perhaps," said Svetlana, "we might get some idea when their envoy arrives."

"Let us hope so," said the king. "Though Saints know when that will finally happen. In the meantime, I suppose we must bide our time."

TROUBLE IN THE CITY

SPRING 1109 SR

"These are nice quarters," said Athgar.

"Yes," agreed Natalia. "They remind me of the rooms the King of Andover provided, although this place feels less like a prison."

"And why would it? You're a celebrated member of the Stormwind family after all."

"Yes, well, let us be thankful Carlingen is less important to the family, or else we'd soon find ourselves in a dungeon."

"Do you really think Svetlana would allow that?"

"She would be hard-pressed to ignore a demand of that nature. When the family speaks, they expect their members to listen."

"How close is she to the Volstrum?"

"I'm not entirely sure," said Natalia. "The last time we were here, I got the impression she was resentful of them."

"And now?"

"I sense there's some frustration with their lack of response. She's asked them for help, though what form that might take is beyond me." She looked across the room to where the Dwarf was examining the legs of a small side table. "Some of us here should guard their words a little more carefully."

Belgast looked up. "Are you talking to me?"

"I am. You almost gave us away when you mentioned Ord-Kurgad."

He waved aside the criticism. "I'm one of the mountain folk; nobody takes us seriously." He paused as his cheeks coloured. "Well… not outside of Therengia."

Katrin threw herself onto a chair. "What do we do now?"

"We rest," said Stanislav. "I don't know about you, but I'm looking forward to finding out just how soft those pillows are."

"I'd like to learn more about the local Therengians," said Athgar.

"I'll go with you," offered Belgast. "We can't have the High Thane running around without protection."

"I shall keep him safe," said Herulf.

"All three of us can go," replied Athgar. "If people are struggling to get to Therengia, we must be able to find some way to help them."

"Good idea," said Natalia. "And I'll go and chat with Svetlana. Hopefully, I can get a better understanding of her relationship with the family."

"Why? What are you thinking?"

She smiled. "We already convinced Reinwick and Andover to ban Stormwinds from their court. Perhaps we can do the same here?"

"And how do you propose to do that? Svetlana is a Stormwind. I can't see her agreeing to ban herself?"

"You forget. Once she marries the king, she won't be a Stormwind anymore."

Athgar shook his head. "But you still are, even though we're bonded."

"True, but it's a Therengian custom where most people have but a single name. In the Petty Kingdoms, it's customary for a wife to take her husband's last name."

"Oh yes. I'd forgotten that, but she'd still be considered one of the family, wouldn't she?"

"That's where things get a little more complicated," said Natalia, "and something I intend to emphasize in my discussions with Svetlana. With a bit of luck, I might swing her over to our way of thinking."

"You mean to tell her of the family's connection to the Halvarian Empire?"

"Not right away, but it might be good to lay some groundwork."

"I'm not familiar with that expression."

"Let's just say I'll plant some seeds of doubt."

"Ah. Now that, I understand." Athgar glanced around the room. "What about the rest of you?"

"Don't look at me," replied Stanislav. "I've a meeting with my bed all planned out."

"Greta and I will wander around the Palace," said Katrin. "Having a good idea of the floor plan might prove advantageous."

"Very well," said Athgar. "We'll meet back here before dinner. I assume that'll be sometime after dark?"

"Yes," replied Natalia. "That's the normal custom in these parts." A wicked grin appeared on her face. "Though it's also the custom to bathe before an important meal."

Athgar returned her gaze with a similar expression. "Then perhaps I should stay and warm your water?"

She chuckled. "Get out of here, bondmate. You've work to do!"

Athgar's laughter echoed down the hallway as they headed off to the streets of Carlingen.

The mud clung to Athgar's boots as he strolled down the street. Herulf insisted on leading the way, constantly looking ahead on the alert for any danger.

"He's dedicated," said Belgast. "I'll give him that."

"He is," replied Athgar, "but his manner puts me ill at ease."

"Why? Because he protects you?"

"I am a simple man by nature, used to looking after myself. Having a bodyguard feels like an act of excessive pride. I'm no better than any other Therengian."

Belgast snorted. "You are the High Thane of Therengia and a master of flame, Athgar. You couldn't be more different if you tried. Still, your modesty befits you." He glanced towards their guide. "Don't worry. You'll grow so accustomed to him, you won't even notice his presence."

"You speak from experience?"

"I do. If you recall, I once told you I served King Haglarith of Kragen-Tor."

"I remember. You were one of his advisors, weren't you?"

"I was, and as such, I was guarded day and night by his Royal Guards. I tried to object and cursed at the inconvenience, but I eventually got used to it." He nodded at Herulf. "He certainly proved his worth in Reinwick. Have you considered making him one of your captains once we return home?"

Athgar opened his mouth to answer, but movement off to his right interrupted him. Over twenty people approached, their eyes locked on him.

Belgast's hand went to his pick, but Athgar stopped him. "They are unarmed."

"They still have fists," said the Dwarf.

The group who approached was a mixed bunch, half men with the rest women and children, but they advanced cautiously. They halted some five paces short, and then an elderly man with a scraggly grey beard stepped forward.

"My lord," he said. "Have you come to lead us?"

"Lead you?" replied Athgar. "I am not the ruler here."

"Yet you have the grey eyes of our race. Are you truly a noble of the Old Kingdom?"

"Therengia has no nobles."

"They had a king, Lord."

Belgast snorted. "He's got you there."

"My name is Athgar, and I have the honour of representing the people of Therengia."

The mention of his homeland sent murmurs through the group.

"Then the rumours are true," the bearded man continued. "The Old Kingdom is reborn."

"Not reborn," said Athgar. "Therengia is not an empire dedicated to conquering other lands. It is a home where people like us can live in peace and harmony with others."

A younger man pushed his way forward. "Peace? You dare to speak of peace? We are descendants of the once great Kingdom of Therengia. For too long, we've been subject to ridicule and oppression. It is time we took back what is rightfully ours!"

"I understand your anger, but if we want to flourish as a people, we must live alongside others, not subjugate them. To do so makes us no better than our enemies."

The older man pushed his younger companion back. "Ignore the harsh words of Athelstan. The passion of youth drives him. He means no offence, Lord."

"A passion I well understand, but I am no lord. Please, call me Athgar."

The man bowed. "Very well, Athgar. I am Haywald, a boot maker by trade."

"Pleased to meet you, Master Cobbler, but something tells me your presence here is no mere coincidence."

"You are correct, my lord. Your arrival in Carlingen was noted, and word soon spread throughout the city."

"And you just happened to gather as I'm out walking?"

"Forgive us, Lord. We followed you to the Royal Palace, and we've watched for your departure ever since."

"To what end?"

"To bring you word of our plight." Haywald glanced around the street. "But here is not the best place to speak of such things."

"Then where would you suggest?"

The old man bowed deeply. "I humbly invite you to my home, Lord, to share bread."

"I would suggest otherwise, Lord," said Herulf. "He may mean you harm."

"Nonsense," said Athgar. "The sharing of bread is an ancient Therengian custom. I'm surprised you're not familiar with it."

"You forget, Lord, I was raised in Reinwick, where they suppressed our culture."

"Then consider this a chance to reconnect with your heritage." Athgar bowed. "I am pleased to accept your invitation, Master Haywald."

The rest of the group appeared happy, although they said nothing.

The old man smiled, displaying a surprisingly good set of teeth. "Then come, my lord, and I shall take you to my home."

Haywald led them down a side street, drawing attention from all they passed. Athgar noted the six men walking alongside, three per side, clubs in hand. "Who are they?" he asked.

"They are our fyrd, my lord. They keep our streets safe."

"You guard your own streets?"

"Only out of necessity, for the king's men dare not tread this section of the city."

"Why not?"

"We learned long ago if we did not protect our own, many lives would be lost."

"That explains the presence of your fyrd but not the absence of the king's men."

"The city is large, and His Majesty lacks the manpower to patrol it properly. As a result, each area must fend for itself." Haywald halted at a crossroad. "The Temple Knights of Saint Agnes patrol the area to our left, while the domain of the Brotherhood is to the right."

"Brotherhood?" said Athgar. "More Temple Knights?"

"No. They are mercenaries, or to be more precise, they were. Now they prey on others, providing their so-called protection for a price."

"And behind us?"

"That is considered the Palace district and thus one of the few areas the king controls. Ahead lies the Therengian district."

"Have you a Dwarven district?" asked Belgast.

"No," replied Haywald. "The mountain folk are scattered throughout the city. For the most part, they're left to their own devices."

"So you're saying the Brotherhood preys on them?"

"Not at all. Not even the Brotherhood would dare upset a Dwarf. To do so would soon find them incapable of procuring weapons."

"Are you suggesting all of my people are smiths?"

"Not at all, Master Dwarf, but an insult to one is an insult to many, and those who are smiths made it clear they will not do business with any who threaten their kin."

"Would that we could all act so," said Athgar.

They continued on their way, the buildings growing more dilapidated as they moved farther into the Therengian district.

"Are all the buildings as bad as this?" asked Belgast. "It's a wonder they don't collapse."

"We're forced to make do with little," said Haywald, "and these are some of the oldest buildings in Carlingen."

"This is worse than Reinwick," offered Herulf. "We might not have had many rights, but at least we had roofs over our heads."

"Why such poverty?" asked Belgast. "You mentioned you were a cobbler, have you no customers?"

"I had a thriving business back in Eidolon, but when we heard Therengia had been reborn, we sold off everything and paid a ship to bring us here."

"I assume you meant to continue on?" asked Athgar.

"We did, but the ship's captain demanded the rest of our coins before setting us ashore, stranding us here. I'm afraid it's a common story amongst our people."

"Have you taken this to the king?"

Haywald shrugged. "We talked to some of his men, but none were inclined to help unless we could pay them."

They halted before a run-down building with two windows looking out onto the streets, their shutters warped with age, while a weather-beaten door graced the entrance. Athgar covered a cough with his hand, for the place reeked of rot and mildew.

The door opened, discharging a pair of children who rushed forth, bumping into Athgar in their haste to get outdoors. Moments later, an older woman appeared, her apron stained with the accumulations of a lifetime spent in a kitchen.

"My apologies, Lord," she said, bowing. Her eyes flicked to Haywald. "I didn't know we were expecting guests."

"This is my wife, Brona."

"And those children?" said Athgar. "Yours?"

"My son's," replied Haywald. "Left in our care on his passing."

"My condolences on your loss. Might I enquire as to how he died?"

Brona teared up, leading her husband to step forward and embrace her. "There, there," he muttered, holding her tight.

Athelstan pushed his way to the front door, turning on Athgar. "Temple Knights beat him to death."

"Which ones?" asked Athgar.

"Does it matter? They're all the same, treating us like we're vermin!"

"I've dealt with Temple Knights before, and those of Saint Mathew were of great help in the past. Even now, they patrol the streets of Ebenstadt, one of Therengia's cities." He paused as he realized what the man meant. "You're talking about the Cunars, aren't you?"

"I am. Why? Are they your friends?"

"No," said Athgar. "Most definitely not. We've fought them twice now."

"And when he says that," added Belgast, "he means we beat them."

"Then help us fight!" said Athelstan.

"I am not here to fight," replied Athgar. "I'm here to learn more about your plight. I promise you this, though: if you truly wish to travel to Therengia, I will do all in my power to make that possible."

Brona broke from her husband's embrace, then straightened her apron. "Come, my lord. Let us share what little bread we have."

She led them inside, leaving the crowd milling around at the front door. The home of Haywald and Brona was little more than one room of a much larger building. The place had the look of an inn or tavern, likely the building's original purpose, but it had seen better days. It now housed multiple families, each home marked by a simple hanging cloth instead of a door.

"We used the doors to fuel the fire our first winter here," explained Haywald.

"Who owns this place?" asked Belgast.

"No one, as far as we can tell. These buildings sat here rotting when we arrived."

"A pity. Their construction has held up well. They must have represented a considerable investment back when they were built."

"This is our home," said Brona, indicating a worn brown blanket adorning an opening. She pushed it aside, leading them all into a small room. A fireplace sat against the far wall, its flames offering scant heat against the day's chill. To the left was a rickety-looking table, upon which Brona had been preparing food. "I'm afraid we haven't much," she said. "Had I been expecting you, I would have seen fit to find something grander." She placed half a loaf of old bread on a platter while everyone sat on the floor.

Her offering was meagre, yet Athgar couldn't help but think it represented a significant portion of their daily food. He considered refusing but knew it would be seen as an insult. Instead, he plucked a tiny morsel from the loaf and popped it in his mouth. Haywald did likewise, then passed what remained of it around the circle.

"You've told me of your past," said Athgar, "now tell me what you hope for the future."

"We are a simple people. Our dream is to live a simple life, free from tyranny and oppression."

"And you believe Therengia would allow you that freedom?"

"I know many see that as wishful thinking, but what is there to life if not hope?"

"That is all we have left," added Brona. "The dream of a better life."

"We must do something," insisted Belgast. "This just isn't right."

"I agree," replied Athgar, "but I am not a wealthy man. I cannot simply spend coins and send these people on their way." He fell silent, his gaze taking in his new acquaintances. "I shall find a way to better your lives," he said at last. "Though at this precise moment, I know not how. From what I've learned, he lacks the men to bring order to the streets of Carlingen. I fear it will be some time before you'll see an improvement in your circumstances."

"So that's it?" said Brona. "You hear of our plight and then abandon us?"

Athgar met her gaze. "I will not abandon you, I promise, but I must consider your circumstances before I attempt to act. To make changes prematurely could lead to the situation worsening."

"Worsening?" said Herulf. "My pardon, Lord, but how in the name of the Gods could it get any worse?"

"You've lived in Reinwick. Have you so soon forgotten the restrictions you were under? Imagine if the king banned these people from carrying weapons. The streets would become a bloodbath."

"He's right," said Haywald. "Only the strength of our fyrd keeps the enemies at bay."

"It's not a fyrd," replied Belgast, "at least not a proper one. Those men are more of a collection of thugs. What you need is someone to come in here and train them."

"You insult us," said Brona. "Those men are the only thing keeping us safe."

"My apologies, madam. I didn't mean to insinuate they weren't useful, merely that they could be better equipped to carry out their duties. Individually, I'm sure they're capable, but a proper fyrd must learn to work together to make a lasting difference. Decent weapons would go a long way to help."

"You make a good point," said Athgar, "yet I fear the cost of arming their fyrd would be prohibitive."

Belgast stared at him. "I know that look. You have something in mind."

"I do, but I'd rather not say more until I've spoken to Natalia." Athgar rose, then bowed towards his hosts. "Thank you, Haywald, Brona, for your hospitality. I hope sometime soon I'll have the opportunity to return the favour."

Everyone else stood, then Athgar left them, deep in thought.

Herulf looked at Belgast. "Looks like our visit is about to get a lot more complicated."

The Dwarf laughed. "That's putting it mildly!"

SVETLANA'S PLEAS

SPRING 1109 SR

Svetlana stared out the second-storey window at the Great Northern Sea, its distant horizon marred by a mist far out over the water. Her attention was so focused that she wasn't aware of someone entering.

"I hope I'm not interrupting anything?" said Natalia, standing beside her. "Enjoying the view?"

"To tell the truth, there's not much to see."

"Yet you still gaze seaward."

"I was trying to imagine what those at the Volstrum are up to."

"The same thing they always are, terrorizing their new students."

"No," said Svetlana. "I meant the matriarch and her advisors. I suppose I should've said Stormwind Manor rather than the Volstrum."

"Stormwind Manor no longer exists. The victim of a fire, I'm told."

"A pity. I always wanted to see it. Have you ever been there?"

"I have."

"And what was it like?"

"Rather unremarkable, to be honest. A large, rectangular building divided into an assortment of stuffy rooms. Nothing as grandiose as the Palace here. You should count yourself lucky."

Svetlana stared down at her hands as she unconsciously wrung them. "I do, yet I feel so abandoned here, as if I've been casually tossed aside as useless. I suppose it must've been quite different for you, considering the strength of your magic."

"The family would have us believe they are everything, but there's more to life than blind obedience."

"It surprises me to hear you say that. It's certainly not what our instructors at the Volstrum preached."

"I'm of the opinion that most of those instructors had minimal real-world experience amongst the Petty Kingdoms."

Svetlana met her gaze. "What are you saying?"

"Serving a cause is one thing, but doing so blindly can lead to a person's ruin. I prefer a more tempered approach."

"That being?"

"Athgar was not the family's choice when it came to bonding, yet I followed my heart."

"Is he the king you said you had an affair with?"

Natalia blushed. "I might've exaggerated a bit there. He's not a king, but he's an accomplished Fire Mage."

"But not a Sartellian? You dared oppose the family's wishes?"

"My situation is not too dissimilar to yours when you think about it."

"I fail to see how."

"You are following your heart in regard to the king, are you not?"

Svetlana blushed. "Yes. I suppose I am."

"Tell me, did you ever notify our superiors of your intent to marry?"

"No. I intend to inform them after the fact when it would be too late to do anything about it. I hope that doesn't upset you?"

"Not at all," said Natalia. "I think it's wonderful. However, I am curious what the family is so interested in when it comes to Carlingen."

"I've sent reports on many things over the years, but I've not received any hint of what draws their interest."

"Yes. The family is like that. They ignore you until they want something, then the fangs come out."

"Fangs?"

"Sorry. I didn't mean to be dramatic. In my experience, they have a singular focus, to the exclusion of all else. I know it's not entirely true, but from our point of view, that's what it feels like. If it were up to them, we'd never even be allowed to have friends. What kind of life would that be?"

"A lonely one," said Svetlana. "I should know. That's precisely what they told me when they sent me here."

"Yet you fell in love with the king. If you don't mind me asking, when did you first realize there was an attraction?"

"He was always polite, even when we were first introduced. When I arrived, he was only a prince and not even the heir. He wasn't meant to be king, you know. He was the youngest of four brothers, but they all died before they could assume the Throne."

"Yet he is named Maksim, like his father."

"His actual name was Horatio, but he changed it when he ascended to the Throne. He believed taking his father's name would promote a sense of continuity. Unfortunately, that didn't quite work out as he hoped."

"When we came through here last year, you said you had him wrapped around your finger."

"That was pure bravado," said Svetlana. "I didn't want a fellow Volstrum graduate thinking I'd gone soft."

"Loving someone is not a weakness; it's a strength."

"Not to the family."

"The family doesn't know everything."

"Don't they? They have a presence in every court of consequence across the Petty Kingdoms. That's a tremendous amount of power."

"It is," said Natalia, "but to what end? What is the purpose of having that amount of influence if they never use it?"

"I'm not sure I understand."

"We attended the same lectures at the Volstrum. Tell me, have wars lessened in the last century?"

"No. If anything, they've increased."

"Precisely. So why doesn't the family employ their influence and diplomacy instead of letting the Continent fall into chaos?"

"You shock me," said Svetlana. "You openly speak of the family with contempt."

"Not the entire family," replied Natalia, "but you must admit, some take advantage of their position to further their own aims. How about the person you report to, for instance? Have they ever even met you?"

"No. As far as I know, my letters could be sitting unread in a box."

"Precisely. Would it be too much to ask for them to respond or at least acknowledge they've read your correspondence?"

Svetlana clenched her jaw. "No, it would not. I've been writing to them about our current circumstances for months, yet I haven't heard so much as a peep. Do you have the same problem?"

Natalia smiled. "I don't concern myself with letters, and chances are, any they've sent would have a hard time catching up."

"You travel that much?"

"Let's just say I've seldom remained in one place for very long."

"You must possess some influence in Karslev," said Svetlana. "Would you consider using it to help us here in Carlingen?"

Natalia contemplated her request. She'd still not revealed the truth of her situation, and she feared to press the woman too much on the matter. Then again, she didn't want to lie outright if she could avoid it. "I have friends I could write to," she finally said, "although it would likely be some time before we hear back."

A look of relief flooded across Svetlana's face. "Thank you, Natalia. I greatly appreciate it."

"Is there anything in particular you'd like me to ask?"

"I'm concerned they won't care for the idea of me becoming queen. What if they recall me to the Volstrum?"

"I can't see them doing that. The family is all about influence, and who better to wield that than a queen? I'd say it's far more likely they'd urge you to use that relationship to push their agenda."

"And if that is contrary to Maksim's wishes?"

"There often comes a time in a person's life when a single decision will have lasting consequences. At moments like that, we must weigh our options and make the choice we can best live with."

"Are you suggesting I take the family's or the king's side?"

"That is a decision only you can make, Svetlana. Regardless of your choice, know I am here to support it." She forced a smile. "Come. It's a nice enough day. Let us cast aside our worries for the moment and concentrate on other more pleasant thoughts."

"Yes, of course. What would you like to talk about?"

"Your impending nuptials. I assume the ceremony will be conducted at the Temple of Saint Mathew?"

"Naturally."

"Did you arrange for the Temple Knights of Saint Agnes to escort you there on the day?"

"No. Why would I?"

"It's not uncommon for them to escort noble brides to the ceremony."

"But not after?"

"That is usually the new husband's prerogative."

"Then I must visit the local commandery."

"We can go together," offered Natalia. "Why not this afternoon?"

"I'm afraid the king asked me to be present when he meets with his barons."

"Then allow me to go and visit the Temple Knights in your stead?"

"Are you sure? That's an awful lot to ask of you."

"Nonsense. It'll be nice to get out and see the city."

"The city is a dangerous place."

"Then I'll take Katrin with me. I can't imagine anyone would dare interrupt the travels of a pair of Stormwinds!"

. . .

On their previous visit, they'd stayed at the Warriors Rest, an inn right across the street from the Commandery of Saint Agnes. Natalia now steered Katrin in that direction while Greta followed along behind, her attention constantly shifting from one building to the next.

The district patrolled by the Temple Knights was in marked contrast to the rest of the city, for people walked the streets without fear, few carrying weapons to defend themselves.

They had only gone half a block before they caught sight of their first Temple Knight patrol: six mounted women riding down the street, their visors up, the better to see around them. Natalia stared, open-mouthed.

"Problem?" asked Katrin.

"I swear I know that knight."

The knights advanced, and then their leader slowed, coming to a halt less than three paces away. "Natalia? Is that you?"

"Sister Cordelia. I didn't expect to run across you here."

"I was promoted to Temple Captain and sent to take over as head of the company here."

"When did you arrive?"

"Six weeks ago, give or take a day. What brings you here? Not hunting for godstone, I hope?"

"Not at all. I happened to be passing through but was invited to a wedding, so I thought I'd stay a little longer. I trust we didn't get you into too much trouble back in Krieghoff?"

"There was a bit of a misunderstanding with the Church's upper echelons, but nothing too terrible."

"What happened to the father general?"

"I couldn't say. He was shipped off to the Antonine, and we haven't heard anything since. Mind you, they're not in the habit of sharing information about punishment, so I suppose we shouldn't be surprised. What of you? Still with Athgar?"

"Yes. In fact, we have a daughter, Oswyn, though I'm afraid she's not here with us."

"Marvellous," said Cordelia. "I'd love to stay and chat, but there's a patrol to see to. Perhaps you'd care to stop by the commandery later?"

"I was on my way there now, actually. I need to talk to you about the upcoming Royal Wedding."

"I wondered when that topic might come to my attention. I assume they want us to escort the bride?"

"Yes."

"Drop by the commandery in a few days, and we'll see what we can do."

"A few days?"

"Yes. I've never escorted a bride before, so I should read up on what's required."

"I'll bring some wine."

"Even better," replied Cordelia. "Now, you must excuse me. Give my regards to Athgar."

"I will." Natalia watched as the Temple Knights rode on.

"You didn't tell me you had friends in the order," said Katrin.

"Only the one, and I had no idea she was here."

"You mentioned Krieghoff. What was that all about?"

"There was a Cunar there, a Father General Gilbert, who led an attack on Ord-Kurgad."

"The Orc village of the Red Hand?"

"Precisely. The intervention of Cordelia and her knights helped us win the day."

"She was a captain?"

"No. Back then she was an equerry, but her captain put her in charge of a detachment of Temple Knights."

"Is this what you do now? Run around making friends wherever you go?"

Natalia laughed. "Yes. I suppose it is."

"How long ago did you meet her?"

"Let's see now—it must be close to five years. Athgar and I sought refuge in the Grey Spire Mountains, where we first met Belgast. It's rather a long story, better told over a nice drink."

"Well, our visit to the commandery has been delayed for a few days. Perhaps we should seek out a tavern instead?"

"I'd prefer to return to the Palace. The atmosphere there is far more welcoming, and the drinks are free."

"Svetlana knows nothing about what we've been up to, does she?"

"No, she doesn't, at least not as far as I'm aware."

"Could the family have filled her in on your past exploits?"

"Anything's possible, but I doubt it. From what she told me, all her communications with the family have been one way."

"She could be lying."

"No, I don't think so. If you recall, she considered herself the very epitome of the high-born Stormwind. If she had designs on arresting me, I doubt she'd keep them to herself. And if she did, why wait? It would have been a relatively simple matter to apprehend us when we first arrived."

"She's still a Stormwind," warned Katrin.

"I'm well aware, but then again, so am I. Are you suggesting I'm not to be trusted?"

"Of course not."

"You were just like her once," said Natalia. "You changed. Why not her? We should at least give her the benefit of the doubt."

"I suppose I'm just jaded. It comes from spending years in the magerite mines. It's like everywhere we go, we're under the eyes of the family."

"It won't be long before we're back in Runewald, where you can learn to relax."

"Runewald?" piped up Greta. "What's it like?"

"Peaceful," said Natalia, "or at least it was when we left."

"Is it like Zienholtz?"

"No. The two are nothing alike. Zienholtz is a city, while Runewald is a country village with fresh air and an abundance of trees."

"Does that mean no cobblestone roads?"

"It does, although if you miss them that much, you can always travel to Ebenstadt. It's not as large as the capital of Andover, but it has plenty of streets."

"When will we go there?"

"Some time yet," replied Natalia. "We're waiting for our friends, Kargen and Shaluhk. I expect they'll have their son, Agar, with them too."

"Is he my age?"

"No. He's almost six, but by Human standards, he's more like ten."

"I'm not sure what you mean," said Greta.

"Orcs mature faster than us Humans. Their younglings reach physical maturity at fourteen and also walk and talk much sooner than Human children."

"And is Agar their only child?"

"He is."

Greta looked down at her hands, almost whispering, "Do Orcs love their children?"

"Of course. What kind of a question is that?"

"I only ask because I was sent to the king's court."

"Did your parents die?"

"No. They couldn't afford to feed me."

"I'm sorry," said Natalia. "That is a terrible burden to bear."

"She won't bear it alone," insisted Katrin. "She's going to live with me once we get to Runewald. I'll raise her as my own."

Natalia noted her classmates' look of determination. It wouldn't be an easy transition, especially after all the hardships they'd been through, but at least Katrin would have a family of her own. "It'll be nice to get home," she said, "and I expect you two will fit in well."

"I'm looking forward to it," said Greta. "I've never had a real home before, at least not one where I was wanted."

"Have you considered what you'd like to do once you settle down?"

"I'm still trying to get used to not living in the Palace hallways."

"Perhaps she'll find a nice Therengian boy to settle down with," teased Katrin.

"I could suggest the same for you," added Natalia. "There are many eligible men in Runewald, and you would be considered quite the catch, being a Water Mage."

"Can I be a Water Mage?" asked Greta.

"I honestly don't know. A person's ability for magic is sometimes determined by an affinity for one of the elements. Have you any particular attachment to water?"

"I'm not sure what you mean by affinity."

"Do you find yourself drawn to water or fascinated by fish?"

"Not particularly, but until I met you, I'd never even seen the sea."

"What about fire?" asked Katrin. "Do you find yourself fascinated by flames?"

"I learned how to build a fire at the Palace, but I wouldn't say it holds my attention."

"That would seem to rule out Fire Magic. How about animals? Any love for forest creatures or birds?"

"I don't particularly like horses. As for birds, they're more of a nuisance when they spend all their time singing."

"Well," said Natalia. "Your circumstances appear to indicate you possess no innate magical ability, but that's far from certain. Athgar only gained his magic through great tragedy."

"Also," added Katrin, "we must bear in mind there is no definitive way to identify a wielder of magic until they come of age."

"Where does magic come from?" asked Greta.

"The prevailing theory," replied Natalia, "is it's in the bloodline. We know the children of mages often have magic, but there's also a theory it can lie dormant for generations."

"And what do you think?"

"It's a lot more complicated. There is an argument to be made that magic is nurtured instead of being natural, which would fit Athgar's background. It doesn't, however, explain mine."

"Why?"

"I manifested magic at a very young age, and that was without the presence of a magical father to guide me in any way."

"Perhaps your mother possessed magic?"

"That is a possibility, but I'm still undecided on that. The breeding program of the Stormwinds has produced some powerful mages over the years, but it's not unknown for two mages to produce a child with no magic. I think what it all comes down to can be summed up in a simple word—complicated."

TURMOIL

SPRING 1109 SR

Upon returning to the Palace, Athgar found Natalia in their room.

"Tired?" he asked.

"Not particularly. I was enjoying a little peace and quiet, but now that you're back, we have things to discuss."

"We do. My trip into Carlingen was very… illuminating, but I sense you also learned something new. Why don't you go first?"

"Very well," said Natalia. "I had a chat with Svetlana."

"And?"

"She's not happy with the family. Given enough time, I believe I can sway her to our way of thinking. She would make a powerful ally."

"Did you tell her about Runewald?"

"Not directly, but I let slip the family doesn't always have her best interests at heart. She feels they've abandoned her, and I can see why. Her superiors at the Volstrum have yet to return any of her correspondence."

"That's good for us, surely?"

"It is," said Natalia, "but I can't help feeling sorry for her. She's lonely here, despite the upcoming wedding. What she really needs is some friends."

"Wasn't she one of those who teased you mercilessly during your stay at the Volstrum?"

"She was, but then again, so was Katrin, initially. The Stormwinds warp the minds of everyone who steps through the doors of the Volstrum; that's not an easy thing to undo."

"I assume that means we'll stay in Carlingen a little longer than we initially planned?"

"We don't need to make a decision just yet. After all, we're still waiting for Kargen and Shaluhk."

"Anything else to report?"

"As a matter of fact, there is," said Natalia. "We set out for the Agnes commandery today to make some arrangements for the wedding, and you'll never guess who we ran across."

Athgar stared back, his mind searching through their shared history. "I give up. Who?"

"Cordelia."

"The Temple Knight?"

"Temple Captain now," corrected Natalia. "She arrived a short time ago to take up her new command. She invited me to come and visit her to discuss the wedding arrangements. Perhaps you'd care to join me?"

"I'd be delighted, and Belgast might like to accompany us. He spent a lot of time in her company."

"While we're there, I thought it would be a good idea to talk to her about the possibility of sending sister knights to Therengia."

"That would mean revealing our true roles."

"Yes, but if you can't trust a Temple Knight, who can you?"

"I might remind you the Cunars are Temple Knights, and we don't trust them!"

"Point taken, but these are Holy Sisters we're talking about, the same order that helped us at Ord-Kurgad."

"You're right, but let's not lead with the idea. We'll stick to the wedding ceremony initially and get a feel for where they stand regarding the whole 'crusade' thing before we start asking for favours."

"That's probably for the best. What of you? Tell me of this illumination you mentioned earlier."

"If you recall, the city is broken into districts, each patrolled by... well, let's call them factions. The Therengians took it upon themselves to form a fyrd, though they pale in comparison to what we have back in Runewald."

"Go on."

"It seems there's been little change since we last left. They don't trust the king, and I can't say I blame them. From the sounds of it, his men are corrupt. Between them and the ship's captain, these people have been robbed blind and deprived of most of their coins. All they want is a home to call their own, but they're trapped in the slums of Carlingen."

"Is there anything we can do for them?"

"We could offer them sanctuary in Therengia, but getting them there is the problem. We don't have the funds to hire boats, and I doubt Kargen will bring enough umaks to take more than a handful."

"True," said Natalia, "yet I can tell you have a plan."

"Am I that obvious?"

She smiled. "Only to me. So, what is it you've come up with?"

"King Maksim wants to control the city streets, and the Therengians already have a fyrd. I propose His Majesty equip them properly and let them expand the area they patrol. It solves the king's manpower problem while at the same time mending fences. After all, it's difficult to be mad at a ruler when he's giving you better equipment. It would also elevate their status amongst the people of Carlingen. I'd still like to see them in Therengia, but this would at least make their lives more bearable."

"It's a good plan," said Natalia, "though who knows what the king will make of it. Perhaps it would be best to win Svetlana over to the idea first, then take it to His Majesty."

"You think that might work?"

"There's only one way to find out. How many Therengians are there in Carlingen?"

"That's something I've yet to determine, but judging from the street I went down, I expect at least a couple thousand. Of course, not all those would be eligible to be part of the fyrd. There's also the matter of women. I doubt the king would allow them to patrol the streets."

"They do in Runewald."

"Yes, they do," replied Athgar, "but this is not Therengia, and we cannot expect Carlingen to adopt the same traditions as us."

Natalia smiled. "You said us."

"You're as much a part of Therengia as I am. In fact, you named the place!"

"Yes, but only because I couldn't think of anything else. I sometimes wonder if that decision didn't just make things worse."

"Nonsense," said Athgar. "If anything, it's helped our cause. Ever since word got out, Therengians have flooded east, swelling our numbers."

"Yes, but at the same time, the other Petty Kingdoms see us as their worst nightmare come to life, which raises the matter of how to present your idea to Svetlana. She might think it strange that I advocate for a people disliked across the Continent. The family certainly wouldn't suggest such a thing."

"Then present it as a cost-effective method for raising a militia to patrol the streets."

"I'm sure she'll ask who will train them."

"I will," replied Athgar. "I've spent more than my fair share of time amongst the Runewald fyrd. I know what's needed."

"Belgast can help you, and what about Herulf?"

"As far as I'm aware, he has little experience with such things."

"He fought off the invasion near Korvoran."

"Yes. He proved to be particularly skilled at deploying archers, or so I'm led to believe. Perhaps I'll have him do the same here."

"They're to be used patrolling the streets," said Natalia, "not going into battle. I doubt bows would be of much use."

"I suppose you're right, but there's something I find a little disturbing about having an improperly formed fyrd. Footmen without bows is like having… I don't know, maybe a Water Mage without an ice spell?"

Natalia laughed. "An ice spell? I'm afraid you'll need to do better than that. Do you mean ice shards, or a frozen portal, perchance? Or did you have something else in mind?"

"Now you're just teasing. You know full well what I meant."

"Yes, I do, and I think I know what has you so vexed."

"Then please enlighten me."

"Sooner or later, these people will travel to Therengia, most likely by foot. For that to happen, they must be able to defend themselves, which is why you want archers."

"Is it? I hadn't considered that, but I suppose that's true. It's not as if the king could afford to provide an escort."

"Hopefully, he won't be upset at them leaving."

"Upset?" said Athgar. "Why would he be upset?"

"Would you go to the expense of arming and equipping a force of men only to see them march off to the middle of nowhere? Arming a militia is a financial investment he might not be willing to part with."

"This is getting more complicated by the moment. Should I try to come up with another solution?"

"We can certainly give it further thought, but what you suggest has merit. The trick will be looking at it from all angles and finding a solution that suits everyone. Give it a couple of days, and then I'll take whatever we've got to Svetlana."

Natalia sat on the floor, staring at a decorative bowl full of water. She concentrated, drawing forth her magic and using her words of power to channel arcane energies into the object of her attention. The surface rippled, then colours swirled around, finally coalescing into the smiling face of Galina Stormwind.

"Good to hear from you," the woman responded. "How are things in Carlingen?"

"Peaceful at present, although the king is concerned about some problems with his neighbour to the south."

"Ostrova?"

"Yes. That's the one. What do you know of it?"

"The last I heard, they were ruled by a king. From a military standpoint, they have a large army, although they keep most of it close to their border with Salovia. I believe that kingdom is their traditional enemy."

"Any idea how big that army might be or what it consists of?"

"Ah, now you're getting into one of my favourite subjects. Naturally, I don't have my notes, but if I recall, it consisted largely of foot troops, close to half, maybe even a little more. I believe their archers make up another thirty percent, with the remainder being horse." Her hand went to her chin. "Let me think. There was something distinct about their cavalry. Oh yes, I remember—they don't use knights."

"Not at all?"

"They had them in the past, but they were involved in a rebellion. After that, the king banned them."

"What do they use instead?"

"Mounted men-at-arms, likely wearing no more than links of mail. Their Royal Family has an almost paranoid fear of being overthrown, so they limit what any one noble can raise, and the horsemen fall under the king's exclusive command, including a Royal Guard that takes to the field on occasion. They are a somewhat backwards country in terms of tactics and strategy, but as you and I know, that can change with the presence of a single individual, so I wouldn't put much stock in that information. Are you expecting trouble?"

"Possibly," said Natalia. "There are rumours the King of Ostrova wants to claim some of Carlingen's territory, but we've yet to receive any official demands."

"Are there any Stormwinds or Sartellians at court?"

"Yes. Svetlana. You remember her?"

"I do. She was someone who asked a lot of questions, but I can't recall if she had much potential. Did they breed her?"

"No," replied Natalia.

"Ah. Well then, you have your answer. Had she a decent amount of power, it would have been the first thing they ordered her to do. She was, if I recall, a high-born and well-regarded."

"The family appears to have abandoned her. She's received no word from them since her assignment here."

"That is the way of the Stormwinds," said Galina. "It's one of the things that bothered Illiana so much. She wanted to strengthen family bonds by doing more for our graduates, but Marakhova was against it."

"I thank you for the insight," said Natalia. "Have you any news concerning things in Reinwick?"

"Not since you left. There was talk of training Reinwick's footmen to fight alongside the men of Andover, but it has yet to be formalized. No, I take that back. There is some news, although relatively minor. They've decided to officially name their arrangement the Northern Alliance. I suspect there shall be a diplomatic effort to bring Eidolon into it, perhaps even Langwal. Both would need to agree to ban the Stormwinds and Sartellians, present company excepted, of course."

"There appears to be a new power on the Continent."

"As long as things continue on their present course, yes, but I imagine it will be some months before we see anything substantial regarding cooperation. I'll let you know if anything else happens before our next communication. Shall we say the same time next week?"

"I look forward to it," said Natalia.

"Very well."

The image faded, replaced by a reflection of Greta.

"What are you doing?" the girl asked.

"Using a spell to communicate with Galina. It's not as versatile as the Orc's method but has its uses."

"How does she know when you're trying to contact her?"

"I arrange the next communication ahead of time."

"So, when the time comes, she just watches her bowl?"

"That's right," said Natalia. "Or has someone watch it on her behalf."

"If I were watching the bowl and she made contact, would I see her?"

"No, that's not quite how it works. You are not the intended recipient, so you'd only notice ripples in the water, no image. Which is usually enough to indicate someone is attempting to make contact, though, so it serves the same purpose."

"Do Fire Mages possess that ability?"

"Some have access to a magic flame which allows a person to project their image, but I'm not aware of the specifics."

"Is there no way for a Fire Mage to contact a Water Mage?"

"As far as I know, only mages within the same discipline can communicate over long distances, and even then, they would both need to know the spell involved. The family's practice has always been to limit knowledge of those types of spells to only its most trusted members."

"And the Orcs?"

"Their spell notifies the person they're trying to contact and is known by all their shamans."

"But not to Humans?"

"Shaluhk tells me there is a Human woman to the west who learned the spell, but she promised not to pass it on to others without the Orcs' permission."

"I imagine a spell like that would be quite valuable."

"Indeed, and highly sought after if its existence was made known, so don't go spreading any rumours about it."

"I would never do such a thing," said Greta. "I promise."

"You know, travelling with us exposes you to a great many dangers."

"Katrin told me all about the family. Don't worry. If there's one thing I learned in Zienholtz, it's when to remain silent."

"Do you regret leaving Andover?"

"No. It felt like a prison. 'Speak only when spoken to,' they said and, 'mind your place.' All I ever learned was to remain silent and slink into the background."

"You're free of all that now," said Natalia. "And though you're still young, eventually, you'll have to make your own decisions. It's our responsibility to enable you to do just that."

"Meaning?"

"Eiddenwerthe is full of different cultures and realms, each with its own idea of proper behaviour. If you are to thrive, we must see to it you learn to recognize what is acceptable when dealing with strangers."

"But I am to live in Therengia, am I not?"

"Yes," said Natalia, "you are, but our home... your home is growing in influence. There will come a day when delegates from across the Continent come seeking our help, and when that day arrives, we shall need you at our side, not as a servant, but as an equal. All we ask of you in return is to listen and learn. I'm not suggesting you remain quiet as you did back in Andover, but it would be best if questions waited until others were not around. Do you understand?"

"I do," replied Greta, falling silent as she was clearly struggling with something.

"You have questions?" asked Natalia.

"If I possess no magic, then how am I to be of help to you?"

"Magic does not define a person's value. Take Belgast, for example, or Stanislav, for that matter. Neither has the capacity for magic, yet they've proven themselves indispensable."

"But I am no mage hunter or smith."

Natalia chuckled. "Belgast is no smith; that's his cousins' role. His gift is much more difficult to define."

"Then why is he here with us?"

"He is a stalwart companion and a dear friend. Someone we count on to have our backs should the need arise."

"So, he's a great warrior?"

"He would be the first to deny that label. He would call himself adequate when it comes to fighting, but his heart is pure. That, above all else, is what makes his advice so compelling." She paused, staring into the girl's eyes. "Do not strive to simply emulate others, Greta. You will find your own path in life, have no fear. It just takes time."

"And until then?"

"I shall ask Athgar to train you in weapons. After all, if you're going to live in Runewald, you'll need them."

"Because Runewald is dangerous?"

"No. Because once you're of age, you'll be required to join the fyrd!"

COURT OF THE KING

Natalia opened the door to see Svetlana standing there, waiting.

"His Majesty invites you to court," the soon-to-be queen said. "He feels you would gain further insight into the politics of the land by seeing him rule first-hand."

"To what end?"

Svetlana lowered her voice. "He seeks your counsel."

"On what?"

"Ruling. You've visited other courts, have you not?"

"I have," replied Natalia.

"Maksim was never properly prepared for the Throne. As I mentioned earlier, his older brothers took precedence in terms of succession, so they overlooked his education. As a result, he finds himself ill-equipped to deal with the pressures of being king. He hoped you'd agree to watch him carrying out his duties and offer suggestions on how he could improve."

"Surely you're just as qualified to tell him that?"

"My training at the Volstrum was the same as yours, yet our careers since graduation differ greatly. While I've been here, in Carlingen, you've travelled the Petty Kingdoms. Is that not true?"

"I suppose it is," replied Natalia. "Very well. Let us go and see the king." They walked through the Palace. "What can you tell me of Carlingen and its nobility?"

"The Barons of Carlingen are all new. Their titles and lands were established only three years ago when King Maksim gained the Crown. His idea was to promote settlement outside the city, but it has proved troublesome, to say the least."

"I assume you're referring to the Baron of Raketsk?"

"Yes. When you alerted us to his misdeeds on your last visit, the king ordered him to court to answer the accusations. Instead, he fled and has since been replaced, but he took most of his wealth, leaving his old lands in a terrible state. The king appointed a new baron, a fellow named Tanger Haus, but he's struggling."

"Was he the heir to Raketsk?"

"No, Georgi Kulikov had no relatives to inherit his title, and even if he did, his flight would invalidate their claims."

"And this Tanger Haus, how did he come by the title?"

"He is the King of Abelard's second cousin. His Majesty considered it prudent to appoint someone with experience running an estate. Of course, it doesn't hurt that he's related to royalty, giving the title an air of respectability."

"How many barons has he?"

"Only three," said Svetlana. "Carlingen is coming apart at the seams, so he hoped by creating the baronies, some of the population might move farther into the countryside."

"I assume that wasn't the case?"

"It ended up being a disaster. The only way to encourage people to move was by offering coins, which, in turn, used up most of the barons' reserves. It will be years before they recover their losses. Meanwhile, they are unable to contribute to the Royal Treasury."

"And what, if I may ask, is the Royal Vault's current status?"

"Close to empty," said Svetlana. "I'm afraid His Majesty's recent attempts to bring order to the city cost us dearly."

"What was his chief expense?"

"He sought to improve the lot of his warriors by increasing their pay, but it has done little, if anything, to curb their excesses."

"Excesses?" said Natalia. "Perhaps you'd care to provide further details?"

"There've been reports of corruption amongst the members of the Royal Army, particularly those who patrol the streets."

"And so he thought to give them more to convince them that bribes were undesirable?"

"Precisely."

"It's unfortunate he didn't take a different approach. I would've dismissed anyone found taking bribes and replaced them with new hires."

"Regrettably, we have trouble recruiting. Few men are willing to take up arms in the king's name these days."

"Unfortunate," said Natalia. "How big is the Royal Army?"

"Theoretically, there are twelve companies, but none are at full strength."

"And their composition?"

"Three companies of crossbowmen, and nine of foot, though only three have decent armour."

"No cavalry?"

"No, but then again, most of the kingdom is thick forest, hardly the type of terrain favourable to their deployment. You must also realize this city accounts for the bulk of its people, thus necessitating a larger contingent of foot to secure the streets."

"An interesting observation," said Natalia, "but I would think cavalry more suited to quelling rebellion and unrest on the city streets."

"They would be, but there are no horse breeders in Carlingen, and the cost of shipping mounts here would quickly empty what remained of our coffers. Of course, there are two companies of Temple Knights within the city, but you know as well as I that they cannot be counted on to help should conflict arise."

"Two companies?" said Natalia. "I knew about the Temple Knights of Saint Agnes, but I wasn't aware any others were present?"

"The Temple Knights of Saint Cunar have a commandery in the city's western district."

"Cunars? Here? I assumed Carlingen too remote to be of interest to them."

"They are relatively new to the region," explained Svetlana. "They began constructing their commandery about four years ago and sent a company two years later."

"Interesting." Natalia wondered at the timing, for it followed the order's defeat at the Battle of the Standing Stones some five years ago. Could this be an attempt at re-establishing a presence in the east? She made a mental note to tell Athgar of her discovery.

"Ah, here we are," said Svetlana as they approached an ornate set of doors. The guard, noting their approach, grasped a handle and then pushed on the door.

It swung open, admitting them into the largest room in the Palace. It had been meant as a great hall but felt cavernous and empty with so few people within it. King Maksim sat on his intricately carved wooden throne while three men, presumably his barons, stood before him, their conversation interrupted by the new arrivals.

"Ah, my dear," said the king. "Come in. I see you've convinced Lady Natalia to join us. She is most welcome."

"I hope we have not disturbed you," said Svetlana.

"Not at all. We were merely discussing ways in which we might improve relations with one of our neighbours."

"I assume you mean Ostrova," said Natalia.

"Yes. I received word the messenger we sent just returned. He will join us shortly."

"He's not here?" asked Svetlana.

"The poor fellow was covered in filth, so I thought it best to allow him time to freshen up. After all, in the grand scheme of things, it's not as if a slight delay would change anything."

Natalia held her tongue. Such a delay would be inconceivable in the other courts of the Petty Kingdoms, but Maksim obviously didn't think that way. She was not one to favour the absolute rule of a monarch, but when someone assumed the Crown, proper protocols needed to be followed. Her training at the Volstrum stressed such things, but then it dawned on her that Therengia was the complete opposite. People there were free to speak their minds, even encouraged to do so. Then again, the Moot appointed the High Thane, so perhaps the same rule didn't apply.

She pushed the thoughts from her mind, concentrating on the current topic instead. "I wonder, Majesty, if you might enlighten me about the message he took to Ostrova?"

"I wrote to their king telling him there were rumours of a border dispute and that I was willing to meet in person to sort out any disagreements."

"And was the tone of that communication conciliatory or resolute?"

"I'm not sure I understand what you're asking?"

"I seek to determine if you might've inadvertently made it sound as if you'd be willing to give up land in exchange for peace."

"Would it be bad if I did?"

"Such a move would be seen as a weakness, Majesty, and might result in similar demands by your other neighbours."

"The only other neighbouring realm is Braymoor, and they're hardly in a position to make any demands unless you're suggesting the wild lands of Zaran would seek expansion?"

"No, Majesty. I'm merely trying to enlighten you on the prevailing politics of the Petty Kingdoms."

"Tell me more of these other kingdoms."

"Most are ruthless, Majesty, willing to take advantage of any weakness they perceive in their immediate neighbours."

The king leaned forward in his chair. "Wouldn't that lead to war?"

"Sometimes it does," replied Natalia, "but the balance of power is maintained through a complex series of treaties and alliances. Only the threat of a major conflict keeps them subdued."

"It seems most volatile."

"And it is. It also means one regional conflict could easily escalate into a Continent-wide war."

"I suppose we should be thankful that it hasn't already begun."

"Indeed, Majesty. Such a conflict would weaken the Petty Kingdoms, allowing the Halvarian Empire to conquer us all."

The king grimaced. "The empire holds no threat to me; they're too distant. We are a remote kingdom here, our borders to the east nothing more than wilderness. We've all been told a Continental war would be disastrous, but it would have little effect on us."

"On the contrary," said Natalia. "If war broke out on such a monumental scale, refugees would soon overwhelm you."

"I hadn't considered that. Still, what am I to do? I have no allies to speak of nor emissaries at my court with which I might negotiate treaties of any kind. We are, it seems, abandoned to a life of solitude. Even your family refuses to acknowledge us."

"With all due respect, Majesty, they sent you Svetlana."

He smiled. "Yes, and for that, I will be forever grateful, yet I can't help but feel we are ignored in the grand scheme of things—that we are insignif-icant in their eyes."

"Even the humblest of farmers has power," said Natalia. "Sometimes, all it takes is for them to learn how to wield it."

"You have me intrigued. Please continue."

"Without farmers, we have no food, and without food, our entire way of life collapses."

"I understand that easily enough, but I'm unsure how it helps me with my current predicament."

"You have people within the city who came here seeking Therengia."

"We have. What of it?"

"Might not some of them be farmers?"

"No doubt they are," said Maksim, "but I fail to see what difference that makes."

"You lack funds, Majesty, and the best way to alleviate that is to rebuild your economy."

"And how do we do that?"

"What is the one thing you have in abundance?"

"Problems?"

"No," said Svetlana. "She means land."

"Yes, of course. But most of it is thickly forested."

Natalia cleared her throat. "I propose you clear the land and offer it as farmland, free of charge."

"Free of charge? That sounds more like a way of using up what few funds remain. Do you know how many men I'd need to hire to do that?"

"On the contrary," replied Natalia. "Your army consumes your treasury. Why not make them earn their pay?"

"A marvellous idea," said Svetlana. "They could begin almost immediately. With a little luck, we might have the fields ready for summer planting!"

"And the seed?" said the king.

"A typical farm should have plenty from last year's harvest. I'm sure what farmers you have would be pleased to part with some for a few coins."

"But that's my problem, don't you see? I haven't the funds for such an expenditure."

"There are other ways to save your funds," said Natalia.

"Such as?"

"I assume your army is one of your larger expenses?"

"It is, but we can't very well leave ourselves undefended."

"Svetlana tells me you recently increased the pay of your warriors to curb their larcenous tendencies."

"I did. Unfortunately, it had little effect."

"In that case, I suggest you dismiss those who indulge in such pastimes."

"Then who would patrol our streets?"

"The people of Carlingen. Instead of allowing the streets to fall into chaos, you grant the right to select groups to act on your behalf. You could equip them with the weapons and armour taken from your dismissed warriors. It is, admittedly, a short-term solution, but one which would lighten the load on your purse strings."

"And how do I decide whom to arm?"

"We can help you with that, Majesty. I would start by approaching the Temple Knights of Saint Agnes and Saint Cunar. They already patrol the districts around their commanderies. Perhaps they can be convinced to increase the range of their patrols? There'd be little cost to yourself for such a solution."

"Would that be enough to secure the city?"

"Likely not, but there is another choice, although it would require a greater investment."

"Go on."

"Grant the Therengians permission to do the same."

"Are you mad?" shouted the king. "Arm them, and we'd be financing our own overthrow!"

"They are already armed," replied Natalia, "and they offer no opposition to your rule. Extend them friendship, Majesty, and they will return it with loyalty."

"What do you think, Svetlana?"

"It is a risk, Majesty, but what choice have we? To continue as we are will only result in financial ruin."

"And if Ostrova presses these unfounded claims for our land?"

"Then we seek allies."

"Where? Braymoor will be of little help to us. They can barely hang on to their own lands."

"You must do as they do in the other Petty Kingdoms," said Natalia. "Seek an alliance with someone who borders your enemy. In this case, that would be Salovia, Zalista, or Therengia."

Maksim frowned. "You mean Novarsk, surely?"

"Novarsk is now under the rule of Therengia, Majesty."

"You would have me ally with the enemy of civilization?"

"Therengia is not your enemy," said Natalia. "Rather, it's a land much like any other. They've also recently demonstrated their prowess on the battlefield, making them more threatening to Ostrova. Of course, there's still a chance you can avert trouble through diplomatic means, but alliances and treaties take time. If you are to pursue such things, it would be best to begin earlier instead of later."

The king turned to his barons. "Well? What do you three think?"

Lord Tanger answered before anyone else could. "All things considered, it is a wise move, Majesty. We know how much the Petty Kingdoms fear the rise of the Old Kingdom. An alliance with them might just work to our advantage."

"I disagree," said Lord Flarik. "An agreement with that upstart of a kingdom would only alienate us from the rest of the Continent. What think you, Thalmund?"

The Baron of Adlinschlot contemplated his answer before replying. "You both make valid points, but what other realm in these parts has an army with a reputation like the Therengians? The only question I have is how we'd go about making overtures. Well, that and what they could gain from an alliance with us. Would they even be open to such a thing?"

"You can but try," replied Natalia. "I should be happy to make some enquiries on your behalf if you wish."

"Please do," said the king, "but let's ensure it's not the only plan we pursue."

"I also know the new Temple Captain of Saint Agnes. Shall I talk to her concerning increasing their patrols?"

"If you would be so kind."

"In that case, I'll visit their commandery first thing tomorrow morning."

"Now," continued Maksim, "we must work out the details of all we have discussed. It's all well and good to reduce our army, but quite another thing to decide whom we dismiss and which men to send to clear the forest."

"On the brighter side," said Svetlana, "such work will give us a surplus of wood which we could then export. I'm sure other kingdoms along the Northern Coast would be willing to pay for our lumber."

"I'll talk to some shipowners," said Lord Thalmund, "and try to work out a deal whereby they ship the wood free of charge and share in the profits."

"Yes," agreed Maksim. "An excellent idea."

"If I may?" said Lord Tanger. "If you intend to arm the local Therengians, you might consider doing that before you dismiss your warriors. The last thing we want is a complete breakdown of the social order."

"My husband has been amongst them," said Natalia. "He can organize the transfer of power if you'd like."

"Very well, but let's wait until we've heard back from the Temple Knights first, shall we? I'd hate to have everything lined up only to find the Church won't do their part."

"I suggest," said Thalmund, "we clear land between the baronies and the capital, Majesty. That will mean more trade and alleviate some of the congestion in Carlingen. We'll also need to invest some effort into clearing the roads if we're to be shipping lumber." The conversation soon devolved into a myriad of details.

Svetlana tapped Natalia on the arm. "Come," she said. "You've done enough for one day. Let us leave the rest to the men."

"Are you not interested in knowing all that transpires in your kingdom? After all, you'll soon be their queen."

"True, but until then, I shall take every chance I can to enjoy the peace and quiet of a tranquil life. Saints know things will get much more hectic in the coming months."

THE COMMANDERY

SPRING 1109 SR

Athgar and Natalia could see their breath as they stepped out onto the streets of Carlingen. They'd left while their companions still slept, the better to conduct their business in private.

"It won't be long now," said Athgar. "Any day, Kargen and Shaluhk will arrive, and then we'll be amongst friends."

"And what do you call our travelling companions?"

"Yes. Well, maybe I should've said we'll be with family?"

"Better," she replied. "I wonder how Oswyn is faring?"

"She's under Shaluhk's care. She'll be fine." He saw the look of concern on her face and decided to change the subject. "How did your visit to court go yesterday?"

"Fine."

"That's it? Just fine? Care to be a little more specific?"

"Let's just say I've planted a seed."

"What kind of seed?"

"I introduced the prospect of an alliance with Therengia to help secure their border."

"And he agreed to it?"

"He didn't dismiss it out of hand, but it takes time to sway someone's attitude, especially where the Old Kingdom is concerned."

"I can well believe it," said Athgar. "Anything else?"

"I made some suggestions to put the kingdom on a more stable financial footing, but once again, they'll take time to implement. That reminds me, the king's messenger returned with news that Ostrova intends to send an envoy. There might be more to this claim of theirs than I thought."

"They finally demanded land?"

"No. They only announced an intended meeting, but I doubt they'd be doing so out of the kindness of their hearts. A kingdom doesn't usually send an envoy unless it wants something."

"Could they be seeking allies of their own?"

"If that's so," said Natalia, "then they picked the wrong kingdom. Carlingen can barely afford to maintain its army. Speaking of which, I introduced the idea of arming the local Therengians."

"And?"

"They still need to work out the specifics, but they seemed to come around to the idea. Much of it hinges on us being successful at the commandery today."

"They're two different things, surely?"

"They are, but Maksim is a cautious man. He'll move forward on giving the Therengians the authority they need to keep the streets safe once the Church has agreed to do their part."

"That must have been an uphill battle," said Athgar. "The nobility's hatred of my people runs deep." He paused for only a moment. "Sorry, I should've said our people."

"I take no offence."

"It'll be nice to see Cordelia again. I wonder what she's been up to?"

"She came here as a Temple Captain. I told you that."

"Yes, but what did she do after all that mess in Krieghoff?"

"You can ask her yourself," said Natalia. "There's the commandery up ahead."

The building was an exact copy of the old Cunar commandery back in Ebenstadt. Athgar was about to say as much when he noted the presence of six grey-clad Temple Knights standing outside its door, staring up at a second-storey window.

"Cunars?" he said. "Here?"

The pair drew closer until they could hear the knights.

"In accordance with Church law, you are hereby ordered to vacate these premises."

"We do not recognize your authority," came the reply. "Return to your own commandery and leave us in peace."

"Is there a problem?" called out Natalia.

The group's leader turned to face them. "This is Church business and none of your concern." He looked back up at the window. "We will return, you have my word, and next time it won't be only the six of us."

"It matters not whether you come back with half a dozen or an entire company. The answer is still the same. We will not relinquish this commandery without the express command of our grand mistress."

"Come!" the Cunar snapped at his companions. "We shall not waste any more time on this errand. If the sister knights want a fight, then so be it!" They turned in unison, making their way up the street, forcing Athgar and Natalia to step aside or risk being trampled.

"What was that all about?" asked Athgar.

"I don't know," replied Natalia, "but I'm guessing Cordelia does."

"Yes, but is she willing to talk about it?"

"Let's go and find out, shall we?" She led them to the door. Moments later, it opened, revealing a pair of scarlet-clad Temple Knights who took up positions on either side of the entrance.

"Come in," came a familiar voice.

"Captain Cordelia?" said Athgar. "Is that you?"

She soon appeared. "My apologies, but it's been a hectic morning. Don't tell me you're here to talk about the wedding? I haven't had time to research the customs in these parts."

"Actually," said Natalia, "we're here about something else."

"Then you should come to my office. The street is not the best place to discuss matters."

They travelled through the commandery, finally arriving at the captain's office on the top floor. Cordelia waited until they both sat before calling in her aide to offer drinks.

"We are here at the king's behest," said Natalia.

"What is it he wants?"

"Your assistance. He would like to know if you could expand your patrols to other parts of the city."

"I shall consider it," said Cordelia, "but there is only one company of Temple Knights here."

"You would not be the only group keeping the streets safe," added Athgar. "The same offer will be made to the Cunars."

"Good luck with that."

"Is there strife between the two orders? I'd hate to think we were in some way responsible."

"This has nothing to do with what happened in Krieghoff; it's an internal matter."

"Meaning we should mind our own business? It's a little late for that, don't you think? We heard them ordering you to surrender your commandery."

"There's been some... issues of late within the upper echelons of the Church."

"What kind of issues?"

"A push to disband the fighting orders."

"All of them?"

"All, save the Cunars. The argument is they represent the Holy Army and, as such, are more than capable of taking up any duties requiring Temple Knights."

"When did this begin?"

"It's been going on for some years," replied Cordelia, "but it got worse a few years back after they suffered a defeat in battle."

"Battle?" said Athgar. "Where was this?"

"Near a place called Ebenstadt, which is now part of Therengia. Shortly after that, a man by the name of Sir Raynald showed up in the Antonine, making all sorts of claims, including that a powerful family had infiltrated the Cunars. I didn't believe the rumours initially, but then an old friend contacted me." She lowered her voice. "I assume you're familiar with the name Stormwind?"

"Yes, I've heard it," said Natalia. "They are a family of Water Mages who supplies advisors to the courts of the Petty Kingdoms."

"I have it on good authority they're aiding the Halvarian Empire, and they're not the only ones. There's also a group of Fire Mages called the Sartellians."

Athgar smiled. "We know all about them and their connection with the empire."

"You do?"

"Yes." He looked at Natalia, who merely nodded in response. "I'm going to tell you a story, Captain, but you must promise to let me finish before you pass judgement."

"Very well. You have my word."

"Natalia's last name is Stormwind. She ran away from this 'family' but they pursued us. Our desire to remain free eventually took us to Caerhaven all those years ago."

"Does that make you a Sartellian?"

"No. I unlocked my magic with help from the Orcs."

"So you're fugitives?"

"We were, but we've found a new home in a village called Runewald."

"I'm not familiar with it."

"Nor would I expect you to be," said Athgar. "It lies within Therengia."

"I can see why you might want to keep that to yourself."

"Oh, there's more."

"Much more," added Natalia. "Athgar is the High Thane, I his Warmaster, and our army was the one who defeated the Cunars."

Cordelia sat back. "Ordinarily, I'd take a statement like that with a big pinch of salt, but I sense you're telling me the truth."

"If you recall, we harbour no love for the Cunars."

"That's something we have in common," said Cordelia. "Now, as to the family, let me tell you my side of the story. If you remember, I served in Ilea."

"Yes, on the Shimmering Sea," said Natalia. "That was your first posting, if I recall."

"It was. I served with someone who later rose to a higher rank within the order, and she's the one who notified me of the part this so-called family, the Stormwinds and Sartellians, played in recent events. I can't help but feel they're up to something here."

"They're not, at least not yet, but I fear their attention may soon be directed to this city. The king's future bride is a Stormwind. I'm working on convincing her to abandon the family, but it's not something I can hurry. One false move, and she'll inform Karslev of our presence here, then the place will be crawling with people trying to kill us."

"I'd love to help you," said Cordelia, "but I've enough troubles of my own. You saw those Cunars; it's only a matter of time before they return in larger numbers."

"Could you ask your regional commander for help?"

"There is none. Carlingen falls outside the normal scope of regional commands, making me the senior ranking member of the order in these parts."

"Might I ask why they sent you here?" said Athgar. "It doesn't seem the kind of place where one would go as a reward."

"Ordinarily, I'd agree, but circumstances have changed. The logic behind sending me here is quite involved but basically boils down to maintaining a presence close to Karslev. You see, we have no commanderies in Ruzhina, so this was the next best thing."

"And if the Church dissolves your order?"

"I shall follow the lawful commands of my superiors, but only our grand mistress can order us to disband. In the meantime, I must find a way to peacefully coexist with the Cunars."

"Perhaps the king could convince them to hold off on seizing the commandery?"

"We all know how obstinate the brother knights can be. It's not like them to back down based on a suggestion from a king. They'd see that as interference in Church business."

"What if I could offer you more?" asked Athgar. "Your order would be welcome in Therengia, although you'd have to build some new commanderies. The Temple Knights of Saint Mathew already keep a detachment in Ebenstadt."

"I'll bear that in mind, but I'm not ready to abandon my post quite yet. Tell me about the king's plan."

"You already patrol around your commandery," said Natalia. "We're proposing you extend your coverage area a few blocks in each direction. Naturally, we'd define those streets where you'd be responsible for keeping the peace, and His Majesty would grant you the power to arrest any troublemakers and deliver them to his guards."

"And you intend to make the same offer to the Cunars?"

"We do, but we'll ensure none of your areas overlap. In fact, if I'm not mistaken, your assigned area is adjacent to the Therengian district."

"Therengian? So other groups are involved?"

"Yes, a few. Why? Is that a problem?"

"That largely depends on who these other people are. I'd hate to think he's involving criminal elements."

"We shall do our best to avoid that," said Natalia, "but his heart is in the right place. So what do you think?"

"It has merit and wouldn't be much of a burden. You may tell His Majesty we agree, on the condition we have some say in defining our responsibilities."

"Excellent," said Athgar. "He'll be quite pleased."

"There is something else," added Natalia.

"Go on," said Cordelia.

"You were the equerry in Caerhaven. How would you like to oversee a horse breeding program?"

"For whom?"

"The king has few horses, and those shipped in from the rest of the Continent are expensive. A breeding program here in Carlingen would go a long way to alleviating that problem."

"And why would I agree to that?"

"Your order will eventually need replacement mounts," said Athgar. "This way, you'd have your pick of them."

"A breeding program is expensive, especially if we import the breeding stock."

"This is a long-term investment, but one that could grow to a considerable size. If your order is disbanded, you'll need funds to support your people unless you intend to give up and abandon it all?"

Cordelia clenched her teeth. "I have no intention of abandoning my vows."

"Good," said Natalia, "because we wouldn't want you to. There are few people in the Continent we can trust, Captain, and you happen to be one of them. If that means bringing you and your entire command to Therengia, then so be it."

"I'm curious why you're being so generous. Temple Knights seldom get involved in regional disputes."

"You're behind the times," said Athgar. "Captain Grazynia used Temple Ships to prevent a seaborne invasion of Reinwick. The time for sitting on the fence has come to an end."

Cordelia nodded. "I knew it would eventually come down to that. I just didn't expect it to be so soon."

"There is time yet," said Natalia, "and who knows, perhaps we'll convince the Cunars to put aside their demands for the time being."

"We can hope."

They sat in silence, pondering things until the Temple Captain finally spoke. "Might I ask what brought you to Carlingen in the first place?"

"We were returning home," said Natalia, "but things took an unexpected turn as usual."

"We were on your route to Therengia?"

"Yes. Friends of ours are meeting us here. The plan is to take boats upstream."

"But won't that have you going through the wildlands?"

"It will," said Athgar, "but that land holds little fear for us compared to the Petty Kingdoms."

"I've heard the place is full of all sorts of fearsome beasts."

"We killed a wyvern on our first trip," offered Natalia, "but that encounter paled in comparison to what we had to put up with in Andover."

"Where lies Therengia from here?"

"The river forming the north and eastern borders of Carlingen snakes down past Ostrova into what used to be Novarsk. Beyond that lies our home."

"Used to be Novarsk?"

"Well," replied Athgar, "it's still there but is now a province of Therengia."

"You conquered it?"

"Not by choice, I assure you. Perhaps I should explain?"

"I think that best," said Cordelia.

"You've heard about the Cunar's defeat at Ebenstadt, but of even greater import are the events that followed. In the wake of their loss, the Temple Knights abandoned the city, leaving it in the grip of a greedy bunch of sellswords. Subsequent events led us to retake the city, but Novarsk devised a similar plan."

"Let me guess—they attacked you?"

"Not right away. After the Cunars left, many took it upon themselves to try to recapture Ebenstadt. They all failed, for, thankfully, none were particularly well-planned. The Queen of Novarsk, however, thought these subsequent campaigns had worn us down to the point where she could march in and take over our lands. We defeated her invasion, then turned things around and invaded Novarsk, capturing their queen. When their nobles then rose up against us, we defeated them and made the entire country one of our provinces."

"You two have been busy."

"Oh, we weren't there for that. We were busy in Reinwick. Kargen organized that campaign."

"Wasn't he the chieftain at Ord-Kurgad?"

"He was," said Athgar. "I named him acting High Thane in my absence."

"You were reunited. That's excellent news. When I learned the Duke of Krieghoff waged war on Holstead, I feared the worst."

"I heard there was a war," said Natalia. "Who won?"

"I don't know if you can say anybody actually won. A large battle occurred outside of Draybourne, but while Holstead technically lost, the Duke of Krieghoff died leading a cavalry charge. In the end, the invading army slunk back to Krieghoff, and there's been an undeclared truce ever since, or at least there still was when I left Caerhaven. There were rumours they wiped out the Orcs of Ord-Kurgad."

"Only those who remained," said Athgar. "Kargen led most of them through the mountains where they settled east of Ebenstadt, joining the other tribes now living in Therengia."

"They willingly put themselves under your laws?"

"They were instrumental in creating the realm," explained Natalia. "They did not join us so much as unite us in a common cause, that of defending their homes."

"And you think they would welcome Temple Knights after what was done to their home?"

"It was not your order who destroyed Ord-Kurgad. Kargen remembers how you came to their aid at a time of great danger. I'm sure he'd welcome your presence now."

"Yes," added Athgar, "and you wouldn't be the only order within its borders. As I mentioned earlier, the Temple Knights of Saint Mathew have a presence there already."

"I'll give it some consideration," said Cordelia, "but I'm not ready to uproot my company just yet. There's still a role to be played here, and if the king thinks it will help bring peace to the city, then I must do all I can to assist."

UNREST

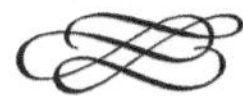

SPRING 1109 SR

The sounds of footsteps running down the hall, accompanied by the familiar jingle of armour and weapons, wrenched Athgar from his slumber. Beside him, Natalia stretched.

"What was that?" she asked as yet more warriors raced down the corridor.

"Guards, from the sound of it. Remind me to mention to His Majesty that the Palace walls need to be thicker."

"We should take a look. I'd hate to be caught sleeping in the middle of an attack."

Athgar sighed. "Very well. Let me put some clothes on, and I'll take a peek."

"No. We'll wake the others, then all go together." She dressed quickly, glancing over as her husband pulled his tunic over his head. "Ready?"

"As ready as I'll ever be." He buckled on his belt, then tucked his axe into it. "Should I take my bow?"

"We're in a building. I doubt it will be of much use."

"I was thinking more of using it if we had to flee."

Their bedroom door burst open, revealing Belgast, his hair wild and his beard badly knotted, evidence of his sudden awakening. "I assume you heard it too?"

"We did," said Athgar. "The others?"

"They're getting dressed even as we speak."

Natalia stifled a chuckle. "We can spare a few moments if you'd like."

The Dwarf looked back with a raised eyebrow. "For what?"

"A comb, perhaps?"

It took a moment for the words to sink in. "Yes, of course. I'll be ready in short order." He closed the door behind him.

They assembled in the suite's main room. Belgast insisted on keeping his pick-axe in hand as Athgar looked out into the corridor.

"Nothing," he said. "Could we have imagined it?"

"All of us?" replied the Dwarf. "I think not!"

"Which way do we go?"

"Left," said Greta. "The great staircase leads down to the ground floor. If someone's trying to break in, that will likely be their target."

"Why would you say that?"

"It's simple. The upper floors are where important guests keep their wealth."

"Follow me, everyone," said Athgar, "but stay close. There's always the chance someone infiltrated the Palace."

They proceeded slowly, Athgar and Natalia in the lead. Stanislav came next, followed by Katrin and Greta. At his own insistence, Belgast brought up the rear, the better to turn and fight should someone come up behind them.

They reached the top of the stairs, where the king's soldiers stood waiting below, their swords already drawn. Athgar descended the first step, but then Natalia grabbed his arm.

"No," she said. "This way. We need to get to a window to understand what's going on out there, and we'll have a much better view from this floor."

Athgar followed her, and they were soon at the front of the Palace, looking down into the darkness, but flickering lights told them all they needed to know. A mob had descended on the Palace, torches held high, while a group of spearmen formed a line blocking their way.

"There'll be bloodshed," said Athgar.

"Not if I can help it," replied Natalia. "Come. We must be quick, or it will be too late."

They ran back to the stairs, then descended, exiting onto the street as the guard captain warned the mob to return to their homes. Athgar pushed through the guardsmen, placing himself between the two groups. He looked over the townsfolk, noting the clubs and rocks they held ready for use.

"Go home," he called out. "Let there be no bloodshed this night!"

"Easy for you to say," came the reply. "You're not living under the iron fist of a despot."

"Nor are you. No doubt you have grievances, but violence is not how to resolve them."

A woman pushed her way to the front of the crowd. "And what would you have us do? Meekly submit?"

Growls erupted from the mob. To Athgar's mind, they were a flask of oil waiting to be lit. Something had to be done, and quickly.

"Talk amongst yourselves," he finally said, "and choose three to speak on your behalf."

"Why? So you can throw them into a dungeon?"

"I will guarantee their safety," said Athgar. "You have my word."

"You are nobody. Why should I trust the word of a stranger to these lands?"

Without answering, he threw his arms upward, sending a streak of flame into the air, silencing the mob. "I am Athgar of Athelwald, Master of Flame."

Out of the corner of his eye, he noticed his wife moving up beside him. "And I am Natalia Stormwind. I, too, guarantee their safety. Now is not the time for the spilling of blood. Come. Choose your representatives, and then let us sit down and discuss things in a civilized manner."

Murmuring broke out amongst the crowd as the woman rejoined them.

"What now?" whispered Athgar.

"We wait," replied Natalia.

"For them to attack?"

"No. A mob like this must be much angrier to risk tangling with Royal soldiers. The crisis is over, but we should be vigilant lest someone stokes the fire again."

The woman returned. "I am Zegota Kotesky, a baker by trade. My friends chose me to represent them."

The crowd pushed a man to the front. "I am Wygurn, son of Erdan, a worker of wood."

The two individuals looked back as someone made their way to the front, pushing people aside in his haste. "I am Raban Engle, our third representative," announced the tall, muscular man.

"Fear not," said Natalia, "for we guarantee your safety. As for the rest of you, go home. These three will return and tell of all that transpires on your behalf."

A few left while many remained, talking amongst themselves.

"Begone!" called out Zegota, waving away the mob. "Else we'll never get anywhere."

Raban moved closer, glaring at Athgar. "This better not be a trap."

"I assure you it's not."

"Now," said Natalia. "Let us go inside where we can speak freely." She lowered her voice. "I sent Katrin to arrange a room."

Athgar stared back at her. "When did you find the time to do that?"

"When you pushed past the guards."

He smiled. "You're a remarkable woman."

"And you, a remarkable man. I suppose that's why we work so well together."

Greta appeared at their side, whispering something Athgar couldn't quite make out.

"This way," said Natalia to their new guests. "A room has been prepared for our use."

Athgar and Natalia sat on one side of the table, the three representatives on the other. Herulf stood behind, alert to any danger as Katrin and Greta entered, bearing drinks.

Raban downed his all at once while the other two took only sips. It occurred to Athgar that this fellow hadn't revealed his trade. "So, here we are," he began, "a baker, a woodworker, and...?"

Raban stared back for a moment before answering. "I've worked many jobs over the years, everything from deckhand to common labourer."

"Yet you don't look it," said Natalia. "I wouldn't have taken you for much past the age of twenty."

"Twenty-three, actually," replied Raban. "But it's of little consequence. Why do you really want us here?"

"I assure you we have only your best interests at heart."

"I find that hard to believe."

"Why is that?"

"Just look at you! You're not from here, and throwing around the name Stormwind like that!"

"What would you know of the Stormwinds?"

"Only what everyone else knows. They're the premier spellcasters on the Continent." He leaned forward, placing his elbows on the table. "You should be supporting us in our endeavours, not trying to make excuses for the so-called King of Carlingen."

"Perhaps," said Athgar, "we might be better served by discussing your grievances?"

Raban leaned back, sneering as he crossed his arms against his chest.

In his place, Zegota sat up straighter. "I'll go first, shall I?" She waited, then, at a nod from Natalia, stood. "I think better on my feet. I hope that's not too distracting?"

"Not at all," replied Natalia. "Please continue."

"The city streets are rampant with crime. Break-ins are increasing, and people are being assaulted in broad daylight, yet the king does nothing! Some folk have taken it upon themselves to take more direct action"—she quickly glanced to Wygurn—"but this has led to clashes with the king's men."

"Can you be more specific?" said Athgar. "You mentioned clashes, but that could mean any number of things."

"The presence of any armed men on the street, other than the king's, typically results in a confrontation—sometimes arrests—even though all these people are trying to do is keep the streets safe."

"How many are we talking about?" asked Natalia.

"Dozens. Why, last night alone, they hauled five more off to the king's cells. What do you intend to do about that?"

"I shall ask to see these prisoners. If they are innocent, as you claim, then I will do all I can to secure their release."

Zegota had expected a fight, but Natalia's answer was the last thing she thought she'd hear. "Thank you," she mumbled as she took her seat.

"Promises are cheap," said Raban. "You'll say anything to keep the king in power."

"We are not in service to the king," replied Athgar. "We are only travelling through Carlingen on our way home."

"Then why are you still here?"

"That is none of your concern. What is, however, is what happens to you and your fellow countrymen from now on." His eyes flicked to Wygurn. "I remember you. You were part of the crowd when I met Haywald."

"I was."

"Then speak freely. You have a sympathetic ear."

The woodworker cleared his throat. "As you know, my people took it upon themselves to patrol our streets, but we've had some difficulties."

"In what way?"

"The king's men prohibit us from arming ourselves in any meaningful way, restricting us to little more than clubs and cudgels, hardly the type of thing that discourages the nastier criminal elements within the city. I ask you, how are we to defend ourselves? The gift of our ancestors is a curse."

"Gift?" said Raban.

"He means the grey eyes," explained Natalia.

"The survivors of the Old Kingdom are a curse upon our city! If the king wants to secure the streets of Carlingen, he should banish them."

"And where would they go?" asked Athgar.

"Who cares? Those grey eyes are a plague upon the civilized lands." Raban stared back, their eyes locking.

"The king is considering arming a fyrd," said Natalia, interrupting the contest of wills.

"What nonsense is this?" demanded Raban. "Surely you're not suggesting he'd allow those heathens to take control of the streets?"

"They would only be authorized to patrol their own district for the time being, but that could easily change."

Wygurn cleared his throat for the second time. "That would be most acceptable."

Natalia turned back to Raban. "And what is your grievance?"

"The Temple Knights of Saint Agnes," the man replied. "They've displayed a heavy hand of late, and the king should banish them from Carlingen."

"That's quite the statement," said Athgar. "Perhaps you'd care to tell us more?"

"What more is there? The sister knights abused their influence to extend their dominion over many city blocks."

"It is their sworn duty to protect women."

"It is, but not to the prejudice of everyone else. I understand they do important work, but their outlook is always one-sided. Many is the man who's fallen afoul of their intemperate use of force. They are a danger that must be curbed, lest the streets fall into mayhem."

"What, precisely, are you suggesting we do?"

"You claim to have the king's ear. Use it to ensure His Majesty banishes them from his kingdom."

"I doubt he would accept that proposition," said Natalia, "and even if he did, I would not be the one to raise such a subject without a thorough investigation. However, I shall see to it personally that the matter is looked into." She paused, looking at each in turn. "Is there anything else you'd like to bring to our attention?"

When no one spoke, Athgar stood. "Return in two days, and we shall speak again. At that time, we'll tell you of our progress, but I warn you, it takes time to make meaningful change, and I will not use the threat of violence to force the king's hand. That would only lead to greater strife."

Raban grunted.

"You have something to add?" asked Natalia.

"This is a fool's errand," the fellow replied. "Mark my words. It will all end in failure. Better, I say, to storm the Palace with an armed mob and be done with it!"

. . .

Natalia looked out the window, noting how the rising sun threw its golden rays across the gardens behind the Palace, bringing them to life.

"Coming to bed?" asked Athgar. "It's been a long night."

"So it has," she replied, "yet I cannot settle my mind." She turned to look at her husband. "What did you make of that group?"

"I'd say they're hiding something, at least that fellow Raban is."

"He's more than he appears."

"Meaning?"

"He was no ship hand, or labourer, for that matter."

"What makes you say that?"

"Observation," said Natalia. "His hands were not calloused, nor his physique fitting for such a role. He has more the look of a warrior about him, don't you think?"

"But if that's true, wouldn't he be working for the king?"

"Do you think all such men work for royalty?"

"No, I suppose not. What about him makes you think he's a warrior?"

"You remember Brother Yaromir?"

"The Temple Knight of Saint Mathew? Of course, but what has he to do with anything here?"

"Temple Knights follow a very rigid training program that has them practicing every single day."

"And?"

"It leads to a particular physique, one with broad shoulders and thick arms, much like Raban."

"Are you suggesting he's a Temple Knight?"

"Or he once was. He was very vague about his background."

"How would one go about leaving a fighting order?"

"That's just it," said Natalia, "aside from those serving Saint Agnes, it's a lifelong commitment. Only the most heinous of crimes against his order would result in being dismissed."

"Yet not so bad they would execute him for his crimes?"

"Precisely, though what that means in real terms is beyond my comprehension."

"Well, the fellow bore no kind words for the sister knights."

"Nor the Therengians, which leads me to believe he has his own agenda."

"Meaning?"

"You heard what he said. He has no interest in seeing a resolution to this crisis. Rather, he seems to relish the idea it will break into actual fighting."

"I agree, but why? What could he possibly have to gain?"

"Instability might benefit Ostrova," offered Natalia. "If they press for land while Maksim is forced to fight for his streets, there's a very real chance he'll be too busy to oppose them."

"Agreed," said Athgar. "Does that mean Raban is working for the enemy?"

"There's no way to tell at this point."

"You don't think he's still a Cunar, do you? We know they threatened Cordelia's knights, and he seemed dead set against them remaining in Carlingen."

"It's a possibility, but why would he threaten insurrection if that were the case?"

"Perhaps it's only that," said Athgar, "a threat meant to pressure the king. We know they want the Agnesite commandery. What better way to gain it than by discrediting the Temple Knights who occupy it?"

"I'm not convinced. There's more to this story. I'm sure of it. Cordelia told us a lot, but she didn't tell us everything. Something's going on in the Church that they don't want to talk about."

"She mentioned they wanted to disband the other fighting orders."

"She did," said Natalia, "which makes me wonder what they're up to, even more. Why force the Agnesites out now? Why not wait until the order is officially disbanded? And another thing, the Cunars already have their own commandery. Why do they need a second one?"

"That's easy enough to explain. They want to bring in more knights of their own."

"But why? At the Volstrum, we called this region the armpit of the Continent, and with good reason. There is very little of value here, and as we've seen for ourselves, the kingdom's treasury is almost empty."

"Then it's not about coins," said Athgar. "It has to be something else." He thought it over, then snapped his fingers. "I have it."

"Go on."

"Do you remember the name Talivardas? If you recall, he was the Cunar regional commander who ordered the Holy Crusade we crushed."

"Yes, I remember now. He was a Stormwind. Is that what this is all about? The family?"

"Think about it," said Athgar. "The Battle of the Standing Stones was five years ago, which is plenty of time for him to advance in the order, even be appointed their grand master."

"I still don't see how that fits in with what's happening here?"

"If the Cunars are under the family's control, then it only makes sense they would mass close to home. What better place than Carlingen."

"Yes, but to actively promote insurrection? What would that gain them?"

"What would happen if the king were overthrown?"

"Someone else would rise to take his place. It's happened often enough throughout the Petty Kingdoms. Are you proposing the Cunars might take over?"

"Why not? They ruled Ebenstadt for years, didn't they?"

"Still, this is all conjecture at this point, and in any case, there are far too many other things to worry about."

"This is what we get for travelling across half the Continent," said Athgar. "It would be nice if, for a change, we could visit someplace that isn't in the middle of a crisis!"

INCIDENT

SPRING 1109 SR

Wendred threw herself onto the forest floor. "I'm done," she announced. "I can't walk another foot."

Her husband, Wigstan, sat down beside her. "We'll take a break. The rest are all strung out along the forest path anyway."

"We've been going for weeks. How much farther, do you think?"

He looked skyward, but the canopy of trees blocked his view of the sun. "According to that map we bought, we should see the border any time now. Of course, that assumes I'm reading it properly."

"And the others? What do they think?"

"They're following our lead. Look, I know it's been difficult, and once we cross that river, we still need to travel clear across the Kingdom of Ostrova, but then we'll be home."

"Home?" said Wendred. "What does that even mean anymore? We're headed to a place we've never seen, to live amongst people we've never met. Only the Gods know what we'll find."

"It's Therengia reborn. Just like all the stories passed down for generations. Do you honestly believe the Gods would abandon us now when we're so close?"

"Close? We're barely halfway there, if that map is any indication. We'll probably starve to death before we ever reach our destination."

"This is not like you," said Wigstan. "You're normally so full of energy and enthusiasm."

"Yes, well, the drudgery of such a trip can wear down even the most enthusiastic of people. It wouldn't be so bad if we didn't need to cross this forest. Honestly, half of these trails turn back on themselves and send us in circles. I feel like I haven't seen the sun for almost a week."

"Come now. We might not be able to see it, but its light filters down through the trees."

"Not enough to navigate by. We're supposed to be heading south, but we could just as easily be going north."

"It's true. I'll not deny it, but the directions showed the path would be confusing." He dug into his bag and pulled forth a worn-out piece of parchment. "There, you see?" he said, pointing at some marks. "We passed that landmark three days ago. Remember the twisted roots?"

Wendred forced a smile. "Yes, we did. Thank the Gods for that." She was about to say more, but something in her husband's demeanour kept her quiet.

"Do you hear that?" he said, peering off into the distance.

"Is that running water?"

"Yes," he replied, a smile breaking out. "That can mean only one thing. We've almost arrived at the border." He stood, holding out his hand for her. "We're so close!"

She reached up, grasping his hand, and he pulled her to her feet.

"Are there a few more steps inside of you?"

"There are," she replied, "but if this turns out to be another disappointment, I'm done."

They proceeded down the trail, the woods opening to a wide river brimming with fast-flowing water.

Wendred gasped. "It's enormous! How will we ever cross?"

"Trust in the Gods, and they will provide an answer."

They continued to the water's edge, then sat, dangling their feet in the cleansing waters.

"It's cold," said Wigstan.

"Aye, but wonderful all the same. And look, the other side's not nearly so thick with trees."

Others emerged from the woods, rushing to slake their thirst in the crystal clear water.

"Well?" said Wigstan. "What do you think? Can we cross?"

"If you're asking if we could swim it, I'd say not. The current looks fast, and we have no idea what might lurk in those waters."

"We must get across somehow. What if we built a raft?"

"That's a grand idea. Have you any experience constructing such a thing?"

Wigstan frowned. "No. The only water back home was a stream, and even that was only waist-deep."

Wendred cast her gaze on the trees behind them. "I suppose we could cut a tree into logs and use it to float across."

"You think that would work?"

"Why not? Wood floats, doesn't it?"

"Aye, it does, but how would we steer?"

"We don't need to," she replied. "We hang on to it and use our legs to cross to the other bank."

"But the current will take us downstream."

"Does that matter? Our objective is to get to the other side of the river. Who cares where we land?"

"Very well. We'll start first thing tomorrow morning."

That evening, the fifteen of them gathered around a fire, all grey-eyed individuals who'd left Carlingen in the hopes of reaching Therengia. They'd pooled their coins to purchase the map, and though others warned them it was a ruse to deprive them of their funds, so far, it had proven remarkably useful.

"Just imagine," said Wigstan. "A few months from now, we'll be nestled in amongst others of our kind, roasting pigs over an open fire."

"Yes," chimed in Arath, a youth of some eighteen summers. "And there I'll find me a friendly woman to take to wife!" His statement brought cheers to those gathered, a rare occasion these days.

"He's got things all planned out," said Hildwyn, the oldest of the group. "I expect by this time next year, he'll have her with child!" Her peal of laughter caused Arath to blush profusely.

"The young are always filled with passion," said Wigstan. "Let him dream while he can. It won't be long before age dampens his ardour."

"What of tomorrow?" asked Hildwyn. "Can we really cross that river?"

"I don't see why not. It won't take much to cut down a tree and drag it to the water."

"That's not the problem," said Arath. "Are we to sit upon a log while it floats across or swim beside it? And in either case, how do we cling to it without it rolling?"

"I can't think of everything," replied Wigstan, "but you raise an important point."

"Where I come from," said Hildwyn, "men would chop down trees, then float them down the river to our home. More remarkable still was the fact they balanced on logs while doing so."

"Surely you're not suggesting we try that?"

"No, some of us are too weak for such things. However, there is an old trick we could use."

"Which is?"

"Lash two logs together, and they will not overturn."

"And with what do we lash them?"

"Surely there's enough spare clothes amongst us we can cut some up into strips of cloth?"

"Strips of cloth?" said Arath. "Would that even be strong enough to hold two logs together?"

"We're trying to cross a river, so they only have to hold for a short time."

"Then it's settled," said Wigstan. "Tomorrow, while we chop down a tree, the rest of you will tear off strips of cloth. With a bit of luck, we'll be across the river by nightfall."

Wigstan pushed the logs farther out into the water while Wendred perched atop, her legs dangling on either side. Her weight forced the logs down, soaking her lower torso, but she was in no danger of sinking. Wigstan, now waist-deep in the river, clung to one side, then kicked off from the shallow bank and out into the main channel. The water grabbed them, pulling them farther out, where the current was considerably faster.

Wendred glanced behind her to where the others followed their example. The wind picked up, blowing loose strands of hair from her kerchief. It was frightening, yet at the same time, exhilarating. Years from now, they would tell of the great adventure that brought them to their new home. The future was full of promise, and she imagined herself living in a fine house with smoke billowing out of the chimney, the smell of roast meat permeating the place.

They drifted downstream, Wigstan kicking out with his feet to propel them closer to the southern bank. The rest of their group followed in their wake, spread out every twenty paces or so.

She saw Arath chatting away with Hildwyn as he pushed them farther into the current, then his smile went slack as an arrow struck him in the face. He slid silently into the water, leaving behind nothing but a trail of blood.

Wendred looked around, trying to find who'd loosed the thing. Were there Orcs about? Panic rose in her chest, threatening to crush her heart. She struggled to breathe, and then an arrow thudded into one of the logs upon which she sat, narrowly missing her hand.

"Stay down," warned Wigstan, but then he tensed, his eyes rolling up into his head before he slipped beneath the river's surface, only to emerge moments later, face down, an arrow protruding from his back.

More arrows whizzed past. She glimpsed movement on the southern bank, just enough to recognize archers preparing to loose another volley. Death was coming for her; of that, she was certain. She closed her eyes, hoping her trip to the Afterlife would be quick, and then someone yelled, "Loose!"

Terrified beyond all reasoning, she dove into the water. She didn't see the arrows descend, but when she came to the surface, there was no mistaking their thuds as they dug into the wood that had so recently been her raft. A log careened past her, narrowly missing her head. A body lay atop it, lifeless arms dangling in the water, but she had no time to worry about who it might be.

She struck out for shore, s, trying not to drown, but living on land had never prepared her for such a thing. The current dragged her down as an arrow struck her hair, tangling in her locks. The water claimed her, and as she sank, she felt only calmness. Her Wigstan was dead, and she readied herself to join him in the Afterlife.

Georgi Kulikov watched from the southern bank. He'd fled Carlingen in the wake of those meddlesome strangers, yet here he was, not even a year later, ready to return and claim the kingdom for his own.

"Cease," came the call.

"So soon?" said Kulikov. "I assumed you'd want to ensure there were no survivors?"

"Those were not warriors," replied Commander Rudger, nodding towards the water as the bodies floated by. An old woman lay atop a pair of logs lashed together, her grey eyes staring up at them. "Therengians," he spat out. "Hardly worth the arrows."

"It's important none live to report what they've seen."

"What they've seen? The only thing they could have witnessed was a group of archers. Are you now proposing they can see our camp?"

"The ground is open here," said Kulikov. "It's not beyond the realm of possibility."

"And what would people like that know of armies? They are a defeated race. Do not worry yourself over them."

"And if a survivor returns to the capital?"

"Even if by some miracle they lived through our volleys, they are Therengians, Lord. Who'd believe them?"

The former Baron of Raketsk watched as the current carried the bodies farther downstream. "You don't suppose they will be carried to the sea?"

"Of course not. The coast is hundreds of miles away. That lot will wash up on the riverbank before nightfall."

"Then you'd best dispatch some men to go and recover the bodies."

"To what end, Lord?" The commander looked at the foreign noble. The fellow held an inflated opinion of his worth, but Rudger's superiors were adamant the noble might be useful, so he must mind his manners. "I shall send men to scour the banks," the commander added before a rebuke came his way.

The baron grumbled something before he turned, storming off to the camp, snarling as he passed another fellow approaching the contingent of archers.

"Problem?" called out the commander.

"Just the usual," answered Captain Falks. "Nothing I can't handle."

"You should be careful. It's said he carries some influence at court."

"He wouldn't be the first to make such claims."

"Nor will he be the last."

"Meaning?"

"You know the king as well as I," said Rudger. "He fixates on something to the exclusion of all else, then one day he'll wake up and decide it's of no further interest."

"And you think that will happen here?"

Rudger considered this carefully. "His Majesty has always been fascinated with history. I doubt his interest in this matter will wane for the foreseeable future."

"So, we must put up with His Lordship a while longer?"

"As long as he's of use to us. Should he become a burden, however, I have permission to cut him loose."

Falks smiled. "Cut him loose? That sounds very permanent."

"I suppose that's one way of interpreting things, not that I necessarily disagree with it."

"So, you'll kill him?"

"It would be better for all of us if he met with an unfortunate accident. After all, this part of the frontier is overrun with dangerous creatures. Who knows what might happen?"

Falks watched as the river carried the bodies around a bend. "Shall I send men to bury them?"

"There's no hurry. They're not going anywhere."

"Might I ask a question, Commander?"

"By all means."

"Why are we here?"

"You mean with this annoying nobleman of Carlingen?"

"Precisely."

"He has his uses," said Rudger. "Why? What do the men think we're up to?"

Falks shrugged. "There's many a rumour circulating through camp."

"Then amuse me with what they're saying."

"Some believe we're invading Carlingen to expand our borders."

"And what do you make of that?"

"There is little of value here, and we have much of our own land still undeveloped, so I doubt that's the case."

Rudger grinned. "Very astute of you. What else do they say?"

"That there is a great treasure hidden somewhere north of the river."

"What kind of treasure?"

"That's just it—nobody knows. Speculation is running rampant, everything from a dragon hoard to buried treasure. Is there some truth to it?"

"There is, though I wouldn't put too much faith in it being coins if I were you."

"Meaning?"

Rudger swept his arm to indicate the far bank. "Somewhere over there lies a treasure that will make us the strongest army on the Continent."

"But you said it wouldn't be coins. What else could give us such power?"

"What is power? To some, it's endless amounts of gold, while to others, influence."

"But you said it would make our army strong. Is it a lost armoury full of weapons and armour?"

"That wouldn't help," replied Rudger. "We'd still need people to carry such things. No, out there lies a treasure that's been lost since the fall of the Old Kingdom."

"Now you're talking in riddles," said Falks.

"Don't worry. I'll fill you in on the details once the rest of our men arrive."

"There are more coming? I thought we were the only ones."

"Oh no. Finding what we're looking for will take far more than this measly command."

"How many more?"

"Almost a thousand," replied Rudger.

The captain's mouth fell open.

"I see you're impressed."

"Why so many, Commander? Surely we're not expecting opposition? The Army of Carlingen is nowhere near us."

"It is not the treasure that's the problem. It's getting across the river."

"So, we're to build boats?"

"No," said Rudger. "A bridge."

"Why?"

"While we know the treasure lies somewhere within the region, we don't possess precise directions. The objective will be to set up a permanent camp on the other side of the river from which we'll send out exploratory groups. To keep them supplied, we'll need to bring wagons across, which, my dear fellow, requires a bridge."

"It would take tons of stone to bridge that river, Commander."

"Not at all. The king has put his best scholars to work on the idea, and they've devised a surprising solution."

"Which is?"

"They will use boats to anchor the bridge. It's been done before, but never on such a scale."

Captain Falk grinned. "That's why you need so many men—to build the thing."

"Well, that and guard it while it's under construction."

"And how long will it take?"

"That's the question, isn't it, and I'm afraid I can't answer with any certainty. I expect weeks, if not months, but I'm not an expert. The king is sending an engineer who'll oversee the entire operation, but until he gets here, there is little we can do to prepare other than ensure the camp on this side of the river is ready."

"This is much bigger than I thought."

"It is, but cheer up. This could well mean a promotion for you."

"For me?"

"Of course. With this discovery, the army of Ostrova will be impossible to defeat. That means we can expand our borders to our heart's content, but that, in turn, requires more men necessitating others to lead them. Mark my words, Captain. This is only the beginning."

"We still need to get across the river."

"We do, but to my mind, it's a trifling problem, easily solved. Oh, it'll take a lot of muscle and sweat, so don't think it'll be easy, but the real challenge"—he pointed across the river—"lies over there."

FRIENDS

SPRING 1109 SR

"I'm worried," said Svetlana, moving closer to the fireplace. "The wedding is only a few weeks away, and I'm concerned the family will demand my return."

Natalia remained in her seat, nursing a mug of mulled cider. "Have you heard something?"

"Nothing but a deafening silence, but that, in itself, is worrisome."

"There's no reason to think they'd interfere. As I mentioned, the marriage works to their advantage."

Svetlana took a deep breath. "I wish I were as certain as you. How do you do it?"

"Do what?"

"Remain so calm and collected. You've been nothing but courteous and respectful the entire time you've been here, while I babble on endlessly."

"You've just caught me at my best, that's all. Believe me. I've had my moments of panic."

"And how did you get through them?"

"I leaned on those around me," replied Natalia. "Especially Athgar."

"What's it like being married?"

"Wonderful. Athgar and I are very happy."

"So, you consider yourself bond-mates?"

It took a moment for Natalia to realize Svetlana was not using the term to speak of Orcs. "Yes, very much so. My husband and I have a mutual respect for each other."

"I'm surprised to hear you say that, him being a Therengian and all. It can't be easy having to deal with that."

"Let me give you some friendly advice," said Natalia. "Look around and see the world as it truly is, not as you've been taught. It may surprise you."

"Are you suggesting our teachings were false?"

"From a certain point of view, yes. I learned far more after graduation than I ever did from our classes."

"Such as?"

"The Continent would be a better place if we treated others with the dignity and respect we wish for ourselves."

"You've grown in wisdom," said Svetlana. "Something that, in my experience, is rare amongst members of the family." She blushed. "Perhaps I've said too much."

"Not at all. You are to be queen. It's only proper you learn to speak your mind."

"Even at the expense of the family?"

"The family is not who you think they are."

Svetlana grew silent for a moment as she stared into the fire. "I sometimes wish the family would leave me alone."

"I thought you said they hadn't contacted you?"

"They haven't, but their mere existence drives me to distraction. Every word I say, and decision I make, must be carefully weighed lest I offend those above us."

"It doesn't need to be that way," said Natalia. "Come, sit. There's something I want to talk to you about."

The future queen moved to take a seat opposite. "Go on."

"What if I told you there was another way?"

"Another way to what?"

"To be free of the family's influence?"

"Is this a test of my loyalty?"

Natalia was about to continue, but a servant entered and then bowed.

"Excuse me, my lady, but a dispatch just arrived."

"Should you not take that to the king?" asked Svetlana.

"He is with the barons and gave strict instructions not to disturb him."

"And?"

The man blushed. "I thought it might be prudent for you to deliver the message. He would hardly object to you interrupting."

"Very well. Hand it over."

The fellow stepped closer, passing her a hastily scribbled note. "It's from the east gate," he explained.

Svetlana read it over, and then her eyes went to Natalia. "It appears we have visitors."

"Let me guess, a delegate from Ostrova?"

"No, something far more unusual—Orcs!"

"That will be our friends. Don't worry. They're not hostile. If you recall, I mentioned someone would be meeting us here to escort us farther into the Continent."

"And you trust those green savages to do that?"

"They are not savages!" snapped Natalia, then took a breath, calming herself before continuing. "The Orcs are a civilized race, and I trust them. Enough, in fact, that I left my daughter in their care."

"I…"

"Perhaps it's time I reveal the truth of the matter."

"I think that would be wise."

Natalia sipped her wine as she gathered her thoughts. "I ran away from the Volstrum shortly after graduation, fleeing south to get as far from the family's influence as possible. My path took me to Draybourne, but bounty hunters came after me. I defeated them with my magic, inadvertently injuring Athgar, who was trying to help me. I nursed him back to health and then accompanied him to Corassus, and we've been together ever since."

"But I don't understand," said Svetlana. "If you fled the Volstrum, why did you return there last year?"

"We went seeking revenge. They came after my daughter, but striking back at them turned out to be an ill-conceived attempt to warn them off."

"You fought the family?"

"Yes, in Karslev itself. Does that surprise you?"

"I suppose it shouldn't," replied Svetlana. "You're certainly powerful enough. Wait, does that mean Katrin was also working against the family?"

"It does. She failed out of the Volstrum and became one of the Disgraced. Have you any idea what happens to those who disappear?"

"No."

"They are sent as slaves to mine magerite. That very ring you wear was dug out of stone by the blood and tears of such people."

"That's ghastly."

"When Athgar and I reached Karslev, we were captured. They enslaved my husband and used threats against his life to make me serve them."

"Yet you're here now?"

"Yes. Thanks to the help of friends, Athgar escaped, and together we burned down Stormwind Manor. After that, we fled west to Reinwick, determined to undermine the family's influence in the courts of the Petty Kingdoms."

"Why are you telling me all this now?" asked Svetlana.

"Because it's time for you to make a choice. Either you cling to the skirts of the family or join us in working against them."

"And who is 'us' exactly? Surely you're not suggesting the two of you possess enough power to take on the Stormwinds?"

"Even with an entire realm behind us?"

Svetlana chugged down the remains of her drink. "I'm afraid you'll need to explain that one to me."

"Athgar is the High Thane of Therengia, and I, his Warmaster."

"Do you realize what you're saying? I could have you arrested. Saints know there are plenty who'd pay a king's ransom for you."

"Yes, you could arrest us… or accept our hands in friendship and throw off the yoke of the family."

"What of King Maksim?"

"Nothing has changed regarding my offer. If you truly seek help from Therengia, all you need do is speak to Athgar, or if you prefer, I can talk to him on your behalf."

"I must think this over carefully. It's a decision that would have lasting consequences."

"Good. I wouldn't have it any other way." Natalia stood. "Now, with your permission, I shall go to my friends and bring them back here to the Palace. Perhaps, once you meet them for yourselves, you and the king will see the wisdom in accepting our offer of aid."

"Very well," said Svetlana. "I'll send some of the king's men to escort you if only to reassure the guards at the gate all is well. The king and I will await your return in the great hall."

Sergeant Brauer escorted them to the gate, assisted by six of the king's guards. As they neared the eastern gate, they couldn't help but notice the men in the gate tower stood with their backs to the city, presumably with crossbows in hand.

"There's no need for that," called out Natalia. "Those Orcs are friendly."

"One can never be sure," replied Sergeant Brauer, "and we must be vigilant lest it's a trap." The fellow halted, then rested his hand on the hilt of his sword. "Open it up," he said, nodding towards the city gates.

They waited as four guards rushed to remove the drop bar, then hauled the doors open to a welcoming sight. Kargen and Shaluhk stood before the tower, the rest of their party behind them. Natalia's eyes, however, only had room for Oswyn.

The four-year-old screamed with delight and ran forward. Agar rushed after his tribe-sister, surprising the guards, who immediately drew their swords. Athgar moved to block them, his hands enveloped in flames.

"Sheath your weapons," he called out. "There will be no bloodshed this day." He let the fire subside.

Natalia crouched, and their daughter barreled into her arms.

"Momma! Momma! I missed you!"

She clutched Oswyn to her, tears streaming down her face.

Having slowed at the sight of the soldiers, Agar cautiously advanced. Behind him, his parents watched, curious about how things might develop. Instead of waiting, Athgar moved to meet them, giving Kargen a firm hug.

"It is good to see you again," said the chieftain.

"How was your trip?"

"Boring, but I think that is about to change now you have returned."

"And you, Shaluhk?"

The shamaness embraced him. "Good to see you again, Athgar."

"I hope Oswyn hasn't been any trouble?"

"Not at all."

Athgar looked past her to another familiar face, along with a dozen Orc hunters he didn't recognize. "Skora, I hope you're well?"

"I am," replied the old woman, "though I must admit your daughter is becoming a handful."

"Papa! Papa!"

Athgar wheeled around, and Oswyn jumped into his arms, almost knocking him over. He crushed her to him, wanting the moment to last forever. Only after he'd stood there for some time did he realize everyone was looking at him.

He ignored them, placing his daughter on her feet. "Let me look at you," he said. "You've grown so much." He reached out, placing his hand on her forehead.

"What's wrong?" asked Natalia.

"She feels warm." He turned to Shaluhk. "Has she been ill?"

"Not at all," replied the shaman. "She is as healthy as a tusker."

"Let me see," said Natalia, placing her own hand on Oswyn's forehead. "She feels cold to me."

"How curious," said Shaluhk. "It appears her gifts have begun to manifest."

"She's only four. Mages don't typically show any affinity for magic until their coming of age."

"Correct me if I am wrong, but did you not show your own manifestations much earlier? I seem to recall Stanislav mentioning you froze water while even younger?"

"She's got you there," said Athgar. "And if she's as powerful as you at that age, it only makes sense. I'm more worried about her temperature, though."

Natalia picked her up. "She's cold, I tell you. Why, she's chilled to the bone."

"She doesn't act like it," he replied. He reached out again, this time touching Oswyn's cheek. "Just as I thought, she's warm. You check, Shaluhk."

The shaman stepped closer, reaching out with her green hand and placing it gently on the young girl's forehead. "There is nothing wrong with her that I can tell." A smile broke out, and she nodded. "I understand now."

"Then perhaps you might explain it to us?"

"If you recall, Athgar, your magic was unleashed when you suffered."

"Are you suggesting Oswyn is suffering somehow?"

"No, but reuniting with her parents after such a long absence is very emotional for her. Her emotions likely unlocked that which lay dormant within her. You have, in essence, allowed her to discover her spark." She turned to Natalia. "You, on the other hand, allowed her to find the source of her Water Magic."

Athgar looked at the concern on Natalia's face. "Do you remember when I rushed into the building back in Ebenstadt to rescue her from the fire?"

She nodded.

"Something quenched the flames. I think it was her."

"I remember," replied his wife. "And at the Battle of the Standing Stones, I felt a burning in my stomach, as if she were on fire." She stared back, her mind trying to make sense of things.

Shaluhk wasn't finished. "Years ago, I predicted your child would one day master both fire and water. This was only made possible when the application of magebane during your pregnancy suppressed her inner capacity for Water Magic long enough for the spark to be born within her."

Natalia nodded. "I suspected such was the case, but even so, now that we see evidence of it, my head is spinning." She laughed quietly at first, then louder. "After centuries of breeding, the family got it all wrong!"

"Wrong?" said Athgar. "I'm not sure I understand. You yourself are a powerful mage. Doesn't that support their idea of selective breeding?"

"But that's just it, don't you see? Had they known this years ago, they could've bred an army of mages trained in both Fire and Water Magic!"

"Momma?" said Oswyn. "Is something wrong?"

Natalia smiled down at her. "Not at all, my dear. We're just so happy to see you."

Agar moved closer, bowing before Natalia. "I have done my best to keep her safe."

"And you did well, Agar, son of Kargen." She paused when she caught sight of his weapon. "Is that an actual metal axe I see in your belt?"

The youngling grinned. "It is. My father awarded it to me after my first kill."

"He saved Shaluhk and I both," said Kargen. "I thought it only fitting he use the axe my father handed down to me."

"Are we going to stay here?" asked Oswyn.

Natalia placed her on the ground and took her hand.

Athgar grabbed Oswyn's other hand, and they turned to face Sergeant Brauer. "You can lead us back to the Palace now, Sergeant."

The man hesitated. "There are a dozen armed Orcs outside the gate, Lord."

"These hunters are members of the Red Hand, as am I. Will you incur my displeasure by denying my tribe-brothers entrance?" He glanced at the Orcs, noting three were female, but thought it better not to correct himself and confuse the fellow.

It looked like Brauer wanted to draw his blade, and Athgar couldn't blame him. Most people in the Petty Kingdoms had been raised on tales of bloodthirsty Orcs eating the flesh of men. It couldn't be easy for the fellow to suppress his panic in their presence.

"I assure you, they're friendly." Still, the obstinate look. "Also, I feel I should point out that an attack on any member of the tribe is considered an attack on us all, myself included."

The sergeant relaxed slightly, then grunted something incomprehensible before barking out an order to his men. They, in turn, took up positions on either side of the roadway while their leader looked Athgar in the eye. "This way, my lord."

Athgar and Natalia waited as Kargen and Shaluhk fell in behind, Skora and the hunters following along.

Agar, however, moved closer to a guard, reaching out to lightly touch the fellow's padded gambeson. "Very nice. I must get one for myself someday."

"You have seen armour before?" asked the guard.

"Yes, but this armour is not links of metal." He looked up at the guard's face. "Is it cumbersome to walk in?"

The fellow stared back, not quite sure how to react.

"Come, my son," said Kargen. "We can speak of such things later. We are guests here in the city and should not keep the king waiting."

"Very well, Father." Agar rushed up to take his place between his parents.

"It seems we are ready now," said Shaluhk.

. . .

"This, Your Majesty," said Athgar, "is Kargen, Chieftain of the Red Hand."

Maksim IV leaned forward on his throne. "Is it not customary amongst the tribes to bow before a king?"

"He is a chieftain," replied Natalia. "In his lands, that grants him equal status."

Maksim raised an eyebrow. "Is that so? Well then. In that case, greetings, Kargen of the Red Hand, and welcome to Carlingen."

"It is an honour to be here, Majesty."

"Tell me, where are your lands?"

"To the south, near Novarsk."

"So, you're near the new Kingdom of Therengia?"

"Yes," replied Kargen. He glanced at Athgar only to see a slight shaking of his head. "You might say we are on very good terms with them. We are primarily hunters, so we roam around looking for food."

"And have you any issues with this new Kingdom of Therengia?"

"None whatsoever."

"I'm curious," said Maksim. "How many warriors have you back home?"

"We have no warriors. In our society, we prize hunters over soldiers. As to numbers, I am not one to count such things. Why do you ask?"

"I was just wondering whether or not I might be able to hire your tribe to fight with us. We've had some trouble with one of our neighbours of late and fear war is coming."

"Surely Your Majesty is being premature?" said Svetlana. "We have yet to receive their envoy."

"I am the king. As such, I must prepare by taking precautions."

"I only brought a dozen hunters with me," said Kargen, "and most have only recently completed their ordeals."

"That's a coming-of-age rite," explained Athgar, "wherein the young hunters must survive by themselves in the wilderness for ten days."

The king swept his gaze over the Orcs. "I am impressed. I confess you've surprised me, Lord Kargen."

"In what way, Majesty?"

"You are most civilized for a race described as savage. It seems my education has been lacking in such matters."

Oswyn ran across the room to stand in front of Kargen. "I am Oswyn," she announced.

Maksim smiled. "Oswyn, is it? I assume you're Athgar and Natalia's daughter?"

"I am."

The king was about to say more, but Agar ran up to stand beside the young girl, axe in hand. "Leave her alone!" he shouted. "You will not hurt her!"

"I assure you, I harbour no such intention," said Maksim, "but I recognize loyalty when I see it, and you possess it in abundance. I commend you on your bravery, young one. Not many children are courageous enough to stand up to a king."

"He meant no offence," said Kargen. "The ways of Human Royalty are strange to him."

Maksim chuckled. "No offence was taken, I assure you."

"You mentioned the possibility of war," said Shaluhk, moving up to stand beside her bondmate.

"I did. And you are?"

"Shaluhk, bondmate to Kargen and Shaman of the Red Hand."

"A shaman, you say. It seems I am doubly blessed this day." Maksim paused, unsure of how to proceed.

"Let us keep no secrets," said Kargen. "Feel free to speak plainly; we promise not to take offence."

"Very well. I fear war is brewing with our southern neighbour. They've informed us they're sending an envoy to this court, but I want to project strength. Having a fellow king present, or in your case, a chieftain, would accomplish such a thing."

"Have you any idea when this envoy is to arrive?"

"I'm afraid not, but until they do, I offer you my hospitality."

Kargen looked at Athgar, who nodded slightly.

"Very well," the Orc Chieftain replied. "In that case, we accept."

WEDDING

SPRING 1109 SR

"Now, that," said Belgast, "is a building to be proud of."

Athgar stared up at the Temple of Saint Mathew. "It must have cost a fortune."

"Aye, but it was well spent. Look at those arches; only a Dwarf would think of something as grandiose as that."

"There are Human architects, you know."

Belgast sighed. "Yes. I suppose you're right, but it seems to me whoever planned this place must have seen the king's chamber in Kragen-Tor. Those pillars in front are almost identical to the Pillars of Truth."

"Which are?"

"When the king interrogates a prisoner, they're lashed between the two pillars. It is said when held there, one is compelled to speak the truth." He looked at Athgar and smiled. "Mind you, it's all nonsense."

"I'm surprised to hear you say that."

"Haglarith once told me the story was invented to lend an air of mystique to the place. Faith in those pillars is so ingrained in the minds of Dwarves that they believe it."

"Thus making the statement true?"

"Precisely. I suppose we should call it a clever ruse, but you can't admit that to anybody."

"No," said Athgar, "of course not." The doors to the temple opened. "Ah, there's Captain Cordelia."

"That's Temple Captain," corrected Belgast. "It's important to use proper titles in ceremonies like this."

"I might remind you the wedding has yet to begin."

"Oh yes, of course. Say, did you have time to look into those prisoners the townsfolk complained about?"

"We did, or rather Natalia did. The king agreed to a general amnesty for everyone but the most violent criminals."

"So he didn't set them all free?"

"Are you suggesting he should have let murderers and thugs back on the street?"

"No, of course not. I always forget how much crime there is in Human cities."

"And I suppose you're going to tell me Dwarven cities experience no such problems?"

"There are crimes of passion from time to time, but most of us mountain folk are good-natured. Of course, we don't imprison the guilty."

"Then what do you do with them?"

"Execute them if it's serious," replied Belgast. "Otherwise, banishment is the order of the day."

"And to where do the banished go?"

"To the Human cities, generally."

Cordelia approached, bowing in greeting. "Belgast, good to see you again, and you, Athgar."

The Dwarf smiled. "It's always a pleasure to see a sister knight."

"All ready for the ceremony?" asked Athgar.

"Yes," replied the Temple Captain. "Not that there's much for me to do. Six of my knights are at the Palace, ready to escort the future queen to the temple, with more inside. As for myself, I've been making sure everything here is in readiness."

Athgar lowered his voice. "If you have a moment, I want to discuss something with you."

"By all means. What is it?"

"There's been rumours of your Temple Knights throwing their weight around."

"I assure you that is not the case. Such behaviour would be unconscionable."

"Might I ask the composition of your patrols?"

"They operate in groups of six," replied Cordelia, "and I alternate who is in each group. I find that tends to keep them on their toes. If anyone is complaining about them, it's likely the criminals. Is there a specific complaint I need to address?"

"When we met with the townsfolk, an individual claimed your knights exclusively sided with women. Natalia and I are convinced he might be a Cunar."

"It would explain the animosity. Somehow, word has travelled about the part I played at Ord-Kurgad, and they're not the types to forgive me for arresting one of their father generals."

"Is that why they demanded you hand over the commandery?"

"I'm afraid I'm not at liberty to reveal much in the way of details, but I've learned the Temple Knights of Saint Cunar have been pushing for a greater role of late."

"A greater role in what?"

"The Church in general, but enough of this melancholy talk. You and Natalia have done well for yourselves to be the king's guests."

"More like guests of the future queen. She and Natalia were fellow students at the Volstrum."

"And has she been informed of your true positions?"

"She has, although the king has yet to learn the truth."

"You are playing a dangerous game here," warned Cordelia. "Lies can only lead to trouble."

"It's not so much a lie as an omission. Don't worry. We'll tell him eventually, but he has enough trouble to deal with for now."

Horseshoes clattered on cobblestones, warning all the wedding party approached.

"Please excuse me," said Cordelia. "I must prepare for the queen's arrival."

"Aye," said Belgast, "and we should get inside before all the best seats are taken."

Trumpets blared, announcing Svetlana as she rolled up in an ornate carriage, six mounted Temple Knights leading. Cordelia opened the door, and the future queen stepped down, her golden dress sparkling in the sunlight. Natalia followed, dressed in less-conspicuous attire, and then they climbed the steps to the Temple of Saint Mathew.

Royal guards stood at the door, snapping to attention as they passed, and then the wedding party was inside, pausing momentarily as the six Temple Knights took up positions on either side.

Stanislav fidgeted in his seat.

"What's the matter?" asked Belgast.

"I'm not one to appreciate weddings," replied the mage hunter, "especially not ones of this… extravagance."

"Is that because your own wedding was… How shall I put this?"

"Disastrous? It's all right. You can say it."

"I was going to say unsuccessful, but since you insist, I'll agree."

"It's not just that. To my mind, a wedding should be a private affair, attended by family and close friends, not a huge spectacle."

"But this is no ordinary wedding. It's royal!"

"Speaking of which, where's the king?"

"Have you no understanding of etiquette?" asked Belgast. "A king can't be seen to wait on a commoner, even a Stormwind."

"So, where is he?"

"Outside, I expect. He'll likely come in a side door after she makes her way to the altar." He craned his neck. "Hush now. Here she comes down the aisle."

Beside Belgast, Agar squirmed. "Why do Humans spend so much time waiting? Have they nothing better to do?" He nudged the Dwarf. "Why is the woman wearing gold?"

"To signify her wealth," replied Belgast.

"Why do knights guard her?"

"Those are Temple Knights of Saint Agnes, an order dedicated to protecting women."

"Why does she need protection?"

"My understanding is that it's merely symbolic."

"So it has nothing to do with the crossbow?"

The Dwarf turned in annoyance. "What are you babbling on about? What crossbow?"

"The one up there," replied Agar, pointing to the balcony.

Belgast twisted in his seat, looking to where the youngling pointed. Whoever constructed this temple had built a balcony below the ceiling, likely to aid in construction but also to provide a spot for people to view the massive chamber without interfering in the proceedings. At the moment, a Royal Guardsman was visible, his blue-and-gold tabard easy to distinguish against the white stone. Unlike the other guards, however, he leaned forward, taking aim with his crossbow. The Dwarf followed the fellow's line of sight and gasped as he realized the future queen was in jeopardy.

"Traitor!" Belgast called out, jumping to his feet and pointing.

His shout echoed through the chamber, but it was too late. A crossbow bolt flew from the man's weapon, racing through the air. Standing beside Svetlana, Natalia turned, her hands moving even as words of power sprung from her lips. A wall of ice appeared before her, sending a chill through the room as the bolt struck, its tip poking through on the other side.

The crossbowman reloaded, but as he leaned forward to release his second bolt, a streak of flame struck him in the chest, tumbling him backwards, out of sight.

Kargen and Shaluhk rushed forward from the front row, weapons drawn, while Athgar searched for more assailants.

Royal Guards charged into the room as those in attendance panicked, several running for the exit, but the Temple Knights of Saint Agnes closed the doors and barred any from leaving. More guards appeared on the balcony, and then Maksim entered from a side door, making his way to his intended.

Sergeant Brauer leaned over the railing. "He's dead," he called out. "No sign of any accomplices."

The Holy Father looked at his king. "You should get to safety, Your Majesty."

Maksim met his gaze. "Continue with the ceremony."

"Surely not!"

"I will not be held hostage by the threat of violence." He paused, looking at Svetlana, who merely nodded in response. "There, you see? It is her wish also that you proceed."

The Holy Father gathered his nerves. "Very well, Your Majesty." He began the blessing.

Athgar sat back, placing his tankard on the table.

"Another?" asked the servant.

"No, thank you. I've had quite enough." He looked at the head table where Maksim and his new queen were enjoying themselves, although Svetlana appeared a little reserved. The sight reminded him of his early days with Natalia. She'd been far more suspicious back then, convinced the family lurked behind every corner, and with good reason.

His gaze wandered to his wife sitting on Svetlana's left, and their eyes met, eliciting a smile from them both.

"Now, now," said Stanislav. "We'll have none of that pining from you. You'll have plenty of time to be with your good wife later."

"Aye," added Belgast. "This is a celebration, and as such, requires imbibing copious amounts of drink!"

"I believe I'll pass on that," replied Athgar. "I haven't forgotten what happened the last time I drank excessively."

"Very well, then. I'll do my part and drink your share for you. I'd hate for us to appear ungrateful."

Athgar stood, drawing the attention of all present. "Your Majesties," he said. "I owe you an apology." The guests grew quiet.

"For what?" replied the king.

"I didn't mean to kill the man on the balcony. Had I taken greater care, we'd have a prisoner to interrogate."

"And had you not, my bride might be the one dead. You did what you felt was best, and I am indebted to you. Indeed, the entire kingdom owes you much. In recognition of your actions, I would grant you a boon. Ask what you want of me, Athgar of Athelwald, and I shall do all in my power to make it yours."

"I ask no reward save for your happiness, Majesty."

King Maksim turned to Natalia. "And what of you, my lady? What boon would fit for one of your calibre?"

"I desire no riches, Majesty, but there may come a time when someone casts doubt upon us. I ask only that should such a thing occur, you give us a chance to explain ourselves."

"You speak in riddles. Would you care to elaborate?"

"This is a time of celebration, not deep discussion. Would it not be wiser to enjoy the company of your new queen and celebrate the day's events?"

Maksim smiled. "It would indeed. Very well, I will accede to your wish. I promise to heed your words if you ever find yourself the object of doubt. After all, a king has two ears and only one mouth, so he must listen twice as much as he talks."

The room burst into applause.

"Thank you, all of you," he continued. "I am deeply honoured you were here with us today, despite the attempt on my queen's life. Rest assured. I shall spare no effort to discover who is behind this heinous plot."

"To the happy couple," roared Belgast, raising his tankard.

The guests echoed the sentiment, downing their drinks. The room soon filled with voices as everyone resumed their previous conversations.

Belgast smiled, looking quite pleased with himself. "Works every time."

"What does?" asked Stanislav.

"Using a toast to break up a long speech."

"Long? But the king hardly said anything."

"That's true, but I sensed him readying to bore us to death."

Kargen, sitting on the other side of Athgar, leaned in close. "Tell me, my friend. Why have you not seen fit to inform King Maksim of your true identity? Do you not trust him?"

"I'm not sure. Svetlana knows, and I don't think the king would arrest us, but my recent experiences in Reinwick lead me to believe there are ears at court who would pass on information to less-desirable people."

"You mean spies?"

"I do."

Kargen grunted. "Humans are far too complicated for me to understand. Just when I feel I have a grasp on their behaviour, something like this happens. Why can the people of the Continent not be more like Therengians?"

"I'm afraid even Therengians suffer," replied Athgar. "King Eadred was not someone to set a good example."

"How much longer will we linger here in Carlingen?"

"I'm not entirely sure. Natalia seems convinced Svetlana wants to join us."

"But you do not?"

"The family is powerful," said Athgar, "and are yet to make their demands. I fear she may buckle under pressure from her superiors."

"All the more reason we should leave sooner rather than later."

"I can't. Not until I find some way to bring the Therengians home."

"That is a long trip, my friend, and we have few umaks."

"Then what about a larger ship?"

"No," said Kargen. "You know as well as I that anything larger would be unable to navigate the upper waters of the river. If they undertake such a trip, it must be over land."

"We can't take them through Ostrova, and they'd never survive the wilderness to the east, not without a lot of help."

"Then we wait."

"You make it sound so simple," said Athgar.

"I have faith the Ancestors will find a way for us to accomplish our goals. The bigger problem is the king's generosity; I doubt he can continue to house us forever. The cost alone to feed us must be enormous."

"It likely is, but we've been trying to help him."

"How?"

"Natalia offered some advice on deepening his coffers, and together, we've been looking at ways to secure the streets."

"Is it truly that dangerous here?"

"I've seen no danger myself, but I've heard the stories."

"And your progress?" asked Kargen.

"The Temple Knights of Saint Agnes have increased the area they patrol, and the king agreed to arm the Therengian fyrd."

"Yet I sense you are nervous about the next step."

"I am," said Athgar. "I must meet with the Temple Knights of Saint Cunar and convince them to do their part."

"Are there no Mathewites here?"

"There are, but only lay brothers, I'm afraid."

"And are there any other factions that might prove useful in keeping the peace?"

"There are a few, but they're no better than gangs. Not the sort of folk we want patrolling the streets."

"I will see if Shaluhk can find any tribes in this region."

"You think that would help?"

"I would not get my hopes up if I were you. Even if some were in the area, I doubt they would entertain coming into a city like Carlingen."

"Then why look for them at all?"

"There is more to keeping the peace than crowding the streets with soldiers," said Kargen.

"Meaning?"

"The presence of a tribe of Orcs in the countryside would likely unite those who perceive them as dangerous."

"Isn't that simply reinforcing their hatred for Orcs?"

Kargen shrugged. "It makes little difference in the long run, and in the grand scheme of things, this kingdom is of little consequence. I am curious, however, why you are making such an effort here. I understand you want to help the Therengians, but you have your own realm to look after."

"I don't like people pushing their weight around."

"I do not understand that expression."

"Ostrova is using its strength to force this kingdom to give up land. If we don't stop them, they'll do the same thing to Therengia."

"Are you suggesting a failure here could lead to war?"

"It makes sense, doesn't it? We know the Petty Kingdoms are always fighting for dominance. If Ostrova has its way, their king's arrogance will have him making demands of his other neighbours."

"But would our strength not be a deterrent?"

"It didn't work for Novarsk," said Athgar, "and if they pick a fight with Therengia, they'll likely convince others to join their cause. The Continent fears us, and fear drives men to take extreme actions."

Kargen shook his head. "Will they never learn?"

"The Old Kingdom fell because all the other lands united against them. We can't afford to push them into the same situation here."

"Yet, if I understand correctly, a war with Ostrova might do that very thing."

"It puts us in a tough situation. We either sit this conflict out and risk them coming for us later or intervene and risk a larger war."

"There is another option," said Kargen. "We send word to Wynfrith to prepare for war. If a conflict does come, we cross the border and defeat them quickly before they can gather allies."

"Very well. Have the army assemble in Novarsk. If there is to be a battle, then best it's done on our terms."

SURVIVOR

SUMMER 1109 SR

A knock drew Natalia's attention away from Oswyn, who was sitting on her mother's lap listening to a story. The young girl jumped down and ran to the door, but it proved too heavy for her to open.

"One moment," called out Natalia as she rose and straightened her dress before crossing the room to see who'd arrived.

A Temple Knight stood there waiting. "My lady," the woman said, "I have news from Temple Captain Cordelia." She produced a sealed letter.

Athgar entered from a side room. "We have visitors?"

"No. It's only a note," replied Natalia, breaking it open. She scanned its contents before looking up at the messenger. "I assume she's expecting a reply?"

"Indeed, my lady."

"What is it?" asked Athgar.

"A Therengian woman has shown up at the commandery."

"And?"

"The letter doesn't give specifics, but Cordelia feels it's in our best interests to hear the woman's story."

"That sounds serious."

"I would go myself, but I promised Svetlana I would attend court to offer advice. Would you consider going in my stead?"

"To court?"

"No, to the commandery." Natalia chuckled. "I know how much you despise the trappings of court."

"As long as that's acceptable to the order?" He looked at the Temple Knight, who merely nodded. "I'll take Belgast."

"Then you'd best go right away before Herulf returns. You know he doesn't like the thought of you going anywhere without him."

"Yes," admitted Athgar. "He's becoming a bit of a nuisance in that regard."

"What about me?" called out Greta.

"You and Katrin are coming with me," said Natalia. "I would value your opinion of the court here."

"My opinion? I was nothing more than a messenger in Andover."

"True, but you were there long enough to see how everything worked. Don't you think it would be interesting to compare your experiences there with how things are done here in Carlingen?"

"Belgast?" called out Athgar.

The Dwarf peered from the doorway. "Yes?"

"How would you like to join me in visiting Cordelia?"

"At the commandery?"

"Yes. There's a visitor there she wants us to meet."

"Give me a moment." Belgast stepped into the room but was staring down at his belt while he fiddled with the buckle.

"Something wrong?"

"It's this belt. It's shrunk."

Natalia chuckled. "I don't suppose it has anything to do with all the food you've eaten of late?"

"Nonsense. Us mountain folk keep on a steady diet." He brushed past her to stand before Athgar. "Come. It's best we don't waste time dawdling around here, or someone might see fit to insult us."

Athgar struggled to contain himself. "I don't think there's any 'us' in the situation."

His companion harrumphed. "Are you coming or not?"

"Very well. After you."

The street was empty when they arrived at the Temple Knight commandery, unlike the last time Athgar had visited. Their guide led them past the two sentries to the second floor, where Cordelia's office lay.

"Just out of curiosity," said Belgast. "Did anyone ever approach the Cunars?"

"I'm afraid we've all been putting it off, but I suppose we can't continue doing so forever, not if we want the streets properly patrolled."

"And if they refuse to cooperate?"

"Then we shall have to look at an alternate arrangement."

"We're here," announced the guide as they arrived at an open door.

"Come in," called out Cordelia.

They entered to find a grey-haired woman sitting before the Temple Captain.

"Natalia apologizes, but she's needed at court." Athgar stepped into the room but stopped at the sight of the malnourished old woman whose sunken grey eyes turned towards him as he entered.

"You are Lord Athgar," she said, her voice weak. "I heard about you in the Therengian district."

"Yes, and this is Belgast Ridgehand, a close friend of mine. Are you well?"

"As well as I can be, considering the circumstances."

"Perhaps you'd best start at the beginning," prompted Cordelia.

"Yes, of course. My name is Wendred. Like you, I am of Therengian descent. My husband and I came to Carlingen after a lifetime of servitude in Abelard."

"Servitude?" asked Athgar.

"Yes. We were serfs for the Royal Family, although perhaps slaves would be a more accurate description. We finally earned our freedom and came east, seeking the kingdom reborn." She paused, gathering her thoughts, but her voice broke as she continued. "M-m-my husband, Wigstan, purchased a map that was supposed to show us the way."

"I'm guessing it didn't?"

"Actually, it proved quite accurate; surprising, now I think back on it. In any case, it led us through the thick forests south of here to the great river forming the border. That's where everything went horribly wrong." Her head lowered, tears running down her cheeks.

"Take your time," said Cordelia. "I know this is difficult for you."

"We needed to cross the river," continued Wendred, "but it was wide, and its current swift. We sought to lash together logs and float across. It would have worked, too, if it hadn't been for those archers."

"Archers?" said Athgar. "Do you mean to tell me someone loosed arrows at you?"

The old woman nodded. "At first, we took them for Orcs, but then we saw men lined up on the other bank."

"You mean the southern bank?" asked Belgast. "But that would be Ostrova, wouldn't it?"

"Yes, that's right," said Cordelia, "but let her continue, I beg of you."

"We were unarmed," said Wendred, "save for the odd knife or axe. We were no threat to them."

"How many archers did you see?" asked Athgar.

"I'm not sure. Perhaps twenty, maybe more?"

"That's an unusually large hunting party," said Belgast.

"They were not hunters," she insisted. "They were lined up in the open with someone giving them orders."

"Soldiers, then," said Athgar. "But why would they aim at people crossing the river?"

"That's easy," said Belgast. "They're hiding something. The Ostrovans, I mean. I'm afraid this poor woman and her travelling companions stumbled across something they weren't meant to see."

"Yes, but what?"

"A buildup of their army?"

"If that's the case, I must warn the king." Athgar turned back to Wendred. "How many of you were there?"

"Fifteen, but I'm the only survivor." Her eyes went blank. "I watched my Wigstan die, an arrow in his back."

"She's in shock," said Cordelia, nodding to their escort. "Let's get her to her room, shall we? And someone should stay with her."

"Yes, Captain."

They waited while the guards escorted the old woman from the room before the Temple Captain broke the silence. "You see why I called you here. If there is an army massing to the south, it can only spell trouble."

"I shall return to the Palace and inform His Majesty," said Athgar. "Not that it'll do much good. If I'm not mistaken, the southern border is a long way from here, and moving an army through that type of terrain would be difficult, even for a trained hunter like me. It's remarkable she made it back here at all. What do you intend to do with her?"

"She'll stay here for now, but we're making some enquiries in the Therengian district to see if we can't find someone willing to take her in."

Athgar noted Belgast stroking his beard, a sure sign he was thinking things over. "Your thoughts?"

"I can't quite wrap my head around the why." The Dwarf looked up to confused faces. "I'm not referring to Wendred and why they travelled south. I'm trying to reason out what Ostrova is up to. From all we've heard, there's nothing down there but forests and rivers. Why in the name of the Gods are they even there? Is there something of strategic value we overlooked?"

"There's still the possibility they might be after godstone."

"If that's the case, why are they waiting?"

"What makes you think they're waiting?"

"Several things," said Belgast. "The presence of archers lends credence to the idea the army is involved. And if they are, why aren't they already across the river? All they need are men and shovels, and they could dig out any godstone in a matter of a few days."

"Could they have just arrived in the area?"

"It's possible, but what are the odds they arrived at almost the exact same time as Wendred's group? They were also formed on the bank, indicating they were watching the river. The big question is, why loose their arrows? Couldn't they have waited until they were across and arrested them all? No, they're hiding something."

"Your argument makes sense, but if not godstone, then what?"

"Give me some time to let it ruminate," said Belgast.

"We'd best get back to the Palace. If Ostrova is preparing to invade, the king must prepare his defences."

"I must admit," said Svetlana, "you are surprisingly well-spoken. I never would have expected one of your kind to be so educated."

"We prize intelligence," replied Shaluhk, "and our shamans oversee the education of our younglings."

"You look after all the children?"

"No, but we offer assistance and guidance to the parents. The selective wisdom of the Ancestors ensures the tribe's growth."

"And these Ancestors are gods?"

"No," said Kargen. "They are the spirits of Orcs who lived before us."

"Are you suggesting you can speak with the dead?"

"When a body dies, the spirit lingers, some longer than others. It is said they remain behind to act as our guides."

"Fascinating," said Svetlana. She turned to King Maksim. "What do you think, Your Majesty?"

"I agree with your assessment. We were always taught Orcs are savage brutes, yet you are more sophisticated than us in many ways."

Kargen grunted. "We are often mistaken as such by the people of the Petty Kingdoms."

"I no longer consider Carlingen one of them," said Maksim. "I turned my back on them after they refused my pleas for help."

"What type of help, Majesty?" asked Shaluhk.

"After the rebirth of Therengia, many came here with the hope of a new life, while others sought to plunder it. What makes matters worse is both groups were disappointed. Now we are stuck with an overabundance of people, most of whom have few productive skills. It has proven difficult to keep them from each other's throats and a challenge to maintain the peace."

"Yes," added Svetlana, "and their poverty only adds to the misery."

A king's guardsman entered. "Your Majesties, Lord Athgar and Lord Belgast are here."

"Escort them in," replied Maksim.

The two newcomers advanced, halting before the king.

"Your Majesty," said Athgar. "We just came from the Agnesite commandery. I fear we bear disturbing news."

"Then speak freely, so we might better understand the situation."

"A group of Therengians travelled south seeking to cross Ostrova into Therengia. They made it as far as the border, where archers attacked them as they crossed the river."

The king leaned forward. "Attacked, you say? Do you mean to imply foreign troops were on our soil?"

"They were on their own side of the river, Majesty, but gave no warning. Of the fifteen travellers, only one escaped."

"And these soldiers said nothing?"

"They did not," replied Belgast. "From the sounds of it, they loosed off an overabundance of arrows to ensure no survivors, but an old woman managed to escape with her life."

"Was there any sign of them on Carlingen's side of the river?"

"No, sire."

"This is an outrage," said Svetlana.

"It is," agreed Maksim, "yet what can I do? There has been no violation of our territory; even if there were, I'm in no position to send troops. An expedition that far south, through that terrain, would prove difficult, if not impossible."

Natalia, who'd been standing to one side, moved up beside her husband. "Have we any word concerning the Ostrovan envoy's arrival?"

"Not at present, although I've been expecting one for some time. Do you believe this could be a pressure tactic to put us ill at ease?"

"It was poorly executed if it was. Volleys of arrows are not the best way to ensure a lone survivor. I can only conclude the woman's survival was pure happenstance."

"That is good," said Shaluhk. "It means our opponent is unaware this knowledge has reached us."

"True," said the king, "but how do we take advantage of that?"

"If I may," said Kargen. "Allow me to take my hunters south and investigate."

"With only a dozen Orcs? That's far too dangerous."

"They are hunters of the Red Hand," said Athgar. "They can move around in that terrain with great ease. A group of archers, even the best, will be of little use against their warbows."

"Warbows?"

"Yes," said Kargen. "Great bows used by members of my tribe, designed for our hunters to utilize their strength. They were Athgar's gift to his tribemates."

"I will go with them," announced Natalia.

"No," said Shaluhk. "I will. It would be better for you to remain here to advise their Majesties. I only ask that you look after Agar during our absence."

"Of course. It would be my pleasure."

"The way south is treacherous," warned Maksim. "There are no roads, and what trails are there are poorly marked, not to mention numerous lakes and rivers to contend with."

"Fear not," said Kargen. "We will be travelling by umak. If enemy archers are on the river, we will find them."

"I suggest," said Belgast, "that once Kargen arrives in the area, he spends more time on the northern side of the river."

The Orc grinned. "You are thinking there is something of value there."

"I am."

"Could it be located on the south side of the river?" asked Svetlana.

"If it were," said the king, "why would there be persistent rumours they want to claim our border region?"

The Orc nodded. "Your logic makes sense. What of you, Master Belgast? Any ideas on what we might find?"

"I've wracked my brain over this for days now and come up with several possibilities, but none explain the presence of warriors."

"I agree," said Athgar. "Do you suppose this could have something to do with the attempt on Svetlana's life?"

The king sat back. "I hadn't considered that possibility, although I'm still not convinced Svetlana was the intended target. He loosed that crossbow as I entered the temple."

"I would agree," said Belgast. "I think the man in the balcony discharged his bolt prematurely because we spotted him."

"And he tried to load a second one," added Athgar, "despite Natalia's wall of ice protecting the queen. Have you any idea who he might work for?"

"Nothing in terms of absolute proof," replied Maksim, "but I have my suspicions."

"I'm guessing you think it's Georgi Kulikov," said Natalia. "Aside from his mistreatment of tenants, what can you tell us about him?"

"Once I elevated him to baron, he always insisted on proper treatment as a noble. Of course, before your previous visit, I bore no reason to suspect he was lining his pockets."

"You say you made him a baron. What was he prior to that?"

"My father's military commander. Not that he ever really had anything to do in that regard."

"So he was in charge of raising and maintaining your army?"

"Precisely," said the king. "Why?"

"It brings into question the loyalty of your troops, sire. I'm told he fled with a large number of coins. Could he be plotting a return?"

"With what?"

"Ostrovan troops," replied Natalia. "Why settle for a bit of land when you can put your own man on the Throne and control the entire country?"

"Yes, but why? Surely the King of Ostrova realizes we're not a wealthy kingdom?"

"I'll bet it's not the kingdom he's after," said Belgast. "He has little to gain by attacking Carlingen, and any campaign from the south must march through very inhospitable terrain. Hardly the type of campaign that would prove successful. However, a friendly king on the Throne makes acquiring the land they're after much easier."

"So, they want to put Kulikov on the Throne? How do they expect to do that without an army?"

"Oh, they have an army, sire, just not the one you think."

"Meaning?"

"I believe that riot out front of the Palace was a taste of things to come."

"But we settled those grievances," said Natalia.

"Did we?" replied Belgast. "Or were we being fed what we wanted to hear? I'm not suggesting those complaints weren't legitimate, but it takes a lot to get a crowd riled up. Someone's pulling strings around here, and unless I miss my guess, we all know who that might be." He looked around the room at blank stares. "Cunars," he said. "I'm referring to their Temple Knights."

SOUTH

SUMMER 1109 SR

Kargen knelt, placing his hands on Agar's shoulders. "You must behave, my son. The Humans in this part of the Continent differ from those back home and may take offence."

The youngling straightened his back. "I am of the Red Hand, Father. I will not disgrace us."

"I am sure you will not."

"How long will you be gone?"

"Likely a couple of ten-days, maybe a little longer. It largely depends on what we find."

"Will it be dangerous?"

"There is always danger when traversing the wild lands, but we are all hunters."

"Mother is a shaman."

Kargen grinned. "True, but she underwent the ordeal like all of us." His eyes flicked to Shaluhk, who stood nearby, watching the exchange. "She was a gifted hunter in her day. I do not doubt her abilities in this regard."

"I shall watch out for Oswyn."

"As you should. Now say farewell to your mother."

Agar rushed over to Shaluhk, who encircled him in a firm embrace. "Be safe, Mother."

"I will," she promised.

He broke off the embrace, making his way back to where Athgar and Natalia waited. Oswyn, being a little more forward, rushed to take Agar's hand and guide him the rest of the way. "Don't worry," she said. "Oswyn will look after you."

Shaluhk turned to her bondmate. "So? I was a gifted hunter in my day?"

He grinned back. "And still are. I merely tried to soothe the heart of our son."

"That is the correct answer." She glanced behind them at the hunters of the Red Hand who'd arranged themselves into three umaks, leaving the rest pulled up on the river's edge. "What do you think?" she asked. "Should we ride with the hunters or take our own umak?"

"Our own. It will give us more privacy."

She chuckled. "We will be on a river, where sound carries. It will not be as secluded as you think."

"Then I shall refrain from more intimate conversation."

She turned a darker shade of green.

Her response left Kargen grinning. "Even after all we have been through, I can still make you blush?"

"Yes. Just as you make my heart beat faster by your mere presence."

"You are enjoying this far too much."

"And why should I not? It is rare for us to travel thus, unencumbered by our duties. Let us enjoy the experience while we have the opportunity."

"Yes, you are right. We should delight in each other's company before the Humans to the south try to kill us."

"It would not be the first time men have tried, nor I suspect, will it be the last."

They arranged themselves in the umak before taking up their paddles, Kargen sitting in the back while Shaluhk sat in front.

"Farewell, my friends," called out Kargen.

Oswyn took a step forward, replying in the language of the Orcs. "*Safe hunting!*"

The umaks pushed off, making their way upriver.

Athgar looked at Natalia and grinned. "It seems our daughter has not been wasting her time in our absence."

"It is true," said Agar, "but she often confuses which language she speaks."

"She'll get used to it," said Natalia. "She's still young."

"Might I ask a question?"

"Of course. What is it?"

"When will she be strong enough to pull her first bowstring? She is already four. By the time I was her age, Laruhk had taken me on my first hunt."

Natalia nodded at her husband. "Perhaps you're better suited to answer that?"

Athgar looked at Agar; not quite six, yet by Human standards, he seemed closer to a ten-year-old, both in size and behaviour. "Do you still have the first bow Laruhk gave you?"

The youngling grinned back. "I do, though it is at the Palace. Why?"

"How would you like to give it to your tribe-sister?"

"Truly?"

"Yes, but you must teach her to respect it. We can't have her running around loosing arrows into people."

"I will do as you ask, Uncle."

"Uncle?"

"Is that not the correct Human term?"

"Yes," said Athgar, breaking into a smile. "I suppose it is." He paused a moment. "You do your father proud, Agar."

"Thank you, Uncle." Agar turned around and raced off back to the Palace, a trio of king's guards rushing to keep up with him.

"You make a good uncle," said Natalia. "And an even better father."

Athgar was about to reply, but then Oswyn touched his leg. He looked down to see her peering up at him, her arms outstretched. He picked her up.

"Where did Agar go?" she asked.

"Back to the Palace. Don't worry. We'll see him shortly."

"Why did he leave?"

"He went to fetch something."

A mischievous grin appeared on her face. "To get me a bow?"

"How did you know that?"

"She may be young," said Natalia, "but she's not deaf."

Svetlana sat, sipping her wine, her feet up on a footstool, warmed by the fire. The door opened, admitting her servant.

"A message has arrived for you, Majesty, and this came with it."

She turned to see Olya clutching a small wooden box. "I don't recall a courier arriving?"

"It came by ship. Their captain dropped it off as a courtesy." She removed the letter from atop the box and handed it to her queen.

"This bears the Volstrum's seal," said Svetlana, fear seeping into her heart as she stared at it. Was the family recalling her? She glanced at the box. No, they'd hardly send a package if that were the case. She broke the seal, then read over the letter. Olya, sensing the gravity of the situation, waited silently.

"Where is Lady Natalia?" asked the queen.

"I believe she and Lord Athgar went to the river to see the Orcs off."

"Please ask her to join me upon her return."

"Yes, Majesty."

The door opened, and Oswyn barrelled into the room, her new bow held high. The Orc youngling followed next, chasing after her, while Athgar and Natalia entered at a more sedate pace.

"You wanted to see us?" asked Natalia. "Or is it only me you wished to speak with?"

Svetlana, who'd been pacing, turned from the fire, brandishing a note. "A letter from the Volstrum just arrived," she said, ignoring the children's presence, "and it appears the family has finally taken an interest in Carlingen. It's from Larissa Stormwind, although I don't know who that is."

"I recognize that name," said Athgar. "Wasn't she the mage banned from Reinwick?"

"I believe she was," added Natalia, "but I know little of her other than that. It's not a name I heard at the Volstrum."

"Might Galina be able to tell us more?"

"Galina?" said Svetlana. "I didn't know she was a member of your party."

"She remained in Reinwick," said Natalia, "but I contact her once a week to keep up on current events."

"You've learned a spell to communicate over long distances? I didn't even know that was possible."

"It is only taught to a select few."

"But you said you ran away. How is it that it came into your possession?"

"That's a rather long story," said Natalia. "Suffice it to say I happened to stumble across it while I was in Karslev. I will teach it to you if you want, and then we can stay in touch once we leave."

"I would like that very much, but at the moment, I have bigger things to occupy my mind." She handed over the letter.

Natalia read through it. "This says you're to build a fleet."

"It does, though to be more precise, I am to persuade the king to build one for them." She pointed at the box. "They sent a generous amount of coins to get things started. No doubt you read they've also indicated I should be on the lookout for you."

"To what end?" asked Athgar.

"They ordered me to see to Natalia's arrest."

Athgar's hand instinctively felt for his axe as a chill crept into the room.

"Of course, I have no intention of doing so," continued Svetlana, "but it makes things a little more complicated."

"In what way?"

"Should the family send an envoy to Maksim's court, we'd have difficulty explaining your presence."

"What does the king think?" asked Natalia.

"I've not seen fit to apprise His Majesty of your current circumstances yet."

"Might I ask why? He is your husband after all."

"He has enough trouble in his court without having to make a decision about such things. Were I to reveal your break with the family, he might feel forced to choose sides."

"But wouldn't he side with you?"

"I hope there is some truth in that, but we cannot discount the family's power and influence."

"They hold no influence here," said Natalia. "His only experience with the politics of the family is through you. Unless you're suggesting you still serve the Volstrum?"

"I'm caught. I want to be free of them, but I also fear their retribution."

Natalia moved forward, taking Svetlana's hands in hers. "Make a clean break from the family, and we will stand with you."

"And if they send someone to court?"

"Then we'll deal with them together. You are not alone anymore, Svetlana. We're here to help."

"And when you leave?"

"I shall teach you the spell that allows us to communicate over great distances. If the family threatens you, all you need do is tell us, and we'll send help."

"And what do I do with the funds they provided?"

"The letter makes no mention of it," said Natalia.

"Yet they sent it with the note."

"Without specific instructions on its use, consider it a gift to spend how you please. It would certainly mitigate the kingdom's current woes."

"And the demands to build a fleet?"

"It makes no definite demands in terms of numbers."

"Meaning?" asked the queen.

"A few boats could be useful for His Majesty's current plans, and even if he began construction on only one, would that not be in the spirit of that letter?"

"I should take this to His Majesty."

"I think it about time you took a great deal more, don't you?"

"Easy for you to say," said Svetlana, "but this puts my entire future at risk."

"Would you rather labour for a thankless mistress or chart your own course?"

Svetlana straightened her back. "You're right. I can no longer live in fear. I shall go to the king and tell him the truth."

Oswyn, who'd been quiet, began fiddling with the box, and the lid popped open, revealing a pile of freshly minted coins. "Look, Momma. Gold!"

Agar moved up beside her, gazing down into the container. "I have never seen coins like this." He held one up to his face. "What are they?"

Svetlana chuckled, moving closer to snatch one herself. "These are golden sovereigns," she said, moving to the window for better light. "Unbelievable!"

"What's the matter?" asked Natalia.

"It seems the pretense of living under a king's rule is no longer the case in Ruzhina."

"I'm not sure I understand what you're implying?"

Svetlana tossed her the coin.

Natalia caught it, then held it up, examining it. "Incredible."

Athgar fidgeted. "Would someone care to explain what's happening here?"

"It appears Marakhova Stormwind has seen fit to adorn the coins of Ruzhina with her likeness."

"But they have a king, don't they?"

"They do," explained Natalia, "but he has no real power. He is, in essence, little more than a puppet, with the Stormwinds pulling the strings."

"No longer, it seems."

"Perhaps," said Agar, "but could the family be making their own coins?"

They all stared at the youngling in surprise.

"Did I say something wrong?"

"Not at all," said Athgar. "In fact, you may have given us the key to the family's downfall."

"Downfall?" said Svetlana. "I fail to see how minting their own coins could be of any concern to the king."

"I can't say for certain, but I doubt the King of Ruzhina likes the idea of being controlled. Those coins prove he is of no consequence, and that, we might be able to use to our advantage."

"But how does this hurt the family?"

"They are flailing around right now," continued Athgar, "and have failed to gain a foothold in Reinwick while the Northern Alliance reduces their influence even more. Added to that is the work of this 'inner circle' Cordelia hinted at."

"What 'inner circle'?" said Svetlana. "I've heard nothing of this."

"Temple Captain Cordelia indicated members of her order were aware of the family's efforts in aiding Halvaria."

"But how would they even know that?"

"I'm not sure, but they're taking steps to reduce the family's influence, and the Temple Knights of Saint Agnes have a presence at every court in the Petty Kingdoms. I don't imagine that sits well with the family."

"You may be onto something," said Natalia. "If the family's influence is failing, it might explain their sudden interest in Carlingen. No offence, Svetlana, but in the grand scheme, your home is of little consequence as a military power."

"It's the fleet!" said Athgar. "They fear the Temple Fleet. That's why they need ships."

"Agreed, but why not build ships themselves?"

Svetlana smiled. "For once, I possess the answers you seek. Do you remember our lessons on regional politics back at the Volstrum?"

"I'm afraid you'll need to remind me," said Natalia. "What in particular are you referring to?"

"In Ruzhina, building ships is the sole prerogative of the king."

"What about merchants?" asked Agar.

"Even merchants need the king's permission."

"And is that difficult to obtain?"

"Not usually, but every Ruzhina merchant pays a tithe to the Crown in return for a shipping license. It's one of the few ways the Crown fills its coffers."

"Don't they have taxes?" asked Athgar.

"They do, but they account for much less in Ruzhina than in other kingdoms, largely because the family doesn't enjoy parting with their coins."

"So the family doesn't build ships in Ruzhina because they don't want to pay the Crown? That would seem to indicate there's some tension between them."

"There likely is, given the state of things."

"Who is the King of Ruzhina?" asked Athgar.

"Yulakov the Seventh, or at least he was, last I heard."

"And do we know much about him?"

"Only that he's quite old," replied Svetlana. "I recall he had several sons, but I can't remember how many or how old they would be now."

"I assume he would have named an heir?"

"Yes, his oldest son, whomever that might be."

"Could that be what's behind this whole affair?" asked Athgar.

"You think there's a new king? I fail to see how that would be a problem for the family."

"A new king, particularly if he's young, is more likely to resent their interference. Perhaps he's trying to assert his authority."

"Why now?"

"With the family struggling to keep control over the courts of the Petty Kingdoms? I think it the ideal time, don't you? They'd be far too busy with events abroad to resist him."

"It would be a mistake to underestimate the family," said Svetlana. "They've had their hand around the throat of that Royal Family for generations."

"All the more reason a new king would resent them. Not that we possess any way to take advantage of the situation at the moment, but it bears further consideration."

"To what end?" asked Svetlana.

"The destruction of the family," said Natalia. "We've danced around them for years, but ultimately, the only way to stop them is to destroy them in their nest."

"You talk as though they're snakes."

"And they are if you think about it. They hold an entire continent in their coils, or rather they did. We are finally seeing cracks in their foundation, and we need to ensure the entire structure collapses."

Svetlana inhaled sharply. "Are you suggesting a war against Ruzhina?"

"No, not Ruzhina—the Volstrum and all it stands for."

"I admire your passion, Natalia, but no one could stand against the power of the family's mages."

"Couldn't they? We've already burned Stormwind Manor to the ground, and that was with very little preparation. Think what we could accomplish if we put our minds to it!"

"Yes, but Carlingen has only a small army, hardly enough to threaten Ruzhina."

"I'm not thinking so much in military terms as in political ones. The family's downfall will not be through a traditional battle: more like a test of wills, and we have the one thing they lack."

"Which is?"

"A sense of true family. There is no power greater than a mother's love." She locked eyes with Svetlana. "One day, Saints willing, you'll have children of your own. Would you see them handed over to the family for training against your will?"

The words sank in. "No. Most definitely not! Still, there are so many mages at their disposal."

"Not as many as you might imagine," said Natalia. "And they're scattered across the Continent in an attempt to cling to power."

"But there's the entire staff of the Volstrum, not to mention their students."

"And how many would support their cause if they knew the truth?"

"But what have we to use against them? You, me, and Katrin: that's only three. Oh, and Galina, apparently, so I suppose that makes four."

Natalia smiled. "You seem to be of the opinion that only the family has mages."

"Who else could provide them in such numbers?"

"That's easy to answer," offered Athgar. "Therengia."

DEMANDS

SUMMER 1109 SR

"I am disappointed," said Maksim.

Svetlana bowed lower. "My apologies, Majesty. I did not mean to cause you such grief."

He sat back. "You must let me finish. I am not disappointed you chose to side with Natalia, merely that you felt you couldn't bring this to me sooner."

A wave of relief flooded through her.

"This letter you spoke of," continued the king. "Do you have it in your possession?"

"I do." She held out her hand, and Olya ran forward to place it in her palm. Svetlana, in turn, presented it to the king. Maksim took it, unfolding it slowly as if its mere presence were a foreboding of doom. The room remained quiet as he silently read it.

"These instructions are quite clear." His gaze shifted to Natalia, who stood amongst her friends. "Tell me, Lady Natalia, why should I not order your arrest? It would be the easiest solution."

"Some time ago, Majesty, you made a promise that should doubt be cast upon us, you would give us a chance to explain ourselves."

"And now you would hold me to it? Very well. I shall grant that request."

Natalia moved to stand before the king. "As Svetlana just revealed, Athgar is the High Thane of Therengia, and I, his warmaster, but there is far more to the story than a quest for power. Rather, it's the opposite. A true desire to live in peace led us down this road."

"Go on."

"I fled the Volstrum to avoid a forced breeding."

"Breeding?"

"Yes. Those in charge of the family wanted me to provide them with a child. The Stormwinds have been trying to create more powerful mages through arranged breeding for generations, and they considered my magic potential exceptional."

"I had no idea such was the case." The king looked at his queen. "Was this true for you also, my dear?"

"They did not consider me a suitable candidate for such things, Majesty."

Maksim shook his head. "I find the entire idea distasteful, but please continue with your story."

Natalia remained quiet, collecting her thoughts before speaking. "I ran as far as I could to escape their grasp, eventually finding myself in Draybourne, where I met Athgar. Unfortunately, they somehow discovered my presence, forcing us to move on, eventually arriving in Corassus."

"And how is this of any consequence to me?"

"I shall get to that shortly, Majesty. While in Corassus, we discovered the family was involved in a plot involving the Temple Knights of Saint Cunar."

The king leaned forward, resting his elbow on the arm of his throne. "What kind of plot?"

"They took slaves and sold them to pirates to line their treasury with gold. In the end, we exposed their duplicity, but because of this, we couldn't remain in the city, so we headed north to find refuge in the Grey Spire Mountains."

"That's where I met them," called out Belgast. "Once again, that order was up to no good, trying to steal godstone from under the noses of the Orcs."

"If I understand you correctly," said the king, "the Cunars are not to be trusted."

"Not necessarily all the Cunars, Your Majesty," replied Natalia. "We learned the family had somehow infiltrated the upper echelons of the order, though in that case, it was the Sartellians rather than the Stormwinds. This was even more evident after we came north to Ebenstadt."

"Ah, yes. I've heard of that. The Battle of the Wilderness. That was back in 1104, wasn't it?"

"Yes. The entire campaign resulted directly from the family's machinations, but I digress. At that time, Athgar and I found the remnants of his people, the Therengians, descendants of those who survived the Old Kingdom's destruction. We planned to settle down and live amongst them, but after our daughter was born, the family tried to take her by force."

Maksim half stood. "They tried to kidnap your child?" He glanced over at Oswyn, who was entranced by a nearby tapestry. "I can't imagine anything worse."

"It's true," added Athgar. "We travelled to Karslev in an attempt to warn them off, but the entire escapade almost ended in disaster. We fled to Reinwick, where we were instrumental in getting the family banned from Andover's court before we sailed here."

"And now you mean to do the same thing here. Is that it?"

"Actually," said Natalia, "we only intended to travel home, but then Svetlana told us of your current circumstances. We seek only to help you, Majesty."

"By suggesting I ban the family?"

"No, by offering you the hand of friendship. We desire to live in peace, Majesty, but the Stormwinds persistently work against us. Join us in fighting this scourge, and you shall have the full weight of Therengia behind you."

"At the risk of sounding ungracious, that would make me an enemy of most of the Petty Kingdoms."

"Perhaps it might've in the past, but recent events suggest otherwise. Reinwick has already recognized us as a kingdom, Majesty, as has Andover. Join us in friendship, and you shall also gain their trust."

Svetlana moved closer, taking Maksim's hand in hers. "It is true, my love. What they offer us is more than mere friendship. It is a future free of the family's influence."

Maksim smiled. "It is a convincing argument that is most appealing, but I am a king and must make choices that benefit not only myself but my subjects as well."

"Then consider this," said Athgar. "Join us, and we will do all we can to transport those willing to Therengia, thus relieving you of much of your congestion."

"Much as that thought pleases me, I must still deal with Ostrova, not to mention this." He hefted the letter. "How do you propose I explain everything to the Stormwinds?"

"Let them think you are following their guidance," said Natalia. "Use their coins to benefit your kingdom as you see fit."

"And when they come to find out where the ships are?"

"Show them what they want to see."

"You have me at a loss for words. How am I to show them ships that don't exist?"

"I'm not suggesting you don't build them," replied Natalia, "merely that you not do so in the numbers they expect."

"You possess a devious mind, Lady Natalia. Or do I refer to you as Warmaster? Perhaps that warrants a 'Your Grace'?"

"Lady Natalia will do fine, Your Majesty."

"It is a fine thing to be offered friendship, but I wonder what you seek in return."

"Merely that you treat Therengians with the same dignity and respect you do the rest of your subjects, and you ban the Stormwinds and Sartellians from court appointments within your realm, excepting, of course, for those of us you are familiar with. In return, you would participate in a defensive alliance wherein if any realm or territory is attacked, it shall be considered an attack on all."

"So Carlingen would become part of the new Therengian Empire?"

"We are not an empire," said Athgar, "we are a collection of like-minded kingdoms. Each land is free to rule as it wishes, provided it adheres to the aforementioned conditions. Of course, if you wanted full-fledged membership in our realm, that, too, would be available, albeit with more stringent conditions."

"Those being?"

"A common set of laws followed by all. You would still hold your title of king, which would be handed down to your successors, but the day-to-day running of your kingdom would be organized a little differently."

"How different could it be? How many ways are there to rule over men?"

"You'd be surprised," said Athgar. "In our lands, village leaders, called thanes, are selected by the townsfolk. These thanes, in turn, elect the leader of Therengia, which is how I became High Thane."

"But you just said I'd remain king?"

"I did, but trained individuals appointed by you would oversee most of the tasks required to run the kingdom."

"So, I would be a figurehead?"

"Not at all, Majesty. You would sit upon the Thane's Council, what we call the Moot, and there you would share your wisdom and knowledge with the other rulers."

"How many rulers have you at present?"

"One from each of the five villages of Therengia. No, make that seven; we've had some growth in the last year. In addition, there's the Triumvirate of Ebenstadt and the Governor of Novarsk."

"Triumvirate?"

"Yes," said Athgar. "The rulership of that city falls under the control of three individuals: Stanislav and Belgast, you already know."

"And the third?"

"A man named Yaromir, a Temple Captain of Saint Mathew, to be more precise."

"By the Saints, you mean to tell me the Church is involved? I would never have expected that."

"They are free to practice their religion, provided it does not interfere with others. That is, after all, one of the chief tenets of the Church, is it not?"

"Yes," said Maksim. "I suppose it is, though it rarely turns out that way. Would you station warriors here if I became a part of Therengia?"

"Not unless you desired it, sire."

"And what of Ostrova?"

"I'm not sure what you're asking."

"Ostrova sits between our two lands. How does that affect things?"

"It would be more convenient if they fell under our rule, but we can just as easily traverse the wilderness to the east."

"That's dangerous, surely?"

"Our people do not fear wild lands, Majesty, and in any case, they would use the river for trade. As long as Ostrova did not attempt to block our boats, I foresee no difficulties."

"Aye," added Belgast. "Both realms would benefit from such trade, for it would give us a route to the Great Northern Sea and all the trade therein. Naturally, Carlingen would be our port of choice, and who knows, with the increase in traffic, you might need to make your docks even bigger."

Maksim returned his gaze to Athgar. "And all of this if we agree to become part of your realm?"

"None of this is conditional, save for membership in the Moot. Should you decide you prefer to be an independent kingdom, we would respect that, but I hope you would see the benefits of increased trade, regardless."

"To put it another way," added Natalia, "you have three choices. You remain independent and isolationist, in which case the Army of Therengia cannot assist you. The other choices are to either ally with us or join our realm. In either case, you would have the support of our warriors. The bigger difference would be what happens once the current crisis is over."

"You have given me much to think about," said Maksim. "I shall weigh the options you laid out for me, but regardless of my decision, I promise imprisoning you is not something I will consider."

"I thank you for that, Your Majesty."

"I am curious whether you offered these options to the Orcs?"

"They were not offered membership in the traditional sense," replied Athgar.

"Meaning you coerced them?"

"No. They've been part of Therengia since its founding. Under our laws, there is no distinction between Human and Orc, save for membership in the Moot."

"I'm afraid you'll need to explain that to me."

"Orcs, for the most part, live in their own villages. Since we Humans outnumber them, each tribe has two members sitting on the Moot, rather than the Human villages, which have one."

"And how do they decide which two shall represent them?"

"One seat is for their chieftain, the other for their head shaman. Kargen and Shaluhk fulfill that requirement for the Red Hand."

"How many tribes are there in Therengia?"

"Four at present," said Natalia, "but more may be joining us."

"How do you know that?"

"The Orcs, like descendants of the Old Kingdom, were driven from their homes and forced to live in less-than-ideal circumstances. Many have expressed a desire to come east to a land that values their contributions."

"And you know this, how?"

"Through magic," said Athgar, "but is it not for me to explain the mysteries of shamans."

"And are there Orcs somewhere within the boundaries of my own realm?" asked the king.

"Not that I'm aware of, Majesty, but if you desire, we can ask Shaluhk upon her return."

"Very well."

"If Orcs are here," offered Agar, "you should consider yourself lucky. It means the land is fertile and the hunting good."

"I shall bear that in mind," said the king. "Perhaps, if we find them, I'll ask them to send a youngling to my court to advise me." His gaze wandered to Agar's companion, standing by his side. "And as for you, young Oswyn, I hope one day my queen and I will be blessed with children. Perhaps then you'd come and visit them?"

"Yes, please," she replied.

"Such manners," said Svetlana. "You do your parents proud."

"When are you going to have a baby?"

The queen cleared her throat. "These things take time and cannot be rushed, but I promise we'll let you know when that happy day arrives."

Oswyn's giggles echoed throughout the great hall and soon proved contagious, with everyone joining in, so much so that King Maksim wiped a tear from his eye.

"Come now," he said, finally regaining his composure. "I have much to attend to, as I imagine you do too. I shall see you all at dinner?"

"Of course, Majesty," said Natalia. She bowed, then led their group from the room, Oswyn's hand in her own.

Belgast collapsed into a chair. "Well, that was not quite what I expected."

"In what way?" asked Stanislav. "He didn't throw us all out, did he?"

"You would know if you'd been there."

"I can't help it if I need to nap occasionally!"

"Come now, you two," said Greta. "You sound like a couple of old women."

"I beg your pardon?"

"I'm sorry." She looked down at her feet. "It's an expression I picked up in Andover."

"Ah, well," said the Dwarf. "I suppose it could have been worse. Thank the Saints the King of Andover wasn't one to swear excessively."

"Oh, but he did," said Greta. "Why, I once heard him call—"

"That's quite enough of that," warned Katrin. "The last thing we need around here is you swearing like a Dwarf." She eyed Belgast. "And yes, I'm talking about you!"

Duly chastised, he sank even lower in his chair.

Stanislav chuckled. "That's the quietest I've seen him in days, but he didn't answer my question."

"The king is weighing his options," said Athgar, "but guaranteed our safety, regardless of his decision."

"Well, I suppose that's something."

"Are there Orcs in Carlingen?" asked Agar.

"You were there at court," said Natalia. "Did you not hear our answer?"

"I did, but sometimes it is not wise to reveal all to others, particularly when you do not know if you can trust them."

"You impress me. Where did you learn about such things?"

"From my parents. They often held meetings in the great hall of Runewald, and I was usually there to hear all that transpired."

"And that interests you?"

"Very much so, yes."

"Fascinating," said Athgar. "Tell me, what did you think of King Maksim's response today?"

"He is cautious. He wants to please his new queen, but at the same time, he does not wish to upset the family. I suspect he sees them as a threat and wishes not to anger them."

"That's a remarkably astute observation for one of your age. Anything else you'd care to comment on?"

"Yes," said Agar. "If there are no Orc tribes in Carlingen, then we should attempt to find one."

"Why?"

"I heard the land to the south is unlikely to be cleared anytime soon, but it would make excellent hunting grounds. Who better to safeguard the kingdom's borders than Orcs?"

"Are you sure you're only six?"

"Come now," said Belgast. "You're forgetting Orcs mature much faster than other folk."

"Even so," added Stanislav, "I'd warrant he has a better understanding than most others, even members of his own tribe. I doubt Laruhk could have made an observation like that."

"Agar is smart," declared Oswyn, "and he's my brother!"

"He is indeed," said Athgar.

"So what do we do now?" asked Belgast.

"We wait," replied Natalia. "The king already agreed to let the Temple Knights of Saint Agnes patrol the streets, but the Cunars are an entirely different matter, considering what we told him."

"And the Therengian situation?"

"You mean the kingdom or the people of Carlingen?"

"Both, I suppose."

"I assume the king will come around to the idea of equipping the fyrd, particularly now he has some spare coins."

Athgar chuckled.

"You find something amusing?" asked the Dwarf.

"I wonder what the family would make of the situation."

"I fail to see how that might be considered humorous."

"Imagine, if you will, Marakhova Stormwind huddled near an open fire, a tankard of ale in hand."

"I doubt she would drink ale," offered Katrin. "It's likely she'd prefer wine."

"Very well. Make it a chalice of wine. She's sitting comfortably, and then a messenger arrives with a letter from Carlingen."

"And?"

"What would her face reveal if they told her the very funds she'd sent to Carlingen to advance her cause were being used against her?"

THE ORCS

SUMMER 1109 SR (IN THE LANGUAGE OF THE ORCS)

Kargen dug deep with the paddle, sending the umak surging forward, past the thick forests on either bank, and though they travelled against the current, their progress was swift. The Windrush River flowed east, along the border with Zaran before turning south, the same route they'd taken to Carlingen, but in reverse. After many days, they turned west, following one of the great tributaries that formed Carlingen's southern border.

As the days raced by, it was easy to forget the purpose of their trip. All was tranquil in the wilds of Carlingen, and the chieftain couldn't help but think of the game that might be found in this forgotten wilderness.

"It is peaceful," said Shaluhk, breaking his reverie.

"Yes, it is. It reminds me of the woods where we grew up. I knew every trail that led to Ord-Kurgad."

"You miss it."

He shrugged, though she couldn't see it, sitting as she was in the front of the umak. "I am content when we are together. What of you? Do you miss our old home?"

She failed to respond, instead staring off to the north.

"Is something wrong?" he called out.

"Bring us to the north shore," said Shaluhk. "There is something strange about the pattern of the trees there."

Kargen steered them to the riverbank, where they climbed out and dragged the umak from the water. The other boats following along behind started heading towards their position.

"Shaluhk has spotted something," he called out. "We will investigate. The rest of you wait here."

The shaman only took a few steps into the trees before she realized what she'd found. "Ruins. I suspect there must have been a great city here some time ago."

"What makes you say that? Surely it is more likely to be a single building?"

"See the stone steps leading down to the water? Would a single dwelling have such a thing? Creating it would have required skilled stonemasons, which indicates a larger settlement."

"Are you suggesting Dwarves made it?"

"Of course not," said Shaluhk. "Dwarves rarely live in thick forests like this. Let us look around some more. We might be better able to determine its size by finding more ruins."

"Very well, but we should remain together lest there be any danger. Before we start, I shall call our hunters ashore to watch over our umak." He did so while his bondmate examined the immediate vicinity.

The area she first discovered turned out to be the remains of a small building—its stone walls having collapsed long ago. Nearby, however, she found something far more interesting, a flat path cutting through the forest in a straight line. She knelt, scraping away a layer of leaves and dirt, only to discover stone. A little more work revealed even more, closely packed together.

"What have you there?" asked Kargen.

"A cobblestone street, by the look of it."

"How long do you think it has been buried?"

"As a hunter, that is more your area of expertise."

Kargen knelt, examining the layer of debris covering the path. "Many seasons, to be sure, perhaps even centuries."

"I know of no such city rumoured to be in this area."

"Nor I," he replied. "Could it be an ancient Elven city?"

"No," said Shaluhk. "This construction looks more Humanlike. Note how the stones are not properly aligned. The Elves would never stand for such imperfections."

"How can you know so much about Elves? We have never met any."

"True, but I have been in contact with Kraloch, who lives amongst the Humans far to the west, and they have dealings with the forest folk. He has told me a great many things about them."

"Even he does not know everything."

"Certainly, but look at where this road leads."

"Deeper into the woods."

"Yes, but in a straight line. The Elves are said to work with nature, not bend it to their will. How, then, do you explain such a path? Surely a more logical way to make a road would have been to wind it around the trees."

"Your argument makes sense," said Kargen. "Let us explore farther afield and see what else we can discover."

The day wore on, leading to the uncovering of many more ruins. As the sunlight faded, Shaluhk found what turned out to be a crucial piece of evidence, a partially intact wall containing the remains of a mural. She pulled away the forest growth, then sat back, the better to take in the entire image. "It depicts a battle."

Kargen moved closer, trying to make sense of the images. "Those are our kind, but they fight beside Humans. Do you realize what this means?"

"I do indeed. At one time, this must have been part of the Old Kingdom. Note how they use their spears in a tight formation. This is said to be how our Ancestors fought. They revived this same tactic in the west."

"There is some writing at the bottom," said Kargen, "but it is partially buried." He drew his knife and dug away the dirt. "It appears you are correct. This is the language of Athgar's people, but it is difficult to read."

Shaluhk called forth an orb of light, then floated it closer.

"That is new," said Kargen.

"I learned it from Lady Aubrey."

"Who is?"

"The Human to the west who has learned much of our magic. She, in turn, taught me this spell."

"It appears there is much to gain from such an exchange."

Shaluhk nodded, then looked back at the mosaic. "This text is archaic, but indicates we are in the Wurgeld Forest, likely their name for this region. The mural depicts an army marching off to war but does not mention who they are fighting."

"Wurgeld? That name means nothing to me."

"Nor me, but neither of us is a scholar. Were Tonfer Garul here, no doubt he would make sense of all of this."

"Wait," said Kargen. "There is something about the warriors depicted here that looks familiar. Do you see it?"

"Yes. They are similar to those I conjure when using warriors of the past."

"How does this all connect? Clearly, this was a city of the Old Kingdom, but what caused it to fall into ruin, and what happened to its inhabitants?"

"I imagine the survivors fled, likely becoming those who founded Runewald and the surrounding area."

"And the Orcs?"

"Perhaps they were the predecessors of the tribes inhabiting our region. Either that or there is another group of Orcs out there somewhere."

"If that were true, would you not be aware of their existence?"

"My magic will not find what is lost. Without knowledge of their existence, how would I contact them?"

"Would not the Ancestors know of them?"

"Who is to say they do not? You know as well as I do the Ancestors are often cryptic. Perhaps there is a reason they have not spoken of such things?"

Kargen grunted. "Sometimes, I feel they are more a curse than a blessing."

"Our more immediate concern is what we do next. Our primary reason for coming here was to investigate what the Humans of Ostrova were up to. Do we now spend time looking further into this mystery or continue on our way?"

"We camp for the night and move on at first light. I would like to learn more about this place, but we lack the time for such things."

"Perhaps there is another way to find the answers we seek," said Shaluhk. "What if I contacted the Ancestors here?"

"Do you believe that would work?"

"I would be willing to give it a try. The spirits of the dead are somehow linked to the place they died. That connection might allow me to discover one who once inhabited this city."

"Very well. Do what you can."

Shaluhk sat back, arranging herself into a comfortable position before she closed her eyes and uttered the words of power. The air buzzed with energy, and as she opened her eyes, they glowed with an intense white light. Moments later, she let out a gasp as she looked around.

"What is it?" asked Kargen.

"Many spirits linger here," she replied. "Far more than I would ever have imagined." She locked eyes with someone beyond Kargen's sight. "You," she called out. "I am Shaluhk, Shaman of the Red Hand. Come here that I might speak with you."

She looked up as if someone was standing over her.

"Who are you?" she asked.

Kargen heard no response, but his bondmate did, for she nodded in understanding.

"What is this place?" Again, a pause.

Her one-sided conversation continued, and he began to share in the excitement. Shaluhk spoke with a long-lost member of their race: what secrets would be revealed?

Finally, her eyes dimmed, and she slumped forward, exhausted. Kargen leaned towards her, grasping her hand in concern.

"I am fine," she said, "but never before have I spoken to one from such an age. It is tiring."

"I thought all spirits were the same?"

"Not so. It is easier to contact the more recently deceased than those who entered the spirit realm far in the past."

"You were able to contact Uhdrig. Surely she died long ago?"

"She did, but this place is older."

"How much older?"

"It is hard to say with any accuracy. The spirit I spoke with did not use a calendar I was familiar with, but I would guess he died over four hundred years ago."

"That fits with what we know of the Old Kingdom," said Kargen. "It faded into obscurity some five hundred years past."

"Yes, mention was made of that. From what I gathered, this city survived the fall of the original Therengia only to meet with disaster some decades later."

"What type of disaster?"

"That, I am unable to determine. The spirit, Ungor, spoke of getting ready to march off with the rest of King Eadwulf's army to a great battle, but he fell ill before he was to leave and passed here, in the city of Beorwic."

"A fascinating tale, and one that deserves looking into further. However, at this moment, we must concentrate on our promise to King Maksim. We will tell of all we learned here when we return to the city, but for now, we should rest and recover our strength. Soon, we will find those we seek and shall need our wits about us."

The men of Ostrova made no secret of their presence. The first sign of them was the sound of chopping wood. Kargen led his group to the southern bank, where they hid their umaks, then proceeded along the shore, their warbows strung and ready for use. They'd expected to find a few warriors, but the sight of hundreds chopping down trees came as a bit of a shock.

"What are they doing?" Kargen said more to himself than anyone in particular. "Are they building a village?"

"I see no sign of it," replied Urag. "They are stacking wood, but there is no indication of buildings anywhere. Perhaps they are planning on building something bigger?"

"She is right," said Shaluhk, pointing. "Look there."

A large knot of people gathered at the river's edge, prodding the riverbed with poles, some advancing waist-deep into the water to carry out their assigned tasks.

"This I do not understand," said Kargen.

"There are boats nearby," said Urag. "Could they be building more?"

"Were that the case, why not build them farther inland and then carry them to the water? It would make construction much easier."

"There are many men here," said Shaluhk. "And every one has the look of a warrior. I suspect they are getting ready to cross the river."

"With so few boats?" said Kargen.

"There is more than one way to cross a river."

"Such as?"

"A bridge," offered Shaluhk. "That would be why they are probing the water with poles."

"Please explain," said Urag.

"A bridge requires support, and to bear the weight, it would need a solid base, namely the riverbed. Were it too soft, the bridge would sink and be useless."

"But the river is wide here. Surely they do not expect to build a bridge of such length?"

"We must learn more," said Kargen.

"And how do you propose we do that?"

Kargen grinned. "By infiltrating their camp at night."

"What good will that do? Even with our night vision, it will be too dark to make out much of anything."

"You must learn the ways of our enemies, Urag. Humans like this tend to take shelter in tents lit by lanterns, making them easy to see at night."

"And what do we do when we find them?"

"We listen." He noted the look of despair on the young hunter's face. "Fear not. I am well aware your command of the Human tongue is weak. Shaluhk and I will proceed into the enemy's lair while you and the others remain close by in case we run into trouble."

"And if they discover you?"

"Then we will call for help. You have my word. The important thing here is to learn what these Humans are up to. Once we possess that information, we withdraw. By any luck, we shall be on our way back to Carlingen by sunrise."

The darkness enveloped them as Kargen led, his axe drawn lest trouble rear its ugly head. Shaluhk followed in his steps, a long knife in hand. Considering their size, a casual observer would have expected them to create quite a lot of noise, but their footfalls were silent, their breath quiet.

Kargen made his way in amongst the enemy's tents, most in darkness, for it was close to midnight, and only a quarter of the moon lit the sky this night, throwing everything into shadows.

The camp's commander was easy to spot as guards patrolled his quarters, each bearing a lantern, while two more sporting spears and shields stood alert outside his tent.

"That is our target," whispered Kargen. "But the guards will prove troublesome. Perhaps we should make our way around the back?"

"Guards do not frighten me," replied Shaluhk. "A simple spell would soon have them asleep."

"True, but then we would leave evidence of our visit. Our objective is to find out what they are up to, not to alert them to our presence."

"And if they spot us, regardless?"

Kargen smiled, his ivory teeth bright even in the gloom. "Then we pretend we know nothing of their language. We will be mistaken for the savage Orcs they expect of our kind."

"Let us hope it does not come to that."

"The clouds are rolling in, and soon the camp will be too dark even for our night vision. Take my hand so we are not separated."

They advanced, slowly working their way behind the tent. The men carrying the lanterns walked back and forth, always taking the same route, pleasing Kargen. Before long, they crouched behind the canvas, their faces lit by the lantern glow from within.

Inside, two Humans were engaged in a heated disagreement, the canvas somewhat muffling their voices. Kargen frowned, unable to discern anything of import. Shaluhk's eyes sparkled with mischief, and she touched his arm, pointing to a nearby copse of trees. He followed her lead and was soon amongst the undergrowth.

"I have an idea," she said. "A spell that might be of use to us."

"What type of spell?"

"An ancient one called spirit walk that allows us to traverse the world of the Ancestors, which lies adjacent to our own."

"And how will that help?"

"We can walk as ghosts, unseen by the living. I shall cast it on you first, but be warned, it is a little disorienting."

"Meaning?"

"The world will appear muted in colour, not that you will notice much difference in the dark. Sounds will also be slightly affected as if you have water in your ears."

Kargen steeled himself. "Very well. You may proceed."

Shaluhk channelled her magic, and then he felt a tingling sensation. Moments later, he heard a snap as if someone had stepped on a twig, and then he floated free of his body, which fell to lie amongst the underbrush.

She then repeated her spell, her own physical form joining his on the leaves of the forest floor.

"Come," she said. "Let us see what we can discover."

He followed her as she walked out into the open, no longer afraid of being seen. They approached the back of the tent where she walked through, leaving Kargen's mind struggling to grasp the concept. He paused, building up the nerve to do as she'd done, but then her hand appeared, grabbing him and pulling him through.

They stood inside the tent, where two men sat on either end of a small table, upon which lay a map. Kargen moved closer, looking down at the crude drawing. "This must represent the river," he said, his voice sounding muted even to himself.

"Yes, and look here." She pointed, her finger going clear through the paper. "This is our present position, or close to it."

"How can you tell?"

"There is a slight bend in the river where we landed the umaks that is quite distinctive." She moved her hand, indicating a spot farther downstream.

"So, it is a bridge after all," said Kargen.

"*I've had enough of this,*" said one man in the Human tongue, wobbling slightly as he stood. "*I shall turn in for the evening, Commander. Perhaps you'll see my reasoning more clearly in the morning.*"

The other fellow got to his feet and bowed slightly. "*I shall give it my undivided attention, my lord.*"

His lordship walked towards the door, passing right through Kargen, who turned to see where the fellow was going.

"He is unimportant," said Shaluhk. "The other one is in charge. Commander is a high rank amongst the Humans of the Petty Kingdoms, and the presence of so many warriors tells us this is more than a scouting mission."

"I would agree, yet, numerous as they are, there are still not enough here for a full-blown invasion." He looked down at the map. "They are interested in something on the northern side of the river, but they do not know the exact location. It appears they intend to cross and begin searching."

"Those ruins we found are in the vicinity. Perhaps that is what they seek."

"To what end? Of what value is a destroyed city to the men of Ostrova?"

"We may never know, but I do not believe we will discover further answers here. We should return to our bodies, then find the others. It is time we went back to Carlingen."

"And how do we go about returning to our bodies?"

She smiled. "Do not worry. I shall show you."

THE FLEET

SUMMER 1109 SR

Belgast stared down at the boat. "Is this what passes for the navy of Carlingen? It's so small! Why, a ship like this isn't even half the size of *Vigilant*."

Svetlana grimaced. "Nevertheless, this and its sister ships constitute our fleet."

"How many do you have?" asked Natalia.

"Five all told, but none have put to sea since I arrived."

"What of the *Bergannon*, the ship we took to Ruzhina last year?"

"That is a trading vessel and has yet to return from its latest journey up the coast."

"How many men could these things carry?" asked Athgar.

"Thirty, providing they don't mind rowing, or, if you prefer, only three and they can use the sail."

"Why three?"

"Two to handle the sail," explained Svetlana, "and one to steer using the rudder."

"And who crews these ships?"

Svetlana shrugged. "That's where things get complicated. In theory, the king's warriors man them, but with the treasury so low these past few years, they've sat ashore, empty. I can't even guarantee they would still float."

Belgast frowned. "And the current king has ruled for how long now?"

"Almost three years, but his father beached the ships shortly before his death. What do you think? Would it take much to get them afloat again?"

"Likely not, but you'd be better off investing in one larger ship, like the *Vigilant*, rather than wasting all your efforts on something as small as these."

"Ignore him," said Natalia. "He doesn't understand the sea. These vessels were made to carry raiding parties, and your coast is not overly large. They're more than suitable for the task at hand."

"And the family?" asked Svetlana. "What do you think they will make of such ships?"

"They would likely see them as unsuitable. Unless I miss my guess, they want a fleet to rival the Temple Knights, and I'm given to understand the *Vigilant* is one of their smaller vessels."

"But we have no one capable of building ships of that size."

"True," said Natalia, "but the Volstrum doesn't need to know that."

"I'm not sure what you're suggesting."

"It's simple," said Belgast. "You begin constructing a ship much like this, though with a longer keel. It shouldn't be too hard to modify the design."

"Would that even be seaworthy?" asked Svetlana.

"That's just it, don't you see? It doesn't need to be. This whole 'building a ship thing' is a ruse to convince the family you're doing your part."

"And when the ship never launches?"

"Leave that to me," replied the Dwarf. "There's nothing like cost over-runs and bad scheduling to delay a project."

"What in the name of the Saints are you talking about?"

"Sorry. It's a Dwarven expression. A project is simply a complicated task one wishes to finish. I've seen my fair share back in Kragen-Tor. Why, King Haglarith once had the warriors guild all up in his beard over building a massive catapult to protect the city."

"What happened?"

"I took over the management of its construction. By the time we were done, there were so many extra expenses, the whole thing had to be scrapped." He noted the look of concern on Svetlana's face. "They weren't any real expenses, merely pretend ones. The king used the funds to build a new orphanage."

"An orphanage?"

"Well, a tavern, actually, but it proved very profitable."

"And if they send someone to inspect the construction?"

"Then you show them nothing more than the skeleton, or whatever you call the frame. I'm not one for nautical terms."

"I like the idea," said Svetlana, "but how many of these frames are you suggesting we build?"

"That largely depends on the family's expectations. Did their instructions give any figures?"

"No. They were very vague on that point, but I suspect we may find ourselves the subject of a visit shortly. For some unknown reason, Carlingen has unexpectedly become of interest to them. Surprising, considering they've ignored me since I arrived." She turned to Natalia. "Don't worry. I've set people to watch the docks. If a ship arrives bearing members of the family, I'll be sure to give you lots of notice."

"Thank you. I appreciate it. Now, as for these boats…"

"Ships," corrected Belgast. "We must use the correct terminology if we are to fool the masters of the Volstrum. And as to their construction"—he bowed deeply—"I would be honoured if you allowed me to make the arrangements. Should you prove agreeable, I shall endeavour to keep you abreast of my progress with regular reports."

"I mean no offence, Master Dwarf, but how do I know you won't pocket the coins for your own use?"

"I would never!"

"Belgast would never do something like that," explained Natalia. "Those who wander the Continent are sworn to be honest and forthright in all things."

"Sworn by whom?"

"The traders guild," said Belgast. "It is a requirement to conduct business outside of our strongholds."

"But surely not every one of your race is a member? What about those born in Human cities?"

"Aye, I'll admit the guild doesn't control everybody, but rest assured, I am a Dwarf of my word."

"In that case, I accept your offer, Lord Belgast."

"You do me a great honour, Majesty. I will make some enquiries this very day and see what might be involved in getting this entire project up and running. Shall we say two days to prepare the report?"

"Report?" said Svetlana.

"Of course. You can't do something this large without proper preparations. Look at Kragen-Tor. The place is immense—we couldn't have built it without detailed planning."

"Your approach is difficult to understand, but I trust you know your business. Very well. Two days, after which I expect a thorough briefing."

Natalia chuckled.

"You find something amusing?" asked the queen.

"Only the thoroughness of Belgast's efforts. You'd best put aside the bulk of the day for his report. He's very meticulous."

"I look forward to it." Svetlana stared seaward towards the various open-topped vessels of old, much like the king's. "You know, when I first arrived here in Carlingen, I found the city very backward. The Volstrum taught us all about the finest palaces on the Continent but neglected the smaller realms."

"That must have been quite the shock," said Natalia.

"It was, and I took it personally for the first few months. Here I was, a high-born, the daughter of powerful mages, yet they never considered me for breeding. Then, to make the insult greater, they sent me to the most backward kingdom they could find." She fell silent.

"What changed your mind?"

"When I took my position at court as an advisor to the previous king, he had little time for my counsel, isolating me even further. Then, as he sickened, his heir prepared to ascend the Throne."

"The current king?"

"No, Maksim's remaining brother, Vinzent. By then, his two other brothers had already succumbed to the wasting sickness. It's a hereditary trait, although my husband has yet to exhibit any symptoms."

"I'll talk to Shaluhk on her return," said Natalia. "There's a good chance she could prevent its onset."

"Truly?"

"I cannot guarantee it, but if a sickness is dormant, I'm sure her magic could keep it at bay, perhaps even cure it."

"I would be most grateful. How can I repay you?"

"I offer her services in friendship, with nothing expected in return."

"That's certainly not the family's way."

"You know," said Natalia, "I occasionally think of abandoning the name Stormwind, but then I realize that such an act would only make the family happy. We need to reclaim our name and show the courts of the Petty Kingdoms not all of us are scheming villains."

Svetlana laughed. "Don't hold back on my account."

"Sorry. It's so frustrating. It seems like the family has burrowed their way into positions of power and influence everywhere we go."

"Well, they have been at it for a long time."

"Longer than you think."

"What makes you say that?"

"I've learned much since I graduated from the Volstrum," replied Natalia, "and even more when I briefly returned. I've come to believe the family is responsible for the fall of the Old Kingdom."

"But the family wasn't founded until years later? At least, that's what they taught us. I can still remember Mistress Nina lecturing us on that very topic."

"That may well be, but it makes sense they would omit their failure."

"Failure? Surely the fall of Therengia was a desired outcome?"

"I don't believe so."

Svetlana shook her head. "Why wouldn't they want to destroy the Old Kingdom?"

"It's more likely they were trying to control it but failed to consider the Therengians' propensity for justice. They are, by and large, honest folk, disinclined to succumb to bribes or corruption. Of course, there are exceptions, but those very beliefs were an important part of their culture."

"And so the family's efforts failed?"

"It makes sense, doesn't it? Especially considering their current hold over Halvaria."

Svetlana's expression went blank. "What's this now? They control the empire?"

"Yes. Didn't I mention that?"

"You most certainly did not. This changes everything!"

"In what way?"

"I cannot support a family who plots the downfall of us all. Are you absolutely certain of this?"

"I found proof," said Natalia, "written in the hand of Illiana Stormwind herself."

"Could you be mistaken? Perhaps you misread her words?"

"There was little room for misinterpretation. Her meaning was clear. It might also be worth mentioning we are not the only group to reach that conclusion."

"Who else?"

"That is not my story to tell, but suffice it to say, others working towards the empire's defeat also made this connection—people who are beyond reproach."

Svetlana reached out, taking Natalia's hand in a firm grip. "I renounce the family and everything it stands for and will do all I can to convince the king it's in his best interest to do likewise. Now, how do we go about prying the Petty Kingdoms out of their grasping hands?"

"I doubt we can ever truly wrest control away from them, but we can at least educate those willing to listen."

"But the presence of even a single Stormwind could spell disaster. How do we make them understand that?"

"To use the words of Mistress Nina, 'the politics of the Petty Kingdoms are complicated,' and let's be honest, kings and dukes would do anything to rise above their neighbours. Having a court mage is one proven way of doing that. What other magic schools of consequence are there besides those of the Stormwinds and Sartellians?"

Svetlana sighed. "I suppose that's true."

"We've made great gains in Reinwick and Andover," said Natalia, "and the territory falling under the administration of Therengia is making strides to end their influence, but these things take time."

"So we just wait?"

"For now. Knowledge is power, and eventually, a Stormwind, or possibly even a Sartellian, will show up here demanding you follow their orders. When that happens, we have the advantage, for we know exactly what they're after, while they have to dance around the subject."

"How does that help us?"

"By weakening them," replied Natalia. "If we can convince them Carlingen is building a fleet, they'll waste precious resources funding it. It will also hamper their plans to wrest control of the Great Northern Sea away from the Temple Fleet. You'll be interfering with their ultimate plan to conquer the Petty Kingdoms, a far more effective approach than using an army."

"Provided we survive the coming months. There's still the prospect of war with Ostrova."

"Which we will deal with in time. Let's not worry too much about that until Kargen and Shaluhk return. Then we'll better understand what we're up against."

"We?"

"Yes," said Natalia. "Providing that's what you desire. We will not leave you to face this alone."

"Were it my choice, we would already be allied, but such a commitment is the king's prerogative. Will you tell him of the family's connection to Halvaria?"

"I think that would be better received coming from his wife, don't you?"

"Doubtless it would, but I must take great care with how I present it to him. I shouldn't like to overwhelm him."

"He is strong, Svetlana. Concentrate on matters pertaining to Carlingen. The empire is a distant threat to his mind, so I doubt it will be as overwhelming as you might think. It serves to prove, however, how distrustful the family can be. Perhaps that's the best argument to persuade him to our cause."

"Cause?" said Svetlana. "You make us sound like one of the great powers of the Continent."

"Who says we're not? There is no limit to what we can accomplish if we work together. We've already liberated some of the northern realms from the family's grip. Who says we can't do the same here in the east?"

"Easy for you to say. You don't live so close to Ruzhina. What if they send an army?"

"And how would an army arrive without a fleet to carry them? They're not going to march through the wilds of Zaran."

"True, but that doesn't mean they're above having someone fight us on their behalf. They could even be the ones spreading rumours about Ostrova."

"I hadn't considered that," said Natalia, "but then again, until now, they've had no reason to doubt your loyalty. If they have a presence at the Ostrovan court, then Therengia will consider taking steps to remove them."

"Surely you're not suggesting war?"

"No. I was referring to diplomatic efforts. Rest assured, however, if they attack Carlingen, it would be highly unlikely we would sit back and do nothing. We can't afford a potentially hostile army on our borders."

"But isn't every kingdom a potential enemy?"

"Not at all. After our trouble in Novarsk, Kargen sent envoys to Zalista, and they provided a delegate to Ebenstadt to represent their interests."

"And they don't fear you?" asked Svetlana.

"We've made it clear we wish no aggression."

"And yet you conquered Novarsk."

"Only after they invaded us. Even then, we intended to return the kingdom's rule to the nobility, but they proved untrustworthy. I would be perfectly happy to leave things as they are, were it not for those calling for another crusade."

"Surely the Church would never condone such a thing? Not after they suffered such a resounding defeat?"

"The Cunars are eager to erase the shame."

"True," said Svetlana. "After all, you destroyed their reputation for being undefeated."

Natalia laughed. "Is that what you think? Let me disabuse you of that notion. The Cunars were defeated before—they just don't speak of it, but news of their loss in the last crusade has spread too widely to be denied. However, it would likely be some years before they could make another attempt with how many Temple Knights they lost. There's also less justification, considering the brothers of Saint Mathew are welcome in our land, as are the sisters of Saint Agnes."

"But not the vaunted Cunars?"

"Now you're just teasing me."

"Sorry, I couldn't resist. Still, it begs the question of how much power the Church has. They were, after all, the organization that organized the

Crusades. If I recall, the first crusades were to chase down the remnants of the Old Kingdom, weren't they?"

"They were," said Natalia, "but as they pushed farther east, they changed their story, claiming they'd discovered worshippers of Death Magic, the same excuse they used to justify their campaign against us."

"I understand what you're saying, but I can't quite grasp their reasoning. What good did prolonging the Crusades do?"

"From their point of view, there were several advantages. The more their Temple Knights fought, the more experience they gained, making them the finest warriors on the Continent. They also focused the anger and resentment of all the Petty Kingdoms on a perceived threat, thus distracting them from what was really going on."

"Which was?"

"The family's influence on Church matters. I'm not trying to suggest everyone in the Church is corrupt, merely a small number in important positions, particularly the Temple Knights of Saint Cunar."

"You believe the family organized the last crusade?" asked Svetlana.

"It makes sense, doesn't it? Had they won, they would have destroyed any resistance to their influence, not to mention the possibility they might have killed or captured me. On the other hand, even their defeat served a purpose."

"How in the name of the Saints would their defeat help the family?"

"Simple," said Natalia. "We know they support the Halvarians, and the Cunars are the biggest deterrent to the empire controlling the rest of the Continent. However you look at it, the entire campaign was to their advantage, regardless of the outcome."

"If that's true, then the Cunar detachment in Carlingen represents a serious threat to us, particularly if we act contrary to Karslev's desires."

"All the more reason we must remain vigilant."

ENVOY

SUMMER 1109 SR

Crown Prince Beringar, son of the King of Ostrova, stood a head taller than most of the court. His youthful energy and thick, blond hair marked him as a man of consequence, while a scar on his cheek warned he was not a fellow to be trifled with.

Once announced, he strode into the great hall with purpose, his boots echoing on the stone floor as he approached King Maksim. Behind him came a pair of warriors carrying a chest between them, their armour rattling as they struggled to transport their burden.

Beringar halted some ten paces from the throne, then bent at the waist in an overly dramatic bow, his arm sweeping the floor. Ignoring the small knot of people off to one side, he addressed the king. "Your Majesty, I come bearing greetings from my father, King Eugene of Ostrova."

"Welcome, Highness. I trust your father is in good health?"

"He is, thank you, and I'm certain he'll be most pleased to hear of your concerns for his well-being. I, too, am well, although I must admit to some fatigue from the long journey. I assume word of my arrival proceeded me?"

"It did," replied King Maksim, "though regrettably, it lacked details. I understand you came by sea?"

"Yes, by way of Braymoor. The roads are better in that part of the Continent. I feared a more direct route would lead me astray in the wildlands to the south."

"Yet these very same wildlands are of interest to your father."

"Indeed," said the prince. "I see news travels fast in these parts."

"Perhaps you might explain why, precisely, you're here."

"Isn't it obvious? I'm here to negotiate the purchase of the south."

"A difficult task, given there are no accurate maps of the area. What part in particular is Ostrova interested in?"

"A strip of land running from the border of Braymoor in the west to the wilderness in the east."

"And when you say a strip, how much are we talking about?"

"To a depth of fifty miles, Majesty, although my father is willing to negotiate a lesser distance if desired."

"That is a substantial amount of my kingdom," said King Maksim. "Might I ask what brought on this sudden desire to expand your border?"

Beringar's smile revealed unnaturally white teeth. "Ostrova does not currently border Braymoor, Majesty, and we aim to improve trade with that kingdom."

"Do not take me for a fool, Highness. Were that the case, he would only need a small parcel of land in the west. Why, then, does he want the rest?"

"Does it matter? The land is undeveloped, and we would be doing you a favour by taking it off your hands."

"You still haven't answered my question."

"Did I mention he will pay handsomely for this land?" The prince stood aside, sweeping his arm to indicate his warriors. "Within this chest is a generous offer for the area in question."

King Maksim waved them forward, and they deposited it at his feet before backing up three paces.

Athgar, watching from the side, stepped forward. "Your Majesty, permit me the honour of opening it."

"Very well. You may do so."

He moved up to the chest and grabbed it by one end, pulling it several paces from the king, concerned lest it be trapped in some manner. He knelt, examining the clasp holding it shut before turning to Belgast and nodding.

The Dwarf joined him, pulling forth a small tube that he placed against his eye before leaning in. After a close examination, he nodded to Athgar, who then lifted the clasp and hefted open the lid.

Inside, a loosely piled amount of gold coins struggled to cover the bottom of the chest. Together, they lifted the back end to display the contents to King Maksim.

His Majesty frowned. "This is a trifle light for such a purchase, don't you think?"

"On the contrary, Majesty," said Prince Beringar. "I deem it most generous. The land in question is thick with trees and requires much effort to be made useful."

"Which only leads me to wonder why you want it." Maksim raised his hand as his visitor opened his mouth. "As you've said, you wish a route to

Braymoor, but that hardly justifies a claim to shrink the entire length of my border by a depth of fifty miles."

"My father wishes to expand settlements into the area."

"To what end? The land south of the border is already yours and far more suitable for such pursuits. Why does he want the added cost of clearing out all those trees on my side of the river?"

The prince shrugged. "I cannot say, Majesty, but if you consider the offer insufficient, you might counter with a larger sum?"

"And you believe your father willing to entertain such a proposal?"

"He told me to expect it, sire."

"What think you, Lord Athgar?"

Prince Beringar raised an eyebrow. "Lord?"

"Indeed," said the king. "He is Athgar of Athelwald, High Thane of Therengia." He smiled as he saw the look of disbelief on his guest. "Surprised, Lord Prince?"

The Ostrovan royal recovered quickly. "Is this some ruse to convince me you have allies? If so, it won't work, Majesty. I've made a careful study of your realm for some time now. You are an isolated kingdom, and a poor one at that."

"Hardly a statement designed to sway me to your father's offer. And as for the High Thane, I assure you he is who I say."

"I am," added Athgar. "But if my name is not known to you, then perhaps my warmaster's is?" He held out his hand, and his wife stepped forward. "This is Natalia Stormwind."

Beringar's gaze flicked around the room. For the briefest of moments, he looked more like a deer caught in an ambush, but then he calmed. "It matters not whom you claim to be, Lord. I am here for King Maksim. It is to him I make this offer on behalf of my father, not the upstart ruler of a doomed land."

"Mind your words," warned Maksim. "They are honoured guests within these palace walls. I will not see them insulted."

"My apologies, Lord King. I mean no insult to your honoured self."

"Yet you refer to my kingdom as isolated and poor."

"I meant that only as a statement of fact, Majesty. After all, you have no alliances, and I'm given to believe your coffers are almost empty. I thought my father's generosity in this offer would be more warmly accepted."

"It appears your so-called 'careful study' yielded very inaccurate information. We are, in fact, allied with Therengia and others."

"Others?" sneered the prince. "Who else could possibly come to your aid? I know it's not Braymoor."

"I recently had discussions with certain Orc tribes."

"I suggest you take care, Majesty. The Orcs are savage brutes likely to turn on you at the slightest provocation. Their involvement will do you no favours in the courts of the Continent."

"I could care less for what the other Petty Kingdoms think," said Maksim. "They've never offered even the slightest interest in us, nor we in them."

"Be that as it may, you must tread carefully. Were you to refuse my father's offer, he might view it as a personal affront."

"Are you suggesting he would declare war?"

"I cannot say for certain," said Beringar. "Even though he's my father, I can't claim to understand his reasoning."

"That's a lie," said Natalia. "You came here to make demands of His Majesty and, when refuted, lowered yourself to threats to achieve your aims."

"Such are the politics of the Petty Kingdoms, my lady. I am, in that sense, no different from any other ruler, or in this case, ruler's son. I might also remind you that, Saints willing, I shall become king one day. Acceptance here today would go a long way to ensuring future goodwill between our two realms."

King and prince locked eyes, a test of wills neither seemed willing to lose.

"I think it best," suggested Natalia, "you give His Majesty some time to consider the offer in private. That way, he can assess the value of the land in question and respond with a counteroffer?"

Beringar forced a smile. "That would be most acceptable, my lady."

"Yes," added the king, "though I doubt the extra time will do much to change my mind."

"This is a negotiation," said Natalia, "and as such may benefit from a less-formal atmosphere where ideas can be exchanged without the burden of the rigours of court."

"An excellent idea, Lady Stormwind. Shall we meet again, Highness? Say in three days? That should give us the necessary time to consider your offer."

The prince bowed deeply. "It would be my pleasure, sire."

"Then I shall have someone show you to your rooms."

Svetlana stood, bowing to her husband. "With your permission, Majesty, I will escort our visitor to his quarters."

"By all means."

All remained quiet as the Ostrovan prince followed the queen out of the great hall.

King Maksim visibly relaxed as the door closed. He turned to Natalia. "I am unlikely to change my mind."

"And I wouldn't expect you to, Majesty, but we must strive to put Prince Beringar at ease if we are to discover his true purpose here."

"I thought that obvious. He wants me to surrender the southern territory?"

"You know as well as I that his offer was woefully inadequate."

"You believe he truly wants war?"

"Yes, but he's trying to stall."

"To what end?"

"I don't know," admitted Natalia. "Perhaps when Kargen and Shaluhk return, they can tell us more."

"Speaking of whom, when do you expect them?"

"It could be some time yet, Majesty."

"But the border isn't that far away, and they went by boat."

"They did, but the trip there is not what will occupy their time; it will be the discovery of whatever the Ostrovans are up to, for Kargen and Shaluhk must remain in the region until they can determine the enemy's plans."

Maksim smiled. "And in the meantime, we must keep our new guest occupied. Is that it?"

"It would work to our advantage, sire."

"On another point," added Athgar, "I assume from your earlier remarks, you've decided to ally with us?"

"Yes, although I only decided that after speaking to that fool of a prince." He paused, deep in thought. "I suppose that means we must work out some details?"

"That was my thought also, although perhaps Your Majesty would like a break after dealing with your newest visitor?"

"Yes. That's a splendid idea." Maksim rose, then looked at his guards. "Prince Beringar seems to have left his chest of coins. Be so good as to deliver it to his quarters." With that, the king strode from the room.

"Well," said Belgast. "That was interesting."

"Interesting in a good way?" asked Stanislav. "Or bad?"

"I'm not entirely sure." The Dwarf glanced at Katrin, who'd been silent the entire time. "What do you think?"

She smiled. "I imagine we'll learn a great deal about Ostrova's intentions over the next few days."

"Really? What makes you say that?"

"In a word, Greta. She's taken it upon herself to spy on him."

"And how does she intend to do that?"

"You'd be surprised what one insignificant girl can get away with in a large Palace. She's been exploring the place since our arrival, committing it to memory, including the servants' corridors and rooms. If there's anywhere to eavesdrop on the prince, she'll find it."

Stanislav lifted his tankard to his mouth, pausing as an idea struck him. "Why is it the king sent his heir?"

"That's easy to answer," replied Belgast. "He carries more weight in terms of influence."

"But wouldn't the King of Ostrova be worried about his son's safety, particularly if he's pushing for war?"

"I hadn't thought of that. Could the prince be in disfavour?"

"Doubtful," replied Katrin. "He's still the Crown Prince after all."

"Then we must be missing something."

"I don't think they actually want a war," offered Stanislav. "In fact, this whole escapade seems like a ruse."

"What makes you say that?" asked Belgast.

"Just a hunch. Perhaps ruse isn't the right word so much as a distraction? Have you ever seen a street magician?"

"I'm not sure where that came from. One moment we're discussing Prince Beringar, the next, you're talking about entertainers?"

"Bear with me. Answer the question."

"Yes," replied the Dwarf. "Of course I've seen street magicians. They use sleight of hand to pass off tricks as true magic. They're a plague on the civilized lands. What is it you're trying to get across?"

"Simply that they purport to do one thing while secretly doing another, like stealing from you."

"Are you suggesting Ostrova is distracting us for some reason?"

"It makes sense," said Stanislav. "The threat of war is very inconvenient, requiring the raising of more troops. That, in turn, costs coins, which Carlingen is in short supply of."

"Let me see if I understand you. You're suggesting they're attempting to bankrupt the kingdom?"

"It is merely one possibility."

"There are others?" asked Belgast.

"Many."

"Then perhaps you'd care to elucidate?"

"Most certainly," said Stanislav, rubbing his hands together. "My first thought was this demand was sincere, yet try as I might, I can see no logical reason why they want this region when their own land is said to be sparsely populated. We've gone over this before, of course. Could it be the presence of shadowbark? Possibly, but if that were the case, why not cross the border and harvest it, or better yet, get permission to cut down the trees and pay a small tithe to King Maksim? It would be a mutually beneficial arrangement. Then I thought of godstone, but that falls from the sky. With the thousands of square miles of thick forest out there, who could even witness such a thing?"

"What of their supposed desire for a border with Braymoor?"

"As King Maksim said, why ask for an entire border region when they only require a small area?"

"Then what are you suggesting?" replied Belgast. "That they're trying to engineer a diplomatic embarrassment for King Maksim's court?"

"I considered that, but who would care? He has no influence in the Petty Kingdoms."

"You're talking in circles."

"Perhaps," said Stanislav, "yet I can't help but remember poor Wendred's story. The King of Ostrova already has men in the area, so it only stands to reason he's up to something. The question is, what?"

"I suppose you'll just have to wait for the Orcs to return."

"Are there any records of the area that might be useful to us?"

"I can make enquiries," said Katrin, "but I doubt it. These people take little interest in record keeping."

"And how would we know that?" asked Belgast.

"As I mentioned earlier, Greta has spent much of her time here getting to know the place."

"And?"

"There is no archive room or even a true library. Oh, there are books scattered here and there, but nothing that passes for official records, save for the office of the king's treasurer."

"Then we must speculate."

"I'm open to suggestions," said Katrin.

Stanislav sipped his ale slowly, then placed his tankard back on the table. "Whatever they're after needs to be something found in the wilderness."

"A dragon's lair?"

"No," replied Belgast. "Those creatures live in the mountains, and I don't believe there are any near Carlingen."

"A lost treasure, then?" suggested Katrin.

"I suppose that has some merit, but who would have lost it? And more importantly, why would it be in the middle of a thick forest?"

"I would tend to agree," said Stanislav. "After all, if it were a lost treasure, it has to be substantial enough to warrant all this effort on their part."

"I agree," said Belgast, "and that being the case, why would someone abandon it in the middle of nowhere?"

"Do we know of any ancient treasure lost in these parts?" asked Katrin.

"I'm afraid you're asking the wrong person. Now, if we were referring to Kragen-Tor, I could tell you all sorts of stories about lost expeditions, but none would have come this far north. What about you? Did you learn anything about this area at the Volstrum?"

"I'm afraid not. Our studies concentrated on the more influential courts of the Petty Kingdoms."

Belgast frowned. "Could they be attempting to drag out negotiations while their army marches on us? You know, a surprise attack, that sort of thing?"

"I highly doubt it," replied Natalia. "Traversing even a small army through a forest that thick would prove difficult, let alone one big enough to capture the capital."

"The Therengians could do it, especially with the Orcs' help."

"No doubt, but Ostrova is not on friendly terms with Orcs. You saw Prince Beringar's disgust at even the mention of them. That looked genuine to me."

"And to me," added the Dwarf. "Which leads us back to the same old question. What are they up to?"

"Whatever it is," said Stanislav, "you can bet your whiskers it won't be good for Carlingen."

Belgast laughed. "By the Saints, you've finally begun using Dwarven terms. My presence must have started rubbing off on you!"

THE FAMILY

SUMMER 1109 SR

Larissa Stormwind stood on the deck, absently watching as they readied a boat to row her ashore. Earning her way back into the good graces of Marakhova had been difficult, considering her failure in Reinwick all those years ago, but she consoled herself that her success here would more than compensate for it.

The *Peregrine's* captain appeared in front of her. "They're ready to row you ashore, my lady."

She ground her teeth together. As a senior Stormwind, he should address her as mistress, yet she could hardly expect a mere ship's captain to be aware of such things.

"Very well," she said, trying her best to sound bored despite her rapidly beating heart. Her future was at stake here. One false move and Marakhova would banish her from the upper echelons of the family.

Larissa climbed into the boat, then the rowers pushed off from the *Peregrine*, digging into the water with their oars, propelling the tiny craft forward. Her gaze wandered to the docks and the city of Carlingen, where many of its worn, windblown buildings looked ready to collapse. How long would she be forced to endure the stench of this place?

Her assignment was simple enough, for the family had already placed one of their own in the Royal Court. All Larissa needed to do was ensure the instructions she'd sent were being followed. It should be a foregone conclusion that all was well, yet the shame of her failure in Reinwick still haunted her, forcing her to question everything.

The boat bumped up against the dock, and she stepped ashore, ignoring the crew's enquiries. She took a moment to get her bearings before heading towards the Palace.

Natalia opened the door to see Svetlana standing there. "Is something wrong?"

"I received word of another visitor," replied the queen. "A ship bearing the flag of Ruzhina dropped anchor. It looks as though the family finally sent someone to investigate. I expect they'll pay their respects to the king soon enough."

"Would it be better if I remain here, out of sight?"

"His Majesty would prefer you be present, along with your companions, including the children."

"Might I ask why?"

"He feels it would show strength," said Svetlana, "especially the presence of the Orcs."

"I'll gather everyone and be there directly. Have we any idea of timing?"

"The messenger left the docks as soon as he witnessed them lowering their boat, so you still have some time."

"Do we know how many to expect?"

"I'm afraid not, but I suspect only one, likely Larissa Stormwind herself. She was, after all, the one who sent that letter."

"I shall bear that in mind."

"Very well. I'll see you shortly in the great hall."

The guards threw open the double doors to the great hall of Carlingen, and Larissa waited to be announced before entering. She looked around as she walked, noting how much smaller it was than even some of the Volstrum's lecture halls, yet it was not without its charms.

The king sat at the far end of the room, an empty throne beside him. She took this as evidence he'd only recently wed, for the latest information in Karslev said nothing of marriage. A handful of people stood off to one side, but they appeared to be of little consequence.

She halted just shy of the king, bowing her head in acknowledgement.

"Greetings, Lady Larissa, or should I call you Mistress Larissa?"

She smiled at the correct form of address. "If you wish."

"Might I enquire as to the reason for your visit?"

"Most certainly, Majesty. I come seeking my sister, Svetlana Stormwind. I understand she is a member of your court?"

"She is indeed," replied Maksim, then leaned to one side, addressing a servant who stood ready to act on his behalf. "Please ask my wife to join us."

"Certainly, sire." The fellow quickly disappeared.

"I must say your visit surprises me," continued the king. "I wasn't expecting another member of the family to come here in person?"

"You didn't? I find that surprising, Majesty. After all, I sent correspondence to Lady Svetlana indicating I intended to visit."

"Really? She said nothing to me."

The door opened, revealing the queen.

"Ah, there you are, Svetlana, my dear. Larissa was just telling me that we were expecting her."

"That comes as a surprise to me, Majesty. Though I received correspondence from her, it did not indicate when such a visit might occur." She crossed the room, sitting down on the second throne.

Larissa knitted her brows. "You're Svetlana Stormwind?"

"I am. I am also now the Queen of Carlingen, so you will address me as, Your Majesty."

The visitor managed a slight bow. "My apologies, Majesty, but word had not reached my superiors of this momentous news, at least not before I left Porovka. My congratulations to you both."

Maksim leaned back, steepling his fingers together. "Tell me the purpose of your visit."

"The King of Ruzhina sends his regards, Majesty, and asks you to join him to rid the Great Northern Sea of a recent scourge."

"A scourge? Can you be more specific?"

"A group of ships operating out of the Five Sisters has been preying on shipping, sire, and King Yulakov is eager to put an end to it."

"The Five Sisters, you say?"

"They are a group of islands, Majesty, off the coast of Reinwick."

"You'll pardon me if I'm mistaken, but isn't that the home of the Temple Fleet?"

Larissa winced. "It is, sire, and they are preying on our shipping."

"And why would they do that?"

"I beg your pardon?"

"It's a simple enough question," replied Maksim. "Why would the Temple Knights of Saint Agnes prey on ships from your kingdom?"

"I'm afraid I couldn't say, but our king was most insistent something needed to be done to curb their excesses."

"And is King Yulakov constructing his own vessels?"

"He is indeed, Your Majesty."

"I'm at a loss to understand why he sent you, Mistress Larissa. You are a representative of the Stormwinds, are you not?"

"I am."

"Then why did you come to Carlingen? Surely a representative of the king's court would be more fitting?"

"I am a member of his court, Your Majesty."

"In that case, you may assure His Majesty, King Yulakov, we will take every step necessary to build and equip ships suitable to the task."

Larissa smiled. Perhaps this wouldn't be so difficult after all? A movement to the left caught her eye, and she turned to see a pale woman with black hair staring at her. There was no mistaking who she was or the young girl beside her.

"What is this?" she hissed, whirling back to King Maksim. "That woman, Natalia Stormwind, is a fugitive. I insist you arrest her at once. And as for that girl"—she pointed at Oswyn—"she is the property of the Volstrum!"

"Slavery is not legal in Carlingen," replied the king, "and Natalia Stormwind is guilty of no crimes in my kingdom."

Larissa unleashed her full fury on Svetlana. "How can you stand by and allow that criminal to remain free? Have you no loyalty?"

"You presume to lecture me on loyalty?" replied the queen. "Must I remind you that you are a guest here?"

"That child is the final product of generations of selective breeding. To give her mother safe haven is a direct violation of your oath to the family. Are you incapable of understanding the repercussions of your actions?"

"My loyalty is to my king, not to the despots of Karslev."

"How dare you take that tone with me!"

Svetlana pushed herself from her chair, stepping forward. "How dare YOU take that tone with ME! I am the queen here, while you are merely a messenger!"

King Maksim reached out, gently taking his wife's hand and urging her to sit. "Come now," he said. "This is a Royal Court, not a tavern in which to come to blows." He locked eyes with Larissa Stormwind. "Despite my wife's irritation with your lack of respect, we've been busy constructing a fleet, or at least the beginnings of one. I should be delighted to arrange a tour of the construction site in a day or two, if that is to your liking?"

Larissa closed her eyes and took a deep breath, slowly returning to a calmer demeanour. "Thank you, Majesty. That would very much be to my liking."

"Good. Then I shall have a servant show you to your quarters." He waved forward one of his men, then waited as the fellow bowed to Larissa.

"If you'll come this way, my lady?" He led her back to the entrance, but as they drew within a few paces of the door, it opened, revealing the countenance of a Temple Knight.

"Temple Captain Cordelia," announced the herald.

Larissa halted, her eyes boring into the new arrival, for people of her ilk had led to her dishonour in Reinwick. She struggled to control her urge to lash out with her magic.

The Temple Captain merely nodded in greeting and then walked past as if Larissa were of no importance. This same act would have brought harsh criticism at any court of the Petty Kingdoms, but here, it appeared to be acceptable. As she swept from the room, Larissa promised herself this woman would pay for her discourtesy.

Cordelia knelt before the king. "Your Majesty, I come bearing a proposal for wider-ranging patrols." She produced a scroll case. "This details the areas of the city my order will undertake the responsibility for patrolling, along with others."

"Others?" said Maksim.

"I've taken the liberty of meeting with several groups, sire, and divided the city into regions, assigning each group to one such area."

"And these other groups would be?"

"The Therengian fyrd, the artisan's guild, the association of dockworkers, and the smith's guild."

"Not the Temple Knights of Saint Cunar?"

"It is not their way to accept orders from an outside entity, Majesty, and since you hold the ultimate authority over these patrols, they see it as a violation of their oath to serve the Church."

"Please correct me if I'm wrong, but could we not say the same of your own order?"

"With all due respect, that would be incorrect. Our primary oath is to protect women, an oath that takes precedence over all others. This proposal fulfills that promise."

King Maksim nodded at one of his guards, who came forward to take the scroll case. "I shall examine this plan of yours with great interest, Captain."

Cordelia rose to her feet and bowed. "You honour me, Your Majesty."

"Since you're here, perhaps you would be able to answer a question for me?"

"If I can."

"Is it true ships of the Temple Fleet are preying on those belonging to Ruzhina?"

"The fleet does not attack merchants," replied Cordelia. "Having said that, they consider pirates fair game. I would put it to you, if they targeted ships out of Ruzhina, it's because they engaged in acts of piracy. Either that or slavery."

"Slavery? In this day and age?"

"Slavery is still active," called out Athgar. "I myself was held as a slave in the mines of Zurkutsk, as was Lady Katrin."

"I thought the Church outlawed slavery?"

"It has," replied Cordelia, "but the vile trade is still carried out, hidden from prying eyes."

"Yet," said the king, "not so hidden in Ruzhina, it would appear."

"My order has no official presence in that country, Majesty. Thus, we are powerless to enforce the ban."

"But not at sea?"

"The Temple Fleet protects honest merchants while hunting down criminals. We operate within the coastal waters of the northern realms with each ruler's permission, save for Ruzhina."

"I don't recall granting your ships permission to operate off my coast?"

"And we don't," replied Cordelia. "We only enter the region when transporting passengers or picking up supplies. The truth is the fleet seldom finds itself this far east."

"And why is that?"

"I'm led to believe there is a lack of friendly ports capable of carrying out repairs. Were you to wish it, I'm sure they would be willing to extend their patrols to your coastline, Majesty."

"And the cost to me would be?"

"Nothing, save for permission to carry out their duties within sight of your coast. Indeed, your city would likely benefit from the arrangement as our ships would occasionally need to replenish their stores. Have you a fleet of your own?"

"In theory, yes," replied the king, "though it hasn't sailed for some years."

"Then perhaps you might consider an alternate arrangement?"

"What are you suggesting?"

"Crewing and keeping ships in working conditions can be time-consuming and expensive. On the other hand, the Temple Fleet is an experienced and active fleet that could increase its presence on short notice if required."

"Are you suggesting we pay you for protection?"

"The fleet accepts donations from most of the Petty Kingdoms bordering the Great Northern Sea, Majesty. They see it as a cost-effective means to keep their waters safe. Since the introduction of the Temple Fleet some dozen years ago, our sea patrols have reduced piracy to almost nothing. As a direct result, trade has flourished, bringing much-needed revenue to even the smallest of treasuries."

"You make it sound so appealing," said Maksim, "but I fear politics would force me to refuse such an offer."

"It is your choice, of course, although I would ask why?"

"I agreed to ally my kingdom with Therengia."

"And?"

The king leaned forward, his interest piqued. "Would not your other supporters balk at dealing with such an entity?"

"Reinwick supports the fleet, Majesty, and they declared Therengia as a friend, if not an outright ally. I see no impedance to considering our offer."

"It's tempting, but I would like to consult with my barons before making a decision."

"I am at your disposal, Majesty, should you have other questions." Cordelia bowed, then withdrew.

Maksim waited until she left to wave Athgar over. "Well? What do you think?"

"It's a most generous offer, Majesty."

"And you have no objection to such an arrangement?"

"None at all. As I've said before, we are a peaceful people with no dreams of conquest."

"Yet you conquered Novarsk and are prepared to do the same to Ostrova, should it prove necessary."

"We seek only to make our lands safe. If the King of Ostrova proved reasonable, we'd have no qualms about leaving them alone."

"So instead, you hope to intimidate him?"

"Therengia is a new kingdom, sire, and as such, must project power to prevent others from coveting our land. If we had not stood against the Holy Army at the Standing Stones, we would not be having this conversation. The same goes for ignoring Queen Rada's invasion of our land. Should we sit back and allow others to dictate our fate or grasp it with both hands?"

"I admire your spirit, Lord Athgar, and I mean no offence by my comments, but I must consider what is best for my kingdom. With the tremendous changes of late, I find myself navigating a difficult path through them."

"It is something we are all called on to do, Majesty, but let me assure you it is not a path you must tread alone."

"Tell me. Were you in my position, would you allow Temple Ships to patrol your waters?"

"Without hesitation."

Maksim raised his eyebrows. "I'm surprised you answered so quickly. I took you for a cautious ruler."

"The Temple Knights of Saint Agnes have proven their worth over the years. This is not the first time we've worked towards a common interest, nor do I believe it will be the last. Might I ask what holds you back from making a decision?"

"Larissa Stormwind. Her presence here complicates matters immensely, and I'm not sure now is the best time to break from them. I'm particularly worried about Svetlana. I know she has little love for them, but they're still her family, and I would not be the one to break that bond, however damaged it might be."

"Your compassion serves you well, Majesty, but the Stormwinds are no family worthy of the name. They are, in brief, more akin to slavers who abduct children from their families, all in the name of advancing the craft of magic. I know Svetlana was born into the family, but I assure you many others, like Natalia, had no choice. They also discard their own when they deem them no longer of any value. Such was Katrin's fate. Speak to your queen if you must, but I doubt she holds any real empathy for the Stormwinds."

CLASH OF WILLS

SUMMER 1109 SR

A knock brought Larissa Stormwind to her feet. She'd taken her meal in her room and now assumed the servants came to cart away the remains, but she opened the door to a tall, well-dressed individual.

"Greetings," the man said. "I don't believe we've met. My name is Beringar, Crown Prince of Ostrova. And you are?"

"Larissa Stormwind, a delegate sent from Karslev."

"Stormwind, you say? I'm honoured to make your acquaintance. Your family has a reputation for being powerful mages. Can I assume that is also your vocation?"

"It is," she replied, "though I'm at a loss as to why you chose to introduce yourself?"

"I heard through a servant there was another distinguished guest here at the Palace and thought it worth investigating."

"To what end?"

"Why, to see if our objectives here align. Might I come in?"

Larissa stood to one side. "By all means." She waited until he took a seat. "I'd offer you something to drink, but I'm afraid the servants here are not very efficient."

"I understand completely. Good help is so difficult to find these days."

"Might I ask your purpose in Carlingen?"

"I'm here at the behest of my father, King Eugene. He desires to expand our border northward into the region currently belonging to King Maksim."

"I can't imagine His Majesty liked that idea."

"To be honest, I didn't expect him to."

"And yet you came anyway?"

Beringar shrugged. "What else was I to do? King Eugene commanded me to after all."

"I'm curious why he sent his heir when a simple envoy would suffice?"

"The idea was to impress upon King Maksim the seriousness with which my father takes the entire affair."

"And did the so-called King of Carlingen take you up on the offer?"

The prince grinned. "No, of course not. It was far too lean for his tastes. Did I detect a note of derision in your voice?"

"Is it that obvious?"

"It is, though it's no surprise to me. Having met the man, I can only describe him as stubborn."

"We appear to have a similar impression," said Larissa. "Prior to my travelling here, it was implied he was a weak king, easily influenced by others. Upon arrival, however, it appears he has developed a backbone."

"I assume that is inconvenient for your plans?"

"What makes you think I have plans?"

"Come now," said Beringar. "One hardly travels all this way simply for a visit."

"I came here on family business."

"Then maybe I can help."

"And why would you do that?"

"Because in return, you might convince your family to send a representative to the Ostrovan court."

"Ostrova is a kingdom of little interest to us."

"Yet you are here, in Carlingen, a realm of even less significance." He paused, letting his words sink in. "You and I both know the family's influence in the courts of the Petty Kingdoms is in decline. In Ostrova, you would be welcome, your counsel valued."

"What is it you think you can do for us?"

"That depends on why you're here," replied the prince.

Larissa considered her guest. He was an educated fellow, clever enough to be familiar with the attitudes of the Continent's courts. The question was whether she could trust him. Then again, what harm could there be if their interests aligned, as he suggested?

"I am here," she finally said, "to arrange the building of ships."

"How very interesting." He stared unblinking at her. "I assume these would be ships of war?"

"Yes. How did you guess?"

"So far as I recall, the family has little interest in merchant shipping. Is this something to do with the Holy Fleet?"

"Not the Holy Fleet—that's down in Corassus. Up here, there's a Temple Fleet to deal with. Those cursed Agnesites have caused us no end of trouble."

"So, you seek to build vessels to counter them. That makes perfect sense. I assume you're also building them in Ruzhina?"

"Yes, but how would you know that?"

"Simple logic when you get right down to it. If I were to build a fleet, I'd use multiple shipyards. That way, you can launch ships simultaneously, possibly outstripping the Church's ability to construct their own vessels."

"It is not the whole Church we have to deal with; it's only one order."

"Interesting you would say that," replied Beringar. "I have it on good authority there has been friction of late between some of the fighting orders. You wouldn't happen to know anything about that, would you?"

Larissa bristled. "What makes you think I know anything of that matter?"

"Come now. The Stormwinds are known for their vast array of knowledge. It's what makes them such effective advisors."

"Why is it of interest to you?"

"I'm looking for anything I can use to my benefit. If there is a rift in the Church, we might turn it to our advantage."

"How?"

"Well, take your problems with this 'Temple Fleet' you so clearly despise. What if you could convince another order to build a fleet?" He paused a moment. "Of course, when I say other order, I speak of the Temple Knights of Saint Cunar. After all, they maintain the Holy Fleet in Corassus. Why not another here in the north?"

"You make a compelling argument."

The prince smiled. "Compelling in a good way or bad?"

"Perhaps a little of both, although I'm not sure how one would raise the subject with an order that so values their independence."

"I would be happy to talk to them on your behalf."

"And what would be in it for you?"

Beringar lowered his voice. "There are rumours the situation here in Carlingen is… volatile. With the right impetus, the people might rise up in rebellion."

"How does that help either of us?"

"I know someone very interested in taking over as ruler of Carlingen, should the circumstances be to his advantage. He would then be indebted to the people of Ostrova for their help in handing him the Throne."

"And this individual is?"

"I'd rather not say just yet, but let it suffice to state he's a legitimate claimant to the Throne. Once he's safely ensconced, I'm sure he'd be more amenable to helping you build a fleet."

"And you think the Cunars would somehow help in this endeavour?"

"They are eager to avenge the loss of Ebenstadt. You have heard of that, haven't you?"

"I am well-versed in the circumstances of that campaign, yes, but I don't see how that leads to an interest in events here."

"Oh, then you haven't heard?"

"Are you teasing me, Highness, or have you actual news to impart?"

He grinned. "I met with the king only yesterday. He informed me he'd allied himself with Therengia, the very same kingdom that defeated the Temple Knights of Saint Cunar."

"Did he, indeed? How interesting."

"It is, isn't it? I imagine the Cunars eager to avenge their disgrace, and what better way to do that than destroying an ally of their greatest foe?"

Larissa thought it over. If what he said were true, it boded ill for the family. Perhaps this foreign prince could be of use after all. "Your idea has merit, but I've yet to see King Maksim's efforts at building a fleet."

"Then think of it as another avenue worth investigating. After all, one can never have too many pokers in the fire."

"The problem with pokers," she replied, "is they often lead to someone getting burned."

Temple Captain Darius withdrew his ring from the wax, examining the seal to ensure its readability. "That's another one out of the way. Anything else?" He looked at his aide, seated on the other side of his desk.

"I'm told you have a visitor, sir."

"A visitor? Here?"

"Yes. A prince, no less, or at least that's what he claims."

"And what would a prince want of us Cunars?"

"He didn't say. Shall I show him in?"

"Let's make him wait a little longer, shall we? It'll teach him humility." Darius dug through the correspondence on his desk, finally locating what he sought. "Any more from Brother Raban?"

"Not as yet, no. For all intents and purposes, those foreigners were true to their word."

"Meaning?"

"They made progress in dealing with the complaints brought about by the citizenry."

"Well," said Darius. "We can't have that, can we? We must take more direct action."

"Are you suggesting we eliminate them, Captain?"

"Unless you can think of an alternate method of getting them to stay out of our business."

"Is this something you want taken care of from within these walls, or would you prefer something more… street worthy?"

The Temple Captain shook his head. "Saints know our order has suffered greatly in the last few years. We don't need something like that to stain our reputation further."

"Of course, sir. I shall see to it at once." The aide hesitated. "And the visitor?"

Darius sighed. "You might as well send him in. At least then we can get it over and done with."

"I shall go and fetch him."

The aide left the room, leaving his captain deep in thought. A visitor was a rare thing in any Cunar commandery, especially one not a member of the Church. Who was this fellow who sought an audience, and what was his purpose in coming here?

A light knock drew his attention.

"The visitor, Captain."

"Send him in."

Prince Beringar entered, ducking to avoid hitting his head. "Interesting," he mused aloud. "I've never seen the inside of a commandery before."

"Do they have none where you're from?"

"Oh, they do, but I've yet to step into one. Pardon my manners, Captain. My name is Beringar, Crown Prince of Ostrova."

"So you claim, but I have a hard time believing a foreign prince would wish to visit one of our commanderies, let alone here, in the armpit of the Continent."

The visitor sat, leaning back and crossing his legs. "Yet here I am, in the flesh."

"I am a busy man," said Darius, "so spare me the platitudes of court and get straight to the point, will you? Why are you here?"

"I rather hoped we might have a bit of a chat."

"About?"

"I am here in Carlingen on a matter of great import to my king."

"And how is that of any consequence to me?"

"King Maksim was not favourably inclined to accept my offer."

"Which was?"

"My father, King Eugene, wants to purchase a parcel of land to the south."

Darius sighed again. "Get to the point, Highness. As I said before, I have things to attend to."

"It occurred to me that if someone else were to rule Carlingen, it would be to our advantage."

"By our, you mean yours. Who rules here is of little consequence to my order."

Beringar chuckled. "A bold lie, Captain. You Temple Knights are interested in the region, or you wouldn't be here. I should also point out that your order successfully ruled over Ebenstadt for some time before your defeat in the wilderness."

Darius clasped his hands on his desktop. "Are you suggesting the Temple Knights of Saint Cunar would overthrow the rightful King of Carlingen?"

"Not at all. I'm merely stating that should the city fall into disorder, it would be your right—nay, your duty—to restore order in the most efficient manner possible."

"The Church does not interfere in secular matters."

"And what do you call the efforts of the so-called Temple Fleet? Are their ships not interfering with events at sea?"

Darius winced, something Beringar noted with pleasure. "I see I've struck a nerve, Captain."

"I'll admit the actions of those of Saint Agnes have been… troublesome of late, but that's what comes of allowing such an order to exist."

The prince adopted a look of surprise. "Don't tell me there is disharmony between the orders? I'm shocked!"

"You are not on the stage, Highness. I suggest you take a more sober approach to the matter."

"Very well. Let's be blunt, shall we? My people want to put someone else on the Throne, but we need somebody to recognize his claim to be successful."

"And you believe an order of Temple Knights would do that for you?"

"Of course. Who better than the premier knights of the Church to restore order?"

Darius chuckled. "You seem to have this all worked out. Let us suppose for a moment I was interested in such an arrangement. You already said you have someone else in mind. Why did you suggest we rule instead of King Maksim?"

"My pardon, Captain. I was merely probing to see where your interests lie. It makes little difference to me who rules in Carlingen, provided it isn't the current monarch. Whether that's you or this other claimant, as long as the result is friendly to Ostrova's aims, then so be it."

"And what are your kingdom's aims?"

"Why, to acquire land. Didn't I mention that already?"

"It must be most important indeed to warrant an overthrow of a king."

"What if I told you there's another reason why he's not fit to sit on the Throne?"

"Why would that matter?"

"I'll tell you what I know," said Beringar, "and then you can decide if it's of any interest to you."

"Very well. I shall listen to your musings a while longer, but I warn you, I have little patience for matters of a trivial nature."

"Then I shall be blunt. King Maksim the Fourth, in all his wisdom, has allied himself with Therengia." Beringar watched the Temple Captain with great interest. The fellow's lack of immediate response was all the confirmation he needed that his words had sunk in.

"Are you certain?" the captain finally asked.

"His Majesty told me so himself, in front of witnesses. Witnesses, I might add, who included the High Thane of Therengia."

"The High Thane? Here in Carlingen? This is outrageous!"

"I thought exactly the same thing, Captain. So you can see why I was so concerned."

"It might have served you better had you led with that."

"Perhaps, but I needed to determine where you stood on matters first. Tell me what you make of this whole affair?"

"That man is an enemy of the Church and should be taken into custody, or better yet, executed."

"And King Maksim?"

"If he is harbouring a criminal of this magnitude, he deserves to feel the wrath of the Church."

"Oh, but there's so much more."

"More?" said Darius. "How much more can there be?"

"Also present was his warmaster, the renegade mage known as Natalia Stormwind. I assume from the look on your face that name is known to you?"

"She was said to have been at the Battle of the Wilderness."

"Ah," said Beringar. "So it was her army that led to the defeat of your order."

The captain slapped his hand on the desk. "I would take great care with my words if I were you, Highness. We do not suffer disrespect from anyone."

"My apologies. I meant only to clarify. Understandably, both of these individuals are of great interest to the Church. The question, at least to my mind, is will it be enough for you to act?"

"I must consider the situation most carefully. I am on the frontier here, many weeks away from my superiors. Thus, I need to measure any proposed actions against what those higher up might wish."

"And you don't think they'd want you to act in this case?"

"They would insist on it," said Darius. "But act, how? I can't storm the Palace and demand the arrest of these two criminals."

"I understand you're in a difficult position, Captain, but what if there were an uprising the king couldn't control? Would you act then?"

"That's hard to answer, for it all depends on circumstances. We'd also need to deal with the other Temple Order."

"Saint Agnes? Surely they wouldn't interfere?"

"As I mentioned earlier, they've been troublesome of late, particularly with that fleet of theirs."

"I was talking about that very subject earlier today."

"To whom?"

"Call them another individual with a vested interest in the politics of Carlingen. They're looking to build ships with which to counter the threat of the Temple Fleet."

"And they would support this uprising you suggest might happen?"

"Given certain assurances, I'm certain they would."

"From your remarks, I assume they would wish whoever came to power to support their shipbuilding efforts?"

Beringar smiled. "We are clearly of one mind in this, Captain."

"We are, but I require some assurances."

"Such as?"

"I must speak to this individual to ascertain whom they represent. Only then will I commit to such an endeavour, and only if I feel it has merit. After all, it's one thing to talk of such things, quite another to have the wherewithal to put them into motion."

RETURN

SUMMER 1109 SR

Kargen pulled the umak onto the riverbank. The other hunters followed his example and were soon ashore.

"Much as I enjoyed your company," said Shaluhk, "it will be nice to see Agar again. I wonder how he fared?"

"He is in Athgar and Natalia's care. No doubt by now, he has the entire court eating from his hands." He paused for a moment. "Is that the correct expression? I am never quite sure."

"It is close enough." She noted the approach of a small group of Humans and a youngling out front racing towards them. Shaluhk embraced their son, then found herself doing the same for Oswyn.

"Sorry," called out Natalia. "They insisted on running ahead."

Kargen grinned. "It is to be expected. I, too, would embrace Shaluhk had we been separated."

His bondmate chuckled. "I remember a fair amount of embracing these last few ten-days."

The mighty Orc Chieftain turned a darker shade of green.

"Welcome back," said Athgar, clutching Kargen's hand. "Much has happened since you left."

"As it has to us," said Kargen. "There is a lot to share, but rather than repeat ourselves, it might be best to visit King Maksim."

"It seems we are of a similar mind, for I was about to suggest the very same thing. I trust the journey there was uneventful?"

"Indeed. The wild lands to the south made for a pleasant trip. The wildlife there is plentiful, and the rivers easy to navigate, making perfect hunting grounds for Orcs."

"Did you spot any signs of them?"

"No. If any of our people are in the area, they did not see fit to reveal their presence. However, you must bear in mind we traversed only a small portion of the region and stayed close to the river."

"And the Ostrovans?"

Kargen frowned. "That is an entirely different matter, but I will speak of it once we are before the king."

With the umaks unloaded, the entire group returned to the Palace, with Sergeant Brauer leading the delegation, keeping curious onlookers at bay.

"You say much has happened," said Shaluhk. "Perhaps it would be best if you gave us the details, so we will be up to date when we talk to His Majesty."

"I'm not sure where to start," said Athgar.

"I am," offered Natalia. "Larissa Stormwind came to court to oversee the family's plans for building a fleet. I can't say it thrilled her to see me there."

Shaluhk nodded. "I can well imagine. Did she demand your arrest?"

"Amongst other things."

"Such as?"

"She wanted the king to turn Oswyn over to the family?"

"I assume he refused?"

"Yes. Then yesterday, an envoy arrived from Ostrova."

"Not just an envoy," said Athgar, "the Crown Prince himself. It appears their king thinks the entire affair is very important."

"And what of the city?" asked Kargen. "Have steps been taken to make it safer?"

"Temple Captain Cordelia presented a plan to His Majesty on that very subject. She proposed dividing the city into five patrol areas, each the responsibility of a select group, none of which, I might add, were the Cunars."

"There's more," piped up Greta.

"What have you heard?" asked Natalia.

"I've spent a lot of time learning the layout of the Palace, and while I wasn't able to find a place to listen in on Larissa Stormwind, I did make a discovery."

"Go on," urged Athgar.

"Prince Beringar went to visit her."

"Any idea what they talked about?"

"No," replied Greta, "but after they finished, I followed the prince as far as the Cunar commandery. He seemed pleased with himself upon his return."

"And you're sure he didn't see you?"

"Absolutely."

"Good work, Greta. Anything else you can tell us about his escapades?"

"He wasn't at the commandery for long before he returned to the Palace."

"Did he make any stops along the way?"

"No, and he went without his guards. Is that important?"

"It could be," replied Athgar, "although I can't say how at this particular point."

"This prince," said Shaluhk, "did he make demands?"

"He offered to purchase a large swath of land," replied Natalia, "but his offer was far from adequate, considering how much of the region they wanted."

"I gather you have a theory as to why that is?"

"You know me too well. He's waiting for the king to make a counterproposal, but it seems like a delaying tactic."

"To what end?"

"His visit to the Cunar commandery indicates he is seeking allies, and I believe I know why."

"Would you care to share with the rest of us?"

"Most certainly," said Natalia. "Do you remember those three townsfolk we told you about?"

"The ones who demanded changes?"

"Yes. Athgar and I found one of them suspicious, so much so we speculated he might be a Temple Knight of Saint Cunar."

"And you believe that is connected with the Prince of Ostrova's visit there?"

"I think that more likely than simple coincidence, don't you?"

"I agree," said Shaluhk, "and we are in possession of knowledge that might back up that suspicion."

"We're here," called out Sergeant Brauer. Guards moved to either side of the gate, allowing the party to enter the Palace and go through to the great hall.

King Maksim sat on his throne with Svetlana at his side, while Katrin, along with Stanislav, Belgast, and Carlingen's three barons, were in attendance.

"Welcome back, Kargen, Chieftain of the Red Hand," said the king. "And honour to you, Shaman Shaluhk. We have sorely missed your presence here."

"Greetings, Noble King," said Kargen. "We have, as promised, returned from the south to report on what we found."

Maksim waved his hand absently. "Let us dispense with formalities, shall we? I think it more important to address the facts. What did you find in the south? Is Ostrova preparing to invade?"

"That is a difficult question to answer. With help from Shaluhk's magic, we infiltrated the Ostrovan camp. There, in spirit form, we gained a greater understanding of their plans, although there are still unanswered questions."

"Is it an invasion?" asked the king.

"I do not believe so, at least not in the traditional sense. They intend to cross the river with a significant force, but in my opinion, they lack the numbers to make it all the way to Carlingen."

"Then what are they after?"

"It appears," offered Shaluhk, "they are searching for something relatively close to the border."

"That explains why they want a strip of our land. Any idea on what they might be after?"

"No, but they are intent on setting up a base on the northern side of the river. We saw plans to construct a bridge." She looked at her bondmate. "There is more, but I do not know if it is relevant."

"Tell us what you know," said Maksim. "If it is unimportant, then no harm is done."

"While exploring the area, we came across some old ruins."

"What kind of ruins?"

"Those of an ancient city."

"And when you say ancient, you mean..."

"I suspect several centuries old, at least. There we found signs of Orcs and Humans working together."

"What kinds of signs?"

"Murals," explained Kargen. "Leading us to believe it may have been part of the Old Kingdom."

King Maksim locked eyes with the Orc Chieftain. "There's something you're not telling us."

"Shaluhk has knowledge of a spell that allows her to speak with spirits. Normally, such magic can only call on those who died in recent memory, but since her encounter with Khurlig, her power has increased significantly."

"Khurlig?" said the king. "I don't believe I know that name."

"She was an Orc shaman," said Shaluhk. "One said to have mastered life and death. Her spirit tried to possess me some time ago, and though she was ultimately defeated, much of her memory remains."

"And how is this relevant?"

"Any shaman can call on the Ancestors, but the spirits who respond to such a spell have been dead for a decade or two. In those ruins, I called on a spirit much older than should be possible under normal conditions."

Maksim took a rushed breath, sitting back in his chair. "Are you saying you can talk to the dead?"

"It is a fact," replied Natalia. "I have witnessed it myself. Our own child was named by the Ancestors."

"Very well. I shall take you at your word. Did the spirit you conjured tell you anything of consequence?"

"He did," said Shaluhk. "He called the city Beorwic. There was to be a big battle in his lifetime, but he fell ill and passed from this world at home rather than as a warrior." She paused, turning to her bondmate. "In those days, his people did not consider themselves hunters."

"Beorwic," said the king. "There's something familiar about that name."

"We also found evidence the region was once referred to as the Wurgeld Forest."

"Did you say Wurgeld?"

"Yes. Why? Does that name mean something to you?"

"It most assuredly does," said Maksim. "As you have no doubt heard, Carlingen is a place for those seeking treasure. As a child, I revelled in such tales, for it seemed like a new adventurer arrived every month, often with stories that sparked my interest." He turned to Athgar. "Are you familiar with the tale of the last city of Therengia?"

"Of course. It was the last holdout of the Old Kingdom, but we always assumed it was Ebenstadt. It even has an old Therengian name: Dunmere."

"When you said Beorwic, I realized I'd heard it before but couldn't place it until you mentioned the Wurgeld. According to legend, King Eadwulf, the last King of Therengia, supposedly made his stand there."

"Supposedly?"

"Well, there are no actual records to indicate where the Wurgeld Forest was, only myth and conjecture, and we all know how the passing of time can twist legends."

"That might explain how my kinfolk came to be in the area," said Athgar. "They likely migrated south and east to escape the alliance that defeated them."

"You're right," said Belgast. "Perhaps they founded Dunmere? What else do we know about the fall of the Old Kingdom?"

"Very little," said Maksim, "though there are legends."

"Such as?"

"The founder of the Old Kingdom was a man named Aeldred."

"Of that, I'm fully aware," said Athgar. "He led a campaign against the Thalamites, defeating them to establish his own dynasty. Even today, the people of Runewald know of him, although they know little of the war that put him on the Throne."

"Ah, but that's where it gets interesting. Many legends surround Aeldred, but the most famous of all is that of his banner."

"I'm familiar with it. It was a flag he carried into battle, said to make an army invincible."

"And you never sought to bring this to my attention before now?" said the king.

"I never connected it to the Last Battle. Wurgeld is not a part of our legends that I'm familiar with. In any case, it's only a story. It can't possibly be real."

"Why do you say that?"

"If the banner of Aeldred was so powerful, why did the Old Kingdom die? Wouldn't its mere presence be enough to guarantee victory?"

"I suppose I hadn't considered that."

"Nothing is infallible," said Natalia. "Even powerful magic has its limitations."

Svetlana spoke up, "Could it be magical in nature?"

"It stands to reason, doesn't it?" suggested Athgar. "We know the Old Kingdom utilized mages."

"What kind of magic could someone put on a flag?" asked Maksim.

"Plenty," replied Natalia, "though the most likely candidates are enchantments."

"What sort of enchantments?"

"I can't say for certain, but several might explain its reputation. One removes fear, which would have a big effect on morale. Then again, there are spells to increase the protection armour affords or allow their weapons to deal greater damage. I could go on, but you get the idea."

"Fascinating," said the king. "And it might very well explain what the Ostrovans are up to. Kargen, you said they planned to cross the river, did you not?"

"I did," replied the Orc.

"And we've speculated at some length about something being in the area. I put it to you all that they believe it to be the banner."

"It's feasible," said Athgar, "but how would they even know where to look?"

"We cannot know for certain," said Maksim, "but what if they have access to some long-forgotten tome or writings? After all, if what Shaluhk tells us is true, someone had to be there to defeat the last Therengian king. It only makes sense they would have written down an account of the final battle somewhere."

"A good point," said Belgast, "and the land now known as Ostrova would have been a convenient place to do such a thing. What do we know of the region from that time?"

"Very little, and we don't even have a date for those ruins."

"Actually, we do," said Shaluhk. "The power required to contact the spirit of Ungor would indicate somewhere close to four centuries, although I am unable to pick an exact year. Does that fit in with what you know of this banner?"

"It does," said Athgar.

"I'm confused," said Stanislav. "Wasn't the Old Kingdom defeated five hundred years ago?"

"That date is the one most often associated with the fall of its capital, but remnants lingered for nigh on a century. The ancient kingdom of Therengia, or as we now refer to it, the Old Kingdom, was defeated by an alliance of smaller realms who banded together to launch the military campaign that destroyed Therengia."

"But didn't you say the banner made them invincible? What am I missing here?"

"A king," continued Athgar, "even a powerful and skilled one, can't be everywhere at once. Outnumbered and already suffering from internal conflict, they were picked apart. The victors, often referred to as the Successor States, fought over the remains of the Old Kingdom, each eager to take possession of the riches of Therengia."

Stanislav bent his head to the side. "And this was how long ago?"

"Their capital fell around five hundred years ago, but many of the Old Kingdom's outlying provinces fought on. Records of that period are largely non-existent, but according to Tonfer Garul, the last great battle occurred some time later when a large host assembled, killing the last King of the Therengians at what we call the Last Battle."

"But if what you say is true, why are there not more records? I think such a great victory would be celebrated?"

"Ah," replied Belgast, "but then you wouldn't be taking into account the aftermath of the war."

"And how would you know?" asked the mage hunter.

"King Haglarith had a particular fondness for military history, and I had the misfortune of listening to him prattle on at length about it."

"I stand corrected. Please continue."

The Dwarf cleared his throat. "It's said that with no common enemy, the Successor States fell in amongst themselves, resulting in a series of wars lasting for close to a century, no doubt destroying much of their history in the process."

"And that is where the Petty Kingdoms come from?"

"Precisely."

"Assuming we're correct," said Natalia, "and Ostrova is looking for Aeldred's Banner, it seems to indicate they intend to go to war. Why else seek an artifact that guarantees victory?"

"Not necessarily," said Stanislav. "They might want it to fend off enemies."

"Then why risk war to obtain it? Surely a small expedition could cross into Carlingen's territory and search for it?"

"They don't know where the city is," said Athgar.

"But wouldn't the standard be at the site of the battle?" asked Belgast.

Athgar grinned. "No. It couldn't be, else one of the victors would have claimed it. And if it wasn't at the final battle, it wasn't in the region at all, or it was left back in Beorwic."

"But if that were the case, wouldn't the descendants have taken it with them when they abandoned the city? There was no sign of it back in Runewald, was there?"

"No. It wasn't amongst King Eadred's treasure," said Natalia, "but perhaps in Ebenstadt?"

"I don't think so," said Athgar. "Imagine the circumstances; King Eadwulf is defeated, his army destroyed. The banner would be a prize worthy of the greatest hero. Rather than let it fall into enemy hands, they likely took it back to Beorwic. Perhaps they intended to carry it farther east, but in the wake of the army's defeat, the victors advanced on the city, intent on destroying it."

"That makes sense," said Shaluhk. "The ruins we found were more than mere abandoned buildings. Walls can collapse over time. That much is true, but an entire city's worth? It is far more likely there was a siege."

"I agree," added Kargen. "And there is something else to consider. Why not keep it as a prize if they captured it? The wealth of the Old Kingdom was said to be legendary, was it not?"

"It was," agreed Maksim, "and all of you make excellent points. You also identified something that works in our favour."

"Which is?"

"We know the location of Beorwic, while our enemy does not. That's assuming you can find your way back there?"

"We can," said Kargen.

"Good. Then it's high time we took steps to secure it."

"Meaning?" said Athgar.

"The time has come to put our army, small as it is, to good use."

PREPARATIONS

SUMMER 1109 SR

Shaluhk opened her eyes. "It is done." The spell had drained her, but she'd had to spend considerable time passing on Natalia's instructions. "Laghul will relay the orders to the Thane's Council. Within days, the Army of Therengia should be on the move and marching towards the border."

Natalia turned to Athgar. "Are you sure this is what you want?"

"There is little choice. If we are to assist Carlingen, we must at least have an army nearby, and we can't do that if we're weeks away from Ostrova."

"And if Ostrova doesn't invade?"

"Then we are no worse off than we are now."

"I'd feel better about this if I were there to lead them," said Natalia.

"As would I," said Athgar, "but we can't abandon King Maksim in his time of need. We must trust our commanders to handle things in our absence."

"Speaking of the king," said Belgast. "What is he up to?"

"He's asked us to look at his men," said Natalia. "I hoped you and Athgar might take it upon yourselves to carry out an inspection."

"Us?" said the Dwarf.

"You're both familiar with the fyrd's organization and training back in Runewald."

"Yes, but that's different."

"Is it?" she said. "The army here serves the same purpose as back home, that of protecting its land."

"True, but these aren't Therengians."

"Meaning what? That they can't be expected to defend their homes?"

"She has a point," said Athgar, "but you must remember the warriors here might not bear the same dedication our fyrd does." He nodded at Natalia. "Don't worry. We'll do our part."

"Good, because I need to discuss strategy with Svetlana. The king wants the beginnings of a strategy by dinner tonight. I'll ensure they assemble the companies on the practice field."

"Which are where?" asked Belgast.

"Two blocks west of the Palace. Don't worry. You can't miss it. It's a big open space squeezed in between city blocks."

"Shall I go with them?" asked Kargen.

"No," said Natalia. "I need you with Shaluhk and me to help map the route south."

"What about the rest of us?" asked Katrin.

"You've received training in strategy, so I'll want you with me. I also thought we could put Stanislav's experience to good use."

"In what way?" asked the mage hunter.

"It occurred to me it might be useful for you to keep an eye on the Cunar commandery. I may be worrying over nothing, but I can't help but wonder what they're up to."

"And what do you have in mind for Greta?"

"Providing she's up to the task, I thought she might do the same for Prince Beringar. Assuming, that is, she doesn't mind slinking around the Palace?"

"Slinking?" The girl smiled mischievously. "I'm especially good at that sort of thing."

"Excellent, but whatever you do, avoid any conflict. And don't, under any circumstances, talk to him directly, or he'll get suspicious."

"I can do that."

"Good. Now, with that out of the way, let's get down to business, shall we? Any thoughts on strategy?"

"Any movement south should be by boat," said Kargen. "Our umaks can lead the way, but does the king possess enough vessels to carry his warriors?"

"That largely depends on how many we're sending," said Natalia."

"A smaller expedition would be better," suggested Athgar.

"To face off against an army?" said Belgast. "Surely you jest?"

"Whomever the king sends will be operating in very rough terrain. Had we a properly trained fyrd, I'd suggest sending them, but we must make do with what we have."

"I don't understand," said Greta. "Why not send every man the king has?"

"In a word, logistics. A large army needs a correspondingly large number of wagons to carry food, wagons that would quickly get bogged down in the thick underbrush. The alternative is to use pack animals, but there's a shortage of horses in these parts."

"What they need is stonecakes," grumbled Belgast.

"Are you offering to make them?"

"What do I look like, a baker?"

"What's a stonecake?" asked Greta.

"A Dwarven meal," explained Belgast. "In appearance, it looks much the same as a piece of coal, but it fills the belly like traditional food. Us mountain folk can live off the stuff for months, but you Humans require a more diverse diet."

"We can't eat stonecakes?"

"Oh, you can, just not for extended periods. A week, maybe two, and then you'd find yourself growing weaker for lack of meat."

"What about Orcs?"

"We have no need of stonecakes," said Shaluhk. "Our hunters gather food as we go."

"Then why not have them hunt for the army?"

"It is a matter of numbers. An army of sufficient size to repel an invader would quickly use up all the game in an area."

"Perhaps there's a better option," said Athgar. "What if we marched the army overland but used boats to carry supplies like tents and food."

"That," said Natalia, "is an excellent idea. I'll suggest it to Svetlana."

"Not all of the king's ships are seaworthy yet," said Belgast, "but I imagine those that are, would have little trouble navigating the river. They'd also be big enough to carry what's needed, providing the expedition isn't too large. Which begs the question of how large should we suggest it be. What are you thinking, Natalia?"

"In theory, King Maksim has an army of around six hundred, assuming each company is at full strength. We must leave some here to protect the Palace, thus reducing the numbers."

"So, what are we looking at—four hundred?"

"That largely depends on what you and Athgar discover when you inspect them. I hope we can muster at least two hundred for the trip, but even that might be a little on the optimistic side."

"It's not enough," said Athgar. "If the King of Ostrova is intent on finding the ruins of Beorwic, he'll have plenty more than that."

"What makes you say that?" asked Belgast.

"First, he has to bridge the river, then spread out over potentially hundreds of miles worth of wilderness. You can't do that with so few. And the more men searching, the more he'll need to watch their camp."

"Can we get more from elsewhere?"

"We might be able to convince some Therengians to join the expedition, but we'd need more time if we want them ready for something like this."

"I'll bring it to His Majesty's attention," said Natalia. "Anyone have anything else to contribute?" She looked around at the group, but nothing was forthcoming. "Very well. I'm off to meet with Svetlana."

Athgar stared at the assembled Carlingen warriors: six companies of footmen, their equipment displaying a surprising diversity. In front of them stood a tall, imposing figure, the sun glinting off his armour so much it forced Athgar to shield his eyes.

"Commander Schoenfeld, I presume?"

The fellow turned, making his way towards the small group.

"You must be Lord Athgar?"

"I am. I'm told you command the Army of Carlingen."

"I have that honour, yes."

"Yet the king hasn't seen fit to make you a general?"

"The army is of insufficient size to warrant such a title." The commander halted, then turned, nodding towards the assembled men. "What do you think of them?"

"Is this all of them?"

"All, save those on duty, my lord."

"A sorry lot," said Belgast, "and not one company at full strength."

"Recruitment has been difficult since the king let the undesirables go, Master Dwarf."

"I suppose we could reorganize them."

"What is it you're suggesting?"

"Merely that we might merge a few of these under-manned companies to create full-strength ones."

"I've heard the crossbowmen are capable," noted Athgar. "Perhaps we could group them with a smattering of those mailed warriors to form the core."

"Core of what?" asked the commander.

"Of the expedition, of course. We could employ the men with lighter armour as a screening force. We'll equip them with axes, the better to clear a path through the heavier parts of the forest."

"How many would we be taking, Lord?"

Athgar frowned. "Initially, I'd expected to take five or six companies, but I now see that was nothing more than wishful thinking. Do you believe the king could spare two companies worth?"

"That's a tall order," said Schoenfeld, "but it's doable. How much time have we?"

"A few days, I expect. We'll know more once His Majesty finalizes his plans."

"A few days? But we must make arrangements for food. You can't march men into the wilderness on a whim. How far will they march? What route will they take? What is the composition of the enemy?"

"All good questions," replied Athgar, "but I'm afraid I can't answer them with any accuracy. Take the distance, for example. We know they'd be marching to the southern border, but without reliable maps, we cannot estimate the distance."

"And the route?"

"A survivor travelled to the border and back by going overland. I'm hoping she'll be able to provide a route. We'll also have Orc hunters leading the way, so I don't expect too much trouble in that regard."

"And the enemy?" pressed the commander.

"That's a little harder to account for. We don't possess an accurate accounting of their numbers, but we know they're building a bridge, so if we can get there before they complete it, we'll be able to oppose their crossing."

"And if not?"

"Then they'll already be in place, and our job will be that much harder. Of course, we'll have mages on our side, so hopefully, that will help sway the situation to our advantage."

"We have no mages, my lord."

"Yes, we do. I'm a master of flame, and Natalia is a Water Mage. In addition, we have the Life Magic of Shaluhk, allowing us to greatly reduce our casualties. I'm not saying it will grant us a guaranteed victory, but it certainly doesn't hurt." He noted the approach of Herulf, who'd proven himself adept at training the Therengian fyrd. "I assume things are going well?"

"They are, Lord. We have word the king consented to release some weapons for them. As you requested, I've been training them in the use of axes."

"And shields?"

"Those, too, though I fear it is not something they take to naturally."

"That only stands to reason. After all, they have little experience in fighting."

"Yes. Most used to be farmers, although apparently rather poor ones, hence the reason for their journey here to Carlingen."

"Has the king provided any armour?"

"Some have quilted jackets," replied Herulf, "while a few count metal helmets amongst their possessions."

"And their morale?"

"High, Lord. They've been readying patrols for the areas designated in the Temple Captain's plan, and their own streets have fallen quiet for the first time in months. The question remaining is whether it will last."

"It's good to hear of their progress. Now," said Athgar, turning back to the king's warriors, "it's time to see if we can do the same with these men." He paused, taking in the view. "Would you be so kind as to advance them fifty paces, Commander?"

"Lord?"

"I want to see how well they keep their lines."

"To what end?"

"I'm trying to ascertain the level of their discipline."

"And having them march will tell you that?"

"Not entirely, but we need to start somewhere."

"Very well." Commander Schoenfeld strode over to stand before the king's warriors, then began yelling commands.

"He's dedicated," said Belgast. "I'll give him that, though he's a little hesitant to obey orders."

"I can understand why," said Athgar. "After all, I'm a foreigner, and a ruler, at that. Hardly the person you'd expect to lead the king's men under normal circumstances."

Herulf watched them advance. "They're not much to look at."

"Oh, I don't know. There's a smattering of good men there."

"They're well-equipped compared to the fyrd, Lord, but I wouldn't trust them to stand in the face of an attack. They have no passion."

"Then we shall do what we can to make them ready."

"And if that still doesn't do the trick?"

"Then we've no hope."

"Well?" asked King Maksim. "What do you make of my army?"

"It has promise," replied Athgar.

"Not exactly the most ringing endorsement."

"May I be honest, Majesty?"

"Of course. I expect no less."

"Your army is poorly trained. I can rectify the situation, but it will take time."

"How much time?"

"Perhaps as little as two weeks, but it depends on how quickly they pick things up."

"I see," said the king. "What does Lord Kargen think?"

The Orc stepped forward. "You need more men, Majesty. From what Athgar tells me, your army lacks the numbers to keep your enemies at bay even at full strength."

"Even before we weeded out the malcontents, we had trouble enough maintaining what few companies we have."

"Considering the number of people who've flooded into Carlingen seeking their fortune, could you not raise additional troops?"

"You would think so, wouldn't you? The trouble is, this city attracts individualists, hardly the type to serve in the Royal Army."

"What of your barons?" asked Athgar.

"They're still struggling to keep their own lands afloat. You must remember I only have the three, and they are relatively new. It will be some years before they can stand on their own feet. If I commanded them to supply troops, I fear I would make them destitute."

"How about mercenaries?" asked Belgast.

"An excellent idea," replied the king. "Know of any hereabouts?"

"Er, no. I suppose not."

"As you are well aware, Carlingen is a remote kingdom. What was it the Volstrum used to call us? Oh yes—the armpit of the Continent."

"Is there no one else you can draw upon?" asked the Dwarf.

"Not unless you're suggesting the Temple Knights?"

"The sisters might be of some assistance," offered Athgar.

"You think they would commit a company to the enterprise?"

"No. They still need to be here to patrol the streets, but a half company might be possible."

"Wouldn't the terrain be most unsuitable for cavalry?"

"Then perhaps they could fight on foot? A few Temple Knights would do wonders for the expedition's morale."

"Do you believe the Temple Captain can be persuaded?"

"Yes," said Athgar, "and she's seen battle before in both Krieghoff and Ilea. Shall I ask her on your behalf?"

"If you would be so kind. What of the Cunars? Could they be of any use?"

"They refused to answer any of our enquiries, Majesty. I fear they've decided to sit out the war rather than stand with you."

The king snorted. "I suppose I should have expected that."

"Have you decided on a strategy?"

"Not as yet. Svetlana tells me she and Natalia have been working on several, but they have yet to decide which one to use. Of course, they all involve moving an army south to the border, but the details are causing the biggest headache. What about Therengia? Any hope of getting help from there?"

Athgar smiled. "We sent word for the army to muster some time ago. With our most recent contact, we ordered them north."

"I thank you for that, but it will be months before they reach the border, surely?"

"On the contrary," said Kargen. "They will be well on their way before sunset."

"That quickly? You surprise me. I assumed organizing something of that magnitude would take weeks."

"The select fyrd stands ready to march at a moment's notice, as does the Thane Guard."

"And will that be enough?"

"They do not come alone. Hunters of the Red Hand, Stone Crushers, Black Axe, and Cloud Hunters, all experienced in war, accompany them. They might not be enough to conquer Ostrova, but they will suffice to draw men away from Carlingen's border."

"There's also the tuskers," added Athgar.

"Which are?" asked the king.

"Huge creatures, easily twice the size of a horse, ridden by the tribe's most experienced hunters. The Holy Army's defeat at the Battle of the Standing Stones was largely due to their presence."

"And have you any cavalry aside from those creatures?"

"We do," replied Athgar. "Thanks to our recent campaign in Novarsk, we now count the Knights of the Mailed Fist amongst our ranks, although I hesitate to use them in battle so soon."

"Why is that?"

"They only recently took an oath to serve us and are yet to prove their loyalty."

"They will serve," said Kargen. "We have been most diligent in rooting out the more fanatical elements of the order."

"As far as I know, Ostrova has no knights of their own," said Maksim. "Not that it matters to us, as the campaign in the south will be in thick forest, hardly the place for horsemen. Still, their lack should help your people once they cross the border. Will this commitment cause problems with your other neighbours?"

"The only other kingdom adjacent to Therengia is that of Zalista to the west, and our relations are cordial."

"Is there nothing to your south?"

"Only if you cross the Grey Spire Mountains, which is enough to stop even the most battle-hardened army."

"I envy you, Lord Athgar. You possess a proven army in sufficient numbers to keep enemies at bay. Would that I had such a force."

"The Army of Therengia is there to keep us safe, sire, not to expand the borders of our kingdom. I would not so easily sacrifice the lives of my people."

"Yet you offer to go to war now in defence of Carlingen."

"I do," said Athgar, "but only to ensure my home's future peace and prosperity. With Ostrova defeated, no enemies remain to threaten our borders."

"Unless you count the Church. Was the Holy Crusade not launched on their orders?"

"It was not the Church, merely the meddling of senior members amongst the Temple Knights of Saint Cunar."

"Then let us pray the same cannot be said here."

TRAINING

SUMMER 1109 SR

Larissa Stormwind looked down at the timbers forming the keel. "Is that all you've accomplished?"

"You must remember," said Belgast. "We only received your letter shortly before your arrival. Then, we had to locate a shipwright, finalize plans, and cut down trees to supply the wood."

"And the others?"

"Plans call for constructing ten more vessels, but we considered it best to complete this one first. That way, we can work out any problems before we continue."

"This vessel is so small."

"It is, but Carlingen has no history of building ships of a larger nature. Our hope is that our work here will give us valuable experience we can apply to a larger vessel."

The Water Mage pursed her lips. The Dwarf's arguments made sense, but she couldn't help but feel King Maksim was dragging his feet. "What is the estimated completion date for this vessel?"

"With the resources at hand, likely six months or so. We could put more people on it, but that would increase the cost significantly. Why? Does that not fit with your schedule?"

"The family needs the ships quickly. Every day we delay, more of our vessels are swept from the sea."

"Then perhaps you should have considered the situation with a more critical eye," said Belgast. "You came to Carlingen, a realm with little experience in shipbuilding. Did you expect us to produce them out of thin air?"

"We gave you ample funds to begin construction."

"True, but there's more to it than simply spending coins. You need an experienced shipbuilder for what you want, and those don't exactly grow on trees." He hesitated for a moment. "Look. I know it's not what you wanted to hear, but I promise you, given enough time, we'll build all the ships you're asking for."

"I find this very frustrating."

"I can well imagine. Might I ask a question?"

"Go ahead."

"What sort of time span were you expecting?"

"My superiors hoped you'd have a dozen ships afloat by next summer."

"That's still quite possible. As I mentioned earlier, this first vessel will likely take six months, but once we get the knack of it, the others will be much easier to construct."

"It will do little good. A ship of this size is far too small for our intended purpose. We need something capable of going one-on-one with the ships of the Temple Fleet."

"Then you should have sought a kingdom more skilled in such things. What about Ruzhina? Do they have the experience necessary?"

"The shipyards of Porovka have previous commitments. They can't even begin construction until early next year."

"And the other Petty Kingdoms along the northern coast?"

"I cannot speak for them," said Larissa. "My responsibility is Carlingen's contribution to the cause."

"I don't know what I can say other than assure you we are making great strides. Were you to come back later in the year, I could tell you more, but as we are only at the beginning of this, we have no idea what difficulties we might encounter."

"How is it you, a Dwarf, found yourself in charge of this endeavour? Surely, as one of the mountain folk, you'd be better employed elsewhere?"

"You would think so, wouldn't you? But the fact is, organizing things is what I do best. The construction itself falls entirely in the hands of the ship-builder, but I arrange everything he needs for the job, freeing him up to do what he does best. I can show you my notes if you wish. I believe in keeping accurate accounts of our expenditures."

"That won't be necessary." Larissa looked around the area. A few men were present, mostly common labourers, but no sign of anyone overseeing them. "I've seen enough. I shall return to the Palace."

"As you wish, my lady."

• • •

Athgar watched the fyrd advance. Herulf kept them at a steady pace, their line remaining straight even if some did still hold their shields too low. "Impressive," he said.

They all smiled, pleased he'd seen fit to praise them.

"They're getting there," said Herulf. "The new shields help a lot."

"Have we any bows?"

"Only a few, Lord, but I've identified the individuals with enough skill to use them."

"I sense a 'but'," said Athgar.

"The bows the king provided are small, nothing like what a real Therengian would use."

"These men are as much Therengian as you or I. Never forget that And as for the bows, we should be thankful they don't have the longer Therengian bows. Such weapons take years to master. What about arrows?"

"There are more than we need, Lord."

"You've been working with these people for some time now. What else can you tell me?"

Herulf nodded at a small group of townsfolk, all a head taller than Athgar. "I thought I might equip those with two-handed axes. Do you think you can convince the king to give us some?"

"I can ask. What are they using at present?"

"Clubs. They're useful for patrolling the street, but they'll be next to useless if we see any real fighting." He took a deep breath before continuing. "There's something else you should know about."

"Never be afraid to speak your mind, Herulf. What is it?"

"Rumours are floating around."

"What kind of rumours?"

"Whispers of rebellion, Lord. Not from these people, of course Your patronage improved their lives, but others call for change."

"What kind of change?"

"A Holy War to wipe Therengia off the face of the Continent."

"That's nothing new," said Athgar. "People have been vilifying us for centuries."

"This is different. They're organized, calling themselves the Saint's Army, and there've been some incidents with our patrols. Nothing we haven't been able to handle just yet, but they're growing bolder."

"I'll bring it to the king's attention. In the meantime, you should increase the size of the patrols. We don't want anyone getting hurt."

"And if this so-called 'Saint's Army' turns violent?"

"Then you must meet it with all the strength and resolve you can muster. If blood is to be shed, you must ensure it's not ours. Am I clear?"

"Yes, Lord."

"Good. I'd like you to remain here, amongst these people. If the situation worsens, send word to the Palace."

"Of course."

"Good work, Captain."

"Captain?"

"As of now, you command the fyrd here. I think the title is only suitable, don't you?"

Herulf grinned. "Of course, Lord."

The magic built, and then Natalia let loose with a streak of ice that raced across the field, striking the ground and sending tiny shards into the air. The footmen, not used to such things, wavered and then broke, running back to the starting line.

Svetlana frowned. "Hmmm. There is a lot of work to do."

"Agreed," added Katrin. "They talked about this back at the Volstrum. Do you remember?"

"Ah, yes. Mistress Nina and her ever-present lectures. We couldn't do anything without some historical note to go with it."

Natalia chuckled. "It takes patience and practice for warriors to get used to magic. It was no different in Therengia."

Svetlana looked at the dozen Orc hunters waiting nearby. "What about them? Did they have reservations about such things?"

"Not at all, but they've grown up around wielders of magic." She paused when she noticed the approach of Kargen and Shaluhk. "I have an idea."

"Which is?"

"We often use Orc hunters to screen the army as they advance. Perhaps their presence could steady these men of Carlingen."

"Or scare them witless," said Katrin. "These people don't live with Orcs on a day-to-day basis, remember?"

"Do you have a better idea?"

"No. Unfortunately, I don't."

"Then let's try it my way, shall we?"

Kargen smiled as he approached. "Are you looking for me?"

"I was. I wondered if your hunters would mind providing a screen as the companies advance."

"If you think that would help."

"I do. If nothing else, they won't flinch when we use our magic, and that should inspire the others to keep their line steady."

"It is worth a try." Kargen wandered over to his hunters, exchanged a few words, and then the Orcs formed a line, spacing themselves out in front of the men of Carlingen, Kargen included.

"He is in his element," said Shaluhk. "He enjoys the challenge of such things; although, if you were to ask, he would deny it."

They waited as the king's companies reformed before beginning the advance anew. Katrin let loose with some ice, and though the line wavered, it didn't fail. Natalia followed with one of her own, as did Svetlana, and this time there was less of an impact on the men of Carlingen.

The companies reached the end of the practice field and broke up into smaller groups, congratulating each other on their success.

Kargen jogged over, a grin spread across his face. "Well? What did you think?"

"A good start," replied Natalia, "yet we still have some work ahead of us."

"I agree," said Svetlana, "but have we the time? Every day we spend here is another the Army of Ostrova can use to build that bridge. How do we know he hasn't already begun searching the northern bank?"

"He probably has," said Kargen. "But if that map of his was any indication, he is still miles away from the ruins of Beorwic."

"Let's hope you're right." The queen fell silent, her gaze turning to the warriors. "Will they be enough?"

"They'll have to be," replied Natalia. "Remember, they don't need to defeat Ostrova, merely delay them until the Army of Therengia crosses the border. Once they hear about that, they'll have no choice but to march south to oppose it."

"And when you defeat them, then what? Will you add Ostrova to your lands?"

"Therengia is not an empire seeking to expand its borders."

"That doesn't answer my question."

Natalia stared back before finally nodding. "If it's anything like Novarsk, as I suspect it is, we shall have to absorb it. That would be good for you, though, as it would place a powerful ally on your border."

"As long as we follow your rules?"

"Our rules, as you call them, are few. You would be free to rule your lands as you see fit, providing you offer no injustice to our people. Is that so much to ask?"

"And would you send warriors to keep the peace in Carlingen?"

"Not unless you asked us to. We are not your enemy, Svetlana—the family is."

"Will there ever be an end to their influence?"

"They'll have their reckoning eventually, though it won't be soon enough for my liking. Were it up to me, I would march an army into Karslev and put an end to their efforts once and for all."

"Come now," said Svetlana. "None of us have that kind of power."

Natalia shook her head, smiling. "You truly have no idea. Now, you must excuse me. I should see if Stanislav has any news about the Cunars."

Svetlana watched her leave. "What was that all about?"

Katrin chuckled. "You don't know about Natalia's discovery at the Volstrum, do you?"

"What discovery? You mean about the involvement with Halvaria?"

"No. I'm referring to the ancient magic."

"What in the name of the Saints are you talking about?"

"She unlocked spells long forgotten by the family, using them to great effect in the west. Then, there's Athgar's training. His knowledge of Pyromancy grew by leaps and bounds when he found the Ashwalkers."

"Ashwalkers?"

"Yes," replied Katrin. "A tribe of Orcs with powerful Fire Mages, or rather masters of flame as they call them."

"Surely the magic of the Orcs can't compare to the Sartellians?"

"Can't it? I saw what he did in Andover, and I doubt the strongest graduate of Korascajan could stand against that. And that's not even the most remarkable development."

"Why?" said Svetlana. "What else transpired?"

"Athgar and Natalia found a way to combine their magic to even greater effect."

"But they're from opposing disciplines of magic. Wouldn't their spells cancel each other out?"

"Couldn't you say the same about the family's desire to breed stronger mages?"

"I'll admit the concept of a Fire Mage and a Water Mage producing powerful offspring is counterintuitive, but history shows it works."

"Yes, it does," said Katrin. "But if we accept that, why is it so hard to believe they can combine their spells to greater effect?"

"How would fire and water even combine?"

"Imagine a waterspout that spits out flames and steam. I didn't see it with my own eyes, but the aftermath was devastating."

"Was it a linked spell?"

"No," said Katrin. "That technique only works when two casters utilize the same spell. No, this was something new."

"Magic has been around for centuries," said Svetlana. "Surely, if it were possible, there would be records of it?"

"You would think so, but I've seen nothing of that nature."

"Nor I, and our classes in the Volstrum certainly made no mention of it. How did they accomplish this arcane feat?"

"The waterspout spell is simple enough in theory, but Athgar found some way of heating the water to a very high temperature, thus releasing an explosion of steam. By all rights, it shouldn't have worked, yet hundreds witnessed it."

"And was this a spell they practiced?"

"No," said Katrin. "Natalia claimed it was Athgar's idea, and they cast it with little advanced warning."

"They must possess a very close bond."

"They do," interrupted Shaluhk. "It is not the first time they have done extraordinary things with their magic. Back in Ord-Kurgad, Nat-Alia stopped Athgar from immolating."

"That's impossible," replied Svetlana. "Once a Fire Mage reaches that point, they're as good as dead."

"Yet Athgar is here, in Carlingen, alive and well."

"And who told you of this?"

"I saw it with my own eyes."

Svetlana struggled to understand it all. "I knew Natalia was powerful, even back at the Volstrum, but this goes beyond everything we ever thought possible. Can you imagine what would happen if the family forced her to its will?"

"That will never happen," said Shaluhk. "She would rather die than submit to them."

"I'm beginning to see why the family has taken such an interest in her. She could rule over the entire Continent with that kind of power."

"It is clear you do not truly understand her. She would never do such a thing."

"Power can be a powerful motivator."

"Not to Nat-Alia. Family is important to her, not the wielding of magic."

"And how would you know?"

"She and I are tribe-sisters. You will find no greater friendship amongst our people save for bondmates."

"I envy you," said Svetlana. "You possess the very things I've always wanted—friendship and family."

"I'm surprised to hear you say that," said Katrin. "You expressed no interest in those things back at the Volstrum."

"It's true. I didn't, but I never understood what I wanted until I came here, and Maksim awakened my passion for life."

"I'm sure that's not the only thing he awakened."

Svetlana blushed furiously.

"We used to be friends," continued Katrin, "and good ones at that. I would have us be so again, providing you were willing?"

"I would like that."

"Then perhaps when this is all done, I'll remain here in Carlingen, along with Greta."

Svetlana smiled. "That would be wonderful."

"What would you do here?" asked Shaluhk. "Become an advisor to the king?"

"Perhaps," replied Katrin, looking at Svetlana with a wicked grin. "Are any of those barons of yours single?"

Temple Captain Darius stared across the table at the Temple Knight.

"Well, Brother Raban, anything to report?"

"Things are going well, Captain. More people join our cause every day, and we'll soon have the numbers we need to accomplish our objectives."

"And you're sure the king has no knowledge of our involvement?"

"No one could make that claim, sir, but I did everything in my power to keep all mention of the order out of it. If His Majesty does hear of our plans, I guarantee he will find no way of connecting it to us."

Darius feared he was treading on dangerous ground here, something far beyond the scope of his authority, yet he knew to do nothing would be unconscionable. If the Temple Knights of Saint Cunar were to regain their former glory, he felt he must take bold actions. And if that involved supporting the overthrow of a king, then so be it. It wasn't as if the royalty here in Carlingen had any actual ancestry tying them to the royal houses of the Continent. In the eyes of the majority of the Petty Kingdoms, they were nothing more than upstarts.

"Captain?"

Startled from his musings, Darius returned to the conversation at hand. "I'm sorry. You said something?"

"I was wondering, sir, when we are to take the next step?"

"It likely won't be for some time."

"Might I ask why?"

"The Army of Carlingen has yet to march south."

"And when it does?"

"Then we shall make our move."

PROBLEMS

SUMMER 1109 SR

I t was a day much like any other, the sun shining down from a cloudless sky, the voices of merchants hawking their wares drifting through the bakery's windows.

Zegota, busy kneading dough all morning, paused to wipe the sweat from her brow. She gazed out the bakery window, expecting to see familiar faces, but an angry mob marched down the street, yelling for the grey-eyes to go home as they took out their anger on anything close at hand. She was no Therengian, but she knew folk like that, caught up in the passion of their hatred, would care little for such distinctions.

One paused by the window, locking eyes with her. He snarled, then yelled obscenities, pointing at her. Zegota abandoned her worktable, fleeing into a back room and closing the door behind her as they charged into her business. She crouched against the far wall in fear, her heart pounding as the sounds of breaking furniture and smashed pots flooded through from the other room.

Someone pulled on the door, and she rushed forward to hold it shut. Whoever stood on the other side must have reasoned it opened away from them, so they kicked at it, eager to discover what lay beyond.

Zegota pressed up against it, adrenaline surging through her veins. Death was coming for her, and she could do nothing about it. Then the sounds beyond changed, and instead of shouts of anger, she heard fear, followed by what sounded like fighting. She closed her eyes, trying to will away the danger until the noises subsided. A light knock on the door startled her, and then a woman's voice called out.

"Is anyone in there? You can come out now. It's safe."

Zegota held her breath, too terrified to speak.

"I am Sister Carmen of the Temple Knights of Saint Agnes. I assure you the danger is gone."

Trembling fingers turned the handle, and then the door swung open revealing an armour-clad warrior of the Church.

"Thank the Saints!" Zegota sobbed.

The damage done by the mob was devastating, but thankfully, Captain Cordelia's Temple Knights had arrived in time to prevent the death of innocents. The instigators of the riot, however, had not fared so well, with two dead while another three nursed serious wounds. She glanced down the street to where the rest of the mob had fled. Lacking the numbers to pursue, she turned to helping those most in need.

The Saint's Army had started by attacking businesses run by Therengians but now targeted many parts of the city, including the merchant district. The cost to the shop owners would be high, possibly forcing some to shutter their doors permanently. Was this their intent?

From all reports, the people responsible for this carnage were religious zealots, yet their attacks seemed well-planned and executed. In each case, they came without warning, destroying people's livelihoods and fleeing before any city patrols could respond. Cordelia sought to counter this strategy by having her knights mount constant patrols, but the city was large, and a single company too few to make a proper effort. Today they'd been lucky, for whoever was behind this riot had not anticipated the quick response from her knights. She noted the approach of a familiar-looking Therengian leading a dozen armed warriors.

"Herulf," she called out. "I'm surprised you're here."

"We were patrolling the next street over and heard the sounds of conflict, but I see you have everything under control." He surveyed the damage, shaking his head. "This makes no sense. I understand them attacking the Therengian district, but why here?"

"My guess is they're trying to destabilize the city."

"I'm not sure I understand what you're hinting at."

"Think of Carlingen as being on the edge of a precipice. On one side are law and order, on the other, complete chaos. A slight nudge at a critical time could well determine the direction of our future."

"Are you suggesting someone wants the city to rise up against King Maksim?"

"That," said Cordelia, "is precisely what I mean. A mob has already marched on the Palace once, and it wouldn't take much to convince it to do so again."

"Agreed," said Herulf. "And I doubt they'd be willing to listen to Athgar and Natalia a second time. But who is behind this?"

"That remains to be seen, although I have my suspicions."

"Anything you'd care to discuss?"

"Not at present," said the Temple Captain. "I shouldn't like to make accusations without proof. In any case, I haven't the knights to investigate further. Our hands are full trying to keep the peace."

"Perhaps there is more that can be done."

"Such as?"

"The fyrd has sufficient numbers to patrol a wider area, but being on foot, we cannot respond within a reasonable time when word of these riots breaks out. I propose we work together. We patrol your section and our own, leaving your knights to form a quick reserve, ready to react to any trouble as it happens."

"The idea has merit, but we'd need some way of communicating where the problems might arise."

"Horns perhaps, or maybe bells?"

"That is easily arranged. We could also find volunteers on each street to sound the alarm when needed."

Herulf nodded. "The beginnings of a good idea, but within the city, it would be difficult to determine the exact location where the bells were ringing."

"Ah," said Cordelia, "but we could assign a specific sound to each region. Say two blasts of a horn for a particular set of streets, or ringing the bell three times, then pausing before the next set."

"It would be a lot of work to arrange it all."

"True, but it would be worth it to end this constant threat of violence. I can see about getting some bells from the temples."

Herulf nodded. "And I'll see what horns are available."

"When you have answers, come visit me at the commandery. In the meantime, I'll create a set of signals for each area."

Prince Beringar leaned back in his chair, sipping an ale. As was usual at this time in the afternoon, the tavern was nearly full, noise permeating the place. Not that it bothered him, for he listened in on all manner of conversations as everyone raised their voices, trying to be heard above the din.

The vast majority of folk were worried about the troubles in the city rather than their southern border, which pleased him greatly. He hadn't organized the so-called Saint's Army, but their activities made it nearly impossible for King Maksim to send any warriors south, giving Commander Rudger the time he needed to complete his search.

He looked up from his musings to see Raban enter, wearing the plain clothes of a commoner rather than the distinctive tabard of his order. Still, there was no mistaking the man's superior attitude or the promise of danger in his stance. It took only a moment for the Temple Knight to spot the prince, then he crossed the room and sat at his table.

"Glad you could make it," said Beringar. "I hope this is not too inconvenient?"

"What is it you want this time?" the Cunar snarled. "Has Lord Georgi changed his mind about seizing the Throne?"

"Would it matter if he had?"

"I've risked too much already."

"Ultimately, it is but a means to an end. Does it matter who rules in this Saint's forsaken land?"

"Are you mad?" said Raban. "You had me convince a Temple Captain to support this mad scheme of yours. Are you now preparing to toss him aside like an old boot?"

"Not at all," said Beringar, "but much is at play. While your order keeps the king busy here, my men are recovering the greatest treasure known to man."

"That was nothing but wishful thinking on Georgi's part. There is no banner, and likely never was."

"That is where you're wrong. It exists, and I am going to recover it. When I do, I shall seize my father's Throne and commence a campaign of conquest. You can be a part of that, too, should you wish. All I ask is that you do your bit and keep encouraging your captain."

The Temple Knight stared back, gauging the prince's sincerity. "Very well. I'll continue to support you in this, but I shall not take the blame should it fall apart."

"Meaning?"

"If Darius fails, he'll bear the consequences alone."

"And you'll advance to assume the position of Temple Captain, is that it?"

Raban grinned. "Someone has to, and I'm the senior knight."

Prince Beringar placed a pair of coins on the table. "I wish you well, my friend. Have a drink at my expense. I won't be remaining in Carlingen much longer, but perhaps I'll see you in Ostrova one day?"

"I look forward to it, Highness."

. . .

Sergeant Brauer stood at the door, his manner indicating the seriousness of the situation. A servant approached, bearing a tray overflowing with food, but as he reached for the door, the sergeant moved to block him.

"The king is not to be disturbed."

"I have his meal."

"He is meeting with Lord Thalmund of Adlinschlot and left strict instructions not to be disturbed for any reason."

The servant shook his head. "I don't understand His Majesty. Why has he surrounded himself with these outsiders? And now, here he is entertaining a baron in a drawing room, of all places. I tell you, it's just not right."

"Who are you to question the decisions of your king?"

The servant shrank back. "I meant no disrespect, Sergeant."

"Then I suggest you be on your way and keep your mouth shut."

The fellow proceeded down the hallway as fast as he could manage without spilling the food.

"I am sympathetic to your cause," said King Maksim, "but you know how dangerous the situation is here in Carlingen. I cannot afford to send men to your lands."

Lord Thalmund frowned. "Not even to secure our safety? I beg of you, Majesty, we need your help." The baron seized on the presence of the other guest in the room. "Perhaps Lady Natalia might give us her thoughts on the matter?"

"By all means, my lord," she replied, "but you've discussed a great many things. To which, in particular, do you refer?"

"That the king sends men to Adlinschlot."

"Listen, Thalmund," said Maksim. "I know you're having similar troubles to what we're seeing in the capital, but I can't send warriors I don't possess!"

"But you do have men, sire. All I'm asking for is a single company."

"They are being sent south to deal with the situation there."

"Surely the security of the baronies is of more importance?"

"It's not a matter of being important or not; it's a matter of numbers."

"Can you not simply raise more?"

"Such things take time, not to mention the added expense of equipping them, and were I to send you men, I would doubtless need to do the same for your fellow barons."

"Is that not your responsibility as king?"

Natalia cleared her throat. "You mentioned troubles, Lord Thalmund. Perhaps you might tell us what in particular you're referring to?"

"There has been resistance to change of late, especially amongst the lower classes, and some have taken it upon themselves to speak out against what they perceive as oppression."

"Can you be more specific?"

The baron wore a blank expression. "I'm not entirely sure what you're asking."

"Have they complained about specific instances of oppression?"

"I… can't really say."

"Surely you've talked to them? At the very least, you should have sent someone to hear their complaints?"

"I don't believe you understand our predicament, my lady. We barons rule by divine right; to question that is tantamount to treason."

"Divine right?" said Natalia. "King Maksim appointed you to the position of baron. Are you now suggesting your right to rule is based on your bloodline?"

"You are confusing the issue," said Lord Thalmund. "You wouldn't understand."

"On the contrary, I understand completely. My training at the Volstrum covered all manner of things, including how monarchs and nobles rule."

"Then you understand our right to rule."

"In order to rule, you must earn the people's acceptance."

"That's absurd."

"Is it?" said Natalia. "Even the most powerful of kings can be toppled if he mistreats his subjects. The Petty Kingdoms are full of examples of such things."

Thalmund jumped up from his seat. "I refuse to stand here and be lectured like this."

"Then don't," snapped the king. "You are free to leave if you are so inclined."

The baron's mouth flapped open a few times, but words escaped him. He finally turned, stomping from the room without saying another word.

King Maksim sighed. "The kingdom is falling apart."

"We are almost at the turning point, Majesty. I urge you to remain strong. The next few days will prove critical to the realm's future."

"That assumes I can keep the crown on my head! Have you heard what's happening out in the streets? Now it's spreading to Adlinschlot. How long, do you suppose, before my two other baronies suffer from this unrest?"

"Likely until we get to the bottom of it, sire."

"Do you know who is responsible?"

"We have our suspicions," said Natalia, "but no proof."

"Then tell me. You may not be able to act, but as king, I can do as I see fit."

"Even you cannot take on the Church, Majesty."

"The Church? Surely you're not suggesting they're behind all this?"

"Not the Church so much as the Temple Knights of Saint Cunar."

"This again?" said Maksim. "I understand your problems with them in the past, but now you're suggesting the entire order is corrupt."

"Is that so hard to believe?"

"They are the might of the Holy Army."

"And what does that do for you, Majesty?"

"They are the preeminent fighting order of the Continent!"

"So they claim," said Natalia, "but I might remind you they were defeated not once but twice. Their involvement here does nothing for you, sire. They neither offer you help nor render assistance in any way, and it's the same story across all the Petty Kingdoms. They say their mere presence is enough to keep enemies at bay, yet when has their order ever deigned to assist a king in need? I'll tell you when—never! You would be far better off to be rid of them."

"To do so would lose me the Church's blessings, and I doubt the general populace would be enamoured of that."

"You are working with the Temple Knights of Saint Agnes, and they hold a far greater sway over the townsfolk than their brother order."

"Still, I'd rather not press my luck."

"Are you aware of the friction between the two orders?"

"No! Why is this the first I'm hearing of it?"

"It was not our story to tell," said Natalia.

"Then why mention it now?"

"Because events are developing far more rapidly than we expected. The recent attacks in the streets are spreading to your barons, and the friction between the Cunars and the Agnesites will only make it harder to keep the city safe."

"What is the nature of this friction?"

"The Cunars claim the sister-knights were ordered to hand over control of their commandery."

"And what did Temple Captain Cordelia make of that?" asked Maksim.

"She refused. She will only pass over the keys if her grand mistress orders it."

"Can we ask the Cunars to leave the sisters alone?"

"I doubt that would work," said Natalia, "though perhaps there is another way."

"Which is…"

"If you officially recognize the Agnesite commandery as belonging to their order, it might convince the Cunars to withdraw their demands."

"I can't imagine that would do much. They don't respect secular law when it goes against their wishes."

"Still, it might buy us some time. Presently, we are assailed on all sides. The barons are begging for help, the streets of Carlingen threaten to fall into anarchy, and the family is breathing down our necks. To make matters worse, Prince Beringar chose this moment to bring his own demands. His timing can't be coincidental."

"Are you suggesting he's behind everything?"

"No, merely taking advantage of the work of others."

"Can we send Larissa Stormwind away?"

"We could," said Natalia, "but we must take care lest the family mark you as an enemy."

"But their influence is waning, isn't it?"

"Do not be deceived, Majesty. They still retain powerful allies."

King Maksim rubbed the arm of his throne, a sure sign of his worry. "Very well. I shall draft a Royal Proclamation recognizing the Agnesite claim to their commandery. With that out of the way, what do you recommend we do with Larissa Stormwind?"

"It might be best if Athgar and I kept ourselves away from court. You could then assure her you've remained loyal to the family and will follow through on their shipbuilding plans."

"And how do I convince her the time has come for her to leave us?"

"I'm not sure you could. Stormwinds can be stubborn, and she needs to redeem herself after her failure in Reinwick. In her eyes, that likely requires an extended stay to oversee the building of the fleet in person."

"Yet we have no intention of allowing that. Could I order her to leave?"

"You are the king, Majesty; she only remains here at your pleasure. Were you to press the issue, she would be forced to leave or else risk a diplomatic incident. Hardly the thing that would endear her to her superiors. The trick is devising a reason for her to leave that she wouldn't see as a mere dismissal."

"Yes." Maksim fell silent but kept glancing at the ceiling as if the view could grant him the answers he sought. He finally lowered his gaze to Natalia. "Larissa Stormwind claimed to represent the King of Ruzhina, did she not?"

"She did. Why? Do you think that might prove useful?"

"It might. According to Svetlana, there's reason to believe some animosity exists between King Yulakov and the family. Do you think that is true?"

"It's possible, though mostly speculation at this point."

"Then I shall write a letter to his court proposing a meeting between us. Unless I'm missing something, it would then be her duty to deliver it."

"A masterful stroke, Majesty. She'd have no way to refuse it without losing face. My only concern is the contents of the letter. If she were to deliver it, you must assume its contents would become known to the Stormwinds."

Maksim smiled. "I wouldn't have it any other way."

TEMPLE KNIGHTS

SUMMER 1109 SR

T he pouring rain drenched Katrin and Natalia on their way to the Commandery of Saint Agnes. Recognizing them, the guards led them inside, and they were soon in Cordelia's office, a hot cup of cider warming them.

"Not the sort of weather to be out and about," said the Temple Captain.

"It can't be helped," said Natalia. "I come bearing a proclamation from His Majesty, King Maksim." She handed over the ornate scroll case containing the document. "It recognizes that this commandery is the property of the Temple Knights of Saint Agnes. I can't guarantee it'll stop the Cunars, but it should give you some breathing room."

"I thank you for this, but that hasn't been on my mind lately. Rather, it's what's happening in the streets of Carlingen. I assume you've heard about the escalating violence?"

"We have, and so has the king. He decided it might be a good time for your order to expand its presence throughout the city."

Cordelia chuckled. "We already have."

"I'd have thought you'd wait for Royal Permission," said Katrin.

"Patrolling the streets has always been amongst our standard duties. Having said that, it's still nice to be given official permission."

"Well," said Natalia. "I can at least convey your thanks to him."

"You can do a great deal more than that."

"Now you're speaking in riddles."

"Not at all," said Cordelia. "I had a very productive meeting with Herulf only yesterday."

"About?"

"How to be more efficient in keeping the streets safe. We've arranged a way for folks to notify us when an attack is imminent. There are still some details to work out, and the entire concept is predicated on finding enough bells, but I believe it will serve us well."

"What do you know about the people responsible for all this madness?"

"Herulf and I reviewed the problems we've had of late regarding this Saint's Army and concluded they are highly organized."

"I agree," said Natalia. "Have you any idea how?"

"Several, but the most probable explanation is whoever is in charge has a mastery of strategy. Very few men could organize something like this while having the wherewithal to encourage others to march."

Katrin leaned forward. "What is it you're suggesting?"

"That they are well-funded. At first, I assumed it was the work of the Temple Knights of Saint Cunar, but they lack the coins necessary to get that many people out on the streets. Then I remembered the problems we had back in Caerhaven."

"So, you're suggesting the family is funding them?"

"It makes sense, doesn't it?" said the Temple Captain. "We already know there's a connection, and the Stormwinds are said to have unending funds at their disposal. Unless you're not telling me something?"

"No," said Natalia. "What you say is reasonable, but I can't see how. The family only recently learned of our presence here, and it would've taken months to set up something like these riots."

"Wait. Could there be someone else funding them? The Crown Prince, perhaps?"

"I find that difficult to believe. Much like the Stormwinds, he would've needed to plan it months in advance, unless…"

"Unless what?" asked Cordelia.

"What do you know of a man named Georgi Kulikov?"

"The name is not familiar. Why?"

"He was the former Baron of Raketsk. We discovered him abusing his power when we passed through here some months ago. When we informed the king, he ordered him arrested, but Kulikov fled, clearing his treasury on his way out."

"But to organize this, he'd still need to be in Carlingen, wouldn't he?"

"Not necessarily. He could have friends here acting on his behalf."

"To what end?"

"Come now. Is it so hard to see?"

"You're suggesting he has designs on the Throne?"

"Why not?" asked Natalia. "We know the corrupting influence of wealth, and by all accounts, he fled with a good deal of it."

"Wouldn't he be better served living out a life of splendour paid for by his ill-gotten gains?"

"Possibly, but the greater the riches, the greater the greed."

"You make a good point," said Cordelia, "but why work with the Cunars, of all people? What do they have to gain from an alliance like this?"

"Overthrowing a king is a difficult proposition, even here in Carlingen. Without a strong army, a usurper would soon succumb to the same fate as his predecessor."

"So this Georgi Kulikov fellow is relying on them to support his claim?"

"That's my guess," said Natalia. "It would also provide him with a disciplined and experienced force of warriors, important should he be forced to fight off others wishing to claim the Throne."

"Your argument is compelling, but the Church forbids interference in secular matters."

"Yet your own order has intervened in the interest of ending piracy, not to mention thwarting the invasion of Reinwick."

"Yes," agreed Cordelia, "but that's a far cry from overthrowing a rightful king."

"Is it? Captain Grazynia took sides in the recent troubles in Reinwick. Can you say this situation is any different? Perhaps the Cunar Grand Master supports Kulikov's claim to the Throne?"

"I doubt he even knows anything about the place. He's more likely busy in the Antonine, trying to disband our order." Cordelia hesitated, realizing she'd said too much. "I don't want you to think it's only us they're after; they want all the fighting orders disbanded, save for their own."

"Yes, you mentioned that earlier. Why do you suppose that is?"

"In light of recent events, I'd say they want to weaken us. You both know of the connection between the family and the Halvarian Empire. Would it surprise you to learn the Cunars have actively worked to reduce their garrisons in the west?"

"By west, I assume you mean along the border with the empire?"

"I do. Few know this, but their abandonment of Arnsfeld led to an invasion. Thankfully, the attack failed, but it's only a matter of time before the empire tries again."

"When was this?"

"Six years ago," replied Cordelia. "I'm surprised you didn't hear of it."

"I was too busy running from the family back then. Political events were of no concern to me."

"But you've travelled to Reinwick since then, haven't you?"

"We did, but there were more immediate problems for the duke to deal with, and events in the west are generally of little consequence to the rest of the Petty Kingdoms."

"A pity. If the kings of the Continent were more involved, Halvaria would never have grown to its current size."

"You said Halvaria was actually beaten?"

"Yes," said Cordelia, "by an army which included Temple Knights."

"I assume they were of your order?"

"We were present, yes, as was a contingent of Mathewites. I'm told they played a crucial part in the battle."

"And the results of this battle?" asked Natalia.

"The empire blamed it all on a rogue commander and retreated behind their border."

"And that's all that happened?"

"What else could be done? It's not as if Arnsfeld could afford to take the fight into Halvarian territory. Have you any idea how large the empire is? I doubt even the combined forces of all the Petty Kingdoms would be enough to carry out a campaign of that magnitude."

"Yet, that eventually must happen. Either that, or we all accept them as our rulers."

"I don't disagree with you," said Cordelia, "but I fear we're getting off topic. The events in the west are of little concern to us at this particular point." She locked eyes with Natalia. "While I appreciate you bringing this message from the king, I can't help but feel there's something else on your mind."

"Too much, if I'm being honest. The king is trying to organize an expedition south to stop Ostrova from infringing on his borders, but with all the trouble here, he can no longer afford to send any men to oppose them."

"So you're suggesting he give up the land?"

Natalia shook her head. "No. If necessary, I'll go south myself. A demonstration of my magic might be enough to persuade Ostrova to remain on their side of the border."

"I hope you're not asking us to send knights. The forest is not exactly terrain conducive to cavalry."

"I would settle for your commitment to helping the king here, in Carlingen."

"I can do that."

"Are you certain? It may bring you into direct conflict with the Cunars again."

Cordelia sighed. "Yes. It wouldn't be the first time our two orders stood on opposite sides."

"You speak of Ord-Kurgad?"

"No. Arnsfeld. The Cunars tried to block a company of our Temple Knights from travelling there. We've been on alert ever since. Well, those who've heard tell of it. It's not officially acknowledged, and I didn't hear of it myself until long after the events. I hate to say it, but a conflict like this has been brewing for some time."

"Could you beat them again?"

"We were lucky at Ord-Kurgad, but I can't guarantee that will hold true here. They are still the finest warriors on the Continent."

"Why would you say that?"

"Cunars are knights well before joining the order. Those who join us Agnesites learn to fight during training, while Cunars have been training nearly their entire lives." She shook her head. "Don't worry. It won't change our resolve in this matter. I just want you to understand what we're up against."

"The Cunars don't frighten me," said Natalia. "We've beaten them before and can do so again."

"And here I thought I was the one with a strong faith."

"I trained as a battle mage, so it comes with the territory. I also have insight into their weakness."

"Which is?"

"I can't speak for all Temple Knights, and I'll grant you those of Saint Cunar are well-trained and highly disciplined, but they lack the ability to see the overall strategy. An army is more than a collection of knights; it includes footmen, archers, and the proper use of magic."

"They have no mages," said Cordelia. "At least none we know of. Mind you, if they've been infiltrated by the Stormwinds, or the Sartellians, for that matter, it may not be an entirely accurate statement. What has the king got?"

"Footmen and archers, no cavalry. However, we are blessed in terms of mages, including myself, Katrin here, and Queen Svetlana, not to mention Shaluhk, who's a shaman."

"That's a Life Mage," added Katrin.

"Yes," said Cordelia. "I remember her from Ord-Kurgad. She was quite accomplished, if I recall."

"Indeed," said Natalia. "And her power has only grown since, but that will be of little help here when we're in the south."

"If the Cunars march on the Palace, it will take more than my Temple Knights to stop them."

"I rather feared as much."

"What do we do?" asked Katrin. "We're caught between a rock and a hard place. Leaving the king's men here will secure the capital while handing the frontier to the enemy, yet if we march against Ostrova, we risk losing the Palace."

Natalia gritted her teeth. "Then we'll need to decide which is the greater risk."

Agar set up the wooden figures, keeping them perfectly aligned. They were a gift from the King and Queen of Carlingen and represented Human warriors, each hand-carved. He was placing the last one when Oswyn rolled a ball, knocking over half of them. He looked over at her, and she giggled.

"It appears," said Kargen, "your tribe-sister is determined to defeat your new army."

"She does not understand battle," said Agar.

"And you do?"

"I know rolling a ball through the lines does not represent a defeat."

"It does if it's made of fire," said Athgar. "Perhaps it's Oswyn's way of representing magic?"

Agar looked down at the displaced figures and grunted. "Then I shall develop a new strategy to counter her magic."

Skora entered, carrying a tray of food. "Anybody hungry?" She set it down on a table. "It's not a full meal, but it should stop your stomachs from growling."

"Thank you," said Natalia. "Now, where was I?"

"You were saying the king needs to keep his men in the capital," said Shaluhk, "which leaves us nothing to take south. How do you propose we deal with the Ostrovans?"

"I hoped between us, we might find a solution."

"I can bring my hunters," offered Kargen, "but a dozen Orcs would be hard-pressed to hold off an army."

"Have you any spells we could use?" asked Stanislav. "We certainly have mages at our disposal."

"Yes, but not enough. Even if Svetlana accompanied us that only gives us three Water Mages, a master of flame, and a shaman. Individually powerful, but of little use against potentially hundreds of enemy footmen, not to mention archers."

"Oh, I don't know," said Belgast. "If we time it right, they'd be stretched out on a bridge."

"And how does that help us?"

"It's the key to this whole affair, don't you see? Destroy that bridge, and they have no way to cross."

"Not true," said Kargen. "They could use boats."

"You saw their base. Did they have enough boats to cross an army?"

"I would say no, but they could have built more."

"Possibly," said Natalia, "but Belgast has the right idea. The bridge is their weak spot. Destroy it, and we'd likely set them back by weeks."

"And how would we destroy it?" asked Shaluhk. "It will take more than a few fire streaks to make it unusable. Magic is powerful against individuals but weak against hundreds of opponents."

"Perhaps not," said Athgar. "What if Natalia called upon some of the magic from that book she got at the Volstrum?"

"It wouldn't work," said Katrin. "In Reinwick, the enemy was massed when she used that water spout. Here, they'd be stretched out along the bridge unless you think we could be there before they complete it?"

"The umaks are fast," said Kargen, "but I doubt they are fast enough for that. We must assume they have already crossed and established a camp on the north side."

"What is the terrain like in that area?"

"Heavily forested. They would need to cut down a lot of trees if they want to set up a camp."

"Is the terrain flat?"

"What is it you are thinking?"

"Natalia and I could try flooding the area. Svetlana, too, if she were present."

"Would that work?"

"I'm not sure," said Natalia. "We'd have to perform a linked spell. We've never tried that before, plus I have a hard time believing we could produce enough water to flood an entire camp. We're trying to defeat an enemy army, not just wet their feet."

"Is there another spell that might prove useful?"

"I shall give it some thought, but I can't think of any off the top of my head."

"What about Beorwic?" asked Athgar. "Could that be of use to us?"

"Yes," said Belgast. "Of course. We find the Banner of Aeldred first. That would guarantee us victory!"

Stanislav frowned. "You're not thinking this through, my friend. That's not the answer."

"Why in the name of Gundar would you say that?"

"If the banner is all it's supposed to be, why did the Therengians lose the battle? Besides, we don't even know if it's there. The victors could have carried it off."

"No," said Athgar. "I can't imagine someone getting hold of something that powerful and not using it. These are the Petty Kingdoms we're talking about!"

"Was there any sign of it when you scouted the ruins?"

"No," replied Shaluhk. "But we knew nothing of its existence."

"Wouldn't it make more sense for the survivors to have carried it off?" asked the Dwarf.

"You would think so," said Athgar, "but if the people of Runewald are the descendants of these survivors, where is it?"

"Yet the King of Ostrova is convinced it exists, assuming our assumptions are correct."

"We've gone over this again and again. What else could they be after?"

"Godstone?" suggested Stanislav.

"The likelihood of that is slim."

"Slimmer than a long-lost magical banner?"

"All right," said Athgar. "I concede the point, although you must admit the presence of that ruined city lends credence to the possibility of the banner's existence. If nothing else, it tells us how far east the Old Kingdom extended. I wonder, was it truly the last city of my ancestors?"

Stanislav shook his head. "I'm sorry, but none of us can answer that."

"Actually," said Shaluhk, "perhaps we can."

Belgast looked at her in surprise. "What is it you're suggesting?"

"Simply that if we returned there, I could talk to the Ancestors."

"You did that already," said Kargen. "We learned the city's name, but they said naught about a banner."

"True, but we knew nothing about it at that time. What do you think, Athgar?"

"It bears investigating, though not at this precise moment."

"Agreed," said Natalia. "We shall visit the place on our journey south."

"And when is that to be?" asked Belgast.

"That remains to be seen."

DECISION

SUMMER 1109 SR

Crown Prince Beringar entered the great hall, his footsteps echoing off the stone floor. He walked with purpose, his stride confident, while inside, he was a bundle of nerves. For years, he'd plotted this mad scheme, confident in its outcome, yet now, with its resolution so close, he had doubts. By all accounts, King Maksim was a weak ruler, easily manipulated, yet somehow, the fool had made some powerful friends. Even more concerning was the presence of Natalia Stormwind. Her reputation as a skilled tactician had spread, and hearing she was allied with the upstart Kingdom of Therengia was too much to bear.

He halted before the king, forcing a smile. "Your Majesty. I trust the day finds you in great health?"

"It does, Highness. Yourself?"

"Couldn't be finer, sire, though I fear the weather is a tad cooler than I would have liked."

"It comes from being on the coast."

"Have you given my father's offer any more consideration?"

"I have," said Maksim. "I cannot, in good conscience, accept it."

"Do you mean to say the terms are insufficient? If so, you are free to make a counteroffer."

"I find it difficult to believe your father wishes to negotiate a tract of land that is naught but wilderness."

Beringar shrugged. "He is of the opinion the area can be settled, the forest there providing wood in abundance."

"Yet your own lands are mostly uninhabited. If you desire forests, why not expand eastward? The wilderness there is full of trees with no other kingdoms claiming them."

"That would put us dangerously close to the emergent Kingdom of Therengia, Majesty. We harbour no wish to start a war."

"Yet you come here demanding my land!"

The Crown Prince took a deep breath, using the time to weigh his response. "I'm sorry if you saw it as such. My father's offer was made in good faith after careful consideration. His advisors met for weeks devising what they determined was a fair and just compensation. As I said before, if you feel it inadequate, you are free to counter with a larger sum."

"This has nothing to do with your coins," said Maksim. "If I cede this land to you, Braymoor would soon be knocking on my door demanding the same."

"Come now, sire. Braymoor is hardly in a position to threaten anyone."

"Nevertheless, a king who willingly parts with his lands would be seen as unworthy to wear the crown." Maksim tilted his head slightly. "Is that your plan here? To force us into rebellion, then annex the whole kingdom?"

Beringar drew in a sharp breath. Had his entire plan come to light? He struggled to find a way out of the situation. "I don't know what your friends from Therengia told you, sire, but we Ostrovans have some experience dealing with them. Since conquering Novarsk, they've made it abundantly clear they covet their neighbours' lands. Allying with them now will only make you subservient to their king's whims."

"He is not a king—he is High Thane, although I wouldn't expect you to understand the difference."

"King, Emperor, High Thane—the title matters not. He is the ruler of a kingdom seeking revenge for hundreds of years of oppression. First, they captured Ebenstadt, then the Kingdom of Novarsk, all in the name of securing their borders. Will there be no end to the growth of their empire?"

"I might remind you, Novarsk began the war that ultimately led to their own defeat."

"Can you blame them? They recognized the threat on their border and acted to defend their lands. What else could a monarch do? Remember, these are the same people who destroyed a Holy Army! Are we to sit back and ignore that?"

"A Holy Army bent on their destruction. You speak with such outrage, Highness, but I've yet to see your kingdom suffer. If you fear their growth, why are you not massing your army to invade them? Instead, you come here, trying to claim my lands!"

"Majesty, it appears my father underestimated the importance you place on your land. If you wish, I shall withdraw the offer and return home. I only ask that you consider your future."

"What's that supposed to mean?"

"Amongst the Petty Kingdoms, alliances shift and twist with surprising regularity. Those who guard your back now may one day be standing with a dagger in hand, ready to plunge it in."

"Is that a threat?" asked Maksim. He sat back, his face a mask. "I find it interesting you choose to visit me when my streets are falling into chaos, and pressures are mounting for me to build a fleet."

"I have no idea what you're talking about," said Beringar.

"Do not take me for a fool. I know you've been in contact with Larissa Stormwind and the Temple Knights of Saint Cunar."

"What of it? Am I not permitted to give my regards to a fellow envoy? And as for the Cunars, I merely paid my respects as befitting a follower of the Church of the Saints. Perhaps the question I should ask is why you had me followed?"

"I didn't. Your actions were reported to me by another interested individual."

"Let me guess, the High Thane, or was it the renegade Water Mage? They have their own agenda, Majesty, and wish to paint me as an enemy, but I assure you I am not."

"And what of your army massing in the south?"

The remark took Beringar by surprise. Someone must have leaked his plans, and now the entire enterprise was at risk. "Army, Majesty? I haven't the slightest notion what you're talking about."

"Come now. I have it on good account you are building a bridge into my territory."

"I assure you we're not."

"My people have seen it with their own eyes."

"I..." The prince lapsed into silence, struggling to extricate himself from this mess. He cleared his throat to buy time, then changed tactics. "If my father has massed an army, I can only surmise he is worried about an invasion."

"Invasion? From me? What nonsense is this?"

"Ostrova is a weak kingdom, Majesty, bordered by Carlingen and Therengia. You yourself admitted the two of you were allied, so it should hardly come as a shock that we have taken defensive precautions."

"I might believe that were it not for the fact there was no alliance until you arrived. There is also the matter of timing unless you claim the ability to communicate over great distances?"

"No, Majesty."

"Then how would your father have even learned of it? And more importantly, how would he have had the time to respond by massing an army and moving it to my border?"

"I'm afraid I'm at a loss to explain it."

"In the light of recent events, I think it best if you return home."

"And my father's offer?"

"Tell him I refuse. In addition, be sure to inform him any movement of his warriors into my lands will be considered an act of war and be dealt with appropriately."

"Dealt with?" said Beringar, his tone mocking. "You barely have enough men to hold on to your Crown, let alone stop an invasion. You should get down on your knees and beg for mercy."

Maksim stood, his guards advancing to take up positions between the two royals. "We are done here," he said. "I give you until nightfall to vacate the city."

The Crown Prince spun around and strode from the room.

Svetlana poured a goblet of wine, passing it to the king, whose hands were still shaking. Maksim sank lower into his seat, pushing his feet closer to the fireplace.

"I shouldn't have let him get to me."

"You did what you had to."

"Did I? Or did I make matters worse? What am I to do, Svetlana? My lands are in jeopardy, and my Crown is at a tipping point, yet I cannot act. If I send my warriors into the streets, the people will rise up against me, yet if I send them south to deal with the Ostrovans, I abandon the city to this so-called Saint's Army. I cannot see a way this ends well. Perhaps it would have been better for you if we had never wed."

"How can you say that?"

He took her hand. "I don't want to see you suffer the same fate as me."

"This is not fate," said Svetlana. "Things are not yet set on a path we cannot change."

"Aren't they? The Petty Kingdoms feared the rise of the Old Kingdom, and now that's come to pass. How long before the rest of the Continent falls under their dominion?"

"Therengia is not the kingdom of old. All they seek is to live their lives in peace."

"Peace? What does that even mean? I tried to rule peacefully, and what did it get me? Nothing. I would have been better off being a despot, ruling by force of arms."

"You did what you thought was best. Carlingen was always going to be a difficult place to rule, and you were not trained for it like your brothers. We are in a challenging position, but there is still a way out."

"If there is, I have yet to hear of it."

"I have an idea, but I'm not sure you'll like it."

"Go on."

"Keep your army here. Allow those citizens who wish it to rise up against you and then crush them."

"And become the type of ruler I so despise?"

"Not at all. I believe you still have the people's support, but there is a power behind this Saint's Army that will only be satiated by bloodshed. We must bring them out into the open to crush them."

"And what about the south?"

"I will see to that myself."

"You will? What is it you intend?"

"I shall take Natalia and the others to confront whoever commands there. Together, we might sway them from their course of action."

"And if you can't?"

"Then we shall unleash the full fury of our magic."

"As you're so fond of telling me, magic is powerful against individuals but does little against an army."

"Not so," said Svetlana. "An army is only as good as its leaders. Remove them, and the rest will fade away to nothing."

"I admire your confidence, but the trip would be dangerous."

"Then send a small contingent to keep us safe—twenty should suffice. Better yet, make them Therengians, allowing your men to stay here."

"Twenty men? To take on an army?"

"Even if you tripled the number, it would still be insufficient, and you need the majority of your men here, in the city. The expedition's goal is to negotiate directly with whoever's in charge, not go into battle."

"Negotiate, or kill?"

"Does it matter?"

"It does to me," said Maksim. "I won't have you throwing away your life on a suicide mission."

"Even if it secures your kingdom?"

"I will not have the kingdom saved only to rule it without you."

"Perhaps there is another way," offered Svetlana. "What if we found the Banner of Aeldred?"

"You think that possible?"

"The Orc shaman, Shaluhk, spoke to an ancient spirit. Could she not use the same magic to ask them where it may be hidden?"

"It's certainly a possibility, and once it's in your hands, you could bring it back here, where it would be out of reach of the Ostrovans."

"Yes, and with it gone, there would be no reason for them to want our land."

Belgast took a bite of venison, the juice dribbling down his beard as he chewed. Once he'd swallowed, he turned to his companion. "So it seems we have our answer. The expedition can finally begin."

"If that's what you want to call it," said Stanislav. "Considering how few are going, I'd be more inclined to refer to it as a forlorn hope."

"Come now. Natalia is powerful, as is Athgar."

"True, yet you and I both know such magic is of little use against an army."

"Svetlana's plan calls for them to find Aeldred's banner, not fight Ostrovans. If we do that quickly and efficiently, we can be in and out of those ruins before the enemy knows we're there."

"It all makes sense," said the mage hunter, "but things seldom go as planned. It might be a different story if we possessed more information about the current state of affairs in the south."

"On that, we can agree, but there's little to do about such things unless you're suggesting Natalia has a spell that might provide us with more information?"

"None that I know of."

"Ah well. I suppose we'll have to take it in stride and improvise."

"How many boats are you taking?"

"You mean 'we,' don't you?"

Stanislav shook his head. "I'm getting far too old for this sort of thing, and someone has to remain behind to look after Oswyn and Agar."

"Isn't that Skora's responsibility?"

"How can you even suggest that knowing how much energy it takes to look after those two?"

Belgast nodded. "Yes. I suppose that's true. You'll be sorely missed, though."

"I somehow doubt that. Still, you haven't answered my question. How many boats?"

"Kargen has enough umaks for us, but we'll need to rely on one of King Maksim's boats to carry the few men he's sending, not to mention the food stores."

"That will slow you down considerably," said Stanislav.

"It can't be helped. The ruins of Beorwic are likely to be extensive, with most of it covered by underbrush, making things even more difficult. Those extra men will help immensely."

"Yet not enough to dissuade the Ostrovans from interfering with the search should they discover you."

"You have the right of it, to be sure, but what choice is there? We can't very well find this banner only to return to discover the city overthrown."

They paused at the sounds of approaching footsteps.

"Athgar?" said Belgast. "Have you any news?"

"We're set to leave at first light tomorrow. The king's ship will meet us at the mouth of the river, and from there, we'll make our way upstream."

"And by we, you mean?"

"You know, the usual lot."

"Yet Stanislav here tells me he's not going? Are there any other absences I should take note of? What about Greta? Will she remain behind as well?"

"That would be Katrin's decision, not mine."

"But she's still a child," insisted Belgast.

"That might be, but she's got a good head on her shoulders, and I doubt Katrin would be willing to leave her behind."

"Any other surprises?"

"Yes," replied Athgar. "Svetlana will accompany us."

"The queen? Surely she'd be better off here?"

"She's acting on behalf of the king in this."

"You know, on second thought," said the Dwarf, "it might be best to bring the children with us. With the Saint's Army roaming around, it could be dangerous here in Carlingen."

"Danger is a curious thing," came Skora's voice as the old woman wandered into the room. "And as for Agar and Oswyn, they've been in danger many times. Don't worry. Lord Stanislav and I shall look after them."

"I'm not a lord," said the mage hunter.

"Of course you are. You're one of the three rulers of Ebenstadt. What else would you be?"

"Hah!" said Belgast. "She's got you there."

"I don't remember asking for your opinion."

"No, but I offered it anyway."

"'Lord' Stanislav does have a nice ring to it."

"I'm sure it'll impress Evira."

"Ah yes," said Skora. "The mysterious woman of Ebenstadt. When will you finally work up the nerve to ask her to marry you?"

The mage hunter blushed. "I've given the matter some consideration of late, but…"

"But what? Don't tell me you're too busy?"

"No, it's not that."

"Then spit it out, man."

"My last marriage didn't fare too well."

"That is no reflection on Evira."

"Perhaps I'm not up to it?"

"Nonsense," said Skora. "By your own admission, your first marriage failed because you spent all your time running around the Continent looking for Water Mages. You're more or less settled now, so it'll be a completely different experience. You love her, don't you?"

"I-I-I do."

"Well then, that's all that matters."

"It's a bit more complicated than that."

"You're making it more difficult than it has to be. Why, you're practically married already. You both live in the same house, and unless I'm missing something, you've even shared a bed on occasion."

Belgast smiled at Stanislav's discomfort. "You should know better than to argue with Skora."

"Yes. I suppose I should. Very well. I shall put the idea of marriage forward upon my return."

"You'll need to do better than that," said the old woman. "She's a living, breathing individual with a heart, not a piece of chattel to be bargained for."

"Pardon me?"

"A little romance wouldn't go amiss."

"What do you recommend?"

"Some nice words, perhaps a gift. Something to show how much you care about her."

"This is starting to sound a lot more complicated."

"And so it should. After all, you're committing to a lifetime together."

"Aye," added Belgast, "although at your age, that's likely not as long as it would be for others." He saw the pain in his friend's face. "Sorry. That one overstepped a little. I meant no offence. If anything, your advanced years should lend more of an immediacy to the entire concept. Why put off the one thing that brings you happiness?"

"That's what Yaromir keeps telling me. Why do all my unmarried friends keep telling me to ask for Evira's hand?"

"I can answer that," said Skora. "Your relationship with her represents their own dreams and ambitions."

"She's right," said Belgast. "You've found a nice woman to settle down with, while most of us fail to. We should be jealous but seeing you two together gives the rest of us hope there's someone out there for everyone."

THE EXPEDITION

SUMMER 1109 SR

Athgar stared back at the boats following in their wake. He and Kargen paddled in the lead umak while Shaluhk and Natalia watched the riverbanks for any sign of trouble. Immediately behind them was Urag, with Katrin, Greta, and Svetlana aboard. Next came the Orc hunters of the Red Hand, with Belgast somewhere in amongst them, swearing up a storm.

Filled with supplies and rowed by Therengians, King Maksim's ship brought up the rear. The vessel was slow compared to the Orcs' lighter boats, and it sat much lower in the water, forcing it to remain in the river's main channel.

"I hope the children will be safe," said Natalia. "Perhaps we should have brought them with us?"

"There might be fighting," replied Athgar, "and that's no place for younglings. Far better to keep them safe at the Palace."

"Even when rebellion threatens?"

"Don't worry. Skora will look after them, and if violence does threaten, she'll abandon the place."

"She was unable to stop Ethwyn," replied Natalia.

"True, but my sister was a Fire Mage. Besides, Stanislav is with them, not to mention Herulf, and he hand-picked the warriors keeping them safe."

"You worry too much, Nat-Alia," said Kargen. "Athgar has the right of it. The danger is far greater in the south."

"It is a mother's place to worry," said Shaluhk. "Perhaps we should discuss other things to keep our fears at bay?"

"A good idea," said Natalia. "Tell me, how have Agar's studies been going of late? Is he still meditating on his inner spark?"

"He is," replied the shaman, "though he grows impatient waiting for it to mature. I explained that it takes time, but he thinks he can will it into maturity."

"Human mages grow into their magic at about the age of thirteen. Do Orcs do the same?"

"It varies. I had a gift for healing in my younger years, but my magic did not come until well after my ordeal. Then again, Agar was engulfed in flames, much as Athgar was. That may result in him manifesting earlier than I did."

"I am fine with that," said Kargen, "as long as he does not set fire to the Palace while we are away."

Athgar laughed. "And it's all right if he does so while we're present?"

"You are a master of flame, my friend. You could easily extinguish the fire. Perhaps you should spend more time worrying about Oswyn, for she shows a capacity for both Fire and Water Magic. If she manifests as early as her mother, there could be no end of worry in your future."

"I hadn't considered that."

"I have," said Natalia. "I've also considered the matter of training mages. If Therengia continues growing, we'll need more wielders of magic. It's time we organized an active training program."

"I agree," said Shaluhk. "The problem is finding those capable of harnessing the arcane powers."

"Stanislav used to seek them out all across the Continent."

"Yes," said Athgar, "but he had the family's resources at his disposal. We, on the other hand, don't. Is there any way to magically detect such potential?"

"There is a spell," said Shaluhk. "The Human Life Mage, Aubrey Brandon, perfected it, but I have yet to learn it."

"Is it even possible to learn a spell over such a distance?"

"Yes, but I have only attempted it once. I shall speak with her at length once we return to Runewald."

"That would save us a lot of time," said Kargen. "In the past, it was often a… How do you Humans say it?"

"A guessing game?" offered Natalia.

"Yes. That is the phrase. Masters would take on an apprentice only to eventually discover they possessed no gift for it."

"I'm curious," said Athgar. "Just how many possess the potential for magic?"

"That largely depends on who you ask," replied Natalia. "The Volstrum taught us only one in ten thousand demonstrated the capacity for magic, but they had no accurate way of measuring that. We know it runs in the bloodline and can often skip a generation, but that doesn't account for those like you, who acquire their magic through extraordinary circumstances."

"It is rare amongst our people as well," said Shaluhk. "Most tribes only produce one or two spellcasters a generation."

"The Ashwalkers have at least five," said Athgar, "but perhaps they were all related. In any case, I've not done my part as a member of the Red Hand in training another master of flame."

"But you have," said Kargen. "You helped Agar with learning to control his inner spark."

"Yes, but he's years away from using it."

"Training mages is a lengthy process," said Natalia, "though I daresay in that regard, the method employed by the Orcs is far superior to the Volstrum's approach."

"I am surprised to hear you say that," said Shaluhk. "I thought your training was more complete than ours."

"Although I learned a lot about using spells in battle, the traditional approach of Humans has always been to have a firm grasp on magical theory before attempting even the simplest of spells. You, however, learn spells right from the start."

"It's true," said Athgar. "The first spell Artoch taught me was create fire, and I learned that soon after being taken under his wing."

"Yes, and he taught you his complete collection of spells in just over a year. Had you been sent to Korascajan, you'd still be learning the basics."

"I'm not so sure about that. Ethwyn trained there and was surprisingly skilled when she showed up in Runewald."

"There are exceptions to everything," offered Shaluhk. "Even amongst the tribes, some learn quickly, while others take months to master the simplest of spells."

"It was the same at the Volstrum," offered Natalia, "but they discarded those they saw as unworthy."

"Like Katrin?"

"Precisely. My approach to teaching magic would require a lot of patience."

"In the west, they created a school to train mages."

"Has it been successful?"

"It is too early to tell," replied Shaluhk. "They only just began instructing their first students, but I understand they are using the Orcish methods."

"What else can you tell us about this academy?"

"Not much, but my counterpart, Kraloch of the Black Arrows, is assisting. I shall endeavour to find out more the next time we speak."

"Good," said Athgar. "With a bit of luck, we'll eventually have dozens of mages at our disposal. Anything else we should be considering?"

"Yes," said Natalia. "The construction of a magic circle that would allow me to traverse great distances using the frozen arch spell. Had we one in Runewald, we'd have been home in mere moments."

"And miss all this fun?" asked Kargen with a grin.

With their progress slowed by the king's boat, nearly a ten-day had passed by the time they arrived at the great forking of the river. Although the river continued south, they needed to follow the western tributary.

Trouble arose almost immediately as the king's boat bottomed out changing course. The rest of the expedition halted while the Therengians jumped off to lighten the load enough to allow it to float free, then climbed back aboard, setting a man at the bow to watch for shallow waters.

As they headed west, the vegetation grew denser on the Carlingen side, branches occasionally reaching out to dip into the water. They camped ashore at night, posting pickets to warn of danger, but the wildlife proved no threat.

By Kargen's estimate, they were only a few days shy of Beorwic. They discussed their next move that evening as they sat by the fire.

"I suggest we take three umaks from this point," said Kargen. "Should the way prove clear, we send one back to fetch the rest of our expedition."

"A good idea," said Shaluhk, "but we should travel at night to avoid detection."

"You think the enemy found the ruins?" said Natalia.

"There is no way of knowing what they have been up to since our last visit, so caution is the order of the day."

"How far is Beorwic from the Ostrovan camp?"

"Nearly half a day's travel. A bend in the river allowed us to get close to their camp while it hid the ruins. Other than trees, the terrain is very flat in these parts, so unless they built a tower, we need not fear discovery."

"Unless they've sent out scouts on the northern bank."

"Yes," replied Kargen. "That is a distinct possibility, which means we must thoroughly search the area before setting up our campfires. The last thing we want is to alert them to our presence, which is why I suggested we take only ourselves and six hunters to ensure the way is clear."

"What of Svetlana and the rest?" asked Natalia.

"Considering none are trained hunters, it is best to leave them here with the remainder of our expedition."

"I'm not the stealthiest of individuals myself."

"True, but the power of your magic will be useful should we find ourselves beset by danger. You can also remain aboard the umak, where hunting skills are not required."

"I can do more than that. I can use my magic to propel the umak without paddles, making us quieter still."

"Hang on a moment," said Athgar. "Rather than all this sneaking around, what if there's a better way? Remember Ash Biter?"

"Who?" replied Kargen.

"A beaver Natalia communicated with. He warned us about the river serpent."

"I see no sign of beavers here."

"True," said Shaluhk, "but that does not preclude the possibility of some other water creature, such as an otter."

"Does your spell work on fish?" asked Kargen.

"No," said Natalia. "I can summon fish but not communicate with them."

"But you could call on an otter?"

"I can cast the spell, but I do not control what it summons. That's entirely dependent on what's in the area."

"Is the creature summoned always friendly?"

"Not necessarily, but just to be sure, I'd suggest waiting for morning."

"Makes sense," said Athgar. "Daylight would enable us to use bows if whatever showed up proved hostile."

The sun peeked through the canopy of trees to the east as they made their way to the riverbank. Kargen spread out his hunters, their eyes searching the forest, watching for any sign of predators. He, Athgar, and Shaluhk stood watch over the river lest Natalia's spell summon something aggressive.

For her part, Natalia waded into the water until knee-deep, then closed her eyes and spread her arms wide, a magical incantation pouring forth. Like the last time, the spell sounded soothing, almost like a lullaby, and Athgar fought off the desire to close his eyes and luxuriate in the words, despite having no idea what they meant.

He wasn't sure how long they stood there before a splash caught his attention. Something approached along the riverbank, occasionally stepping ashore to snap a twig. Then a thin, sinewy creature appeared, its brown back complemented by a lighter-coloured belly.

Natalia stopped, holding her hands out and kneeling as the otter approached, chattering loudly. She responded with more of the melodic words of power, the two of them talking back and forth for some time.

Once again, Athgar felt the pull of nature as if chatting away with such a creature were the most ordinary of things. Natalia stood up abruptly as the otter swam off upstream.

"Well?" said Athgar. "What did you learn?"

"Splash Paw talked about the great floating log spanning the river and that Humans were still working on it. I can only assume that means they are yet to finish the bridge."

"And are there men on the north side?"

"Most assuredly, though not in great numbers. She was also familiar with the ruins but said there have been none like us near it since the green-skins came some time ago."

"I assume she's referring to Kargen and Shaluhk's previous visit?" said Athgar.

"More than likely, yes. Unfortunately, she could not give me an exact count of how many warriors were there. The concept of large numbers is lost on creatures like Splash Paw. The good news is the Ostrovans don't seem particularly concerned about keeping watch, at least not so far as Splash Paw could tell. More than once, she snuck ashore and liberated some fish from what sounded like a bucket."

"Good," said Kargen. "It means we are less likely to be discovered. Did she indicate how far away the bridge is or these men on the northern bank?"

"There's a possibility some might be on the outskirts of Beorwic."

"So much for less chance of discovery."

"Still," said Athgar, "it's more information than we had previously. And now that we have a better idea of what to expect, we can all travel together, landing just east of the remains of the ancient city."

Kargen, Shaluhk, Athgar, and Natalia proceeded towards Beorwic while everyone else remained with the umaks, waiting for the king's ship to arrive.

They were soon amongst the ruins of the old city, the remains of walls poking out from beneath towering trees and underbrush. The roads ran in a square pattern, and Athgar tried to imagine what it had looked like at the height of its glory.

"It's immense," he said with wonder. "This place makes Ebenstadt look like a country village."

"It's likely bigger," replied Natalia, "at least in area, although I suspect most buildings were shorter. Therengians of old didn't generally like tall buildings. Those in Ebenstadt are from after the fall of the Old Kingdom."

"So, how do we proceed from here?"

"I shall contact the Ancestors," said Shaluhk, "but we must ensure we are safe before I do. The last thing I need is an Ostrovan patrol happening upon us while I use my magic."

"You once used a spell to check on Oswyn while she was in my womb," said Natalia. "Could such a spell work to find the enemy?"

"It would, provided they were close enough. The range is quite limited."

"And yet," said Kargen, "you possess all the memories of Khurlig. Might that not increase the range of your magic? It certainly made your warriors of the past more powerful."

"Yes, it did. Very well, I shall see what I can do." Shaluhk picked a relatively open area and began casting. Moments later, she opened her eyes, revealing glowing white orbs. She scanned the vicinity, twisting around to ensure she didn't miss anything. "Signs of life surround us, but none appear large enough to be Human."

"Then is it time to contact the Ancestors?"

"To ensure success, we should find the same spot as before. While we do that, the rest should split up and search the area. We don't want anything dangerous to stumble across us while I am casting."

Kargen stopped mid-step. "But you detected nothing of consequence?"

"Not true. I detected nothing Human-sized, but even small animals can be a threat. Do you not remember the snake bite you received as a youngling?"

"You knew about that?" said Kargen. "I thought my mother kept such things from common knowledge."

"Your mother was a remarkable Orc, but she could never resist telling stories of your escapades."

"And here I believed you only took an interest in me when I was older."

"You have always been a fascinating individual."

Athgar cleared his throat. "I'll take word to the others."

He disappeared into the trees, leaving Natalia with the two Orcs. "I can't imagine how much energy is required to speak with the Ancestors. Is it even more draining when they are from such a long time ago?"

"It is," replied Shaluhk. "My mentor, Uhdrig, taught me that the spirits of the dead weaken over time, which explains why those recently deceased are relatively easy to contact. As a shaman grows in power, she learns to locate those of a weaker nature, suggesting they have been in the spirit realm far longer."

"And the spirit you contacted here on your last visit?"

"He was bound to this place because he died here, but that occurred long ago. It took nearly all my power to make contact with him."

INTRUSION

SUMMER 1109 SR

Belgast looked up from inspecting the stone roadway to discover he was alone. Somehow, he'd wandered away from the Orc hunters accompanying him through the ruins.

He looked around, searching for any signs of them, but then the presence of an extensive circular structure up ahead distracted him. It reminded him of an amphitheatre, but the upper levels had long since collapsed, leaving little but broken columns and crumbling walls. As a Dwarf, he appreciated the beauty of stone, and if the remaining columns were any indication, far greater care had been spent on the construction of this place than any of the surrounding buildings.

A doorway beckoned, though its door had long since rotted away. Belgast stepped through to behold a magnificent sight. Concentric ledges ran around the inside of the structure, the debris from the upper levels filling the seats like an audience waiting for a play to begin.

The middle of the building lay far below the seating, allowing a great host to witness whatever had happened there, reminding him of stories about ancient Thalamites who were said to have put slaves into pits to battle for their lives. These ancient traditions were commonly believed to be the precursors to the jousting tournaments so common amongst the Human lands today.

He wrinkled his nose at the thought. His people rejected such notions, preferring to fight only when given no other choice. The mountain folk were not a numerous people, and to his mind, to throw away a life, any life, was a complete waste of potential. True, criminals were executed on occasion, but they'd broken sacred vows, something considered unconscionable in Dwarven society.

His gaze wandered back to the centre area, noting a statue of some sort. Hoping to get a better view, he'd gone no more than a dozen paces when he heard the crunching of feet on stone. He looked around, expecting to spot his escort of Orc hunters but instead noted the presence of a trio of men descending into the flat area, having come in from another entrance somewhere. Their armour indicated they were soldiers, but their ages suggested inexperienced ones.

Belgast dodged behind a pillar, eager to hide his presence, then tilted his head to the side just enough to watch as they continued on until they reached what he considered the fighting pit. There, they began making their way towards the other end, searching the ground as they went, occasionally stopping to toss aside a stone as if they were looking for something.

Was this the Army of Ostrova hunting for Aeldred's banner? He chided himself, for they hadn't come with him from Carlingen, so who else could they be?

His hand went to his pickaxe as he considered attacking. He knew he could take out one, or maybe two, but the third would most likely flee. The prospect of a fight wasn't what worried him, but if any escaped, they'd warn others and return in greater strength.

He looked back at his point of entry, but to reach it, he must climb up a few tiers, thus exposing his presence. All he could do now was remain in hiding and wait them out. Belgast cursed himself for his foolishness. Had he paid more attention, he wouldn't have lost his escort and been stuck here.

A crash of metal on stone rang out, and he peered from cover once more to see one of the warriors using a shovel to force up a paving stone. His two companions gathered round, but all three released an audible sigh of disappointment before continuing their search, bringing them closer to his hiding spot.

Belgast dropped to all fours to avoid detection, hoping the debris would obscure his presence. He wasn't sure how long he remained there, but his leg began to cramp and then spasm, knocking aside a small stone, and making enough noise to garner the attention of one of the Humans.

"Who's there?" the fellow called out.

The ridiculousness of the situation overwhelmed Belgast, and he almost stood up and yelled, "Me!" but came to his senses in time. Slowly, he drew his pickaxe, small by Human standards, but in the hands of a Dwarf, it could prove quite lethal. He looked around, searching for anything that would give him an advantage but saw nothing of use. His heart pounded at the thought that they might soon be upon him, but then a yell from the other side of the structure distracted them. Clearly, these men had not travelled here alone.

He raised his head, peering past the rocks to spot them passing by the statue, heading towards a fourth, wearing garb similar to their own. More importantly, they were moving farther away from his hiding place.

Something about the statue drew his attention. It depicted a woman carrying a bow, clearly an attempt to represent the goddess Tauril. Then everything fell into place. This was not an amphitheatre designed to entertain the masses. No, it was a place of worship to the goddess of the woods!

Belgast said a silent prayer to her and then made his way back to the entrance, promising to pay more attention to his escort in the future.

Shaluhk closed her eyes, calling on her inner magic to provide a conduit to the spirit realm. She felt the familiar tingle, then opened her eyes to apparitions floating around her. They were easy to see, yet at the same time, indistinct, as if their outlines were blurred.

The shaman kept up her spell as she called out in the Orcish tongue, "*Ungor!*"

A presence grew more distinct, taking the form of an ancient warrior wearing silver mail of Orcish design, the likes of which had not been seen amongst the living world for centuries.

He halted before her. "*We meet again, Shaluhk of the Red Hand. Why have you returned?*"

"*We come seeking your guidance, ancient one.*"

"*Then ask your questions, and I shall do my best to answer them.*"

"*We seek something called the Banner of Aeldred. Have you heard of it?*"

"*Yes. Our king, Eadwulf, carried it aloft at the last battle.*"

"*So, it does exist?*"

"*Very much so.*"

"*What happened to it?*"

"*It marched with the last host to face our enemies but was not enough to ensure victory. I am told it now lies at Tauril's feet.*"

"*And the people who once lived here? Where did they go?*"

"*Some were slaughtered by our enemies, while others fled using the arch.*"

"*Arch?*"

"*Yes. A trio of stones, with one set above the others, forming a gateway.*"

"*Standing stones? Here?*"

"*You are familiar with such things?*"

"*There is one close to our home. You say your people used it to escape?*"

"In our days of glory, the arches were used to traverse great distances."

"Then why are there not more scattered across the Continent?"

"As the kingdom collapsed, we destroyed those we could no longer secure, denying their use to our enemies."

"But they were ancient, were they not?"

"While it is true many predated the formation of Therengia, the most powerful of our mages studied them, eventually building ones of their own. They tightly guarded the secret of the stones, so much so that our mages died rather than reveal how they operated."

"And where did these arches lead?"

"All across Therengia. Doubtless, some remain, as does yours, for even the great mages of old could not destroy them all."

"Therengia has been reborn," said Shaluhk. *"A kingdom where Orcs and Humans live in peace and friendship once more."*

"It will not last," said Ungor. *"It is the fate of Orcs to be hunted by skrollings."*

"Skrollings? That's a Therengian term that means outsiders."

"What better way to refer to those who crushed our civilization?"

"And the banner, can it save us?"

"Only time will tell..." Ungor faded away, and the world snapped back into focus.

Kargen leaned forward, placing his hand upon hers. "Are you well, Shaluhk?" he asked in the Human tongue. "You are pale."

"I am fine."

"What did the spirit of Ungor tell you?"

"Give me a chance to take everything in. My mind is whirling." She glanced around at Athgar and Natalia, who watched with concern, but the Orc hunters guarding the place stared silently into the forest.

"The banner is here," she said at last.

"Any indication as to where?" asked Athgar.

"He said at the feet of Tauril, whatever that means."

"Tauril is the goddess of the forest. I don't suppose you could narrow it down a little?"

"I am afraid not," said Shaluhk. "He also suggested some survivors may have fled through a magical archway."

"Archway?" said Natalia. "You mean like my frozen portal spell?"

"Yes, but more permanent. His description sounded a lot like the standing stones back home. They were situated all across the Old Kingdom, but as they lost ground, they destroyed them rather than let them fall into their enemy's hands."

"Are you suggesting there's one here in Beorwic?"

"Unless they destroyed it like the others."

"This is certainly worth investigating." Natalia rose, her gaze wandering over the area. "The standing stones back home can enhance a person's magical power. If the same is true of this one, we should be able to sense it."

"Agreed," said Shaluhk, "provided we were close enough."

"Perhaps I'm missing something," said Athgar. "How do standing stones help us destroy that bridge?"

"Don't you see?" said Natalia. "It's much more than just the bridge. Based on what we've learned, those stones are the ancient equivalent of a magic circle, meaning I can use them to amplify my magic."

"Understood, but the bridge is still some distance away." Athgar rubbed his chin. "I think I'm beginning to understand. If those standing stones are like circles, Natalia can use them with her frozen arch spell, correct?"

"I assume so," said Shaluhk.

"Which would give us a way home," added Kargen.

"Not quite. Just like a magic circle, she has to commit them to memory. To do that, we have to travel back to Runewald."

"Yes," said Athgar, "but on the bright side, it makes returning here very easy. Did he say where the stones came from?"

"Ungor told me the mages of the Old Kingdom discovered the secret of their construction."

"Good enough for me. If they learned it back then, it can be learned again."

Greta yawned. "Somehow, I imagined this would be a little more exciting. All we've done is sit by the river and wait."

"Be careful what you ask for," replied Katrin. "Excitement often means danger, and we've experienced our fair share of that." She screamed as a figure emerged from the trees, then breathed a sigh of relief as she realized it was only an Orc. Beside her, Svetlana struggled to contain her amusement.

"We found the stone archway," said Urag. "It was so overgrown, we almost missed it."

Natalia looked up from where she sat. "Is it close by?"

"It lies at the easternmost extent of the city. I am afraid it will take some time to get there."

Shaluhk stood. "Nat-Alia and I will investigate while the rest of you stay here. Urag, take us to it."

The Orc hunter bowed. "It is this way."

"Hold on," came Belgast's voice as the Dwarf burst into the clearing, gasping for air. "There's a problem!"

"What kind of problem?" asked Natalia.

"I was out exploring the ruins when I stumbled across something. The architecture here is most interesting, but I found one particular building that quite took my fancy."

"Much as I'd like to hear your thoughts on such things, perhaps you should concentrate on this problem you speak of?"

"Yes, of course. The enemy is amongst us!"

"Our hunters have found no evidence of them," said Urag.

"That may well be, but I know what I saw, and four men are searching through the ruins as we speak."

"Where?" asked Natalia.

"Some distance to the west. At some point, I imagine it must have been the outskirts of Beorwic. I found the ruins of a circular building with a large statue in the centre of an open area. It reminded me of one of those round theatres. Do you know what I mean?"

"I do. There's one in Ebenstadt, though I fear it's not been used in decades. You say there were four men?"

"Yes. Warriors, by the look of them. I managed to escape, but I fear they may have discovered my presence." He looked around. "Where are Kargen and Athgar?"

"They took an umak upstream to scout out the bridge. They'll return by nightfall. What were these men doing?"

"Searching the area, digging up stones. If they're looking for the banner, they seem to believe it's buried somewhere."

"And so it is," said Shaluhk. "Likely in the forest."

"What makes you say that?"

"I contacted the ancient warrior, Ungor, who told me it lay buried at Tauril's feet."

"Then we must act with all haste," said Belgast. "That statue I mentioned is of the goddess herself. If what Ungor said is true, the enemy is close to finding it."

Shaluhk turned to the Orc hunter. "Gather the others. We must strike before they find what they are looking for."

"And the stone archway?" asked Urag.

"That will wait. Now be off with you. We have precious little time in which to act."

"What archway?" asked Belgast.

"A stone archway, similar to the standing stones back home."

"Here? In the middle of the forest?"

"Why does that surprise you?" replied Natalia. "Beorwic was once a thriving city. What better place to build such a structure?"

"Are you suggesting they built one themselves? I thought those things predated the Old Kingdom?"

"And with that belief, you would be in agreement with most of the Continent's scholars, but the mages of Therengia unlocked the secret of their creation."

"Is it still usable?"

"That we have yet to determine. We were about to go and see for ourselves, but then you showed up with the news our enemy is close."

"Is it of any use to us?"

"That remains to be seen," said Natalia. "Assuming it's similar to the one back home, it would act like a magic circle, enhancing any spells cast in the vicinity."

"How near would you need to be to feel its benefit?"

"Closer than we are now, or we would've already felt its power. While the stones are useful for enhancing spells, I suspect they have an even greater potential as a gateway for travel, though it would require far more time for me to discover how to use them in such a way."

Urag returned with the other hunters. "We are ready."

"Katrin and I will remain here and watch the umaks," suggested Svetlana.

Greta jumped to her feet. "What about me?"

"Oh no," said Katrin. "You're staying here, where I can keep an eye on you."

"Very well," said Shaluhk. "Lead on, Master Belgast, but quietly. With some luck, we might surprise these interlopers."

"We're close," Belgast said. "I suggest we draw weapons here. Those warriors may have expanded their search area." He drew his pickaxe, then moved ahead slowly, ensuring his feet didn't dislodge any loose stones. Urag spread the hunters out to either side, their warbows at the ready.

"Careful," whispered Natalia. "In the time it took Belgast to bring word to us, those soldiers may have reported back to their superiors. We could find ourselves outnumbered here." She spotted the Dwarf waving them forward. They crept up to Belgast, who'd crouched behind the remains of a wall.

"That building over there is where I saw them," he said. "At first, I took it for an amphitheatre, but the inside has these thick columns obstructing the view. Then there's the statue of Tauril sitting in the middle."

"And you're sure it was Tauril?"

"She was sculpted with a bow. I know of no other god that would be depicted thus, do you?"

"Could it have been an Elf?" asked Shaluhk.

"No. The ears were round, not pointed. Besides, I've seen enough statues of her to know."

"I did not think Dwarves worship the goddess of the woods."

"We pay homage to all the Gods, though Tauril is not the sort of deity you pray to very often when you live in the mountains. We tend to spend more time thanking Gundar, our creator. Of course, he doesn't answer like your Ancestors do."

"They say the Gods lead in mysterious ways," said Natalia, "but now is not the best time to discuss such things. I might remind you the enemy is near."

"Yes, of course," said Belgast. "My pardon." He tightened his grip on his pickaxe as he scanned the ruins. "Follow me." He crept out from behind the cover of the wall and advanced, his head darting back and forth, looking for any signs of danger. He paused near the remains of a doorway, its sides towering over him.

Another wave brought Shaluhk and Natalia closer while Urag and his hunters continued fanning out to the sides.

"Is there any other way out?" whispered Natalia.

"I assume so. Those soldiers got there somehow, but they didn't go past me." He poked his head out into the open, peeking through the opening.

"Blast it!" he shouted, no longer trying to remain silent. "They spotted me!"

SKIRMISH

SUMMER 1109 SR

Greta stooped to fill the bucket, only to be interrupted by Svetlana. "There's no need for that. Here, hold still."

The Queen of Carlingen drew upon her power, the bucket growing heavier as crystal-clear water filled it to its brim.

"Handy spell, that."

"It's nothing," said Svetlana. "Creating water is one of the first spells we learned at the Volstrum." She smiled. "No. I tell a lie. Stilling water was the first, followed by freezing it."

"What was it like, going to all those classes?"

"Exciting, yet at the same time, terrifying. Everything was so new and different."

"But you came from a magical family, didn't you?"

"I did, but my parents didn't spend much time with me."

"Why is that?" asked the girl.

"It is not the Stormwind way. You see, having children was a way to serve the family. My father was a Stormwind, my mother a Sartellian, but they were much too busy to concern themselves with child-rearing, so servants raised me."

"At least you had someone who loved you."

"Did I? I sometimes wonder. I used to think I was better than everyone else. I was a high-born, one of the elite families of Karslev. My future should have been guaranteed, yet the family wouldn't even consider breeding me."

"But that's a good thing, surely?"

"I didn't think so at the time." Svetlana squinted downriver. "Where is that boat? It should be here by now."

"It likely hit another sandbank," said Greta. "I hear the river is full of them." She regarded her older companion. "Now that you're queen, I suppose you'll have children of your own."

"There's a lot to consider."

"You don't want children?"

"Oh, I do, but I don't much fancy the idea of the family showing up and demanding I send them off to the Volstrum."

"But your kingdom is allied with Therengia now. Surely Natalia wouldn't allow them to do something like that?"

"Having allies is not a foolproof way of ensuring safety. Look at her and Athgar's experiences. The family has come for their daughter on numerous occasions. I'd hate to think the same fate might await my child."

"They wouldn't dare," said Greta. "Any child of yours would be a royal. Something like that could cause a war."

"You're very astute for someone of your age. Have you ever considered becoming a courtier?"

"I've seen enough of court to last a lifetime, so I'll stick with helping out Katrin. How did you two get along back at the Volstrum?"

"We were good friends for a while," said Svetlana.

"Only awhile?"

"I developed an irrational distaste for Natalia due to her low-born status. I know now it was ridiculous, but I'm afraid my upbringing was very strict on such things."

"And Katrin befriended her, thus betraying you?"

"That's how I saw it at the time. We all make mistakes, Greta. The important thing is not to let them define you."

A twig snapped, drawing their attention to Katrin walking up along the riverbank.

"Any sign of the boat?" asked Svetlana.

"Yes. They got hung up on some reeds, but they're free of them now. They'll be here shortly, and then we can set up a proper camp."

Boots thudded on the stone tiles, and then a soldier appeared in the doorway, his sword drawn. Belgast didn't wait, taking the fellow in the stomach, his weapon penetrating the man's leather jacket, digging in until the head of it scraped up against the spine. The soldier fell forward, almost yanking the pickaxe from the Dwarf's hand.

Natalia stepped into the opening, targeting the first she saw with a streak of ice, but the fellow dove behind a pillar, narrowly avoiding an icy death. When a crossbow bolt came out of nowhere, she jumped back, once more out of the line of sight.

"How many did you see?" asked Shaluhk.

"Three, maybe four, but my view was restricted."

"Are you injured?"

"No. Thankfully, their aim was bad."

Shouts arose from within the ruins, and then a trio of men came from around the side of the building. Shaluhk called upon warriors of the past to protect them. The ghostly visages took form, and their mere appearance was enough to convince the enemy to abandon their planned assault. The Ostrovans quickly disappeared behind the building, their shouts of triumph turning to ones of dismay.

Belgast risked another look through the doorway. The object of Natalia's ice shard remained, nearly hidden from view. "This one's mine," he said, rushing in.

Natalia readied another spell before following, prepared to lend a hand should it be necessary. She glimpsed the Dwarf disappearing behind the pillar, then all she heard were the sounds of weapons striking each other.

Belgast let out a grunt before staggering back from the fight. At first, she thought him injured, but then his opponent stumbled forward, falling face-first onto the ground.

"That was harder than I expected," said the Dwarf.

"You didn't need to fight," said Natalia. "My spell could have dispatched him."

"It's not the fight that did me in; it was the rush to get to him. Dwarven legs aren't made for sprinting."

Orcish shouts of victory echoed in the distance.

"It is done," said Shaluhk. "They have all fled."

"Perhaps," said Belgast, "but they'll return."

"How can you be so sure?"

"Those men will take word back that we've come here, which confirms they're searching in the right spot. They didn't come all this way to abandon the hunt now."

Natalia led them through the doorway, down to the tiers where the statue stood. "That is definitely Tauril. Where did you say the banner was supposed to be?"

"At her feet," said Shaluhk, moving up beside her tribe-sister. She dug her toe into the ground near the base of the statue. "It appears there is a stone floor beneath all this dirt."

"Let me see," said Belgast. He squeezed past them, falling on all fours and using his hands to brush away the accumulated years of dust and dirt. "Just as I suspected—a tiled floor. If we dislodge the right one, I imagine we'll reveal a small hiding place. At least, that's what I'd do if I were trying to hide something like the banner. How big did you say this thing is supposed to be?"

"I did not," said Shaluhk. "It was not something I asked from the spirit."

"Still, it was meant to be carried into battle. That means it's a considerable size. Not much point in flying a flag if no one can see it. What do we know of Therengian flags? Anything?"

"I believe they would have hung it from a cross beam," said Natalia. "These days, the Petty Kingdoms use a simple flagpole, but it was common to hang them vertically back then."

"Well, these folks would've been in a hurry, and the flag itself is what's valuable. They likely stuffed it into a box before burying it to prevent it from rotting."

"How big would a box like that be?"

"That's hard to say," said Belgast. "Was the flag made from linen or something heavier?"

"If it's empowered with magic, as we suspect, it has to be made of something more valuable than simple cloth."

"Such as?"

"Silk would be my guess."

"Ah yes. That would make it easier to hide."

"Making it more difficult for us to find."

"Not at all. It's likely in a small box, which means they could have easily hidden it under one of these tiles. The question now is which one."

"The one directly under Tauril's feet," said Natalia.

"Yes, but did that particular turn of phrase refer to the one she's standing on? If so, we'll need to move the statue."

"I doubt that is the case," said Shaluhk. "They lost a battle and were preparing to evacuate the city. They needed to bury it quickly, so they had no time to move a statue." She crouched, tapping the tile directly in front of the figure's feet. "This is where we should dig."

"Say no more," said Belgast as he hauled back on his pickaxe and struck down. The tip barely made a scratch, careening off to one side and slipping from his grasp. He jumped away, eager not to be hit by his own weapon. "Yes, well. Best let me try this another way." He retrieved his pick and, placing it carefully between two tiles, used a leveraging action to raise the stone at Tauril's feet. Natalia and Shaluhk reached out, grasping the edge and hoisting it upright, but beneath it was naught but dirt.

"Don't worry," soothed the Dwarf. "That's to be expected." He knelt again, using his hands to dig away at the soil until his fingertips scraped wood. "Aha! I've found something."

Together, they dug around the object's edge, unearthing a rectangular box about a forearm in width and twice that in length, with an animal head carved into its top.

"A stag," said Natalia. "I believe that was the symbol of Aeldred."

"An interesting choice," said Belgast. "In heraldry, a stag represents someone who won't fight unless provoked. From what I've learned about the man, it fits him perfectly."

"As it does my husband. Let's open this box and see what's inside, shall we?"

"Let's get the box out of the ground first. I shouldn't like to set off any sort of trap."

"You think they'd do that?"

"I would if I were hiding something this valuable, but I can't speak for those of the Old Kingdom. Better to be careful, if you ask me."

"Very well."

They used their hands to excavate all around the box. In short order, they lifted it from its hiding place and put it on top of another tile.

Belgast carried out a thorough inspection before pronouncing it safe. "There is a lock here," he warned, "but nothing I can't handle. Shall I open it, or do you want to wait for Athgar?"

"Best open it now," said Natalia. "I don't know how long we've got before those Ostrovans return in greater numbers."

"Very well. Stand back." He lifted his pick, quickly bringing it down onto the lock with great precision, shattering the hasp. He then held his breath and opened the box. Inside lay a folded, green piece of material shimmering with light as if engulfed in the sun's rays.

"Remarkable," said Shaluhk. "I can feel its magic."

"As can I," added Natalia. "It must be very powerful indeed."

"Shall I pull it out of the box?" asked Belgast.

"Yes, of course."

He unfolded it, revealing a golden embroidered stag head that matched the one on the box. The flag was so large that it almost touched the ground as Belgast held it aloft.

"Remarkable," he said. "I've never seen it's like. It hardly weighs a thing."

"Likely due to its magic," said Natalia.

"Can you tell what kind of magic it has?"

"Not the exact spells, at least not without further study, but whoever made this was accomplished. See the gold thread—it's what holds the spell's power. In magic circles, they often use runes of gold to hold on to the magic."

"Hold on to the magic?"

"Yes, allow it to build up as the mage casts her spells. It's called spell amplification."

"Like the standing stones?"

"The stones have no gold, so they must rely on some other technique."

"Such as?"

"That's just it," said Natalia. "We don't know."

"But magic has been around for thousands of years."

"Yes, but despite constant study, there is still much we don't understand."

"How can that be?"

"The Volstrum considers itself the foremost authority on the subject, but in some ways, the Orcs are more advanced in their understanding of the arcane arts."

"I'm surprised to hear you say that," said Belgast.

"Humans are, for the most part, obsessed with power. The Stormwinds and the Sartellians both stress the channelling of vast amounts of arcane energy, yet more is not always better. Artoch taught Athgar to use a more measured approach, a technique I myself have adopted to great effect. There is also the matter of mastery."

"Mastery of what?"

"The Volstrum wants us to master the elements, whereas the Orcs teach us to respect them, which is, at the fundamental level, a superior approach."

"Does that mean Orcs are more powerful casters?"

"They can be," said Natalia. "Shaluhk is the most gifted shaman I've ever met, but it's more than just raw power. Students at the Volstrum take years to master their craft, while Orcs complete their training in far less time."

"All this is fascinating, but it's not safe here," said Belgast. "We should take this back to camp." He looked down at the hole in the ground and smiled. "I have an idea."

"Which is?"

"Give me a hand replacing this tile. No sense in telling them we've found what they're looking for."

"The box too," suggested Shaluhk. "If they discover it is empty, they might assume it was lost long ago."

"It's worth a try. Now, help me with this flag."

They held the banner with great reverence as they folded it, then Shaluhk took it while the other two placed the box back in its hiding place.

"Will it fool them?" asked Natalia.

"It should," replied the Dwarf. "I doubt a warrior would take the time to look for details like freshly dug dirt. In fact, there's a good chance they may not find it. After all, they haven't got an ancient spirit guiding them." He chuckled as he kicked some dirt overtop the box.

"You find something amusing?"

"I was just imagining someone digging this up centuries from now and finding it empty. What would they think?"

"Likely that the legend of the banner was little more than a myth. History, however, will show them otherwise."

"You mean to use it in battle?"

"Well," said Natalia, "perhaps battle is too big a word. Skirmish might be a little more appropriate."

"And if we defeat them?"

"You mean when."

"Yes. Very well, when. What happens after that?"

"I'm not sure what you're asking."

"It's quite simple," said Belgast. "Once this trouble is… let's call it resolved, what happens to the Banner of Aeldred? We found it in Carlingen's territory. Does that make it his, or do we claim it for the Old Kingdom reborn?"

"To be honest, I haven't given it much thought. Until now, we weren't even sure it existed, and we have no idea of its powers."

"Still, it would be a shame to waste it on such a small army."

"Waste it?" said Natalia. "We are not about to launch a campaign to subdue the Petty Kingdoms."

"True," said Belgast, "but aside from this current mess, I can't see anyone else threatening Carlingen. Therengia, however, has an entire Continent united against us, not to mention the Church."

"Hardly the entire Continent. The Northern Alliance, as it's now called, has recognized us. Others will soon."

"Still, you can't deny we're looked upon by distrustful eyes."

"And you think this banner can change that?"

Belgast shrugged. "Probably not, but we can dream, can't we?" He mulled things over as he filled in the hole with dirt. "You know, the mere possession of it could be enough to get us some help."

"Help?"

"Yes. If I were to take word to Kragen-Tor, the king might see fit to send a company of warriors. Who knows, he could even include some arbalesters. Now that would be a sight to behold."

"I doubt the mere possession of the banner would induce him to commit warriors to our cause."

"You never know. Stranger things have happened."

"How far away is Kragen-Tor?"

"It sits astride the northern side of the Grey Spire Mountains, along the southern border of Zalista. With the recent acquisition of Novarsk, we're practically neighbours. A treaty of defence with Therengia would be just what the King of Kragen-Tor needs. We only need convince him of it."

"Who is the current king?"

"You know, I'm not entirely sure. The last I knew, Lord Farin Greybeard succeeded Haglarith, but he was old when he took the Throne."

"And if he died, would his son rule?"

"Not necessarily," said Belgast. "Dwarven Lords pick their own successor, and they're not always a blood relative."

"Why is that?"

"They choose someone they feel will continue ruling in a similar style, not upset the ore cart by making changes." He slipped the stone tile back into place. "There. All done. Now, let's return to camp and meet up with the others, shall we?"

STANDING STONES

SUMMER 1109 SR

Kargen crouched in amongst the reeds. "I know the water is cool, yet I do not feel it. This spell of yours is most remarkable."

"Don't get too comfortable," replied Athgar. "It won't last forever, and though you don't feel it now, your wet clothes will have you shivering on our way back."

"It would not be the first time that has happened to me, nor, I suspect, will it be the last. I have often gone hunting in winter only to discover the ice was not as thick as I thought."

"You should be more careful. Something like that could lead to you freezing to death."

"Orcs do not feel the cold as you Humans do. Though it is unpleasant to be embraced by icy water, it is not the death sentence it seems to be for your race. Then again, a Human is less likely to fall through the ice due to their weight."

"One more difference between our two peoples."

"And yet we are united by our common goals," said Kargen.

"We are, which brings me to the bridge." He nodded upriver where the Ostrovans had constructed a floating bridge, using boats to support it. These, in turn, were anchored by ropes fore and aft to prevent them from drifting. It spanned the entire river, yet more work needed to be done, for men were still laying planks along the outer edges to allow the passage of wagons.

"It is well-guarded," said Kargen, "and we lack the numbers for a direct assault. Could your magic destroy it?"

"I could set it on fire, but I doubt that would do enough damage to destroy it, not when the water is so close. Mind you, fire in the right places would certainly dissuade them from crossing. Do they have any mages?"

"Shaluhk and I saw no sign of them amongst their camp, but that was some time ago. What about Nat-Alia? Does she have a spell that could destroy it? You talked of her using a water funnel in Andover. Would that work here?"

"I used my magic to heat it to steam, but it would do little to wood."

"Would it not injure the enemy warriors?"

"Yes, but the bridge represents a long and narrow crossing point. The spell wouldn't have the reach to affect more than a handful, hardly the force of destruction we need in this instance. We might have better success going at it with axes."

"Getting close enough to do that without raising the alarm would be very difficult. Could we swim to the boats and cut away the securing ropes?"

"No," said Athgar. "If they raised the alarm, we'd be easy targets. We'll have to think of something else."

"We have a little time. From all appearances, there is only a small force on the northern bank, enough to guard one end but not enough to threaten our position back in Beorwic."

"Agreed, and they have yet to cross any horsemen, which also works in our favour. How long before they're ready to send more men across?"

"I do not think them in any rush. From their point of view, there is little to threaten them aside from wild animals. However, if they discover our presence, they may accelerate their plans."

"If they do that, there's not much we can do to stop them."

Kargen nodded his agreement. "We should return to our camp. I will send three of my best hunters to watch the bridge and report back on any activity. In the meantime, let us take our concerns to the others and see if we can think of a solution."

"It would've been easier if we'd brought some of the king's men."

"True, but they were needed back in Carlingen. There would be little point in recovering the banner if we lost the capital."

"Assuming we even find it," said Athgar. "This whole expedition may prove fruitless."

"You must have faith, my friend. If the Banner of Aeldred is here, Shaluhk will find it."

Urag slowed. "The standing stones are ahead, nestled within those trees."

Natalia proceeded cautiously, trying to avoid tripping in the thick underbrush, while Shaluhk, occasionally using her knife to clear the way, appeared unfazed, as if cutting her way through such obstacles were the most ordinary thing imaginable. "I can feel it," she called out. "Can you?"

"Yes," replied Natalia. "The hairs on my arms are standing on end. I wonder if the stones are somehow responsible for all this growth?"

"That is something I had not considered, but it makes sense. The most logical person to create such a structure would be a master of earth, and we know from experience that kind of power affects nature."

"No. There's more to it than that. I'm sure of it."

Shaluhk pushed through the forest into a small clearing where two immense stones sat on the ground. She looked up at a smaller one lying horizontally across the top of the others, forming an archway half again as tall as her. All three were covered in moss and ivy, hiding them from those who did not know what they were looking for.

"Impressive," said Natalia, coming up beside her and laying her hand on a stone. "This pulsates with energy like the one back home."

"I did not feel anything," said Urag.

"Likely because you possess no inner magic."

"Shall I remain while you examine it?"

"No," said Shaluhk. "I would have you go and seek out Katrin and Svetlana. Their thoughts on this would be most appreciated."

"They were waiting on the supply boat," said Urag, "but I expect it to have arrived by now. I shall return with them."

He disappeared back into the woods, though Natalia and Shaluhk were far too engrossed in their discovery to pay much attention.

"There are runes on the stones back home," said Shaluhk.

"This likely has them, too, but we must clear away some of this growth if we hope to find them."

"It is a pity we did not bring one of the Stone Crushers. They could make short work of it. Once cleared, will you be able to understand how this place works?"

"I believe so," said Natalia. "The language of magic is common to all races. Runes are a manifestation of the chants required to unleash the magic. The trick is putting them in the right order to accomplish the desired effect. In that sense, this is a glorified magic circle. Simply by casting a spell, a mage taps into the stored magical potential of the place..." Her words trailed off.

"Is something wrong?"

"I seem to recall reading something back at the Volstrum years ago. All across the Continent are places where magic is stronger. I asked Mistress Tatiana about it once, and she said it was due to something called 'ley lines.'"

"I believe Lady Aubrey has referenced those on occasion," said Shaluhk. "She said they are lines of magical energy crossing the entire land."

"Yes. They run north-south, carrying immense amounts of power."

"Not only north-south. Our friends to the west believe other lines cross east-west. The power is greatest at the point where these lines meet. They used the term 'nodes'."

"That would certainly explain why they're all over the Continent, or at least they were. It is thought that many amongst the Petty Kingdoms saw them as pagan worship sites and destroyed them. However, your recent discovery indicates the Therengians were the ones who did that."

"Well, at least this one survived," said Shaluhk, "and one other, which means there may be more that avoided destruction, just waiting to be redis-covered. Who knows, perhaps we can unlock the secret of their construc-tion as the Old Kingdom did. Athgar certainly seems to think it possible."

"I know it's possible to create a magic circle. I even know the spell to do so, but it requires a lot of gold to imbue the magic it needs to operate. However, with this"—Natalia glanced at the stones and shrugged—"we have no idea what holds the magic in place."

"If this truly is a magic node, then gold is unnecessary. The power is already there, deep beneath the surface."

"Yes. That makes sense. It's a good thing you're here. I never would've thought of that myself."

"You would have come to that conclusion eventually," said Shaluhk. "You just needed time to ruminate on it."

"If you're right, these standing stones would be placed at the points where the ley lines intersect."

"Yes, and that explains why they built Beorwic amidst a thick forest. That would also infer they knew some way of detecting the ley lines."

"Most mages can detect magic. I wonder if that would work?"

"There is only one way to find out." Shaluhk began casting, letting the magic build inside her. After completing her spell, she stood perfectly still, a gasp of shock escaping her lips.

"I assume the spell worked?" asked Natalia.

"It did indeed. An intense glow infuses the ground surrounding the stones."

"Remarkable."

"I suspect this raw power would be added to any spell cast in its vicinity."

"I imagine so," said Natalia, "for that's precisely the effect magic circles have."

"Yes, but the magic here is likely much more powerful."

"I have brought them," called out Urag.

Katrin waved as she approached. "The supplies finally arrived, so we thought you might like to join us for something to eat." She slowed as she entered the area. "Is this what you were looking for?"

"Yes, it's a magical archway," explained Natalia, "like the one back in Therengia."

Greta cocked her head as she moved closer. "Very interesting."

"Careful," warned Svetlana. "We don't know what it's capable of."

"Oh yes, we do," said Natalia. "It's a funnel for magical energy. You remember learning about ley lines at the Volstrum?"

"Vaguely."

"Well, our friends to the west discovered they run in two directions. The points where they intersect are called nodes and hold great power."

"Friends in the west? You mean Reinwick?"

"No," said Shaluhk. "She talks of those in Merceria, a land on the far side of the Great Halvarian Empire."

"And how would you know all of this?"

"Our shamans have been in contact for years through our magic."

Svetlana stared back, struggling to understand the ramifications of such power.

"I like it," said Greta. "Who built it?"

"Mages of the Old Kingdom," replied Natalia.

"How do you know that?"

"Shaluhk spoke to an Ancestor who lived here long ago."

Greta moved closer, placing her hand upon a stone.

"Remarkable," said Svetlana. "And to think it's been here all this time without us realizing it."

"Hardly surprising," said Natalia. "The capital is far too distant to detect anything of this nature."

"Yes, but fortune seekers have been coming to Carlingen for centuries. It's remarkable no one ever discovered this."

"Who says they didn't? To an explorer, this part of the forest is no different from any other save for the ruins, and even they yield little of value to a treasure seeker."

"Yet the banner is here, somewhere, isn't it?"

"Indeed," said Shaluhk. "Would you like to see it?"

"You found it?"

"It is in my satchel." Shaluhk opened the flap, displaying the green silk held within.

"I must say, it doesn't look very remarkable. Are you sure it holds magic?"

"Very much so," replied Natalia. "It becomes more apparent when it's unfurled. I suspect it holds several enchantments."

"A pity," said Svetlana. "I hoped it might benefit those of us with Water Magic."

"It was designed for a battlefield—hardly the place where our skills can be put to best use."

"Then what does it do?"

"We're not exactly sure. We haven't had much time to examine it." Natalia was about to say more but noticed Greta hugging one of the stones. "Whatever are you doing?"

"I can feel it vibrating," replied the girl. "It's almost as if there's water running on the other side of it."

Natalia looked at Shaluhk. "Do you realize what this means?"

"Yes. Greta appears to possess the potential for magic, though I have no idea which type."

"Identifying magic potential is difficult at the best of times," said Svetlana. "That's why the Volstrum employed so many mage hunters to travel the Continent investigating rumours."

"If I'm magical," said Greta, "can you not use a spell to confirm it?"

"No," said Shaluhk. "Well, there is, but we do not possess it."

"There is?" said Natalia. "I've never heard of one."

"I have been told that in the spirit realm, a person with the potential for magic will emit a unique aura that identifies the element in question. A master of fire, for example, would display a red aura around them."

"So you could identify the magical school for potential mages?"

"In theory, yes, but from what I know, only Human Life Mages can see these auras. Orc eyesight, while superior at night, is unable to make out the subdued colours."

"Let me guess. You learned this from Lady Aubrey?"

"Of course," said Shaluhk. "No other Human has ever travelled the spirit realm. At least none we know of."

"Could you not take someone into the spirit realm with you?" asked Greta.

"I could, but it would not impart the ability to see the magical aura. As far as I know, only the caster of the spell can do that, and it requires the knowledge of what you Humans call Life Magic."

"She is an Enchanter," offered Urag.

They all turned to the Orc hunter.

"What makes you say that?" asked Shaluhk.

"Logic indicates a potential master of magic displays some affinity for their inner power, does it not?"

"It does, but I fail to see how that applies in this instance."

"I have heard she finds her way around the Palace easily, despite its confusing layout. Could that not be seen as being indicative of an Enchanter?"

"I suppose it could," replied Shaluhk, "though I have little knowledge of that particular branch of magic."

"I know all about what Enchanters can do," said Natalia. "The Volstrum saw to that, but how you would go about identifying one is beyond me. If Stanislav were here, he'd likely have an idea."

"How?" said Svetlana. "He spent his time hunting down Water Mages."

"True, but he often turned the discovery of other potential mages into some extra coins. I suspect he'd have some idea of what to look for."

Athgar poked the fire. "It seems the time has come to make some decisions."

"Now that we found the banner," said Svetlana, "I propose we attack the bridge and burn it."

"We haven't the numbers."

"Then we'll send word to King Maksim. I'm sure he'd provide us with more men."

"He can't," said Natalia. "Like it or not, they're needed in Carlingen to put down any signs of revolt. I'm afraid we're forced to deal with this with what we have."

"Let us look at our strengths," said Kargen. "We have the Banner of Aeldred and those standing stones to channel magical power. In terms of numbers, we have twelve hunters, twenty Therengians, and a few extra men to oversee the king's boat. When it comes to magic, we're very strong, with three Water Mages, a master of fire, and a shaman."

"Our strength definitely lies in our magic," said Athgar. "The tricky part is figuring out how to leverage that."

"A direct assault on the bridge is unwise," offered Natalia. "Their archers would prevent us from getting close enough to damage it."

"We could try luring them away," said Urag, "which would allow our spellcasters to get closer."

"That might do the trick, but what magic would we employ? Athgar is the only one capable of setting the bridge alight, but I doubt even his power is great enough to destroy it. As for us Water Mages, there's little we can do."

"Ice shards?" suggested Athgar.

"Useful against warriors, but not much use against something so large."

"Perhaps we could float ice downriver to damage the bridge?"

"While we could freeze the water," replied Natalia, "I doubt it would be enough to damage the bridge."

"You used it to great effect against pirates down near Corassus."

"I did, but that was a ship. The bridge here is much larger, and if you recall, all I did was freeze it in place."

"Well," said Belgast, "we can't just pack up and return to the capital. King Maksim is depending on us. I say we stop fearing their archers and attack the thing! If they rain arrows down on us, then so be it!"

"That's it," said Natalia, a grin spreading across her face. "Rain!"

BATTLE

SUMMER 1109 SR

The stones sat silent despite the life thrumming within them. Once they finished clearing away the moss and ivy that covered them, the sheer number of runes revealed surprised Natalia.

"Remarkable," said Svetlana. "Though I fail to see how this can help us defeat the Ostrovans."

"These stones will make our spells more powerful."

"I understand that, but this is miles from the bridge. I know of no spell we could use here to affect such a distant target."

"Wait," called out Katrin. "What about that book we rescued from the Volstrum? Does it have anything that might be of use?"

"You stole a book?" said Svetlana.

"She did—one hidden in the Inner Sanctum filled with spells only the most powerful mages can cast."

"And has it one that would be useful to us?"

"No," replied Natalia.

"Then why are we wasting time here, at these stones?"

"It occurs to me we might yet be able to use them."

"How? By your own admission, there is no spell useful to us."

"Then I must invent one."

"Invent one? Don't be absurd. It takes years to perfect a new spell."

Natalia turned to her old classmate. "Svetlana, that's what they taught us at the Volstrum, but I've recently realized that such is not always the case."

"What are you implying?"

"Simply that in the west, where they are not forced to abide by strict rules set out by such institutions, they forged a new path, one which I am happy to follow."

"That doesn't make any sense."

"Magic is all about manipulating the energy residing within us, and we know the combination of magical words gives a spell its unique characteristics. What is to stop us from doing so in new combinations?"

"But there would be no way to predict the results? Only a Wild Mage would attempt such folly!"

"I've learned much during my time with the Orcs. We Stormwinds claim to understand magic, but our logic is flawed. Each word invokes a particular element, and most of our spells start with the same phrase."

"Of course they do," said Svetlana. "We practice Water Magic. What else would they begin with?"

"Yes, but you fail to grasp the meaning of the words that follow."

"And you think you do?"

"Perhaps not completely, but I know enough to destroy that bridge."

"How?"

"By making it rain."

"Rain?" said Katrin. "Is that all? I doubt the Ostrovans will be bothered much by getting a little wet. In any case, even if they were, we don't know a rain spell."

Natalia smiled. "Come now. We all learned how to create water; it was one of the first spells we mastered."

"Agreed, but that's a far cry from making it rain."

"Is it? The concept is the same."

"Even if we could," said Katrin, "the three of us lack sufficient energy to produce more than a drizzle."

"Ah, but then you wouldn't be considering using the stones. This archway is more than a magic circle—it's a direct funnel into raw power. If I can tap into it, we can bring a storm the likes of which hasn't been seen for centuries."

Svetlana shook her head. "Don't be ridiculous. There's no way you could control that much magic!"

"I must try. Or are you eager to give up your husband's kingdom?"

"No, of course not."

"I'm in," said Katrin. "How do we start?"

"For this to work, we must collectively create enough magical energy to direct the power skyward."

"And how do we do that?"

"You've heard of linking spells?"

"Of course," said Svetlana. "We learned about that back at the Volstrum but were never taught how."

"I'll show you. It's easier than you might think."

"If that's true, why wasn't it shown to us?"

"I imagine the family feared someone would use it against them."

"But how did you learn it?"

"I first witnessed it in Corassus," replied Natalia. "The pirates there used Air Mages to calm the wind, stranding their prey. It got me thinking that I might be able to do something similar. Of course, back then, I had no other Water Mages with which to work. It wasn't until Athgar and I combined our spells in Andover that I truly understood how to combine magic."

"So what do we do?"

"I shall show you both a slight modification to the basic spell of creating water. You'll then target me, and I, in turn, will direct it towards the stones."

"And that's all there is to it?"

"As far as casting goes, yes."

"But?"

"We are dealing with magical energy on an unprecedented scale. Once this spell begins, it may prove very difficult to stop."

"You're afraid it might consume us," said Svetlana. "That's always a danger when dealing with such things."

"Yes," added Katrin. "We need someone to warn us."

"I can do that," offered Greta. "What do I do?"

Katrin looked at her ward. "You must watch us for any signs of injury."

"Injury? I don't understand. How do you get injured casting spells?"

"Mages draw on energy that exists within, but a finite amount is available each day. If we exceed that reservoir, the magic draws on our physical bodies. Such injuries usually manifest as nosebleeds, though sometimes the blood comes from the ears or even the eyes. If it continues for too long, it can cause internal bleeding, leading to death."

"And if you start to bleed, then what?"

"Then you must do what you can to interrupt the spell."

"What if I were to fetch Shaluhk before you begin?"

"Clever girl," said Natalia. "I should have thought of that myself. Yes. Get her while I teach Svetlana and Katrin how to link spells."

"And the others?"

"You'll need to explain to Athgar what we're about to attempt. It'll be his and Kargen's responsibility to keep the Ostrovans pinned down on the bridge."

"Why?"

"So that when the river crests, we can eliminate as many of the enemy as possible."

"And how long will that take?"

"I'm afraid I can't say for sure. In effect, we'll be building storm clouds, but to create enough rain to flood the river, we need to channel an extraordinary amount of power."

"But the bridge is upriver."

"It is," said Natalia, "yet there is no chance of causing flooding if we create only a small cloud. Instead, we must use the power of the ley lines to unleash a torrent of rain. As far as I know, such a thing has never been attempted before. Thus, we cannot predict how long it will last."

"So they are to keep them on the bridge forever?"

"Not forever. Tell him to watch the sky. That is the best indicator."

Greta ran off, eager to help.

"Can this even work?" asked Svetlana.

"Trust her," said Katrin. "Anything's possible after what I saw her do in Andover."

Kargen peered out from behind the tree. "It appears they are not expecting us. That is a good sign."

"Yes," agreed Athgar, "yet at least one survived the attack at Tauril's statue. I thought they'd have been alerted to our presence."

"The ruins of Beorwic are some distance away. Could something have happened to them?"

"I can't say. Do we know how many escaped?"

"No, though we suspect at least two. I would suggest they perished in the forest, but little is there to cause them harm."

"Then we must assume they've given warning."

"You suspect this is a trap?" asked Kargen.

"If it is, it's an ill-conceived one. More likely, they dispatched men to Beorwic."

"And left this place less defended?"

"Our people never actually saw those survivors. That likely means they have no idea who attacked them. Whoever is in charge here is either stretched to the limit or has very bad judgement. Let's hope it's both." Athgar nodded at the bridge. "They have more men working on it now than when we were here earlier. They appear to be in a hurry to complete it."

"Perhaps they received word about the Therengian Army massing on their southern border."

"It's certainly been long enough, and if that were the case, they'd want to hurry up and find the banner."

Kargen shook his head. "I still do not understand the need for this bridge. I would send boats if I were looking for something like the banner. After all, it is only a flag."

Athgar stared at the monstrosity of wood. "You make a good point, but what if they have something else in mind?"

"Such as?"

"An actual invasion?"

"They would need to traverse a thick forest to get to the capital."

"Yes, but if the city was already in a state of unrest, there would be no opposition. They could send a new ruler ahead with a small group and bring up the remaining army later to instill order."

"Are you thinking of someone in particular?"

"Yes, Kulikov."

"That makes it even more imperative we succeed here."

"My thoughts exactly." Athgar sought out Athelstan, the young Therengian from Carlingen who'd been eager to fight. "You know what to do?"

"Yes, Lord. We move out of the trees and form a line with the banner behind us."

"Now remember, you're not to fight, merely to draw them towards you."

"I will do as you command, Lord." The young man ran back to join the Therengians.

Athgar looked at Kargen. "He's enthusiastic."

"He wishes to please you," replied the Orc. "You have that effect on people."

"Are your hunters ready?"

"Need you ask?"

Athgar looked skyward at the gathering clouds, a sure sign Natalia's magic was building. "This had better work," he muttered, then rose from his hiding place and strolled onto the flat area the Ostrovans had cleared. Athelstan's men followed, forming a ragged line behind the High Thane of Therengia. He ordered the banner unfurled, waiting for the inevitable cries of alarm.

The Ostrovans were a diligent lot, occupied for the most part by the business at hand, namely finishing the bridge. A bucket boy who'd fetched water from the river and was making his way towards the northern end of the bridge was the first to notice the interlopers. A shout of alarm escaped his lips, and then he dropped his buckets and ran for the safety of the bridge.

It didn't take long for others to realize what was happening, and then the workers rushed for the weapons they'd laid aside while they laboured.

Athgar kept a close eye on the enemy yet saw no sign of archers. Fifteen men took up a position in front of the bridge, blocking access to it while others rushed to lend what assistance they could. He knew once the numbers swelled, the fighting would begin.

He heard murmurs behind him. "Hold your positions," he called out. "They are not a danger to us, but our time will come." An unusual sense of pride grew within him, and he wondered if it was due to the banner's presence. He risked a look over his shoulder to see it hanging limply in the still air. Even so, it glowed with an inner light, making his heart soar. He imagined legions of the Old Kingdom marching to their assistance, their axes gleaming in the brightness of day.

Common sense took hold. There would be no help. They would succeed or fail based solely on the actions of those present this day. He glanced again at the sky to see the clouds darkening, feeling the first raindrops on his face.

The enemy grew bolder, with a line of thirty men now in front of the bridge while someone yelled at them to advance.

"Here it comes," said Athgar, waiting as the enemy approached. Slowly they came, and then the neatly ordered line became a mob as some keener than the rest rushed to engage the small group of Therengians.

The first arrow took the lead man in the chest, and he pitched forward, almost tripping the person behind him. Arrows kept coming from the forest, and six more fell under their onslaught. Kargen's hunters picked their targets carefully, using their warbows to great effect. The attack stalled as the survivors fell back, leaving the wounded calling out in agony.

"We won!" shouted Athelstan.

"It's not over," said Athgar. "They'll be back, and in greater numbers."

The rain began in earnest, drowning out the cries of the wounded. Athgar's cloak did little to keep him dry from the unrelenting deluge of water. He considered using a spell of warmth, but to do so would expend a portion of his inner spark. Better to preserve it for the fight that would soon come.

Whoever commanded here likely saw the rain as a blessing, for any archers would now be at a significant disadvantage. Sure enough, the Ostrovans advanced, this time with more than double their previous numbers.

Arrows flew from the shoreline, striking down a few in the front rank, but others quickly filled their places, the advance continuing as they rushed forward to engage the line of Therengians.

Athgar stepped back, taking up a position on the right flank, then threw out his arms, sending a streak of magical fire directly into the enemy. The individual he struck fell back, the flames quickly disappearing in what was fast becoming a torrential downpour.

The noise of the rain striking helmets and armour overshadowed the sounds of fighting. Athgar, now face to face with a swordsman, quickly parried with the handle of his axe while simultaneously sending a wall of flame bursting forth from his left hand. His opponent backed up in a panic, but the fire did little damage.

A few Ostrovans attempted to push out on the flank, but Kargen's hunters picked them off with carefully placed arrows. Athgar saw two of his men go down—one fell face-first into the mud while another lay on his side, screaming as he clutched his blood-soaked stomach, but the Therengians held their line.

Athgar struck out, his axe digging deep into his opponent, and then the enemy was on the retreat again, limping back to the relative safety of the bridge.

Kargen appeared at his side. "How much longer?"

Athgar looked skyward but could see little, so fierce was the storm. "Let's get under cover of the trees. No sense is getting any wetter than we are."

"What does it matter? We are already soaked."

"True, but the ground here will soon become a quagmire. I'd rather the enemy have to deal with that than us."

Georgi Kulikov stared across the river, the heavy rain obscuring his vision while he remained dry beneath his canopy. He noted the approach of Commander Rudger. "You have news?"

"Yes," the commander replied. "We've run into a little opposition on the north bank."

"What do you mean, 'opposition'? You said no one was in the area."

"And so we thought, but a small group of men now blocks our way."

"Then crush them."

"Easier said than done, Lord. They have archers armed with powerful bows."

"How powerful?"

"Enough that they can puncture our armour with ease."

"And how many are there?"

"Difficult to say. Some report thirty, while others swear it's less than ten. Such is the confusion of battle."

"Battle?" the baron sneered. "This is no battle. Send over more men and sweep them aside."

"I might remind you the bridge is not yet complete."

"It looks good enough to me."

"That may be," said Rudger, "but the engineer urges caution. If we put too much weight on it, we risk it collapsing."

"And if we don't, we risk losing any chance of crossing the river. Order two companies forward, Commander, or I'll inform the Crown Prince you failed in your duty." Kulikov noticed Rudger clenching his jaw. He was a typical warrior, more prone to caution like those sycophants in the Ostrovan court. Still, the baron knew he must work with what he had. "Win this day," he continued, "and you shall be covered in glory!"

"Very well, my lord, but the enemy may have more men concealed in the woods. If I am to commit to this, I'll send enough to guarantee victory."

"That's the spirit."

Commander Rudger stepped back into the downpour, shouting orders. The sound of rain striking the canopy soon drowned out his voice.

The baron grinned in anticipation. All it had taken were a few words of encouragement. The men of Ostrova would flood across the bridge, and all opposition would melt away. He imagined himself in Carlingen, marching in triumph towards the Palace. Once the Throne was his, he would mete out revenge on those who'd slandered him. A new age was about to be born —the reign of the Kulikovs!

CARLINGEN

SUMMER 1109 SR

Oswyn stood by the window, staring outside.

"What are you doing there, girl?" said Skora. "You should be getting ready for bed."

"I'm looking at the pretty lights."

"Lights? What in the name of the Gods are you talking about?"

The old woman moved closer, pressing her face against the cool glass. They had a good view of the city, though there wasn't much to see at this time of night. From their perspective, the rooftops were little more than a dark smear with the odd lantern glinting back at them.

Agar moved to stand on the other side of his tribe-sister, following her gaze. "I see them too," he said. "Off to the east."

Skora squinted, but her eyes were not what they used to be. "It's probably nothing. Just a group of warriors patrolling the streets."

"Those are not lanterns," said the Orc youngling. "They are torches and lots of them. It appears trouble is on the way. We should alert the king."

"Very well. Let's get your cloak on, Oswyn. There's a chill in the air this night."

"I will take care of her," said Agar. "You should fetch your own cloak while there is still time." Skora went into her room to gather her things.

Agar knelt before his tribe-sister, the better to keep her attention. "This may get dangerous, Oswyn. Have you the bow and axe I gave you?"

"I do," she said. "They're in my room."

"Then go and fetch them while you can."

Skora reappeared, narrowly avoiding a collision with the young girl. "Here now, where are you off to?"

"She is fetching her weapons," said Agar.

"Surely you're not suggesting she fight at her age?"

"No, of course not, but they are the only things of value she has here in Carlingen. It will serve to keep her attention focused."

Oswyn returned, the axe in one hand, her bow clutched firmly in the other.

Agar gently took the axe from her, tucking it in her belt. "Now remember," he said. "You must listen carefully. This is not a game. Do you understand?"

"I do."

"Good. Hold on to Skora's hand and follow me."

He opened the door, then jumped back in surprise at the figure in the hallway.

"Sorry," said Stanislav. "I was just about to knock. I assume you saw the torches?"

"We did," said Agar. "We must inform the king."

"Already done. I ran across one of his guards on the way here. Their orders are to assemble in the great hall. I suggest we do the same."

"Wait," said Skora. "What about that other Stormwind? What was her name, Larissa?"

"What of her?"

"She's still here, isn't she? Can we trust her?"

"Likely not," said Stanislav, "and I don't much fancy the idea of running across her in the Palace halls."

A yell came from down the hall, and Stanislav dived into the room, knocking Agar aside as ice shattered against the door frame.

"Close that door!" shouted the mage hunter.

Agar moved quickly, slamming it shut and pressing his back against it to prevent it from opening.

Skora dragged a chair over. "Here. Use this to jam it shut."

The door shuddered as something struck it, frost forming on the inside.

"Lucky us," said Stanislav. "It appears we've located our missing visitor."

King Maksim stepped out of the Palace, his men lined up across the street, ready to block the fast-approaching mob. He spotted Sergeant Brauer and made his way over to him. "How are the men?"

"Nervous, sire. Reports are filtering in that the mob is much larger than last time. Shall we hold here or fall back into the Palace?"

"And let them believe we are in retreat? I think not."

"We have few men, Majesty, and may quickly be overwhelmed."

"Has word been sent to Commander Schoenfeld?"

"It has, though we've yet to hear a response."

"Then we shall have to trust in the steadfastness of these men." The king fell silent as the mob's chanting pierced the still of the night. "I can't make out what they're saying, can you?"

"Something about the Saints, I suspect. After all, they do call themselves the Saint's Army." The sergeant tapped a man on the shoulder. "Take a step back. You're making the line uneven." He turned to his king, his grim countenance betraying his concern. "The men are nervous, sire."

"Yes. So you said."

"They might be less so if you were safe indoors, Your Majesty."

"I will not abandon the streets of my kingdom to these thugs."

A shout of alarm came from behind them. Maksim wheeled around to see a large group of men heading towards them, many wielding axes. Then the sergeant let out a sigh of relief. "It's the Therengians, sire. Come to help."

The newcomers halted, then one stepped forward, offering a bow.

"Herulf, isn't it?" said Maksim. "You've arrived at a most opportune time. I assume you know what's happening?"

"Aye, Majesty, and we're prepared to stand at your side. Tell us where you want us, and we'll do the rest."

King Maksim looked at Brauer. "I'll leave their disposition up to you, Sergeant."

"Very well, sire." He yelled out the necessary orders.

The king stepped back, giving them room to manoeuvre. The Therengian fyrd wasn't as well-equipped as his soldiers, but what they lacked in equipment, they more than made up for with their enthusiasm. The king's own men, bolstered by the appearance of allies, settled into their positions, no longer shifting nervously.

The noise of the mob increased, and then the first ones came into sight, torches infusing their faces with an inhuman glow. They tossed bottles and rocks even though the distance was still too far to do any damage. At the sight of the king's thin line of men, they rushed forward as if they were a river flooding over its banks.

A shiver ran down Maksim's spine. He felt an overwhelming urge to flee but gritted his teeth and remained where he was, determined to set an example for his men.

"Steady," he called out, his words quickly lost to the mob's yelling and screaming. They struck his warriors, pushing them back several steps, but the line held. The Saint's Army had attacked with bravado, but their fury soon waned at their lack of success. They fell back, leaving a handful of people in the street, either dead or crying out in pain.

Sergeant Brauer stood firm, maintaining their formation even as a few more stones came their way, easily blocked by shields. As the mob receded, Maksim wondered if they would give up and go home. They'd been unable to break the line; why weren't they running? It then struck him they were waiting for something—the question was, what?

Temple Captain Darius looked over his command with great pride. The Temple Knights of Saint Cunar were the finest warriors on the Continent. This day, they would restore order to the City of Carlingen and, in doing so, establish their rule of the kingdom. His order had been disgraced at the Battle of the Wilderness. This was the opportunity he needed to show everyone they were not an organization to be trifled with.

He took up his place at the head of the column and then gave the command to advance. Horseshoes echoed off the cobblestone streets as the brother-knights rode four abreast in his wake. They were the hammer of the Church—their righteousness would prevail!

Bells rang out across the city, filling him with pride. He imagined himself riding at the head of a grand procession, garlands in his hair proclaiming him the new ruler of Carlingen. Members of his order would travel from across the Continent to pay homage to him, celebrating his glorious victory over the corrupt rule of King Maksim. He was a power to be reckoned with, and nothing could stop him from achieving his goal.

They turned onto the road heading to the Palace, but a single rider blocked their way. Darius slowed, taking in the offending individual.

"Temple Captain Cordelia," he said. "You're the last person I expected to see here. Make way. The Temple Knights of Saint Cunar are riding for the Palace."

"I can't let you do that," she replied.

"I beg your pardon?"

"I cannot permit you to interfere in this matter."

"You're hardly in a position to stop me."

"Aren't I?" said Cordelia. "You are a Temple Captain, same as me. Thus, you lack the authority to intercede in what should be considered a domestic issue."

"I have never heard such ridiculous drivel in my life."

"Yet here I am."

Darius raised his hand, halting his men before he urged his horse forward until he was within spitting distance. "By your own admission, you are interfering in a domestic issue yourself. How do you justify that?"

Cordelia shrugged. "I have permission from my superior."

"I doubt that very much."

"Then you are behind the times, Captain. Have you not heard about the events in Arnsfeld or Reinwick? Unlike yours, my order decided to fight for what we believe in. Now, return to your commandery before I'm forced to engage in direct battle with your men."

Darius laughed. "You? Fight my men? Now that, I'd like to see." He shifted in the saddle. "Go home while you've still got a commandery to retreat to."

"I shall not." Cordelia whistled, and scarlet-clad Temple Knights rode out from the side streets, forming up behind her. "What will it be, Captain? Will you follow the tenets of the Church or attempt to force your way through to the Palace?"

"This is outrageous! What do you hope to accomplish with this behaviour?"

"Isn't that obvious? We're here to prevent your overthrow of the legitimate ruler of Carlingen."

"I order you to step aside!"

"If you intend to ride to the Palace, you'll have to go through us first."

"If that is your only answer, then so be it." Darius drew his sword, raising it on high. "This is your last chance, Captain. I intend to order my knights to advance. If you refuse to stand aside, I will not be responsible for the consequences."

Cordelia remained calm. "I have hung from the mast of a Halvarian warship, Captain. Your threats pale in comparison to that. Advance if you must, but know you will be held accountable for the results."

"Attack!" screamed the Cunar captain as he urged his horse forward, reaching out with his sword to strike the Agnesite. Cordelia parried, knocking the blade aside and then hefted her shield. Darius moved closer until their feet were almost touching before he struck again, his weapon scraping off her vambrace.

She felt the strength behind it, yet it failed to dislodge her from the saddle. With a flip of her head, her visor came down, protecting her face, then she struck back, the tip of her sword hitting his helmet.

He rained blows down on her, one after the other, and she struggled to keep up. Out of the corner of her eye, she glimpsed the other Cunar knights, who'd remained rooted in their positions despite their captain's orders to advance.

A calm washed over her as she looked at the fight dispassionately. They could do little damage to each other thanks to their plate armour, yet Darius continued to lash out with his sword, hammering away without concern for technique. How low had this captain sunk?

He attacked again with a long, overhead strike against her shoulder. Her pauldron stopped it, but in his haste, he revealed a weakness, for he'd stood in the stirrups to give more weight to his blow.

Her horse crashed into his, the impact knocking the weapon from his hand, and then she reached out and grabbed his wrist. Pulling with all her might, she yanked him out of his saddle, and as he fell, he clutched at her, trying to halt his descent, but there was no hope for him. Captain Darius struck the cobblestones headfirst, twitched, and then went still.

Cordelia dismounted as two of her sister-knights came forward on foot. They took the horses while she removed the Cunar captain's helmet. Blood oozed from the man's ear, and she feared he might be dead, but then a gasp of air escaped his lips. A shadow loomed over them both, and she looked up to a Cunar staring down at her.

"You've killed him!" he shouted.

"No. He lives still, but we must get him to the Mathewite mission if he is to survive. Do you know of it?"

"I do." He glanced around, realizing the sister-knights surrounded him. "Will you allow us passage?"

"Yes, but only those needed to bring him. My own knights will escort you."

His gaze flicked back and forth between Cordelia and his captain, finally settling on her. "Very well. I agree to your terms."

"What is your name, Brother?"

"I am Temple Knight Raban, senior brother here after Temple Captain Darius."

"Very well, Brother Raban. Pick your escort, and dismiss the rest back to their commandery. If we are to see to your captain's health, we must act quickly."

He returned to his men and exchanged words, and then nearly the entire column turned around and rode up the street while three dismounted, preparing to lift their captain into his saddle.

"You would be better off bearing him on foot," suggested Cordelia. "He's sustained a serious head wound. The ride might well kill him."

Raban straightened. "Then he shall die in the saddle like a true Temple Knight should."

· · ·

Larissa Stormwind stood before the closed door. "Hand over the girl! She is the property of the family."

"She doesn't want to go with you," came the reply.

She recognized the voice. "Come now, Stanislav. You know she'll end up with us, eventually. Better to hand her over while she's still too young to understand what's happening."

"You can't have her!"

"You seem to think there's a choice involved. Very well. I'll give you two options: I can slay you all and take her, or you can hand her over and live. Which will it be?"

She heard murmuring but couldn't make out any words.

"I'll destroy this door if I have to," she warned.

"One moment."

Again, she waited, trying to determine the reason for the delay.

The mage hunter finally spoke. "Let me unblock the door." What sounded like wood scraped across the floor, then the door opened to reveal the old fool. He backed up, allowing her entry.

The child stood to one side, her face obscured by a hooded cloak. At first, Larissa thought it a ruse, perhaps a makeshift dummy but then the girl shuffled her feet.

"Stay back, Stanislav, or I'll use a blast of ice to freeze your lungs."

He held up his hands to show they were empty. Larissa moved closer, her eyes remaining on the old man. Convinced he would rush her, she extended her right arm, ready to loose a spell should it prove necessary.

She kept the child in her peripheral vision as she advanced, then reached out, seizing the girl's hand. "Come," she said. "It's time we took you away from all this."

Pain lanced up her arm as the child suddenly grew taller. She turned in a panic to see an axe buried in her forearm, its handle held by a green-faced savage now chest-high to her.

"You shall not have her!" shouted Agar, pulling back the axe for another strike.

Larissa cast a spell despite the pain. Her right hand whipped around, ready to kill the upstart Orc youngling, but as she released her power, Stanislav tackled her, driving her to the floor. Her head struck a chair, and the room began spinning, then everything went black.

Agar stared down at the Water Mage. "That was close."

"It was," agreed Stanislav. "How are your knees?"

"They are fine."

"I don't think I could've stood like that for long."

The Orc shrugged. "It was but a moment and the ruse worked. What do we do with her?"

Skora came out from another room, holding Oswyn's hand. "Tie her up for now. I don't suppose you brought any magebane?"

"I'm afraid not," said Stanislav. "And why would I? It's been years since I went looking for mages."

"Then we'll need to gag her for now." She rolled the body over. "She's still breathing but is going to have a massive headache." Skora leaned in closer. "That's always assuming the blow hasn't rendered her simple-minded."

"My mother could cure her," said Agar.

"Yes, but it will be some time before they return from the south. In the meantime, we must do our best to keep her alive."

"Even after she tried to take Oswyn?"

"She only did what she thought she had to. If there's one thing I've learned these last few years, it's that people can change. We must give Larissa Stormwind the same option."

"And if she doesn't join us?"

Skora shrugged. "Then we lock her up for the rest of her life. It makes little difference to me, so long as we tried."

TORRENT

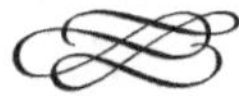

SUMMER 1109 SR

Raw power spewed upward, invisible to most, yet to those capable of wielding magic, it was a bright beacon that lit the sky. Natalia kept her focus on the clouds to the west, but the effort wore on her. Never before had she felt such a magical force. She'd intended to use her own magic to funnel the power of the ley lines, but the unexpected happened once her spell was underway. Now, the earth's power flowed through her rather than being directed by her, and the fierce energy threatened to burn her with its intensity.

Her flesh felt like it was crawling, and she feared the power would consume her entire body. Moisture ran from her eyes, reaching her lips, the taste of blood shocking her. This was it—the final spell—the magic that would end her life forever.

A hand rested on her shoulder, a soothing touch that allowed a coolness to envelop her. She risked a glance to see Shaluhk, hands glowing, using her magic to stem the bleeding. The effort almost cost her concentration, for the pillar of energy veered suddenly, threatening to tear away from her control.

Natalia fought, willing the pillar to turn westward once more, and then it occurred to her that it fought back like a living creature. She changed tactics, imagining a giant funnel, but tried nudging it east instead of pushing it west. Sure enough, the power revolted, moving in the opposite direction with a vengeance.

She closed her eyes, relying on her magical sense to direct it instead of sight. Her muscles ached, her head throbbed, yet she kept at it despite feeling as though she hadn't slept for weeks. Exhaustion threatened to overwhelm her, but she fought on, knowing that stopping now could only lead to disaster.

She felt a drop in power, and then Katrin collapsed. Out of the corner of her eye, she saw Shaluhk place glowing hands on the poor woman. Svetlana fell next, fainting as her magical reserves gave out, leaving Natalia as the only mage left standing.

A strange sensation washed over her, and she realized with a start, her own power was gone. Instead, the energy of the ley lines coursed through her like a raging river. Part of her mind rebelled at the notion, and then she calmed herself as lightning flashed overhead, followed by the roar of thunder.

The storm was in full swing now, drenching everyone, yet the water soothed her, and she embraced the feeling until everything around her began to swirl, and she plummeted into an endless pool.

Seeing Natalia fall, Shaluhk rushed over, eager to heal her yet unsure why her tribe-sister had collapsed. She utilized her magic to detect signs of life, finding only a faint glimmer. Natalia appeared to be in a coma, unresponsive to the outside world, yet still breathing.

The shaman looked skyward where the beam of light feeding the storm had dimmed, its energy no longer under control. Shaluhk spotted Greta and waved her over. "Help me move her under the cover of the trees."

They lifted Natalia, dragging her towards safety, soon joined by Svetlana and Katrin, who, despite their weariness, insisted on lending a hand. Once beneath the welcoming boughs of the forest, they were offered partial protection from the storm.

Katrin raised her voice to be heard over the driving rain, "What happens now?"

"We wait," replied Shaluhk. "Nat-Alia has done what she set out to do. Now we must let nature do what it does best."

"I knew she was powerful," said Svetlana, "but I never believed her capable of this." She glanced up, but trees blocked their view of the dark clouds.

"Her magic did not allow this to happen; the power that flows along the ley lines did."

"Perhaps, but it took her energy to focus it. I doubt any other mage in all the Continent could have done what she did today." Svetlana looked down at the pale face. "Will she live?"

"Most definitely, but her body is in a dormant state. I am unable to determine how long she will remain thus."

"Then we shall stay here and guard her."

The Orc shaman nodded. "Long will I remember the day when Nat-Alia of the Red Hand controlled the very lifeblood of the land."

"Lifeblood?"

"Does the energy of the ley lines not flow across this land like blood through veins?"

"I suppose it does."

"Agreed," said Katrin. "But even more important than this weather is how much magic was released this day. We cannot afford to let our enemies learn how to unleash this power. The results would be catastrophic."

"Even still," said Svetlana, "the ruins of Beorwic have sat undisturbed for centuries."

"They will not remain hidden now," said Shaluhk. "Not after revealing their true power."

"Then when I return to the capital, I shall convince the king to resettle Beorwic. I can think of no other way to safeguard the standing stones."

"A good idea," said Katrin. "I doubt you'll have any difficulty finding volunteers. It will also help relieve some of the overcrowding back in Carlingen. Of course, he'll need to appoint someone to run the place. Another baron, perhaps?"

"No. It must be somebody who fully understands the power contained in those standing stones."

"Such as?"

"How about you?" asked Svetlana.

"I'm no baron."

"No, but you are a Stormwind, despite the family's attempts to erase your existence."

"Still, I know nothing of running a city, especially a ruined one."

"We can discuss the details later."

The wind whipped around, a crack echoing through the forest, followed by a tearing noise. Athgar watched as a tall pine toppled over. "It's getting a tad dangerous here."

"That is putting it mildly," said Kargen. "Yet where else would you have us go? Back to the river, where there is no cover at all?"

"It's either that or we get crushed by falling trees."

"Then come. Let us return to the bridge and see what havoc the weather has wrought."

They made their way through the forest, the thick underbrush hampering their progress while the pelting rain did nothing to make the trip any easier. They arrived at the clearing near the bridge's northern end to see hundreds of men crossing it, making it look like a great snake was advancing. As the lead elements reached the middle of the span, the bridge itself sagged, and for a moment, Athgar thought the entire thing might sink into the river. Then they passed the centre point and continued northward, the span remaining intact.

"So much for that idea," said Athgar. The rain finally slackened a bit, and he looked skyward. "We have failed."

Kargen turned to the west. "Do you hear that?"

"What?"

"A roaring as if a great beast approaches."

It took Athgar a moment to register the distant sound that was rapidly growing closer as if something charged towards them.

"That is no beast," called out Urag. "It is the roar of water."

"Nonsense. No waterfalls are near here, or we would have heard them sooner."

The roar grew to a crescendo, the river rising along with the sound. The bridge, floating on boats but overloaded with hundreds of men, lay close to the surface. The first waves sloshed over it, knocking a few off their feet while others grabbed on to ropes to avoid disaster.

The bridge groaned as the river rose higher still, crashing against the waists of those trying to cross. A terrible wail erupted as men lost their grips, the roar of the water silencing their cries.

Ropes snapped, wood cracked, and the middle of the great span began to flounder as one of the boats holding it in place sank beneath the surging tide.

With nothing left holding it, the strain tore the middle section of the bridge from its moorings. It broke up quickly, sending even more men to their deaths. A small group of Ostrovans tried jumping off the bridge, but as they hit the water, another part collapsed, and large chunks of lumber and heavy rope swirled in amongst them.

Athgar watched in horror as a massive wave tore apart what remained of the bridge as if the Gods themselves had swatted it away. Debris floated downriver in a great tide of flotsam, killing anyone with the misfortune of being in its way, washing the bodies to the ends of the world.

The tide rose higher, the water surging over the bank, rushing towards where Athgar's group stood watching. "Hold on," he called out, grabbing a nearby tree.

Kargen managed to wrap his arms around a trunk, but Urag was not so lucky. The branch he clutched snapped off as the water rose to his waist, carrying him for a hundred paces before he dug his axe into a nearby trunk, barely avoiding the same fate as the would-be invaders.

Athgar felt his tree bowing to the river's power, but the flood had crested, and the water level dropped fast. He looked at Kargen. "Are you all right?"

"I am fine," replied the Orc, "though I fear Urag did not fare so well." They both looked eastward to see the Orc hunter making his way back towards them.

"And the others?" asked Athgar.

They took a moment to count heads. "All present and accounted for," said Athelstan, "at least those who survived the initial attack."

Athgar wandered over to what remained of the bridge's northern end— little more than two poles and shredded rope, the rest having washed downstream. "Gods," he said. "Look at the devastation."

Kargen moved up beside him. "It is safe to say the Ostrovans are no longer a threat."

"How many do you think perished?"

"Two hundred at least, possibly even three?"

"The falling rain made it hard to see, but I would say there were likely that many again on the southern bank, yet take a look. The river over-flowed across all that flat land, taking a good portion of them with it. How many people did you and Shaluhk estimate were there?"

Kargen shook his head. "Not as many as who died on that bridge. They must have received reinforcements, not that it did them any good. Rather, it served to increase their casualties when the flood came."

"What do we do now?"

"I will send hunters to watch the riverbank. Any Ostrovan who tries to cross will be quickly dispatched."

"And those who survived the flood?"

"If the river has not already killed them, we shall."

"Even after all they've gone through?"

"We do not possess the numbers to take prisoners, but if it puts your mind at ease, we can offer them the chance to swim back to Ostrovan terri-tory. Does that suffice?"

"It does."

"Good. Now come. We must return to Beorwic and see how Nat-Alia has fared. The conjuring of a storm of this magnitude must have drained her."

Shaluhk looked up as the others entered the camp. "Nat-Alia is worn out."

"Is she sleeping?" asked Athgar.

"She has gone into a meditative state. I suspect she will awaken once her energy returns. Did her efforts prove rewarding?"

"They did," said Kargen, moving to sit beside his bondmate. "The bridge washed away, as did most of the Ostrovan army. That spell proved most effective."

"Good, but let us hope it is never again needed. The effort almost killed Nat-Alia."

Athgar moved to sit beside his wife, taking her hand and pressing it to his heart, a tear running down his face. "Had I known it would be so dangerous, I would never have allowed her to attempt it."

"The choice was hers to make," said Shaluhk. "You know as well as I, she would have ignored such a request."

"I do, yet I cannot bear the thought of losing her."

Natalia stirred. "Athgar? Is that you?"

"I'm here."

"What happened?"

"The enemy is defeated. Your storm was a big success. Now rest, my love. You need to regain your strength."

She closed her eyes and was soon fast asleep.

"Thank the Gods for that," said Athgar, "but especially you, Shaluhk. I'm sure she would have perished without your magic."

Shaluhk shrugged off the compliment. "I did what I had to do to ensure the survival of my tribe-sister. After all, who else can I trust to look after Agar?"

"You do have a brother."

"Yes, but he is a bad influence. Now, let us light the fire and begin cooking. I have worked up quite the appetite."

They remained in Beorwic for three more days, ensuring the Ostrovans abandoned their attempts at conquest. When they finally pushed their boats into the river, there was a sense of elation, as if they were putting all their troubles behind them. That elation soon turned to concern as they saw the devastation downriver. The great flood produced by the storm had subsided quickly, but the high water had done extensive damage on its way eastward, ripping up trees and clogging the river with broken branches and logs.

The floodwaters would eventually reach the Great Northern Sea through Carlingen, but the river widened as it wound its way north. The waters at its mouth would undoubtedly rise for a day or so, but not nearly to the extent they'd done at the bridge.

A delegation headed by Temple Captain Cordelia waited for them on the riverbank as they arrived back in the capital.

"I assume you found success?"

"We did," said Athgar. "Did you ever have any doubt?"

"I suppose I should know better by now."

"And here?"

"We've had our share of difficulties, but nothing we couldn't handle." She noted Belgast carrying a bag with great reverence. "Is that the banner?"

"King Maksim told you about it?" asked the Dwarf.

"Once we put down the uprising, yes."

"Uprising?" said Svetlana.

"A mob descended on the Palace, or at least it tried to."

"And the Cunars?" asked Natalia.

"The king banished them. They've sailed for Abelard."

"You have been busy. I'm surprised you found the time to come down and welcome us back."

"Oh, I'm not here for you," said Cordelia. "I was sent to escort the queen." She looked at Svetlana. "Your Majesty? I have a horse waiting."

"Very well. I shall see the rest of you back at the Palace, but there's no rush. The king and I have some catching up to do."

They rode off.

"Well, well," said Belgast. "I'd be willing to bet there will soon be a new heir in Carlingen."

Athgar looked at his colleague. "It just occurred to me we didn't see you at the bridge. Where were you when that storm broke out?"

"Like any good Dwarf, when I learned what Natalia planned, I sought refuge in the ruins." He waved the bag. "I also took it upon myself to safeguard this. Good thing, too, or it would've been washed away by the flood, never to be seen again."

"But Beorwic didn't flood, did it?"

"No, but it could have. I was simply safeguarding our future."

Oswyn barrelled out of the gatehouse. "Momma! Momma!"

Natalia ran forward, scooping her up into her arms. Athgar was there moments later, hugging them both.

A tired-looking Agar made his way to the riverbank at a more sedate pace.

"Agar," said Shaluhk. "Why the long face?"

"I am pleased to see you both, but Oswyn wore me out."

"Where is Skora?"

"Back at the Palace with Stanislav. They did all they could for Lady Larissa, but I fear your magic may be needed."

"Why? What has happened?"

"In the course of events, she ended up hitting her head. She has yet to awaken but is being kept under guard, just in case. Shall I bring you to her?"

"No. If she has lasted this long, she can wait a little longer." She hugged her son, then watched as Kargen placed his hand on Agar's shoulder.

"It is good to see you well," said the chieftain. "You must tell us of all that transpired in our absence."

"I shall be happy to, Father, but I think it would be best we wait until you are back at the great hall. Much has happened, and I only witnessed part of it."

"You are becoming quite the diplomat," said Kargen. "Very well, my son. Lead on."

King Maksim sat before the fire, a drink in hand. "I'm pleased to see you returned to me, my dear. I have greatly missed your presence."

"That was evident by your attention last night," she replied.

"What was it you said earlier about resettling Beorwic?"

"I thought we might offer it to the Therengians. Saints know they would have a vested interest in rebuilding it, considering it will provide a gate to Therengia."

"An excellent idea, but that's not what I was referring to. You said something about a new governor?"

"Yes. I think it best if you offered it to Katrin."

"I understand that, considering the nature of those standing stones, but why not make her a baroness?"

"The title implies something inherited by right of birth."

"And?"

"Whoever rules there should be appointed based on merit, not bloodline, ensuring future custodians of the city possess an understanding of magic."

"I see no flaw in your reasoning."

"So you agree so easily?"

"Of course. I value your opinion, and it's not as if I'm the mage in the family."

"Have you considered what you'll do with Aeldred's banner?"

"Yes. I'm giving it to Athgar and Natalia. It was the property of the Old

Kingdom, and Therengia is the natural descendant of that once great realm." He smiled. "Did I tell you what we found when we seized the Cunar commandery?"

"No. What?"

"A substantial contribution to our treasury. I don't know much about these things, but I thought building a magic circle here in the Palace might be useful. I've heard it can be used to transport across great distances. Is that true?"

"With the proper spell, yes. And Natalia has agreed to teach it to me."

"Good. Then it's settled. Now, how do we go about building one?"

EPILOGUE

SUMMER 1109 SR

Two king's men dragged Crown Prince Beringar into the throne room, his shackles scraping along the flagstones with every step. King Eugene watched dispassionately as they forced his eldest son to kneel before him.

"So, the wayward heir returns. Did you really think I wouldn't discover your treachery?"

"I don't know what they told you, Father, but it's all lies. Why would I depose you when I am your heir?"

"You have always been impatient, a trait you share with your late mother, but you've gone too far this time, Beringar. You sent armed men into Carlingen and then visited their court in my name without my authorization! Your actions put this entire kingdom in peril. Even as we speak, the Therengians mass at our border."

"It is a bluff, Father, meant to frighten you."

"Then they succeeded." The king leaned forward on his throne. "Much as it pains me to admit, you are unfit to be the Crown Prince."

Beringar straightened his back. "I did what I believed best for Ostrova."

"You plotted to seize my Throne! That is an unforgivable sin, one you will pay for with your life." He nodded to the guards. "Take him away."

The guards lifted Beringar to his feet.

"No! You can't do this!" shouted the prince. "Please, Father. I beg of you!"

King Eugene clenched his jaw but said nothing, standing motionless as they dragged his son away. Only after the doors closed behind the disgraced prince did the king move, sitting heavily upon his throne. "Zoryana, your thoughts?"

A woman stepped forward, her robes iridescent in the light of the candles. "He was your son, Majesty. His betrayal is particularly vile, and you can longer trust him. You did the right thing by ordering his execution."

"He and I didn't see eye-to-eye, but I never expected this."

"What will you do now?"

"Whatever I must to secure the kingdom."

"Including going to war?"

"Are you mad?" said the king. "This new Therengia is on a rampage and will soon grow to engulf the entire Continent."

"Come, Majesty. Surely you overestimate their strength?"

"Do I? They defeated a Holy Army, and that was well before they took on Novarsk. How do I stand against a realm so strong? I will likely need to cede territory to them just to keep my head!"

"The eastern region is sparsely populated, sire. Its loss would hardly be noticed. Placate them with this gift, and then use your time to build an alliance."

"An alliance?"

"Of course. The rise of Therengia has been feared for generations. Now that it's here, we need to band together, as we did in times of old. The Petty Kingdoms will once more unite to defeat their enemies."

"The Petty Kingdoms can't even unite to stave off the Halvarian Empire. What makes you think they'll lift a finger to help us?"

"With all due respect, Majesty, Therengia is no empire. The time to strike is now before they consolidate their holdings."

"But it would take months, if not years, to form a coalition of allies."

"Then we best get started sooner rather than later."

King Eugene stroked his beard. "Yes. I suppose that makes sense." He looked up at his aide. "Your counsel is wise, Zoryana. Surprising, considering your vocation as an Enchanter."

"I may not be a Stormwind, sire, but I make it a point to know my enemies."

"But you did not see my son's treachery?"

"Nor did you, Majesty."

"Point taken. How do we start?"

"With your permission, sire, I shall travel to the kingdoms closest to us. As you said, it will take some time, but I'm confident we can assemble an alliance capable of dealing a death blow to this reborn kingdom of old."

<<<<>>>

Review Torrent

Read the next book - Cataclysm

If you liked *Torrent*, then *Servant of the Crown*, the first book in the *Heir to the Crown* series awaits.

Start Servant of the Crown

A FEW WORDS FROM PAUL

The events in Torrent have been a long time in the planning. Natalia has grown in power since her time at the Volstrum, and though her journey has been difficult, it has allowed her to come to a true understanding of the nature of magic. She's taken everything she learned throughout the series and developed her own unique spells.

Likewise, Athgar is at the height of his mastery of fire, while Shaluhk has unlocked long-forgotten magic of her own, thanks to the memories of Khurlig. They, along with Svetlana, Katrin, and a host of others, must now work together to end the power of the Stormwinds once and for all.

The story of Athgar and Natalia continues in Cataclysm, the final book in The Frozen Flame series.

I owe a huge debt of gratitude to my wife, Carol Bennett, for her unwavering support and efforts as editor, marketer, and social media coordinator. Were it not for her, these tales would have long ago been abandoned. My thanks also go to my daughters Amanda Bennett, Stephanie Sandrock, and Christie Bennett, for their interest and enthusiasm, and Brad Aitken, Jeffrey Parker, and Stephen Brown for being the awesome gamers they are.

In addition, I'd like to thank the following for their valuable input and support as part of my Beta team: Rachel Deibler, Michael Rhew, Phyllis Simpson, Don Hinckley, Charles Mohapel, Debra Reeves, Susan Young, Anna Ostberg, Mitchell Schneidkraut, Keven Hutchinson, Joanna Smith, James McGinnis, Jim Burke, Lisa Hanika, and Lisa Hunt.

Lastly, thank you, my readers, for your kind words and encouraging feedback. Reviews are always a good way of communicating with authors like me, so please feel free to leave a comment or two with your thoughts on Torrent.

CAST OF CHARACTERS

MAIN CHARACTERS:
Agar - Son of Shaluhk and Kargen, Red Hand Tribe
Athgar - Fire Mage, High Thane of Therengia, bondmate to Natalia
Belgast Ridgehand - Dwarf Entrepreneur, friend of Natalia and Athgar
Beringar - Crown Prince of Ostrova
Cordelia - Temple Captain of Saint Agnes
Greta - Young girl, Katrin's ward
Herulf - Athgar's self-appointed bodyguard, Therengian
Kargen - Chieftain, bondmate to Shaluhk, Red Hand Tribe
Katrin Stormwind - Water Mage, former student of the Volstrum
Larissa Stormwind - Water Mage, Ruzhina
Maksim IV - King of Carlingen
Natalia Stormwind - Water Mage, Warmaster of Therengia, bondmate to Athgar
Oswyn - Daughter of Athgar and Natalia
Shaluhk - Shaman, bondmate to Kargen, Red Hand Tribe
Skora - Friend of Athgar and Natalia, Therengian
Stanislav Voronsky - Former Mage hunter, friend of Natalia
Svetlana Stormwind - Water Mage, school acquaintance of Natalia

CARLINGEN:
Arath - Therengian
Athelstan - Therengian
Brauer - Sergeant, King Maksim's army
Brona - Wife of Haywald
Carmen - Temple Knight of Saint Agnes
Darius - Temple Captain of Saint Cunar
Flarik Wallen - Baron of Wallenston
Haywald - Cobbler, Therengian
Hildwyn - Therengian
Olya - Servant
Parzifal Schoenfeld - Commander, Army of Carlingen
Raban Engle - Citizen
Tanger Haus - New Baron of Raketsk
Thalmund Hargold - Baron of Adlinschlot
Vinzent - Third son of Maksim III

Wendred - Wife of Wigstan, Therengian
Wigstan - Husband of Wendred, Therengian
Wygurn - Son of Erdan, Therengian
Zegota Kotesky - Baker

ORCS:

Artoch (Deceased) - Master of Fire, Athgar's mentor, Red Hand Tribe
Khurlig - Ancestor
Kraloch - Shaman, Black Arrows
Laghul - Shaman, Black Axe Tribe
Tonfer Garul - Scholar, Ebenstadt
Uhdrig (Deceased) - Shaman, Shaluhk's mentor
Ungor - Ancestor
Urag - Hunter, Red Hand

STORMWINDS:

Aramon - Water Mage, Ruzhina
Galina - Water Mage, Reinwick
Graxion - Water Mage, Ruzhina
Gregori - Water Mage, Ruzhina
Illiana (Deceased) - Former head of family, Natalia's Grandmother
Marakhova - Head of family
Nina - Water Mage, Instructor at the Volstrum
Tatiana - Former head of Volstrum

OTHERS:

Aeldred - First King of the Old Kingdom of Therengia
Ash Biter - Beaver
Aubrey Brandon - Life Mage, Baroness of Hawksburg, Merceria
Brotherhood - Local Gang, Carlingen
Eadred (Deceased) - Past Ruler of Runewald
Eadwulf - Last King of Old Therengia
Ethwyn - Fire Mage, sister to Athgar
Eugene - King of Ostrova
Evira - Stanislav's girlfriend, Ebenstadt
Falks - Captain, Army of Ostrova
Farin Greybeard - King of Kragen-Tor
Friedrich Hartman - Duke of Krieghoff
Georgi Kulikov - Former Baron of Raketsk
Gilbert - Father General of Saint Cunar
Grazynia - Temple Captain, Commander Temple Ship *Vigilant*

Gundar - God of the Earth, creator of Dwarves
Haglarith (Deceased) - Former King of Kragen-Tor
Rada - Former Queen of Novarsk
Raynald - Knight Errant
Rothgar (Deceased) - Father of Athgar
Rudger - Commander, Army of Ostrova
Splash Paw - Otter, Carlingen
Talivardas - Temple Commander of Saint Cunar
Tauril - Goddess of the Woods
Wynfrith - Governor of Novarsk, Therengia
Yaromir - Temple Knight of Saint Mathew, Ebenstadt
Yulakov the Seventh - King of Ruzhina
Zoryana - Enchanter, Ostrova

PLACES

PETTY KINGDOMS:

Andover - Kingdom, south of Reinwick
Arnsfeld - Kingdom, Northern Coast
Braymoor - Kingdom, west of Carlingen
Carlingen - Kingdom
Eidolon - Kingdom, Northern Coast
Hadenfeld - Kingdom
Holstead - Duchy, south of Grey Spire Mountains
Ilea - Kingdom, Southern Coast
Krieghoff - Duchy, south of Grey Spire Mountains
Langwal - Kingdom, west of Andover
Ostrova - Kingdom, north of Novarsk
Reinwick - Duchy, Northern Coast
Ruzhina - Kingdom, Northeastern Coast
Salovia - Kingdom, south of Ostrova
Zalista - Kingdom, west of Novarsk
Zaran - Region, between Ruzhina and Carlingen

CITIES:

Athelwald (Destroyed) - Therengian village, Holstead
Beorwic - Ruins of ancient Therengian city, Carlingen
Caerhaven - Capital, Krieghoff
Carlingen - Capital, Carlingen
Corassus - City-state, Southern Coast
Draybourne - Capital, Holstead
Ebenstadt (Dunmere) - City, Therengia

Halmund - Capital, Novarsk
Karslev - Capital, Ruzhina
Korascajan - City, Home of Sartellian Academy
Korvoran - Capital, Renwick
Ord-Kurgad (Destroyed) - Orc Village, Red Hand Tribe, Holstead
Porovka - Port city, Ruzhina
Raketsk - Barony, Carlingen
Rizela - City, Ilea
Runewald - Village, Therengia
Zienholtz - Capital, Andover

OTHER PLACES:

Adlinschlot - Barony, Carlingen
Great Northern Sea - Northern Coast
Grey Spire Mountains - Mountain range, south of Therengia
Kragen-Tor - Dwarf Kingdom, Grey Spire Mountains
Northern Alliance - Reinwick and Andover
Novarsk - Province, Therengia
Old Kingdom - Original Therengia
Pillars of Truth - Kragen-Tor
Shimmering Sea - Southern Coast
Stormwind manor - Ancestral home of Stormwinds, Ruzhina
The Five Sisters - Group of islands, Reinwick
Volstrum - Stormwind Academy, Karslev
Warriors Rest - Inn, Carlingen
Wurgeld - Forest, south of Carlingen
Zurkutsk - Mine, Ruzhina

OTHER INFORMATION:

ORC TRIBES:

Ashwalkers - Reinwick, masters of fire
Black Arrows - Merceria
Black Axe - Therengia
Cloud Hunters - Therengia, masters of air
Red Hand - Therengia, masters of fire
Stone Crushers - Therengia, masters of earth

SHIPS:

Bergannon - Carlingen
Peregrine - Ruzhina
Vigilant - Temple Fleet

BATTLES:

Battle of Ord-Kurgad (1104 SR) - Orcs of the Red Hand defeated Army of Krieghoff

Battle of the Standing Stones (1104 SR) - Therengian/Orc army defeated Holy Army

Battle of the Wilderness (1104 SR) - Human name for the Battle of the Standing Stones

Battle of Wurgeld (date unknown) - Successor States defeats Old Kingdom of Therengia

Holy Crusades - Church-supported military campaigns

Last Battle - Alternate name for Battle of Wurgeld

TERMS:

Disgraced - Failed Volstrum student

Fyrd - Therengian levy

High Thane - Ruler of Therengia

Magerite - Rare gem, indicates magical power

Master of Earth - Orc term for an Earth Mage

Master of Flame - Orc term for a Fire Mage

Moot - Meeting of Thanes Council

Ordeal - Orc coming of age rite

Order of the Mailed Fist - Novarsk order of chivalry

Skrolling - Therengian term for non-Therengian Human

Successor States - Precursor to Petty Kingdoms

Thalamites - Ancient Civilization, Shimmering Sea

Thane - Elected ruler of a Therengian Village

Thane Guard - Elite Therengian warriors

Thane's Council - Ruling council of Therengia

Tusker - Huge animal ridden by Orcs

Umak - Orc boat, similar to a canoe

ABOUT THE AUTHOR

Paul J Bennett (b. 1961) emigrated from England to Canada in 1967. His father served in the British Royal Navy, and his mother worked for the BBC in London. As a young man, Paul followed in his father's footsteps, joining the Canadian Armed Forces in 1983. He is married to Carol Bennett and has three daughters who are all creative in their own right.

Paul's interest in writing started in his teen years when he discovered the roleplaying game, Dungeons & Dragons (D & D). What attracted him to this new hobby was the creativity it required; the need to create realms, worlds and adventures that pulled the gamers into his stories.

In his 30's, Paul started to dabble in designing his own roleplaying system, using the Peninsular War in Portugal as his backdrop. His regular gaming group were willing victims, er, participants in helping to playtest this new system. A few years later, he added additional settings to his game, including Science Fiction, Post-Apocalyptic, World War II, and the all-important Fantasy Realm where his stories take place.

The beginnings of his first book 'Servant to the Crown' originated over five years ago when he began a new fantasy campaign. For the world that the Kingdom of Merceria is in, he ran his adventures like a TV show, with seasons that each had twelve episodes, and an overarching plot. When the campaign ended, he knew all the characters, what they had to accomplish, what needed to happen to move the plot along, and it was this that inspired to sit down to write his first novel.

Paul now has four series based in his fantasy world of Eiddenwerthe and is looking forward to sharing many more books with his readers over the coming years.